BRITISH FUTURE FICTION

CONTENTS OF THE EDITION

A woman of the twentieth century dressed for air travel: from Albert Robida's *Le Vingtième Siècle* (1883)

BRITISH FUTURE FICTION

Volume 4
Women's Rights: Yea and Nay

Edited by
I. F. Clarke

Routledge
Taylor & Francis Group

LONDON AND NEW YORK

First published 2001 by Pickering & Chatto (Publishers) Limited

2 Park Square, Milton Park, Abingdon, Oxon OX14 4RN
711 Third Avenue, New York, NY 10017, USA

Routledge is an imprint of the Taylor & Francis Group, an informa business

First issued in paperback 2017

BRITISH LIBRARY CATALOGUING IN PUBLICATION DATA

British Future Fiction: 1700–1914
1. Science fiction, English
I. Clarke, I. F. (Ignatius Frederick)
823'.08762

LIBRARY OF CONGRESS CATALOGUING IN PUBLICATION DATA

British future fiction / edited by I. F. Clarke.
p.cm.
Includes bibliographical references and index.

1. Science fiction, English. 2. Forecasting—Fiction. I. Clarke, I. F. (Ignatius
Frederick)
PR1309.S3 B75 2000
823'.0876208–dc21
00–051036

ISBN-13: 978-1-85196-617-2 (set)
ISBN-13: 978-1-1387-5084-5 (hbk)
ISBN-13: 978-1-138-11134-9 (pbk)

Typeset by Pickering & Chatto (Publishers) Limited

CONTENTS

THE REVOLT OF MAN

The emergence of the 'woman question' was long delayed in future fiction. For close on half a century – from the appearance of Mary Wollstonecraft's *Vindication of the Rights of Woman* (1792) to the argument for the education of women in Tennyson's 'The Princess' in 1847 – the historians of things-to-come had little to say about half the human race. And yet, the rights of women could have become a major issue, if men had read and accepted what the Marquis de Condorcet said in his essay on *The Admission of Women to the Rights of Citizenship* (1798). He took his stand on the equality of all human beings, and protested against 'the exclusion of women from the rights of citizenship'.

> Either no individual of the human species has any true rights, or all have the same; and he or she who votes against the rights of another, whatever may be his or her religion, colour, or sex, has by that fact abjured his own.[1]

Alfred Tennyson presented the case for the education of women fifty-two years later in 'The Princess'. That most romantic poem should be required reading for all who wish to understand an eminent Victorian's view of relationships between the sexes. The narrative begins in Tennyson's favourite setting – Arcadian and patrician – on a summer's day, when Sir Walter Vivian opens his estate to his tenants. Seven young gentlemen, from 'our set' at college, talk of the heroic family history. They recall the most admired of them all – that heroine of the past, who 'drove her foes with slaughter from her walls'. Where lives such a woman now? The answer begins with the education of women:

> Quick answer'd Lilia 'There are thousands now
> Such women, but convention beats them down:
> It is but bringing up; no more than that:
> You men have done it: how I hate you all!
> Ah, were I something great! I wish I were
> Some mighty poetess, I would shame you then,
> That love to keep us children! Oh I wish
> That I were some great Princess, I would build
> Far off from men a college like a man's,

And I would teach them all that men are taught;
We are twice as quick!'

The vehement words were, in effect, a declaration of war against a patriarchal society. In the Britain of 1847, when 'The Princess' first appeared, there were schools and some university places for boys. Girls, if they were fortunate, were taught at home by a governess, but had no hope of going to university. For women, education was the first great question demanding a future solution. As Tennyson saw the matter, however, Princess Ida and her university for ladies could not be the whole answer to the problem. Tennyson was careful to go behind immediate appearances in order to present those conventional attitudes that then decided relationships between men and women. There is the lord of the universe:

Man is the hunter: woman is his game:
The sleek and shining creatures of the chase,
We hunt them for the beauty of their skins;
They love us for it, and we ride them down.

And there is the patriarch who holds that the everlasting laws of nature assign to men and women their proper place and role in life:

Man for the field and woman for the hearth:
Man for the sword and for the needle she:
Man with the head and woman with the heart:
Man to command and woman to obey;
All else confusion.

And there is Tennyson's evolutionary doctrine of concord, reciprocation and the mutual dependence of men and women:

The woman's cause is the man's: they rise or sink
Together, dwarf'd or godlike, bond or free
For she that out of Lethe scales with man
The shining steps of Nature, shares with man
His nights, his days, moves with him to one goal.

That poem and those sentiments were one sign that the times were changing. The campaign for the education of women started in the 1850s; and from 1871 onwards the rights of women began to find a place in future fiction. Edward Bulwer-Lytton was the first to introduce the new model Eve in *The Coming Race*. He gave a chapter to the women of the subterranean Vril-ya people, and in the first paragraph he makes his major point: the Gy-ei 'are in the fullest enjoyment of all the rights of equality with males, for which certain philosophers above ground contend'. With that nod to John Stuart Mill, Bulwer-Lytton takes his stand with the great systematiser of political and philosophical ideas, who had published his famous essay on *The Subjection of Women* in 1869. Bulwer-Lytton read and accepted Mill's arguments, especially the proposition that: 'The generality of the male sex cannot yet tolerate the idea of living with an equal.' Indeed, Bulwer-Lytton went further than Mill, since he gave the women of the Vril-ya the dominant role in their subterranean world: 'All arts and vocations allotted to the one sex are open to the other, and the Gy-ei arrogate to themselves superiority in all those abstruse and mystical branches of reasoning, for which they say the Ana are unfitted by a duller sobriety of understanding, or the routine of their matter-of-fact occupations.'[2] More than that, Bulwer-Lytton teases the reader by presenting the Gy-ei as the final triumph of Darwinism: 'Whether owing to early training in gymnastic exercises or to their constitutional organization, the Gy-ei are usually superior to the Ana in physical strength (an important element in the consideration and maintenance of female rights).'

In the 1870s it became standard practice for the male authors of utopian projections to include the political equality of women in the desiderata of their ideal future worlds. The first blast in this new war for women's liberation came from the uncertain trumpet of John Francis Maguire, Member of Parliament for Cork from 1865 until his death in 1872. He goes forward twenty years in *The Next Generation* (1871). As this text has it, by 1891 women will have achieved all their objectives: equality in the professions, their own university in London, a third of the seats in the Commons, and Selina Bates will be the Chancellor of the Exchequer. Maguire could not contain his enthusiasm for the advancement of women. They do better than the men in parliamentary business, for they 'never went off on a wrong track, or expended their energies in vain'. The House of Commons is the setting for many decorous affairs in which Irish MPs are said to excel themselves. Moreover, Irish political aspirations are to be realised in a federal union with England, and the perfect symbol of that union will be the marriage of the Prince of Wales with 'the daughter of a great Irish house'. One reviewer thought that Maguire had been 'unfortunate in the choice of a theme...':

> Had he wished to satirize the movement in favour of the enfranchisement of women, his story might have been more amusing. He might have raised a laugh, even if it was impossible for him to impede the reform. Satire being out of the question, it is, on the other hand, plain that a sketch such as this in no way strengthens the position of the liberators...The sole result of the futurity of the story is to make it farcical rather than humorous.[3]

Futurity remained a male preserve, however, and men went on describing new societies in which women were to secure what men thought their rightful place should be. For Edward Maitland in *By and By* (1873) this meant the ending of old restrictions: 'The days happily are long past, in which, while to man all careers were open, to women there was but one, and it depended upon the will of individual men to accord them that.' Women elect their own representatives for the House of Female Convocation, which 'serves as a place for initiating the discussion of questions especially affecting women and children'. Maitland borrows the phalanstery from Fourier in order to reconcile the different interests of the individual, the family, and the community. His intention is to bring 'facilities for comfort, fellowship, and culture otherwise unattainable within easy reach of every rank and grade of life, without detriment to domesticity or individuality'. The Triangular Principle decides where and how all shall live:

> The determining idea of all these institutions is derived from the fundamental plan of human life. They consist, therefore, of three departments, each distinct and complete in itself, yet all inseparably united to form an harmonious whole. One angle of the building is devoted to men, another to women, and the third to both in common with their families.[4]

The most complacent proposition of all was the invention of 'Her Most Adorable Majesty, the Empress of the Earth, and Sovereign of the Human Race' in W. D. Hay's *Three Hundred Years Hence*. As the Emblem of United Humanity she is supreme in all things, save that her role is entirely ceremonial:

> Thus, in the system of government set up by united Humanity, Woman finds her station. Nominally the head of all government in the abstract, yet the Empress possesses not one particle of actual power over the decisions of the cumenic wisdom. This is as it should be, for the faculties of women are not capable of following out the highest intellectual processes, since she has a less degree of pure reason than the man.[5]

A year after W. D. Hay had put woman in her proper place – with words of treason against his sovereign Queen Victoria – an anonymous male writer published the first full-length story devoted entirely to the future of women. He proved to be Walter Besant, a popular author, biographer, and historian, who had spoken out for the poor and the weak in *All Sorts and Conditions of Men* (1882). Today, at the end of the twentieth century Besant's tale of subservient males reads as a far from subtle burlesque history of the coming women, their swift rise and rapid fall. His Victorian readers, however, took to *The Revolt of Man* with great enthusiasm. Within two months it had sold some 9,000 copies, and reviewers were talking of

> ...considerable humour...The impossible is described with so much seriousness and verisimilitude that the reader has no difficulty in lending himself to the deception...a state of things in which woman is supreme, and 'the subjection of man' is discussed in daring themes of female philosophers and revolutionary girl graduates. England is transformed; everything is unsexed; Government, Parliament, the Universities, the professions, society in its thousand shapes, are dominated by women. There is a plethora of muliebrity.[6]

Had that reviewer had a glimmering of the changes that were to transform society in the twentieth century, he would have been more circumspect in his talk of muliebrity. Like Besant, and like most Victorian males, he could not imagine a time would come when satellite television would show viewers throughout the world the power of latterday muliebrity – parliaments listening in silence to the words of Golda Meir, Indira Gandhi, and Margaret Thatcher.

Notes

1. Marie Nicolas Condorcet, Marquis de Caritat, *Esquisse sur l'Admission des Femmes au Droit de Cité*, as translated in: Dr Alice Drysdale Vickery, *The First Essay on the Political Rights of Women* (Letchworth: Garden City Press, 1910), pp. 5–6. Dr Vickery wrote in the preface: 'We form one half of the human race, and need recognition by the law as much as the other half of the race.'
2. See vol. 1, p. 102.
3. *The Athenaeum*, 2271, 6 May 1871, p. 537.
4. Edward Maitland, *By and* By (London: Richard Bentley, 1873, 3 vols), vol. 1, p. 61.
5. (London: Newman and Co., 1881). See vol. 2, p. 149.
6. *The Athenaeum*, 2844, 29 April 1882, p. 537.

CHAPTER I.

IN PARK LANE.

THE
REVOLT OF MAN
BY
WALTER BESANT
NINTH EDITION
WILLIAM BLACKWOOD AND SONS
EDINBURGH AND LONDON
MDCCCXC

BREAKFAST was laid for two in the smallest room – a jewel of a room – of perhaps the largest house in Park Lane. It was already half-past ten, but as yet there was only one occupant of the room, an elderly lady of striking appearance. Her face, a long oval face, was wrinkled and crow-footed in a thousand lines; her capacious forehead was contracted as if with thought; her white eyebrows were thick and firmly drawn; her deep – set eyes were curiously keen and bright; her features were strongly marked, – it was a handsome face which could never, even in early girlhood, have been a pretty face; her abundant hair was of a rich creamy white, the kind of white which in age compensates its owner for the years of her youth when it was inclined to redness; her mouth was full, the lower lip slightly projecting, as is often found with those who speak much and in large rooms; her fingers were restless; her figure was withered by time. When she laid aside the paper she had been reading, and walked across the room to the open window, you might have noticed how frail and thin she seemed, yet how firmly she walked and stood.

This wrinkled face, this frail form, belonged to the foremost intellect of England: the lady was none other than Dorothy Ingleby, Professor of Ancient and Modern History in the University of Cambridge.

It would be difficult, without going into great detail, and telling many anecdotes, to account for her great reputation and the weight of her authority. She had written little; her lectures were certainly not popular with undergraduates, partly because undergraduates will never attend Professors' lectures, and partly because the University would not allow her to lecture at all on the history of the past, and the story of the present was certainly neither interesting nor enlivening.

As girls at school, everybody had learned about the Great Transition, and the way in which the Transfer of Power, which marked the last and greatest step of civilisation, had been brought about: the gradual substitution of women for men in the great offices; the spread of the new religion; the abolition of the monarchy; the introduction of pure theocracy, in which the ideal Perfect Woman took the place of a personal sovereign; the wise measures by which man's rough and rude strength was disciplined into obedience, – all these things were mere commonplaces of education. Even men, who learned little enough, were taught that in the old days strength was regarded more than mind, while the father actually ruled in the place which should have been occupied by the mother; these things belonged to constitutional history – nobody cared much about them; while, on the other hand, they would have liked to know – the more curious among them – what was the kind of world which existed before the development of culture gave the reins to the higher sex; and it was well known that the only person at all capable of presenting a faithful restoration of the old world was Professor Ingleby.

Again, there was a mystery about her: although in holy orders, she had always refused to preach; it was whispered that she was not orthodox. She had been twice called upon to sign the hundred and forty-four Articles, a request with which, on both occasions, she cheerfully complied, to the discomfiture of her enemies. Yet her silence in matters of religion provoked curiosity and surmise – a grave woman, a woman with all the learning of the University Library in her head, a woman who, alone among women, held her tongue, and who, when she did speak, spoke slowly, and weighed her words, and seemed to have written out her conversation beforehand, so pointed and polished it was. In religion and politics, however, the Professor generally maintained silence absolute. Now, if a woman is always silent on those subjects upon which other women talk oftenest and feel most deeply, it is not wonderful if she becomes suspected of heterodoxy. It was known positively, and she had publicly declared, that she wished the introduction – she once said, mysteriously, the return – of a more exact and scientific training than could be gained from the political, social, and moral economy which formed the sole studies of Cambridge. Now, the Heads of Houses, the other professors, the college lecturers, and the fellows, all held the orthodox doctrine that there is no other learning requisite or desirable than that contained in the aforesaid subjects. For these, they maintained, embrace all the branches of study which are concerned with the conduct of life.

The Professor threw aside the 'Gazette,' which contained as full a statement as was permitted of last night's debate, with an angry gesture, and walked to the open window.

"Another defeat!" she murmured. "Poor Constance! This time, I suppose, they must resign. These continual changes of Ministry bring contempt as well as disaster upon the country. Six months ago, all the Talents! Three months ago, all the Beauties! Now, all the First-classes! And what a mess – what a mess – they make between them! Why do they not come to me and make me lecture on ancient history, and learn how affairs were conducted a hundred years ago, when man was in his own place, and" – here she laughed and looked around her with a certain suspicion – "and woman was in hers?"

Then she turned her eyes out to the park below her. It was a most charming morning in June; the trees were at their freshest and their most beautiful; the flowers were at their brightest, with great masses of rhododendron, purple lilac, and the golden rain of the laburnum The Row was well filled: young men were there, riding bravely and gallantly with their sisters, their mothers, or their wives; girls and ladies were taking their morning canter before the official day began; and along the gravel-walks girls were hastening quickly to their offices or their lecture-rooms; older ladies sat in the shade, talking politics; idlers of both sexes were strolling and sitting, watching the horses or talking to each other.

"Youth and hope!"murmured the Professor. "Every lad hopes for a young wife; every girl trusts that success will come to her while she is still young enough to be loved. Age looks on with her young husband at her side, and prides herself in having no illusions left. Poor creatures! You destroyed love – love the consoler, love the leveler – when you, who were born to receive, undertook to give. Blind! blind!"

She turned from the window and began to examine the pictures hanging on the walls. These consisted entirely of small portraits copied from larger pictures. They were arranged in chronological order, and were in fact family portraits. The older pictures were mostly the heads of men, taken in the fall of life, grey - bearded, with strong, steadfast eyes, and the look of authority. Among them were portraits of ladies, chiefly taken in the first fresh bloom of youth.

"They knew," said the Professor, "how to paint a face in those days."

Among the modern pictures a very remarkable change was apparent. The men were painted in early manhood, the women at a more mature age; the style was altered for the worse, a gaudy conventional mannerism prevailed; there was weakness in the drawing and a blind following in the colour: as for the details, they were in some cases neglected altogether, and in others elaborated so as to swamp and destroy the subject of the picture. The faces of the men were remarkable for a self-conscious beauty of the lower type: there was little intellectual expression; the hair was always curly, and while some showed a bull-like repose of strength, others wore an expression of meek and gentle submissiveness. As for the women, they represented with all the emblems of authority – tables, thrones, papers, deeds, and pens.

"As if," said the Professor, "the peeresses' right divine to rule was in their hearts! But, in these days, the painter's art is a rule of thumb."

There was a small stand full of books, chiefly of a lighter kind, prettily bound and profusely gilt. Some were novels, with such titles as 'The Hero of the Cricket Field,' 'The Long Jump,' 'The Silver Racket,' and so on. Some were apparently poems, among them being Lady Longspin's 'Vision of the Perfect Knight,' with a frontispiece, showing the Last Lap of the Seven-Mile Race; Julia Durdle's poems of the 'Young Man's Crown of Glory,' and Aunt Agatha's 'Songs for Girls at School or College.' There were others of a miscellaneous character, such as 'Guide to the Young Politician,' being a series of letters to a peeress at Oxford; 'Meditations in the University Church;' 'Hymns for Men;' the 'Sacrifice of the Faithful Heart;' 'The Womanhood of Heaven; or, the Light and Hope of Men,' with many others whose title proclaimed the nature of their contents. The appearance of the books, however, did not seem to show that they were much read.

"I should have thought," said the Professor, "that Constance would have turned all this rubbish out of her breakfast-room. After all, though, what could she put in its place here?"

As the clock struck eleven, the door opened, and the young lady whom the Professor spoke of as Constance appeared.

She was a girl of twenty, singularly beautiful; her face was one of those very rare faces which seem as if nature, after working steadily in one mould for a good many generations, has at last succeeded in perfecting her idea. Most of our faces, somehow, look as if the mould had not quite reached the conception of the sculptor. Unfortunately, while such faces as that of Constance, Countess of Carlyon, are rare, they are seldom reproduced in children. Nature, in fact, smashes her mould when it is quite perfect, and begins again upon another. The hair was of that best and rarest brown, in which there is a touch of gold when the sun shone upon it. Her eyes were of a dark, deep blue; her face was a beautiful and delicate oval; her chin was pointed; her cheek perhaps a little too pale, and rather thin; and there was a broad edging of black under her eyes, which spoke of fatigue, anxiety, or disappointment. But she smiled when she saw her guest.

"Good morning, Professor," she said, kissing the wrinkled cheek. "It was good indeed of you to come. I only heard you were in town last night."

"You are well this morning, Constance?" asked the Professor.

"Oh yes!" replied the girl, wearily. "I am well enough. Let us have breakfast. I have been at work since eight with my secretary. You know that we resign to-day."

"I gathered so much," said the Professor, "from the rag they call the 'Official Gazette.' They do not report fully, of course, but it is clear that you had an exciting debate, and that you were defeated."

The Countess sighed. Then she reddened and clenched her hands.

"I cannot bear to think of it," she cried. "We had a *disgraceful* night. I shall never forget it – or forgive it. It was not a debate at all; it was the exchange of unrestrained insults, rude personalities, humiliating recrimination."

"Take some breakfast first, my dear," said the Professor, "and then you shall tell me as much as you please."

Most of the breakfast was eaten by the Professor herself. Long before she had finished, Constance sprang from the table and began to pace the room in uncontrollable agitation.

"It is hard – oh! it is very hard – to preserve even common dignity, when such attacks are made. One noble peeress taunted me with my youth. It is two years since I came of age – I am twenty, – but never mind that. Another threw in my teeth my – my – my cousin Chester" – she blushed violently; "to think that the British House, of Peeresses should have fallen so low! Another charged me with trying to be thought the loveliest woman in London; can we even listen to such things without shame? And the Duchess de la Vieille Roche" – here she laughed bitterly – "actually had the audacity to attack my Political Economy – mine; and I was Senior in the Tripos! When they were tired of abusing me, they began upon each other. No reporters were present. The Chancellor, poor lady! tried in vain to maintain order; the scene – with the whole House, as it seemed, screeching, crying, demanding to be heard, throwing accusations, innuendoes, insinuations, at each other – made one inclined to ask if this was really the House of Peeresses, the Parliament of Great Britain, the place where one would expect to find the noblest representatives in the whole world of culture and of gentlehood."

Constance paused, exhausted but not satisfied. She had a good deal more to say; but for the moment she stood by the window, with flashing eyes and trembling lips.

"The last mixed Parliament," said the Professor, thoughtfully – "that in which the few men who were members seceded in a body – presented similar characteristics. The abuse of the liberty of speech led to the abolition of the Lower House. *Absit omen!*"

"Thank heaven," replied the Countess, "that it was abolished! Since then we have had – at least we have generally had – decorum and dignity of debate."

"Until last night, dear Constance, and a few similar last nights. Take care."

"They cannot abolish us," said Constance, "because they would have nothing to fall back upon."

The Professor coughed drily, and took another piece of toast.

The Countess threw herself into a chair.

"At least," she said, "we have changed mob-government for divine right."

"Ye – yes." The Professor leaned back in her chair. "James II., in the old time, said much the same thing; yet they abolished him. To be sure, in his days, divine right went through the male line."

"Men said so," said the Countess, "to serve their selfish ends. How can any line be continued except through the mother? Absurd!"

Then there was silence for a little, the Professor calmly eating an egg, and the Home Secretary playing with her tea-spoon.

"We hardly expected success," she continued, after a while; "it was only in the desperate condition of the Party that the Cabinet gave way to my proposal. Yet I did hope that the nature of the Bill would have awakened the sympathy of a House which has brothers, fathers, nephews, and male relations of all kinds, and does not consist entirely of orphaned only daughters."

"That is bitter, Constance," sighed the Professor. "I hope you did not begin by saying so."

"No, I did not. I explained that we were about to ask for a Commission into the general condition of the men of this country. I set forth, in mild and conciliating language, a few of my facts. You know them all; I learned them from you. I showed that the whole of the educational endowments of this country have been seized upon for the advantage of women. I suggested that a small proportion might be diverted for the assistance of men. Married men with property, I showed, have no protection from the prodigality of their wives. I pointed out that the law of evidence, as regards violence towards wives, presses heavily on the man. I showed that single men's wages are barely sufficient to purchase necessary clothing. I complained of the long hours during which men have to toil in solitude or in silence, of the many cases in which they have to do housework and attend to the babies, as well as do their long day's work. And I ventured to hint at the onerous nature of the Married Mothers' Tax – that five per cent on all men's earnings."

"My dear Constance," interrupted the Professor, "was it judicious to show your whole hand at once? Surely step by step would have been safer."

"Perhaps. I ventured next to call the serious attention of the House to the grave discontent among the younger women of the middle classes, who, by reason of the crowded state of the professions, are unable to think of marriage, as a rule, before forty, and often have to wait later. This was received with cold disapprobation: the House is always touchy on the subject of marriage. But when I went on to hint that there was danger to the State in the reluctance with which the young men entered the married state under these conditions, there was such a clamour that I sat down."

The Professor nodded.

"Just what one would have expected. Talk the conventional commonplace, and the House will listen; tell the truth, and the House will rise with one consent and shriek you down. Poor child! what did you expect?"

"A dozen rose together. Lady Cloistertown caught the Chancellor's eye. I suppose you know her extraordinary command of commonplaces. She asked whether the House was prepared to place man on an equality with woman; she supposed we should like to see him sitting with ourselves, voting with the rudeness of his intellect, even speaking with the bluntness of the masculine manner. And then she burst into a scream. 'Irreligion,' she cried, 'was rampant; was this a moment for bringing forward such a motion? Not only women, but even men, had begun to doubt the Perfect Woman; the rule of the higher intellect was threatened; the new civilisation was tottering; we might even expect an attempt to bring about a return of the reign of brute force – ' Heavens! and that was only a beginning. Then followed the weary platitudes that we know so well. Can no one place truth before us in words of freshness?"

"If you insist upon every kind of truth being naked," said the Professor, "you ought not to grumble if her limbs sometimes look unlovely."

"Then let us for a while agree to accept truth in silence."

"I would we could!" echoed the elder lady. "I know the weariness of the commonplace. When we are every year invaded by gentlemen at Commemoration, I have to go through the same dreary performance. The phrases about the higher intellect; the sex which is created to carry on the thought, while the other executes the work of this world; the likeness and yet unlikeness between us due to that beautiful arrangement of nature; the extraordinary success we are making of our power; the loveliness of the new religion, revealed bit by bit, to one woman after another, until we were able to reach unto the conception, the vision, the realisation of the Perfect "Woman – "

"Professor," interrupted Constance, laying her hand on her friend's shoulder, "do not talk so. Strengthen my faith; do not destroy what is left of religion by a sneer. Alas! everything seems falling away; nothing satisfies; there is no support anywhere, nor any hope. I suppose I am not strong enough for my work; at least I have failed. The whole country is crying out with discontent. The Lancashire women cannot sell their husbands' work. I hear that they are taking to drink. Wife-beating has broken out again in the Potteries. It is reported that secret associations are again beginning to be formed among the men; and then there are these county magistrates with their unjust sentences. A man at Leicester has been sentenced to penal servitude for twenty years because his wife says he swore at her and threatened her. I wrote for information; the magistrate says she thought an example was needed. And, innocent or guilty, the husband is not allowed to cross-examine his wife. Then look at the recent case at Cambridge."

"Yes," said the Professor; "that is bad, indeed."

"The husband – a man of hitherto blameless character, – young, well-born, handsome, good at his trade, and with some pretensions to the higher culture – sentenced to penal servitude for life for striking his wife, one of the senior fellows of Trinity!"

The Professor's eyes flashed.

"As you are going out of office to-day, my Lady Home Secretary, and can do no more justice for a while, I will tell you the truth of that case. The wife was tired of her husband. It was a most unhappy match. She wanted to marry another man, so she trumped up the charge; that is the disgraceful truth. No fish-wife of Billingsgate could have lied more impudently. He, in accordance with our, no doubt most just and well-intentioned, laws, becomes a convict for the rest of his days; she marries again. Everybody knows the truth, but nobody ventures to state it. She banged her own arm black and blue herself with the poker, and showed it in open court as the effects of his violence. As for her husband, I visited him in prison. He was calm and collected. He says that he is glad there are no children to lament his disgrace, that prison life is preferable to living any longer with such a woman, and that, on the whole, death is better than life when an innocent man can be so treated in a civilised country."

"Poor man!" groaned Constance. "Stay; I have a few hours yet of power. His name?" she sprang to her desk.

"John Phillips – no; Phillips is the wife's name. I forgot that the sentence itself carries divorce with it. His bachelor name was Coryton."

Constance wrote rapidly.

"John Coryton. He shall be released. A free pardon from the Home Secretary cannot be appealed against. He is free."

She sprang from the table and rang the bell. Her private secretary appeared.

"This despatch to be forwarded at once," she said. "Not a moment's delay."

"Constance!" The Professor seized her hand. "You will have the thanks of every woman who knows the truth. All those who do not will curse the weakness of the Home Secretary."

"I care not," she said. "I have done one just action in my short term of office. I – who looked to do so many good and just actions!"

"It is difficult, more difficult than one ever suspects, for a Minister to do good. Alas! my dear, John Coryton's case is only one of many."

"I know," replied Constance, sighing, "Yet what can I do! Our greatest enemies are – ourselves. Oh, Professor! when I think of the men working at their looms from morning until night, cooking the dinners and looking after the children, while the women sit about the village pump or in their clubs, to talk unmeaning politics – Tell me, logician, why our theories are all so logical and our practice is so bad?"

"Everything," said the Professor, "in our system is rigorously logical and just. If it could not be proved scientifically – if it were not absolutely certain – the system could never be accepted by the exact intellect of cultivated women. Have not Oxford and Cambridge proclaimed this from a hundred pulpits and in a thousand text-books? My dear Lady Carlyon, you yourself proved it when you took your degree in the most brilliant essay ever written."

The Countess winced.

"Must we, then," she asked, "cease to believe in logic?"

"Nay," replied Professor Ingleby; "I said not that. But every conclusion depends upon the minor premiss. That, dear Countess, in the case of our system, appears to me a little uncertain."

"But where is the uncertainty? Surely you will allow me, my dear Professor," – Constance smiled, – "although I am only a graduate of two years' standing, to know enough logic to examine a syllogism?"

"Surely, Constance. My dear, I do not presume to doubt your reasoning powers. It was only an expression of perplexity. We are so right, and things go so wrong."

Both ladies were silent for a few moments, and Constance sighed.

"For instance," the Professor went on, "we were logically right when we suppressed the Sovereignty. In a perfect State, the head must also be perfect. Whom, then, could we acknowledge as head but the Perfect Woman? So we became a pure theocracy. Then, again, we were right when we abolished the Lower House; for in a perfect State, the best rulers must be those who are well-born, well-educated, and well-bred. All this requires no demonstration. Yet – "

But the Countess shook her head impatiently, and sprang to her feet.

"Enough, Professor! I am tired of debates and the battles of phrase. The House may get on without me. And I will inquire no more, even of you, Professor, into the foundations of faith, constitution, and the rest of it. I am brave, when I rise in my place, about the unalterable principles of religious and political economy: brave words do not mean brave heart. Like so many who are outspoken, which I cannot be – at least yet – my faith is sapped, I doubt."

"She who doubts," said the Professor, "is perhaps near the truth."

"Nay; for I shall cease to investigate; I shall go down to the country and talk with my tenants."

"Do you learn much," asked the Professor, "of your country tenants?"

The Countess laughed.

"I teach a great deal, at least," she replied. "Three times a-week I lecture the women on constitutional law, and twice on the best management of husbands, sons, and farm-labourers, and so forth."

"And you are so much occupied in teaching that you never learn? That is a great pity, Constance. Do you observe?"

I suppose I do. Why, Professor?"

"Old habits linger longest in country places. What do you find to remark upon, most of all?"

"The strange and unnatural deference," replied the girl, with a blush of shame, "paid by country women to the men. Yes, Professor, after all our teaching, and in spite of all our laws, in the country districts the old illogical supremacy of brute force still obtains, thinly disguised."

"My dear, who manages the farm?"

"Why," said the Countess, "the wives are supposed to manage, but their husbands really have the whole management in their own hands."

"Who drives the cattle, sows the seed, reaps, ploughs?"

"The husband, of course. It is his duty."

"It is," said the Professor. "Child, a few generations ago he did all this as the acknowledged head of the house. *He does not forget*."

"What do you mean?"

"I mean, my dear Countess, that things are never so near their end as when they appear the firmest. Now, if you please, tell me something more of this great speech of yours, which so roused the wrath of assembled and hereditary wisdom. What did you intend to say?"

Constance began, in a quick, agitated way, nervously pacing the room, to run through the main points of the speech which she had prepared but had not been allowed to deliver. It was a plea for the intellectual elevation of the other sex. She pointed out that, although there was legislation in plenty for their subjection, – although the greatest care was taken to prevent men from working together, conspiring, and meeting, so that most work was done in solitude or at home – and when that was not the case, a woman was always present to enforce silence – although laws had been passed to stamp out violence, and to direct the use of brute strength into useful channels, – little or nothing had been done, even by private enterprise, for the education of men. She showed that the prisons were crammed with cases of young men who had "broken out;" that very soon they would have no more room to hold their prisoners; that the impatience of men under the severe restrictions of the law was growing greater every day, and more dangerous to order; and that, unless some remedy were found, she trembled for the consequences.

Here the Professor raised her eyes, and laughed gently.

The Countess went on with her speech. "I am not advocating, before this august assembly, the adoption of unconstitutional and revolutionary measures, – I claim only for men such an education of their reasoning faculties as will make them reasoning creatures. I would teach them something of what we ourselves learn, so that they may reason as we reason, and obey the law because they cannot but own that the law is just. I know that we must first encourage the young men to follow a healthy instinct which bids them be strong; yet there is more in life for a man to do than to work, to dig, to carry out orders, to be a good athlete, an obedient husband, and a conscientious father."

Here the Professor laughed again.

"Why do you laugh, Professor?"

"Because, my dear, you are already in the way that leads to understanding."

"You speak in parables."

"You are yet in twilight, dear Constance." The Professor rose and laid her hand on the young Countess's arm. "Child, your generous heart has divined what your logic would have made it impossible for you to perceive – a great truth, perhaps the greatest of truths. Go on."

"Have I? The House would not allow me to say it, then; my own friends deserted me; a vote of want of confidence was hurriedly passed by a majority of 235 to 22; and" – the young Minister laughed bitterly – "there is an end of my great schemes."

"For a time – yes," said the Professor. "But, Constance, there is a greater work before you than you suspect or dream. Greatest of the women of all time, my child, shall you be – if what I hope may be brought to pass. Let not this little disappointment of an hour vex you any longer. Go – gain strength in the country – meditate – and read."

"Oh, read!" cried the girl, impatiently; "I am sick of reading."

"Read," continued the Professor; "read – with closed doors – the *forbidden books*. They stand in your own castle, locked up in cases; they have not been destroyed because they are not known to exist. Read Shakespeare."

Events which followed prevented the Countess from undertaking this course of study; for she remained in town. From time to time the Professor was wont to startle her by reading or quoting some passage which appealed to her imagination as nothing in modern poetry seemed able to do. She knew that the passage came from one of the old books which had been put away, locked up, or destroyed. It was generally a passage of audacity, clothing a revolutionary sentiment in words which burned themselves into her brain, and seemed alive. She never forgot these words, but she dared not repeat them. And she knew herself that the very possession of the sentiments, the knowledge that they existed, made her "dangerous," as her enemies called her; for most of them were on the attributes of man.

The conversation was interrupted by a servant, who brought the Countess a note.

"How very imprudent!" cried Constance, reddening with vexation. "Why will the boy do these wild things? Help me, Professor. My cousin, Lord Chester, wants to see me, and is coming, *by himself*, to my house – here – immediately."

"Surely I am sufficient guardian of the proprieties, Constance. We will say, if you like, that the boy came to see his old tutor. Let him come, and, unless he has anything for your ear alone, I can be present."

"Heaven knows what he has to say," his cousin sighed. "Always some fresh escapade, some kicking over the limits of convention." She was standing at the window, and looked out. "And here he comes, riding along Park Lane as if it were an open common."

CHAPTER II.

THE EARL OF CHESTER.

"Edward!" cried Constance, giving her cousin her hand, "is this prudent? You ride down Park Lane as if you were riding after hounds, your unhappy attendant – poor girl! – trying in vain to keep up with you; and then you descend openly, and in the eyes of all, alone, at my door – the door of your unmarried cousin. Consider me, my dear Edward, if you are careless about your own reputation. Do you think I have no enemies? Do you think young Lord Chester can go anywhere without being seen and reported? Do you think all women have kind hearts and pleasant tongues?"

The young man laughed, but a little bitterly.

"My reputation, Constance, may just as well be lost as kept. What do I care for my reputation?"

At these terrible words Constance looked at him in alarm.

He was worth looking at, if only as a model, being six feet high, two-and-twenty years of age, strongly built, with crisp, curly brown hair, the shoulders of a Hercules, and the face of an Apollo. But to-day his face was clouded, and as he spoke he clenched his fist.

"What has happened now, Edward?" asked his cousin. "Anything important? The new groom?"

"The new groom has a seat like a sack, is afraid to gallop, and can't jump. As for her nerve, she's got none. My stable-boy Jack would be worth ten of her. But if a man cannot be allowed – for the sake of his precious reputation – to ride without a girl trailing at his heels, why, I suppose there is no more to be said. No, Constance; it is worse than the new groom."

"Edward, you are too masterful." said his cousin, gravely. "One cannot, even if he be Earl of Chester, fly in the face of all the *convenances*. Rules are made to protect the weak for their own sake; the strong obey them for the sake of the weak. You are strong; be therefore considerate. Suppose all young men were allowed to run about alone?"

The Professor shook her head gravely.

"It would be a return," she said, "to the practice of the ancients."

"The barbarous practice of the ancients," added Constance.

"The grooms might at least be taught how to ride," grumbled the young man.

"But about this disaster, Edward; is it the postponement of a cricket-match, the failure of a tennis game – "

"Constance," he interrupted, "I should have thought you capable of believing that I should not worry you at such a moment with trifles. I have got the most serious news for you – things for which I want your help and your sympathy."

Constance turned pale. What could he have to tell her except one thing – the one thing which she had been dreading for two or three years?"

Edward, Earl of Chester in his own right, held his title by a tenure unique in the peerage. For four generations the Countesses of Chester had borne their husbands one child only, and that a son; for four generations the Earls of Chester had married ladies of good family, certainly, but of lower rank, so that the title remained. He represented, by lineal descent through the male line, the ancient Royal House; and though there were not wanting ladies descended through the female line from old kings of England, by this extraordinary accident he possessed the old royal descent, which was more coveted than any other in the long lists of the Red Book. It was objected that its honours were half shorn by being transmitted through so many males; but there were plenty to whisper that, according to ancient custom, the young Earl would be none other than King of England. So long a line of only children could not but result in careful nursing of the estate, which was held in trust and ward by one Countess after another, until now it was one of the greatest in the country; and though there were a few peeresses whose acres exceeded those of the Earl of Chester, there was no young man in the matrimonial market to be compared with him. His hand was at the disposal – subject, of course, to his own agreement, which was taken for granted – of the Chancellor, who, up to the present time, had made no sign.

Young, handsome, the holder of a splendid title, the owner of a splendid rent-roll, said to be of amiable disposition, known to be proud of his descent – could there be a husband more desirable? Was it to be wondered at if every unmarried woman in a certain rank of life, whether maid or widow, dreamed of marrying the Earl of Chester, and made pictures in her own mind of herself as the Countess, sitting in the House, taking precedence as Première, after the Duchesses, holding office, ruling departments, making eloquent speeches, followed and reported by the society papers, giving great entertainments, actually being and doing what other women can only envy and sigh for?

It was whispered that Lady Carlyon would ask her cousin's hand; it was also whispered that the Chancellor (now a permanent officer of the State) would never grant her request on account of her politics; it was also whispered that a certain widow, advanced in years, of the highest rank, had been observed to pay particular attention to the young Earl in society and in the field. This report, however, was received with caution, and was not generally believed.

"Serious news!" Constance for a moment looked very pale. The Professor glanced at her with concern and even pity. "Serious news!" She was going to add, "Who is it?" but stopped in time. "What is it?" she said instead.

"You have not yet heard, then," the Earl replied, "of the great honour done to me and to my house?"

Constance shook her head. She knew now that her worst fears were going to be realised.

"Tell me quickly, Edward."

"No less a person that her Grace the Duchess of Dunstanburgh has offered me, through the Chancellor, the support and honour of her hand."

Constance started. This was the worst, indeed. The Duchess of Dunstanburgh! Sixty-five years of age; already thrice a widow; the Duchess of Dunstanburgh! She could not speak.

"Have you nothing to say, Constance?" asked the young man. "Do you not envy me my happy lot? My bride is not young, to be sure, but she is a Duchess; the old Earldom will be lost in the new Duchy. She has buried three husbands already; one may look forward with joy to lying beside them in her gorgeous mausoleum. Her country house is finer than mine, but it is not so old. She is of rank so exalted that one need not inquire into her temper, which is said to be evil; nor into the little faults, such as jealousy, suspicion, meanness, greed, and avarice, with which the wicked world credits her."

"Edward! Edward!" cried her cousin.

"Then, again, one's religion will be so beautifully brought into play. We are required to obey – that is the first thing taught in the Church catechism; all women are set in authority over us. I must therefore obey the Chancellor."

His hearers were silent.

"Again, what says the text? – 'It is man's chiefest honour to be chosen: his highest duty to give, wherever bidden, his love, his devotion, and his loyalty.'"

The Professor nodded her head gravely.

"What martyrs of religion would ask for a more noble opportunity," he asked, "than to marry this old woman?"

"Edward!" Constance could only warn. She sees no way to advise. "Do not scoff."

"Let us face the position," said the Professor. "The Chancellor has gone through the form of asking your consent to this marriage. When?"

"Last night."

"And when do you see her?"

"I am to see her ladyship this very morning."

"To inform her of your acquiescence. Yes; it is the usual form. The time is very short."

"My acquiescence?" asked the Earl. "We shall see about that presently."

"Patience, my lord!" The Professor was thinking what to advise for the best. "Patience! Let us have no sudden and violent resolves. We may get time. Ay – time will be our best friend. Remember that the Chancellor *must* be obeyed. She may, for the sake of courtesy, go through the form of proposing a suitable alliance for your consideration, but her proposition is her order, which you must obey. Otherwise it is contempt of court, and the penalty – ”

"I know it," said the Earl, "already. It is imprisonment."

"Such contempt would be punished by imprisonment for life. Imprisonment, hopeless."

"Nay," he replied. "Not hopeless, because one could always hope in the power of friends. Have I not Constance? And then, you see, Professor, I am two-and-twenty, while the Chancellor and the Duchess are both sixty-five. Perhaps they may join the majority."

The Professor shook her head. Even to speak of the age of so great a lady, even to hint at her death as an event likely to happen soon, was an outrage against propriety – which is religion.

"My determination is this," he went on, "whatever the consequence, I will never marry the Duchess. Law or no law, I will never marry a woman unless I love her." His eye rested for a moment on his cousin, and he reddened. "I may be imprisoned, but I shall carry with me the sympathy of every woman – that is, of every young woman – in the country."

"That will not help you, poor boy," said the Professor. "Hundreds of men are lying in our prisons who would have the sympathies of young women, were their histories known. But they lie there still, and will lie there till they die."

"Then I," said the Earl, proudly, "will lie with them."

There were moments when this young man seemed to forget the lessons of his early training, and the examples of his fellows. The meekness, modesty, submission, and docility which should mark the perfect man sometimes disappeared, and gave place to an assumption of the authority which should only belong to woman. At such times, in his own castle, his servants trembled before him; the stoutest woman's heart failed for fear: even his guardian, the Dowager Lady Boltons, selected carefully by the Chancellor on account of her inflexible character, and because she had already reduced to complete submission a young heir of the most obstinate disposition, and the rudest and most uncompromising material, quailed before him. He rode over her, so to speak. His will conquered hers. She was ashamed to own it; she did not acquaint the Chancellor with her ward's masterful character; but she knew, in her own mind, that her guardianship had been a failure. Nay, so strange was the personal influence of the young man, so infectious among the men were such assertions of will, that any husband who happened to witness one of them, would go home and carry on in fashion so masterful, so independent, and so self-willed, even those who had previously been the most submissive, that they were only brought to reason and proper submission by threats, remonstrances, and visits of admonition from the vicar – who, poor woman, was always occupied in the pulpit, owing to the Earl's bad example, with the disobedience of man and its awful consequences here and hereafter. Sometimes these failed. Then they became acquainted with the inside of a prison and with bread and water.

"Let us get time," said the Professor. "My lord, I hope" – here she sunk her voice to a whisper – "that you will neither lie in a prison nor marry any but the woman you love."

Again the young man's eyes boldly fell upon Constance, who blushed without knowing why.

Then the Professor, without any excuse, left them alone.

"You have," said Lord Chester, "something to say to me, Constance."

She hesitated. What use to say now what should have been said at another lime and at a more fitting opportunity?

"I am no milky, modest, obedient youth, Constance. You know me well. Have you nothing to say to me?"

In the novels, the young man who hears the first word of love generally sinks on his knees, and with downcast eyes and blushing face reverentially kisses the hand so graciously offered to him. In ordinary life they had to wait until they were asked. Yet this young man was actually asking – boldly asking – for the word of love – what else could he mean? – and instead of blushing, was fixedly regarding Constance with fearless eyes.

"It seems idle now to say it," she replied, stammering and hesitating – though in novels the woman always spoke up in clear, calm, and resolute accents; "but, Edward, had the Chancellor not been notoriously the personal friend and creature of the Duchess, I should have gone to her long ago. They were school-fellows; she owes her promotion to the Duchess; she would most certainly have rewarded her Grace by refusing my request."

"Yet you are a Carlyon and I a Chester. On what plea?"

"Cousinship, incompatibility of temper, some legal quibble – who knows? However, that is past; forget, my poor Edward, that I have told what should have been a secret. You will marry the Duchess – you – "

He interrupted her by laughing – a cheerfully sarcastic laugh, as of one who holds the winning cards and means to play them.

"Fair cousin," he said, "I have something to say to you of far more importance than that. You have retired before an imaginary difficulty. I am going to face a real difficulty, a real danger. Constance," he went on, "you and I are such old friends and playfellows, that you know me as well as a woman can ever know a man who is not her husband. We played together when you were three and I was five. When you were ten and I was twelve, we read out of the same book until the stupidity and absurdity of modern custom tried to stop me from reading any more. Since then we have read separately, and you have done your best to addle your pretty head with political economy, in the name and by the aid of which you and your House of Lawmakers have ruined this once great country."

"Edward! this is the wildest treason. Where, oh where, did you learn to talk – to think – to dare such dreadful things?"

"Never mind where, Constance. In those days – in those years of daily companionship – a hope grew up in my heart, – a flame of fire which kept me alive, I think, amidst the depression and gloom of my fellow-men. Can you doubt what was that hope?"

Constance trembled – the Countess of Carlyon, the Home Secretary, trembled. Had she ever before, in all her life, trembled? She was afraid. In the novels, it was true, many a young man, greatly daring, by a bold word swept away a cloud of misunderstanding and reserve. But this was in novels written by women of the middle class, who can never hope to marry young, for the solace of people of their own rank. It was not to be expected that in such works there should be any basis of reality – they were in no sense pictures of life; for, in reality, as was deplored almost openly, when these elderly ladies were rich enough to take a husband and face the possibilities of marriage, though they always chose the young men, it was rare indeed that they met with more than a respectful acquiescence. Nothing, ladies complained among each other, was more difficult than to win and retain a young man's love. But here was this headstrong youth, with love in his eyes – bold, passionate, masterful love – overpowering love – love in his attitude as he bent over the girl, and love upon his lips. Oh, dignity of a Home Secretary! Oh, rules and conventions of life! Oh, restraints of religion! Where were they all at this most fatal moment?

"Constance," he said, taking her hand, "all the rubbish about manly modesty is outside the door: and that is closed. I am descended from a race who in the good old days wooed their brides for themselves, and fought for them too, if necessary. Not toothless, hoary old women, but young, sunny, blooming girls, like yourself. And they wooed them thus, my sweet." He seized her in his strong arms and kissed her on the lips, on the cheeks, on the forehead. Constance, frightened and moved, made no resistance, and answered nothing. Once she looked up and met his eyes, but they were so strong, so burning, so determined, that she was fain to look no longer. "I love you, my dear," the shameless young man went on, – "I love you. I have always loved you, and shall never love any other woman; and if I may not marry you, I will never marry at all. Kiss me yourself, my sweet; tell me that you love me."

Had he a spell? was he a wizard, this lover of hers? Could Constance, she thought afterwards, trying to recall the scene, have dreamed the thing, or did she throw her arms about his neck and murmur in his ears that she too loved him, and that if she could not marry him, there was no other man in all the world for her?

To recall those five precious minutes, indeed, was afterwards to experience a sense of humiliation which, while it crimsoned her cheek, made her heart and pulse to beat, and sent the blood coursing through her veins. She felt so feeble and so small, but then her lover was so strong. Could she have believed it possible that the will of a man should thus be able to overpower her? Why, she made no resistance at all while her cousin in this unheard-of manner betrayed a passion which ... which ... yes, by all the principles of holy religion, by all the rules of society, by all the teaching which inculcated submission, patience, and waiting to be chosen, caused this young man to deserve punishment – condign, sharp, exemplary. And yet – what did this mean? Constance felt her heart go forth to him. She loved him the more for his masterfulness; she was prouder of herself because of his great passion.

That was what she thought afterwards. What she did, when she began to recover, was to free herself and hide her burning face in her hands.

"Edward," she whispered, "we are mad. And I, who should have known better, am the more culpable. Let us forget this moment. Let us respect each other. Let us be silent."

"Respect?" he echoed. "Why, who could respect you, Constance, more than I do? Silence? Yes, for a while. Forget? Never!"

"It is wrong, it is irreligious," she faltered.

"Wrong! Oh, Constance, let us not, between ourselves, talk the foolish unrealities of school and pulpit."

"Oh, Edward!" – she looked about her in terror – "for heaven's sake do not blaspheme. If any were to hear you. For words less rebellious men have been sent to the prisons for life."

He laughed. This young infidel laughed at law as he had laughed at religion.

"Have patience," Constance went on, trying to get into her usual frame of mind; but she was shaken to the very foundation, and at the moment actually felt as if her religion was turned upside down and her allegiance transferred to the Perfect Man. "Have patience, Edward; you will yet win through to the higher faith. Many a young man overpowered by his strength, as you have been, has had his doubts, and yet has landed at last upon the solid rock of truth."

Edward made no reply to this, not even by a smile. It was not a moment in which the ordinary consolations of religion, so freely offered by women to men, could touch his soul. He took out his watch and remarked that the time was getting on, and that the Chancellor's appointment must be kept.

"With her ladyship, I suppose," he said, "we shall find the painted, ruddled, bewigged old hag who has the audacity to ask me – *me* – in marriage."

Constance caught his hand.

"Edward! cousin! are you mad? Are you proposing to seek a prison at once? Hag? old? painted? ruddled? And this of the Duchess of Dunstanburgh? Are you aware that the least of these charges is actionable at common law? For my sake, Edward, if not your own, be careful."

"I will, sweet Constance, And for your sake, just to our two selves, I repeat that the painted – "

"Oh!"

"The ruddled – "

"Oh, hush!"

"The bewigged – "

"Edward!"

"Old hag – do you hear? – OLD HAG shall never marry me."

Once more this audacious and unmanly lover, who respected nothing, seized her by the waist and kissed her lips. Once more Lady Carlyon felt that unaccountable weakness steal upon her, so that she was bewildered, faint, and humiliated. For a moment she lay still and acquiescent in his arms. Worse than all, the door opened and Professor Ingleby surprised her in this compromising situation.

"Upon my word!" she said, with a smile upon her lips; "upon my word, my lord – Constance – if her Grace of Dunstanburgh knew this! Children, children!" – she laid her withered hand upon Constance's head – "I pray that this thing may be. But we want time. Let us keep Lord Chester's appointment. And, as far as you can, leave to me, my lord, your old tutor, the task of speech. I know the Duchess, and I know the Chancellor. It may be that the oil of persuasion will be more efficacious than the lash of contradiction. Let me try."

They stood confused – even the unblushing front of the lover reddened.

"I have thought of a way of getting time. Come with us, Constance, as Lord Chester's nearest female relation; I as his tutor, in absence of Lady Boltons, who is ill. When the Chancellor proposes the Duchess, do you propose – yourself. She will decide against you on the spot. *Appeal to the House*; that will give us three months' delay."

CHAPTER III

THE CHANCELLOR.

THE CHANCELLOR, a lady now advanced in years, was of humble origin – a fact to which she often alluded to at public meetings with a curious mixture of humility and pride: the former, because it did really humiliate her in a country where so much deference was paid to hereditary rank, to reflect that she could not be proud of her ancestors; the latter, because her position was really so splendid, and her enemies could not but acknowledge it. She had plenty of enemies – as was, of course, the case with every successful woman in every line of life – and these were unanimous in declaring that she proclaimed her humble origin only because, if she attempted to conceal it, other people would proclaim it for her. And, indeed, without attributing extraordinary malice to these ladies, the Chancellor's unsuccessful rivals and enemies, this statement was probably true – nothing being more common, during an animated debate, than for the ladies to hurl at each other's heads all such facts procurable as might be calculated to damage the reputation of a family: and this so much so, that after a lively night the family trees were as much scotched, broken, and lopped as a public pleasure-garden in the nineteenth century after the first Monday in August.

At this time the Chancellor had arrived at a respectable age – being, that is to say, in her sixty-sixth year. She was a woman of uneven temper, having been soured by a long life of struggle against rivals who lost no opportunity of assailing her public and private reputation. She had remained unmarried, because, said her foes, no man would consent to link his lot with so spiteful a person; she was no lawyer, they said, because her whole desire and aim had been to show herself a lawyer of the highest rank; she was partial – this they said for the same reason, because she wanted to be remembered as an upright judge. They alluded in the House to her ignorance of the higher culture – although the poor lady had taught herself half-a-dozen languages, and was skilled in many arts; and they taunted her with her friendship for, meaning her dependence upon, her patron, the Duchess of Dunstanburgh. The last accusation was the burr that stuck, because the poor Chancellor could not deny its truth. She was, in fact, the daughter of a very respectable woman – a tenant-farmer of the Duchess. Her Grace found the girl clever, and educated her. She acquired over her, by the force of her personal character, an extraordinary influence – having made her entirely her own creature. She found the money for her entrance at the Bar, pushed her at the beginning, watched her upward course, never let her forget that everything was owing to her own patronage at the outset, and, when the greatest prize of the profession was in her grasp, and the farmer's girl became Chancellor, the Duchess of Dunstanburgh – by one of those acts of hers which upset the debates and resolutions of years – passed a Bill which made the appointment tenable for life, and so transferred into her own hands all the power, all the legal skill of the Chancellor. It was the most brilliant political *coup* ever made. Those who knew whispered that the Chancellor had no voice, no authority, no independent action at all; her patron regulated everything. While this terrible Duchess lived, the Court of Chancery belonged to her with all its manifold and complicated powers. She herself was, save at rare intervals, Prime Minister, Autocrat, and almost Dictator. Certainly it was notorious that whatever the Duchess of Dunstanburgh wanted she had; and it was also a fact not to be disputed, that there were many lawyers of higher repute, more dignified, more learned, more eloquent, and of better birth, who had been passed over to make room for this *protégé* of the Duchess – this "daughter of the plough."

Lord Chester, accompanied by the Countess of Carlyon and Professor Ingleby, arrived at the Law Courts at twelve, the hour of the Chancellor's appointment, and were shown into an ante-room. Here, with a want of courtesy most remarkable, considering the rank of the ward in Chancery whose future was to be decided at this interview, they were kept waiting for half an hour. When at length they were admitted to the presence, they were astonished to find that, contrary to all precedent, the Duchess of Dunstanburgh herself was with the Chancellor. In fact she had been directing her creature in the line she was to take: she intended to receive the hand of the Earl from her, and to push on the marriage without an hour's delay. It was sharp practice; but her Grace was not a woman who considered herself bound by the ordinary rules. Any lesser person would have made her petition for the hand of a ward, and waited until she had received in due course official notification of acceptance, when an interview would have been arranged and the papers signed. All this, owing to the delays of Chancery, generally took from a twelvemonth upwards; and in the case of poor people who had no interest, perhaps their petitions were never decided at all, so that the unfortunate petitioner waited in vain, until she died of old age, still unmarried; and the unlucky ward lived on, hoping against hope, till his time for marriage went by. The Duchess possessed even more than the dignity which became her rank. She was rather a tall woman, with aquiline features; her age was sixty-five, and in her make-up she studiously affected, not the bloom and elasticity of youth, but the vigour and strength of middle life – say of fifty. All the resources of Art were lavished upon her with this object: her hair showed a touch of grey upon the temples, but was still abundant, rich, and glossy, and was so beautifully arranged that it challenged the admiration even of those who knew that it was a wig; her eyebrows were dark and well defined – her enemies said she kept a special artist continually employed in making new eyebrows; her teeth were of pearly whiteness; her cheeks, just touched with paint, showed none of the wrinkles of time – though no one knew how that was managed; her forehead, strong and broad, was crossed by three deep lines which could not be effaced by any artist. Some said they were caused by the successive deaths of three husbands, and therefore marked the Duchess's profound grief and the goodness of her heart, because it was known that one of them at least – the third, youngest, and handsomest of all, upon whom the fond wife lavished all her affections – had given her the greatest trouble; indeed, it was even said that – and that – and that with many other circumstances showing the blackest ingratitude, so that women held up their hands and wondered what men wanted. But her Grace's enemies said that her famous wrinkles were caused by her three great vices of pride, ambition, and avarice; and they declared that if she developed another such furrow, it would represent her other great vice of vanity. As for that third husband – could one expect the poor young man to fall in love with a woman already fifty-eight when she married him?

The Duchess was richly but plainly dressed in black velvet and lace; her figure was still full. As she rose to greet the Chancellor's ward, she leaned upon a gold-headed stick – being somewhat troubled with gout. Her smile was encouraging and kind towards the Earl; to Constance, as to a political enemy who was to be treated with all external courtesy, she bowed low; and she coldly inclined her head in return to the profound act of deference paid to her by the Professor. The Chancellor, a fussy little woman with withered cheeks, wrinkled brow, and thin grey locks, sat at her table. She hardly rose to greet her ward, whom she motioned to a chair. Then she looked at Constance, and waited for her to explain her presence.

"I come with Lord Chester on this occasion," said Constance, "as his nearest female relation. As your ladyship is probably aware, I am his second cousin."

The Chancellor bowed. Then the Professor spoke.

"I ask your ladyship's permission to appear in support of my pupil on this important occasion. His guardian, Lady Boltons, is unfortunately too ill to be present."

"There is no reason, I suppose," said the Chancellor, ungraciously, and with a glance of some anxiety at the Duchess, "why you should not be present, Professor Ingleby; – unless, that is, the Earl of Chester would rather see me alone. But the proceedings are almost formal."

Lord Chester, who was very grave, merely shook his head. Then the Chancellor shuffled about her papers for a few moments, and addressed her ward.

"Your lordship will kindly give me your best attention," she began, with some approach to blandness. "I am glad, in the first place, to congratulate you on your health, your appearance, and your strength. I have received the best reports on your moral and religious behaviour, and your docility, and – and – so on, from your guardian, Lady Boltons, and I am only sorry that she is not able to be here herself, in order to receive from me my thanks for the faithful and conscientious discharge of her duties, and from the Duchess of Dunstanburgh a recognition of her services in those terms which come from no one with more weight and more dignity than from her Grace." The Duchess held up a hand in deprecation; the Professor nodded, and lifted up her hands and smiled, as if a word of thanks from the Duchess was all she, for her part, wanted, in order to be perfectly happy. The Earl, one is sorry to say, sat looking straight at the Chancellor without an expression of any kind, unless it were one of patient endurance. The Chancellor went on.

"You will shortly, you now know, pass from my guardianship to the hands and care of another far more able and worthy to hold the reins of authority than myself."

Here Constance rose.

"Before your ladyship goes any farther, I beg to state to you that Lord Chester has only this morning informed me of a proposal made to you by her Grace of Dunstanburgh, which is now under your consideration."

"It certainly is," said the Chancellor, "and I am about – "

"Before you proceed," – Constance changed colour, but her voice was firm, – "you will permit me also to make official and formal application in the presence of the Duchess herself, who will, I am sure, be a witness, and Professor Ingleby, for the hand of Lord Chester. There is, I think, no occasion for me to say anything in addition to my simple proposal. What I could add would probably not influence your ladyship's decision. You know me, and all that is to be known about me – "

"This is most astonishing!" cried the Duchess.

"May I ask your Grace what is astonishing about this proposal? May I remind you that I have known Lord Chester all my life; that we are equals in point of rank, position, and wealth; that I am, if I may say so, not altogether undistinguished, even in the House of which your Grace is so exalted an ornament? But I have to do with the judgment of your ladyship, not the opinion of the Duchess."

The Chancellor turned anxiously to her patroness, as if for direction. She replied with dignity.

"Your ladyship is aware that, as the earlier applicant, my proposal would naturally take precedence in your ladyship's consideration of any later ones. I might even demand that it be considered on its own merits, without reference at all to Lady Carlyon's proposal, with regard to which I keep my own opinion."

Constance remarked, coldly, that her Grace's opinion was unfortunately, in most important matters, exactly opposite to her own and to that of her friends, and she was contented to disagree with her. She then informed the Chancellor that as no decision had been given as to the marriage of Lord Chester, the case was still before her, and, she submitted, the proposals both of herself and of the Duchess should be weighed by her ladyship. "And," she added, "I would humbly submit that there are many other considerations, in the case of so old and great a House as that represented by Lord Chester, which should be taken account of. Higher rank than his own, for instance, need not be desired; nor greater wealth; nor many other things which in humbler marriages may be considered. I will go farther: in this room, which is, as it were, a secret chamber, I say boldly that care should be taken to continue so old and illustrious a line."

"And why," cried the Duchess, sharply, and dropping her stick – "why should it not be continued?"

Here a remarkable thing happened. Lord Chester should have affected a complete ignorance of the insult which Constance had deliberately flung in her rival's teeth: what he did do was to turn slowly round and stare, in undisguised wonder, at the Duchess, as if surprised at her audacity. Even her Grace, with all her pride and experience, could not sustain this calm, cold look. She faltered and said no more. Lord Chester picked up the stick, and handed it to her with a low bow.

"I am much obliged to you, Lady Carlyon," said the Chancellor, tapping her knuckles with her glasses; "very much obliged to you, I am sure, for laying down rules for *my* guidance – MINE! – in the interpretation of the law and my duty. That, however, may pass. It is my business – although I confess that this interruption is of a most surprising and unprecedented nature – to proceed with the case before me, which is that of the proposal made by the Duchess of Dunstanburgh."

"Do I understand," asked Lady Carlyon, "that you refuse to receive my proposal? Remember that you *must* receive it. You cannot help receiving it. This is a public matter, which shall, if necessary, be brought before the House and before the nation. I say that your ladyship must receive my proposal."

"Upon my word!" cried the Chancellor. "Upon my word!"

"Perhaps," said the Duchess, "if Lady Carlyon's proposal were to be received – let me ask that it may be received, even if against precedent – the consideration of the case could be proceeded with at once, and perhaps your ladyship's decision might be given on the spot."

"Very good – very good." The Chancellor was glad to get out of a difficulty. "I will take the second proposal into consideration as well as the first. Now then, my Lord. You have been already informed that the Duchess has asked me for your hand."

Here the Duchess made a gesture, and slowly rose, as if about to speak. "A proposition of this kind," she said, in a clear and firm voice, "naturally brings with it, to any young man, and especially a young man of our Order, some sense of embarrassment. He has been taught – that is" (here she bent her brows and put on her glasses at the Professor, who was bowing her head at every period, keeping time with her hands, as if in deference to the words of the Duchess, and as if they contained truths which could not be suffered to be forgotten), "if he has been properly taught – the sacredness of the marriage state, the unworthiness of man, the duties of submission and obedience, which, when rightly carried out, lead to the higher levels. And in proportion to the soundness of his training, and the goodness of his heart, is he embarrassed when the time of his greatest happiness arrives." The Professor bowed, and spread her hands as if in agreement with so much wisdom so beautifully expressed. "Lord Chester," continued the Duchess, "I have long watched you in silence; I have seen in you qualities which, I believe, befit a consort of my rank. You possess pride of birth, dexterity, skill, grace; you know how to wield such authority as becomes a man. You will exchange your earl's coronet for the higher one of a duke. I am sure you will wear it worthily. You will – " Here Constance interrupted.

"Permit me, your Grace, to remind you that the Chancellor's decision has not yet been given."

The Duchess sat down frowning. This young lady should be made to feel her resentment. But for the moment she gave way and scowled, leaning her chin upon her stick. It was a hard face even when she smiled; when she frowned it was a face to look upon and tremble.

The Chancellor turned over her papers impatiently.

"I see nothing," she said, – "I see nothing at all in the proposition made by Lady Carlyon to alter my opinion, previously formed, that the Duchess has made an offer which seems in every way calculated to promote the moral, spiritual, and material happiness of my ward."

"May I ask," said Lord Chester, quietly, "if I may express my own views on this somewhat important matter?'

"You?" the Chancellor positively shrieked. "You? The ignorance in which boys are brought up is disgraceful! A ward in Chancery to express an opinion upon his own marriage! Positively a real ward in Chancery! Is the world turning upside down?"

The audacity of the remark, and the happy calmness with which it was proffered, were irresistible. All the ladies, except the Chancellor, laughed. The Duchess loudly. This little escapade of youth and ignorance amused her. Constance laughed too, with a little pity. The Professor laughed with some show of shame, as if Lord Chester's ignorance reflected in a manner upon herself.

Then the Chancellor went on again with some temper.

"Let me resume. It is my duty to consider nothing but the interests of my ward. Very good. I have considered them. My Lord Chester, in giving your hand to the Duchess of Dunstanburgh, I serve your best and highest interests. The case is decided. There is no more to be said."

"There is, on the contrary, much more to be said," observed Constance. "I give your ladyship notice of appeal to the House of Peeresses. I shall appeal to them, and to the nation through them, whether your decision in this case is reasonable, just, and in accordance with the interests of your ward."

This was, indeed, a formidable threat. An appeal to the House meant, with such fighting-power as Constance and her party, although a minority, possessed, and knew how to direct, a delay of perhaps six months, even if the case came on from day to day. Even the practised old Duchess, used to the wordy warfare of the House, shrank from such a contest.

"You will not, surely, Lady Carlyon," she said, "drag your cousin's name into the Supreme Court of Appeal."

"I certainly will," replied Constance.

"It will cost hundreds of thousands, and months – months of struggle."

"As for the cost, that is my affair; as for the delay, I can wait – perhaps longer than your Grace."

The Duchess said no more. Twice had Lady Carlyon insulted her. But her revenge would wait.

"We have already," she said, "occupied too much of the Chancellor's valuable time. I wish your ladyship good morning."

Lord Chester offered his arm.

"Thank you," she said, accepting it, "as far as the carriage-door only, *for the present*. I trust, my lord, that before long you will have the right to enter the carriage with me. Meanwhile, believe me, that it is not through my fault that your name is to be made the subject of public discussion. Pending the appeal, let us not betray, by appearing together, any feeling other than that of pure friendship. And I hope," viciously addressing Constance, "that you, young lady, will observe the same prudence."

Constance simply bowed and said nothing. The Chancellor rose, shook hands with her ward, and retired.

The Duchess leaned upon the strong arm which led her to her carriage, and kissed her hand in farewell to the young man with so much affection and friendly interest that it was beautiful to behold. After this act of politeness, the young man returned to Constance.

"Painted" – he began.

"Edward, I will not allow it. Silence, sir! We part here for the present."

"Constance," he whispered, "you will not forget – *all* that I said?"

"Not one word," she replied with troubled brow. "But we must meet no more for a while."

"Courage!" cried the Professor, "we have gained time."

CHAPTER IV.
THE GREAT DUCHESS.

IMPOSSIBLE, of course, that so important a case as the appeal of Lady Carlyon should be concealed. In fact Constance's policy was evidently to give it as much publicity as possible. She rightly judged that although, in her own Order, and in the House, which has to look at things from many points of view, motives of policy might be considered sufficient to override sentimental objections, and it was not likely that much weight would be attached to a young man's feelings; yet the Duchess had many enemies, even on her own side of the House – private enemies wounded by her pride and insolence – who would rejoice at seeing her meet with a check in her self-willed and selfish course. But, besides the House, there was the outside world to consider. There was never greater need on the part of the governing caste for conciliation and respect to public opinions than at this moment – a fact perfectly well understood by all who were not blind to the meaning of things current. The abolition of the Lower House, although of late years it had degenerated into something noisier than a vestry, something less decorous than a school-board in which every woman has her own hobby of educational methods, had never been a popular act. A little of the old respect for so ancient a House still survived, – a little of the traditional reverence for a Parliament which had once protected the liberties of the people, still lingered in the hearts of the nation. The immediate relief, it is true, was undoubtedly great when the noise of elections – which never ceased, because the House was continually dissolved – the squabbles about corruption, the scandals in the House itself, the gossip about the jobs perpetrated by the members, all ceased at once, and as if by magic the country became silent; yet the pendulum of opinion was going back again – women who took up political matters were looking around for an outlet to their activity, and were already at their clubs asking awkward questions about what they had gained by giving up all the power to hereditary legislators. Nor did the old plan of sending round official orators to lecture on the advantages of oligarchical and maternal government seem to answer any longer. The women who used to draw crowded audiences and frantic applause as they depicted and laid bare the scandals and miseries and ridiculous squabbles of the Lower House, who pointed to session after session consumed in noisy talk, now shouted to empty benches, or worse still, benches crowded with listless men, who only sat bored with details in which they were forbidden to take any part, and therefore had lost all interest. Sometimes the older women would attend and add a few words from their own experience; or they would suggest, sarcastically, that the Upper House was going the way of the Lower. As for the younger women, either they would not attend at all, or else they came to ask questions, shout denials, groan and hiss, or even pass disagreeable resolutions. Constance knew all this; and though she would have shrunk, almost as much as the Duchess, from lending any aid to revolutionary designs, she could not but feel that the popular sympathy awakened in her favour at such a moment as the present might assume such strength as to be an irresistible force.

How could the sympathies of the people be otherwise than on her side? These marriages of old or middle-aged women with young men, common though they had become, could never be regarded by the youth of either sex as natural. The young women bitterly complained that the lovers provided for them by equality of age were taken from them, and that times were so bad that in no profession could one look to marry before forty. The young men, who were not supposed to have any voice in the matter, let it be clearly known that their continual prayer and daily dream was for a young wife. The general discontent found expression in songs and ballads, written no one knew by whom: they passed from hand to hand; they were sung with closed doors; they all had the same *motif*; they celebrated the loves of two young people, maiden and youth; they showed how they were parted by the elderly woman who came to marry the tall and gallant youth; how the girl's life was embittered, or how she pined away, or how she became misanthropic; and how the young man spent the short remainder of his days in an apathetic endeavour to discharge his duty, fortified on his deathbed with the consolations of religion and the hopes of meeting, not his old wife, but his old love, in a better and happier world. Why, there could be nothing but sympathy with Constance and Lord Chester. Why, all the men, old and young alike, whose influence upon women and popular opinion, though denied by some, was never doubted by Constance, would give her cause their most active sympathies.

She remained at home that day, taking no other step than to charge a friend with the task of communicating the intelligence to her club, being well aware that in an hour or two it would be spread over London, and, in fact, over the whole realm of England. The next day she went down to the House, and had the satisfaction of finding that the excitement caused by her resignation – a ministerial resignation was too common a thing to cause much talk – had given way altogether to the excitement caused by this great Appeal. No one even took the trouble of asking who was going to be the new Home Secretary. It was taken for granted that it would be some friend of the Duchess of Dunstanburgh. The lobbies were crowded – reporters, members of clubs, dinersout, talkers, were hurrying backwards and forwards, trying to pick up a tolerably trustworthy anecdote; and there was the *va et vient*, the nervous activity, which is so much more easily awakened by personal quarrels than by political differences. And here was a personal quarrel! The young and beautiful Countess against the old and powerful Duchess.

"Yes," said Constance loudly, in answer to a whispered question put by one of her friends – she may have observed two or three listeners standing about with eager ears and parted lips – "yes, it is all quite true; it was an understood thing – this match with my second cousin. The pretensions of the Duchess rest upon too transparent a foundation – the poor man's money, my dear. As if she were not rich enough already! as if three husbands are not enough for any one woman to lament! Thank you; yes, I have not the slightest doubt of the result. In a matter of good feeling as well as equity one may always depend upon the House, whatever one's political opinions."

The Duchess certainly had not expected this resistance to her will. In fact, during the whole of her long life she had never known any resistance at all, except such as befalls every politician. But in her private life her will was law, which no one questioned or disputed. Nor did it even occur to her to inquire, before speaking to the Chancellor, whether there would be any rival in the field. Proud as she was, and careless of public opinion in a general way, it was far from pleasant, even for her, to reflect on the things which would be said of her proposal when the Appeal was brought before the House – on the motives which would be assigned or insinuated by her enemies; on the allusions to youth and age – the more keen the more skilfully they were disguised and wrapped in soft words; the open pity which would be expressed for the youth whose young life – she knew very well what would be said – was to be sacrificed; the sarcastic questions which would be asked about the increase of her property by the new marriage, and so forth. The plain speech of Peeresses in debate was well known to her. Yet pride forbade a retreat: she would fight it out; she could command, by ways and by methods only known to herself, a majority; yet she felt sure, beforehand, that it would be a cold and unsympathetic majority – even a reproachful majority. Nor was her temper improved by a visit from her old friend, once her schoolfellow, Lady Despard. She came with a long face, which portended expostulation.

"You have quite made up your mind, Duchess?" she began, without a word of explanation or preamble, but with a comfortable settlement in the chair, which meant a good long talk.

"I have quite made up my mind." Between such old friends, no need to ask what was intended.

"Lord Chester," said Lady Despard, thoughtfully, "who is, no doubt, all that you think him – worthy in every way, I mean, of this promotion and your name – is, after all, a very young man."

"That," replied the Duchess, spitefully, "is my affair. His age need not be considered. I am not afraid of myself, Julia. With my experience, at all events, I can say so much."

"Surely, Duchess; I did not mean that. The most powerful mind, coupled with the highest rank, – how should that fail to attract and fix the affection and gratitude of a man? No, dear friend; what I meant was this: he is too young, perhaps, for the full development either of virtues – or their opposites, – too young, perhaps, to know the reality of the prize you offer him."

"I think not, Julia," the Duchess spoke kindly, – "I think not. It is good of you to consider this possibility in so friendly a way; but I have the greatest reliance on the good qualities of Lord Chester. Lady Boltons is his guardian; who would be safer? Professor Ingleby has been his tutor; who could be more discreet?"

"Yes, – Professor Ingleby. She is certainly learned; and yet – yet – at Cambridge there is an uneasy feeling about her orthodoxy."

"I care little," said the Duchess, "about a few wild notions which he may have picked up. On such a man, a little freedom of thought sits gracefully. A Duke of Dunstanburgh cannot possibly be anything but orthodox. Yes, Julia; and the sum of it all is that I am getting old, and I am going to make myself happy with the help of this young gentleman."

"In that case," said her friend, "I have nothing to say, except that I wish you every kind of happiness that you can desire."

"Thank you, Julia. And you will very greatly oblige me if you will mention, wherever you can, that you know, on the very best authority, that the match will be one of pure affection – on both sides; mind, on both sides."

"I will certainly say so, if you wish," replied Lady Despard. "I think, however, that you ought to know, Duchess, something of what people say – no, not common people, but people whose opinions even you are bound to consider."

"Go on," said the Duchess, frowning.

"They say that Lord Chester is so proud of his hereditary title and his rank that he would be broken-hearted to see it merged in any higher title; that he is too rich and too highly placed to be tempted by any of the ordinary baits by which men are caught; that you can give him nothing which he cannot buy for himself; and, lastly, that he is already in love, – even that words of affection have been passed between him and the Countess of Carlyon."

Here the Duchess interrupted, vehemently banging the floor with the crutch which stood at her right hand.

"Lord Chester in love? What nonsense is this, Julia? A young nobleman of his rank – almost my rank – in love! Are you mad, Julia? Are you softening in the brain? Are you aware that the boy has been properly brought up? Will you be good enough to remember that Lady Boltons is beyond all suspicion, and that he could never have seen Lady Carlyon alone since he was a boy?"

"I answer your questions by one or two others," replied her friend, calmly. "Are you, Duchess, aware that these two young people have had constant opportunities of being alone everywhere – coming from church, going to church, in conservatories, at morning parties, at dances, in gardens? Lady Boltons is all discretion; but still – but still – girls will be girls – boys love to, flirt. My dear Duchess, we are still young enough to remember – "

The Duchess smiled: the Duchess laughed. Good-humour returned.

"What else, Julia? You are a retailer of horrid gossip."

"This besides. On the very morning when he waited on the Chancellor, he rode to Lady Carlyon's – "

"I know the exact particulars," said the Duchess. "Lady Boltons wrote to me on the subject to prevent misunderstanding. Professor Ingleby, his old tutor, was there. He rode there alone because his guardian could not go with him. Of course he was properly attended. Lady Carlyon is his second cousin. Properly speaking, perhaps he should have remained at home until the Professor came to him. But a man of Lord Chester's rank may do things which smaller men cannot. And, besides, this impulsiveness – this apparent impatience of conventional restraint – seems to me only to prove the pride and dignity of his character. Is that all, Julia? Have you any more hearsays?"

They were brave words; but the Duchess felt uneasy.

"I have; there is more behind, and worse. Still, in your present mood, I do not know that I ought to say what I should wish to say."

"Say on, Julia. You know that I wish to hear all. Perhaps there may be something after all. Hide nothing from me."

"Very good. They say that Lord Chester is, of all men, the least submissive, the least docile, the least manly – in the highest sense of the word. He habitually assumes authority which belongs to Us; he flies into violent rages; he horsewhips stable-boys; he presumptuously defies orders; he almost openly derides the laws which regulate man's obedience. He questions – he actually questions – the fundamental principles on which society and government are based."

"Quite as it should be," said the Duchess, folding her hands. "I want my husband to obey no one in the world – except myself: he shall accept no teaching, except mine; no doctrine shall be sacred in his eyes – until it has received my authority."

"Would you like the Duke of Dunstanburgh to horsewhip stable-boys?"

The Duchess shrugged her shoulders.

"Why not? No doubt the stable-boys deserve it. We cannot, of course, allow common men to use their strength in this way. But, my dear, in men of very high rank we should encourage – within proper limits – a masterfulness which is, after all, nothing but the legitimate expression of legitimate pride. What is crime in a clown or an artisan, is a virtue in Lord Chester; and, believe me, Julia, for my own part, I know how to tame the most obstinate of men."

She folded her hands and set her teeth together. Julia thought of the late three dukes, and trembled.

"No one should know better, dear Duchess. There remains one thing only. You tell me that the proposed match is to be one of pure affection – on both sides. I am truly rejoiced to hear it. Nothing is better calculated to allay these silly reports about Lady Carlyon and the Earl. Still you should know that outside people say that, should the Appeal go in your favour –"

"'Should'! Julia, do not be absurd. It *must* go in my favour. '*Should*'!"

"In that case, the Earl has declared before witnesses that he will absolutely refuse, whatever the penalty, to accept your hand. How am I to meet such stories as this? By your authorised statement of mutual affection?"

"Idle gossip, Julia, may be left to itself. The Earl is only anxious to have the matter settled as soon as possible. Besides, is it in reason that he should have made such a declaration? Why, he knows – every man knows – that such a refusal would be nothing short of contempt – contempt of the Sovereign Majesty of the Realm. It is punishable – ay, and it *shall* be punished – that is, it should be punished" – the face of the Duchess darkened – "by imprisonment with hard labour for life – Earl or no Earl."

"Then, Duchess," said Lady Despard, with a smile, "I say no more. Of course, a marriage of affection should be encouraged; and we women are all match-makers. You will have the best wishes of all as soon as things are properly understood."

"Julia," the Duchess laid her hand upon her friend's arm, "I am unfeignedly glad that you have told me all this. We have had an explanation which has cleared the air. I refuse to believe that my future husband has so lost all manly feeling as to fall in love. Imagine an Earl of Chester falling in love like a sentimental rustic! Your *canards* about private interviews trouble me not; I am well assured that so well-bred a man will obey the will of the House without a murmur – nay, joyfully, even without consideration of his own inclinations, which, as I have told you, are already decided. And, upon my honour as a peeress, Julia, I am certain that when you come to my autumn party at Dunstanburgh in November next, you will acknowledge that the new Duke is the handsomest bridegroom in the world, that I am the most indulgent wife, and that there is not a happier couple in all England."

Nothing could be more gracious than the smile of the Duchess when she chose to smile. Lady Despard, although she knew by this time what the smile was worth, was nevertheless always carried away by it. For the moment she believed what her friend wished her to believe.

"My dear Duchess," she cried, with effusion, "you *deserve* happiness for your part; and, upon my word, I think that the boy will get it, whether he deserves it or not."

The smile died out from the Duchess's face when she was left alone. A hard, stern look took its place. She took up a hand-glass, and intently examined her own face.

"He is in love with the girl, is he?" she murmured; "and she with him. Why, I saw it in their guilty, stolen looks; her accents betrayed her when she spoke. It is not enough that she must cross me in the House, but she would rob me of a husband. Not yet, Lady Carlyon – not yet." ... She looked at herself again. "Oh, that I could be, again, what I was at one-and-twenty! It is true, as Julia said, that I have nothing to give the boy in return for what I ask of him – his affection. I am an old woman – sixty-five years of age. I suppose I have had my share of love. Harry loved me when I was young – because I was young. Poor Harry! I did not then know how much he loved me, nor the value of a man's heart. Well ... as for the other two, they loved me after their fashion – but it was not like Harry's love; they said they loved me, and in return I gave them all they wanted. They were happy, and I had to be contented." She mused in silence for a time; then she roused herself with an effort. "What then? Let them talk. I am the Duchess of Dunstanburgh. She shall have her whim; she shall have her darling, and if he chooses to sulk, she will punish him until he smiles again. Wait, my lord, only wait till you are safe on the Northumberland coast, and in my castle of Dunstanburgh."

CHAPTER V.
IN THE SEASON.

WOMEN, especially politicians, are (or rather were, until the Revolt) accustomed to the publicity of photographs, illustrated papers, paragraphs in society papers, and to the curiosity with which people stare after them whereever they show themselves. They used to like it. Men, who were, on the other hand, taught to respect modest retirement and that graceful obscurity becoming to the masculine hand which carries out the orders of the female brain, shrank from such notoriety. It was a curious sensation for young Lord Chester to feel, rather than to see and to hear, the people pointing him out, and talking about him.

"Courage!" whispered the Professor. "You will have to encounter a great deal more curiosity than this before long. Above all, do not show by any sign or change of expression that you are conscious of their staring."

This was at the Royal Academy. The rooms were crowded with the usual mob, for it was early in June. There were the country ladies – rosy, fat, and jolly – catalogue and pencil in hand, dragging after them husbands, brothers, sons – ruddy, stalwart fellows – who wearily followed from room to room – ignorant of art, and yet unwilling to be thought ignorant, – flocking to any picture which seemed to contain a story or a subject likely to interest them, such as a horse, or a race, or a match of some kind, and turning away with a half-conscious feeling that they ought to rejoice in not liking the much-praised picture, instead of being ashamed of it, so unlike a horse did they find it, so unfaithful a representation of figure or of action. There were artistic ladies, with their new fashion of dress and pale languid airs, listlessly exchanging the commonplace of the fashionable school; there were professional ladies, lawyers, and doctors, "doing" all the rooms between two consultations in an hour; there were schoolgirls from Harrow, yawning over the Exhibition, which it was a duty they owed to themselves to see early in the season, unless they could get tickets, which they all ardently desired, for the fortnight's private view; there were shoals of men in little parties of two and four, escorted by some good-natured uncle or elderly cousin. The crowd squeezed round the fashionable pictures; they passed heedlessly before pictures of which nobody talked; they all tried to look critical; those who pretended to culture searched after strange adjectives; those who did not, said everything was pretty, and yawned furtively; the ladies whispered remarks to each other, with a quick nod of intelligence; and they received the feeble criticism of the men with the deferent smile due to politeness, or a half-concealed contempt.

This year there were more than the usual number of pictures – in fact, the whole of the five-and-twenty rooms were crowded. Fortunately, they were mostly small rooms, and it was remarkable that the same subjects occurred over and over again. "The same story," said the Professor, "every year. No invention; we follow like sheep. Here is Judith slaying Holofernes" – they were then in the Ancient History Department – "here is Jael slaying Sisera; here are Miriam and Deborah singing their songs of triumph; here is Joan of Arc raising the siege of Orleans, – all exactly the same as when I was a girl forty years ago and more. Ancient History indeed! What do they know about Ancient History?"

"Why do you not teach them, then, Professor?" asked Lord Chester.

"I will tell you why, my lord, in a few weeks – perhaps."

There were a great many altar-pieces in the Sacred Department. In these the Perfect Woman was depicted in every attitude and occupation by which perfection may best be represented. It might have been objected, had any one so far ventured outside the beaten path of criticism, that the Perfect Woman's dress, her mode of dressing her hair, and her ornaments were all of the present year's fashion. "As if," said the Professor, the only one who did venture, "as if no one had any conception of beauty and grace except what fashion orders. Sheep! sheep! we follow like a flock."

The pictures were mostly allegorical: the Perfect Woman directed Labour – represented by twenty or thirty burly young men with implements of various kinds; this was a very favourite subject. Or she led Man upwards. This was a series of pictures: in the first, Man was a rough rude creature, carrying a club with which he banged something – presumably Brother Man; he gradually improved, until at the end he was depicted as laying at the altar of womanhood flowers, fruit, and wine, from his own husbandry. By this time he had got his beard cut off, and was smooth shaven, save for a pair of curly moustaches; his dress was in the fashion of the day; his eyes were down-dropped in reverential awe; and his expression was delightfully submissive, pious, and *béate*. "Is it," asked Lord Chester, "impossible to be religious without becoming such a creature as *that*?"

Again, the Perfect Woman sat alone, thinking for the good of the world. She had a star above her head; she tried, in the picture, not to look as if she were proud of that star. Or the Perfect Woman sat watching, in the dead of night, in the moonlight, for the good of the world; or the Perfect Woman was revealed to enraptured man rising from the waves, not at all wet, and clothed in the most beautifully-fashioned and most expensive modern garments. These two rooms, the Sacred and the Ancient History Departments, were mostly deserted. The principal interest of the Exhibition was in the remaining three-and-twenty, which were devoted to general subjects. Here were sweetnesses of flower and fruit, here were lovely creamy faces of male youth, here were full-length figures of athletes, runners, wrestlers, jumpers, rowers, cricket-players, and others, treated with delicate conventionality, so that the most successful pictures represented man with no more expression in his face than a barber's block, and the strongest young Hercules was figured with tiny hands or fingers like a girl's for slimness, for transparency, and for whiteness, and beautifully small feet; on the other hand, his calves were prodigious. In fact, as was always maintained at the Academy dinner, the Exhibition was the great educator of the people in the sense of beauty. To know the beautiful, to recognise what should be delightful, and then take joy in it, was given, it was said, only to those women of culture who had been trained by a course of Academy exhibitions. Here men, for their part, who would never otherwise rise beyond the phenomenal to the ideal, learned what was the Perfect Man – the man of woman's imagination. Having learned, he might go away and try to resemble him. Women who could not feel, unhappily, the full sense of the beautiful, might learn from these models into what kind of man they should shape their husbands.

"The drawing of this picture," said the Professor aloud, before a picture round which were gathered a throng of worshippers – for it was painted by a royal academician of great repute – "is inaccurate. Did one ever see a man with such shoulders, and yet with such a waist and such a hand? As for the colouring, it is as false as it is conventional; and look at the peach-like cheek and the feeble chin! It is the flesh of a weakly baby, not of a grown man and an athlete."

There were murmurs of dissent, but no one ventured to dispute the Professor's opinion; and indeed most of the bystanders had already recognised Lord Chester, and were staring at the hero of so much talk.

"He is better looking," he overheard one schoolgirl whispering to another, "than the fellow on the canvas, isn't he?"

The "fellow on the canvas" was, in fact, the Ideal Man. He was meant by the artist to represent the noblest, tallest, strongest, straightest, and most dexterous of men. He carried a cricket - bat. It would have been foolish to figure him with book, pencil, or paper. Art, literature, science, politics, all belonged to the other sex. Only his strength was left to man, and that was to be expended by the orders of the superior sex, who were quite competent to exercise the functions for which they were born – namely, to think for the world.

Of course, all the artists were women. Once there was a man who, assuming a female name, actually got a picture exhibited in the Academy. He was a self-taught man, it was afterwards discovered; he had never been in a studio; he had never seen a Royal Academy. He painted an Old Man from nature. There was a faithful ruggedness about his work which made artists scoff, and yet brought tears to the eyes of country girls who knew no better. When the trick was discovered, the picture was taken down and burnt, and the wretched man – who was discovered in a little country cottage, painting two or three more in the same style – went mad, and was locked up for the rest of his days. Presently Lord Chester grew tired of the pictures and of the staring crowd. "I have seen enough, Professor, if you have. They are all exactly like those of last year – the gladiators, and the runners, and all. Are we always to go on producing the same pictures?"

"I suppose so," she replied. "They say that the highest point of art has been reached. It would be a change if we were only to deteriorate for a few years. Meanwhile, one is reminded of the mole, who was asked why he did not invent another form of architecture."

"What did she reply?"

"He, not she, my lord, replied that science could go no farther; and so he goes on building the same shaped hill."

The crowd gathered at the foot of the stairs of the Academy and made a lane for Lord Chester quite to his carriage. It was a crowd of the best people in England, composed of ladies and gentlemen. Yet was it no insignificant sign of the times that many a handkerchief was waved to him, that all hats were lifted, and that one girl's voice was heard crying, "Young men for young wives!" at which there was a general murmur of assent.

In the evening there were the usual engagements of the season, beginning with a lecture on the Arrival at the Highest Level. The lecturer – a young Oxford woman – was learned and eloquent, though the subject was, so to speak, wellnigh threadbare. Yet the discontent of the nation was so great, that it was necessary continually to raise the courage of the people by showing that if Ministries failed, it was only because the right Cabinet had not yet been found. On this night, however, no one listened. All eyes were turned to the young lord, who, it was everywhere stated, had announced his rebellious intention not to obey the law if Lady Carlyon's appeal went against her. The men whispered; the elderly ladies assumed airs of virtuous indignation; the younger ones looked at each other and laughed.

Then there was a dance, at which Lord Chester was seen, but only for a quarter of an hour, because the rush made by all the girls who could get au introduction for his name on their cards was almost unseemly. The Professor therefore took him home.

In the Park the next afternoon, at the theatre in the evening, the same curiosity of the multitude. Indeed the play, as happened very often in those days, was entirely neglected. Glasses were levelled at Lord Chester's box; the whole audience with one consent fell to talking among themselves; the actors went on with the piece un-regarded, and the curtain fell unnoticed.

Perhaps the perfection of the drama was the thing on which the new civilisation chiefly prided itself, unless, indeed, it was the perfection of painting and sculpture already described. The old tragedies, in which women played the secondary part, were long since consigned to oblivion. The old style of farce, which was simply brutal, raising laughter by the representation of situations in which one or more persons are made ridiculous, was absolutely prohibited; the once favourite ballet was suppressed, because it was below the dignity of woman to dance for the amusement of the people, and because neither men nor women wished to see men dancing; the comic man naturally disappeared with the farce, because no one ever wrote anything for him. It was resolved, after a series of letters and discussion in the 'Academy,' the only literary paper left – it owed its continued existence to the honourable associations of its early years – that laughter was for the most part vulgar; that it always rudely disturbed the facial lines; that to make merriment for others was quite beneath the notice of an educated woman; and that the drama must be severe, and even austere – a school for women and for men. Such it was sought to make it, with as yet unsatisfactory results, because the common people, finding nothing to laugh at, came no more to the theatre; and even the better class, who wanted to be amused, and were only instructed, ceased to attend.

When, therefore, the curtain fell, the scanty audience rushed to the doors of the house, and there was something very much like a demonstration, a report of which, the Professor felt with pleasurable emotion, could not fail to be carried to the Duchess.

The next day there came a letter to Lady Boitons – who was still confined to her room with gout – from no less a person than the Duchess of Dunstanburgh, suggesting that the publicity thrust upon Lord Chester through the unconstitutional action of his cousin might produce an injurious effect upon a mind so young. In other words, her Grace was already sensible of the sympathy which was growing up for what was believed to be a love affair, cruelly blighted by herself. If Lord Chester was kept in retirement until the case was decided, he would, perhaps, be forgotten. As for Lady Carlyon, the Duchess rightly judged that the sympathy which one woman gets from another in such cases is generally scant.

No doubt she was right, but unfortunately she was too late. The young Earl had been seen everywhere; his story, much altered and improved, was in everybody's mouth; his likeness was in all the shop windows, side by side with that of Lady Carlyon, or, as if to give emphasis to the difference beeween the two suitors, he was placed with the Duchess on his left and Lady Carlyon on his right. The young men envied him because he was so rich, so handsome, and so gallant ; the young ladies looked and sighed. He was nearer the Ideal Man than any they had ever seen; his bold and daring eyes struck them with a kind of awe, which they thought was due to his rank, ignorant of the manhood in those eyes, which attracted and yet daunted them. They bought his photograph by thousands, and spent their leisure hours, or even the hours of study, when they ought to have been "mugging bones," or drawing contracts, or reading theology, in gazing upon that remarkable presence. Older ladies – those who had established positions and could think of marriage – wished that such young men were within their reach; and very old ladies, looking at the photograph with admiring eyes, would wag their heads, and tell their grandsons how their grandfather, dead and gone, had been just such another as Lord Chester – so handsome, so strong, so brave, and yet withal the most dutiful and obedient of husbands. They did not explain how the virtue of submission was compatible with such frank and fearless eyes.

The mischief, therefore, was done. So far as the sympathies of the people were concerned, Constance could rest content. There remained, however, the House.

Lord Chester appeared no more in public. He went to none of the cricket-matches and athletics which made the season so lively; nor was he seen at any balls or dinners; nor did he ride in the Row. He was kept in almost monastic seclusion, a few companions only being invited to play tennis on his own lawns. But the Professor was with him constantly – Lady Boitons continuing to be laid up with her gout – and they had long talks in the gardens, sitting beneath the shade of the trees, or walking in the lawns. During these conversations the young man would clench his fist and stamp his foot with rage; or his eyes would kindle, and he would stretch out his right hand as if moved beyond control. And he became daily more masterful, insomuch that the women were afraid of him, and the men-servants – whom he had cuffed until they respected him – laughed, seeing the dismay of the women. Never any man like him! "Why," said the butler, a most respectable old lady, "if he goes on like this, he'll be like the Duchess of Dunstanburgh herself. She'll have a handful, whichever o' their ladyships gets him. Beer, my lord? At twelve o'clock in the morning! It isn't good for your lordship. Better wait – oh dear, dear! Yes, my lord, in one minute."

One afternoon, towards the end of June, a little party had been made up for his amusement. It consisted of half-a-dozen young men of his own age, and a few ladies whose age more nearly approached that of the Professor. The young men played one or two matches of tennis, changed their flannels for morning dress, and joined the ladies at afternoon tea. The one topic of conversation possible at the moment was forbidden in that house: it was, of course, that of the great Appeal, and how some said that the Countess wanted it pushed on, so as to take advantage of the public sympathy, and the Duchess wanted it delayed, so as to give this feeling time to cool down; but the Duchess had sworn by everything dear to her that she would marry the young lord whether the House gave a decision in her favour or not; how Lady Carlyon declared that she would carry him off under the very nose of the Duchess; with a thousand other *canards*, rumours, little secrets, whispers on the best authority, and so forth. As, of course, that could not be entered upon in Lord Chester's own house, the afternoon was dull to the ladies. They pumped the Professor artfully, but learned nothing. She was enthusiastic in her praises of her pupil, but was reticent about his previous relations, if any, with either of his suitors; nor would she reveal anything, if she knew anything, about his inclinations – if he had any preference. As for his character, she spoke openly; he was certainly, – well, say masterful – that could not be denied – in a way which would be unbecoming in a man below his rank; as for his religion, no one could more truly love and revere the Perfect Woman than did Lord Chester; as for his abilities, they were far beyond the common: and for his reading, "I have always considered," said the Professor, "his rank as of more importance than his sex; and though I have, perhaps, given him a wider and deeper education than is generally considered prudent for the masculine brain, I believe it will be found, in the long-run, a course productive of great good. In fact," she whispered, "I believe that Lord Chester is a man likely to be the father of daughters, illustrious not only by their birth, but also by their strength of intellect and force of character."

"No man," said one of the guests – one of those persons who always know how to find the right commonplace at the right time, – "no man can have a more worthy object of ambition. To sink himself in the family, to work for them, to reproduce his own virtues in their higher feminine form in his own daughters, – I hope his lordship will obtain this happiness."

"But he can't," cried another – one of those persons who always say the wrong things, – "he can't if he marries the Duc –"

"Hush!" said the Professor. "My dear madam, we were talking, I think, about Lord Chester's character. Yes, he is in many respects a most remarkable young man."

"But is he," asked another lady, "is he quite – are you sure of what you say, Professor, about his orthodoxy?"

Professor Ingleby smiled. All smiled, indeed, because her own faith had been greatly suspected, as everybody knew.

"As sure," she said, "as I am of my own. Oh! I know what wicked people have hinted at Cambridge. But wait; have patience; I will before long prove my religious convictions, and satisfy the world once for all, in a way that will perhaps astonish, but certainly convince everybody, what my faith really is, and how truly orthodox – and I will answer for my pupil."

Then the young men appeared, and they began to talk about the games over their tea. Presently they pressed Lord Chester to sing. No one had a better voice, or sang with greater expression. He refused at first, on the ground of being tired of the words of all his songs, but gave way and sang, with a laughing protest at the sentiment of the song and the inanity of the words, the following ballad, just then popular: –

"Through sweet buttercups, through sweet hay
    Rolled in swathes by the southern wind:
Side by side they wended their way;
The sloping sun on their faces lay,
    And dragged long shadows behind.

Eighteen he, and stalwart to see;
    Muscles of steel and a heart of gold.
Cheeks hot-burning, and eyes down-dropped, –
What did he think when she suddenly stopped,
    And gave him her hand – – to hold?

She was but thirty; her lands around
    Lay with orchards and corn-fields spread;
Meadow and hill with the sunlight crowned,
Wealth and joy without stint or bound,
    And all for the lad she would wed!

He listened in silence, as young men should,
    While she pictured the life to come;
In tangled copse, in the way of the wood,

With new spring flowers and old leaves strewed
   She spoke of a love-lit home.

Only a year: and the hay again
   Lies in swathes, like the weed on the shore;
Lone he wanders with troubled brain,
Crying, 'When will she come again?'
   Poor fool; for she comes no more.
Forgotten her troth; and broken her oath;
   His love will return no more."

"The air is not bad," said the singer, when he had finished, rising from the piano, "but the words are ridiculous. As if he were likely to care for a woman eighteen years his senior!"

These words fell among them like a bomb. There was a dead silence. No one dared raise her eyes except the Professor, who looked up in warning.

Presently an old gentleman, who bad been half asleep, shook his head and spoke.

"The songs are all alike now. A young fellow gets made love to, and is engaged, and then thrown over. Then he breaks his heart In real life he would have called for his horse and galloped off his disappointment."

"Come, Sir George," said the Professor, "you must allow us a little sentiment – some belief in man's heart, else life would be too dull. For my own part, I find the words touching and true to nature."

"How would it do?" asked Lord Chester, smiling, "to invert the thing? Could we have a ballad showing how a young lady – she must be young – pined away and died for love of a man who broke his promise?"

They all laughed at this picture, but the young men looked as if Lord Chester had said something wonderful in its audacity. Most certainly, thought the Professor, his words would be quoted in all the clubs that very day. And what – oh! what would the Duchess say? And although she had no legitimate power over the ward of Chancery, she could do what she pleased with the Chancellor.

There was one young fellow present, a certain Algy Dunquerque, who entertained an affection for Lord Chester amounting almost to worship, No one was like him; none so strong, so dexterous, so good at games; no one so clever; no one so audacious, no one so gloriously independent.

They were talking together in a low whisper, unregarded by the ladies, who were talking loudly.

"Algy," said Lord Chester, "you said once that you would come to me if ever I asked you, and stand by me as long as I asked you. Are you still of the same mind?"

"That kind of promise holds," said Algy. "What shall I do?"

"Be in readiness."

"I am always ready. But what are you going to do? Shall we run away together?"

"Hush! I do not know, – yet. All that a desperate man can do."

CHAPTER VI.
WOMAN'S ENGLAND.

THE next day was Sunday, and of course Lord Chester went to church with the Professor, who was always careful to observe forms.

The congregation was large, and principally composed of men. The service was elaborate, and the singing good. Perhaps the incense was a little too strong, and there was some physical fatigue in the frequent changes of posture. Nothing, however, could have been more splendid than the procession with banners, which closed the service; nothing sweeter than the voices of the white-robed singing-girls. It was a large and beautiful church, with painted glass, pictures having lights burning before them; and the altar, on which stood the veiled figure of the Perfect Woman, was heaped with flowers.

The sermon was preached by the Dean of Westminster, whose eloquence and fervour were equalled by her scholarship. No one, except perhaps Professor Ingleby, was better read in ecclesiastical history, or knew more about the beginnings of the New Religion. She had written a book, showing from ancient literature how the germs of the religion were dormant even in the old barbaric times of man's supremacy. Even so far back as the middle ages men delighted to honour Woman. Every poet chose a mistress for his devotion, and ignorantly worshipped the type in the Individual. Every knight became servant and slave to one woman, in whose honour his noblest deeds were done. Even the worship of the Divine Man became, first in Catholic countries, and afterwards in England, through a successful conspiracy of certain so-called "ritualists," the worship of the Mother and Child. At all times the effigies of the virtues, Faith, Hope, Love, had been figures of women. The form of woman had always stood for the type, the standard, the ideal of the Beautiful. The woman had always been the dispenser of gifts. The woman had always been richly dressed. Men worked their hardest in order to pour their treasures into the lap of woman. All the reverence, all the poetry, all the imagination with which the lower nature of man was endowed, had been freely spent and lavished in the service of woman. From his earliest infancy, women surrounded, protected, and thought for men. Why, what was this, what could this mean, but a foreshadowing, an indication, a revelation, by slow and natural means, of the worship of the Perfect Woman, dimly comprehended as yet, but manifesting its power over the heart? The Dean handled this, her favourite topic, in the pulpit this morning with singular force and eloquence.

After touching on the invisible growth of the religion, she painted a time of anarchy, when men had given up their old beliefs and were like children – only children with weapons in their hands – crying out with fear in the darkness. She told how women, at last assuming their true place, substituted, little by little, the true, the only faith – the Worship of the Perfect Woman, the Feminine Divinity of Thought, Purpose, and Production. She pointed out how, by natural religion, man was evidently marked out for the second or lower creature, although, by the abuse of his superior strength, he had wrested the authority and used it for his own purposes. He was formed to execute, be was strong, he was the Agent. Woman, on the other hand, was the mother – that is to say, the Creative Thought; that is, the Sovereign Ruler. In the animal creation, again, it is the male who works, while the female sits and directs. And even in such small points as the gender of things inanimate, everything of grace, usefulness, or beauty was, and always had been, feminine. Then she argued from the natural quickness and intelligence of women, and from the corresponding dulness of men, from the lower instincts of men compared with the spiritual nature of women; and she showed how, when women took their natural place in the government of the nation, laws were for the first time framed on sound and economical principles, and for the benefit of man himself. Finally, in a brilliant peroration, she called upon her male hearers to defend, even to the death if necessary, the principles of their religion; she warned the women that a spirit of questioning and discontent was abroad; she exhorted the men to find their true happiness in submission to authority; and she drew a vivid picture of the poor wretch who, beginning with doubt and disobedience, went on to wife-beating, atheism, and despair, both of this world and the next.

The sermon lasted nearly an hour. The Dean never paused, never hesitated, was never at a loss. Yet, somehow, she failed to affect her hearers. The women looked idly about them, the men stared straight before them, showing no response, and no sympathy. One reason of this apathy was that the congregation had heard it all before, and so often, that it ceased to move them; the priestesses of the Faith, in their ardour, endeavouring constantly to make men intelligent as well as submissive supporters, overdid the preaching, and by continual repetition ruined the effect of their earnest eloquence, and reduced it to the level of rhetorical commonplace.

The Professor and her pupil walked gravely homewards.

"I think," said Lord Chester, "that I could preach a sermon the other way round."

"You mean – "

"I mean that I could just as well show how natural religion intended man to be both agent and contriver."

"I think," said the Professor, "that such a sermon had better not be preached, at least, just yet. It was *rather* a risky thing to make that remark of yours about the ballad which you sang yesterday. Such a sermon as you contemplate would infallibly land its composer – even Lord Chester – in a prison – and for life."

Lord Chester was silent.

"Do you speculate often," asked his tutor, "in these theological matters?"

"Of late," he replied. "Yes, this perpetual admonition about Authority worries me. Why should we accept statements on Authority? I have been looking through the text-books, and I conclude – "

"Pray do not tell me," she interrupted, laughing. "For the present, let me not know the nature of your conclusions. But, Lord Chester, for your own sake, for every one's sake, be guarded – be silent." She pressed his arm; he nodded gravely, but made no reply. When they reached home they learned that the Chancellor herself was waiting to see Lord Chester. She wished to see the Professor as well.

The Chancellor was in a great worry and fidget – as if this unhappy business of the Appeal was not enough for her – because, whatever decision was arrived at by the House, she would have to defend her own, and there was little doubt that her enemies would not lose so good a chance of attacking her; and now the boy must Deeds get saying things which were repeated in every club of London.

"I must say, Lord Chester," she began, irritably, "that a little respect – I say a little respect – is due to a person who holds my office. I have been waiting for you a good quarter of an hour."

"Had I known your ladyship's wish to see me, I would have saved you the trouble of coming here, and waited upon you myself. I have but just returned from church."

"Church!" she repeated, in mockery; "what is the good of people going to church if they fly in the face of all religion? Do not answer me, pray. Your lordship thinks yourself, I know, a privileged person. You are to say, and to do, anything you please. But I am the Chancellor, remember, and your guardian. Now, sir, I learn that you make dangerous, revolutionary remarks – you made one yesterday – openly, on the impossibility of a young man marrying a woman older than himself."

"Pardon me," said Lord Chester; "I did not say the impossibility of marrying, but of loving, a woman twenty years his senior."

"The distinction shows the unhappy condition of your mind. To marry a woman is to love her. What would the boy want? what would he have? Professor Ingleby, have you anything to advise? He is your pupil. You are, in fact, partly responsible for this deplorable exhibition of wilfulness."

"With your ladyship's permission," replied the Professor, softly, "I would venture to suggest that, considering recent events, it would be much better for Lord Chester to be out of London as soon as possible."

"What is the use of talking about leaving town when Lady Boitons is ill?"

"If your ladyship will intrust your noble ward to my care," continued the Professor, "I will undertake the charge of him at my own house for the next three months."

The Chancellor reflected. The plan seemed the best. Since Lady Boitons was ill, there was really no one to look after the young man, while, at the present moment of excitement, it seemed most desirable that he should be out of town. If the boy was to go on talking in this way about old women and young men, there was no telling what might not happen ; and the Duchess would be pleased with such an arrangement. That consideration decided her.

"If you really can take charge of him – you could draw on Lady Boitons for whatever you like, in reason – it does seem the best thing to do. Yes – he would be safer out of the way. When can you start?"

"To-morrow."

"Very good; then we will settle it so. You will accompany Professor Ingleby, Lord Chester; you will consider her as your guardian – and – and all that. And for heaven's sake, let us have no more folly!"

She touched his fingers with her own, bowed slightly to the Professor, and left them.

"My dear boy," said the Professor, when the door was shut, "I foresee a great opportunity, And as for that sermon you spoke of –"

"Well, Professor?"

"You may begin to compose it as soon as you please, and on the road I will help you Meantime, hold your tongue."

With these enigmatic words the Professor left him.

There was really nothing very remarkable in Lord Chester's leaving London even at the height of the season. Most of the athletic meetings were over; it was better to be in the country than in town: a young man of two-and-twenty is not supposed to take a very keen delight in dinner-parties. Had it not been for the Appeal and the way in which people occupied themselves in every kind of gossip over Lord Chester – what he said, how he looked, and what he hoped – he might have left town without the least notice being taken. As it was, his departure gave rise to the wildest rumours, not the least wild being that the Duchess, or, as some said, the Countess, intended to follow and carry him off from his own country-house.

Without troubling themselves about rumours and alarms of this kind, the Professor and her pupil drove away in the forenoon of Monday morning. The air was clear and cool ; there was a fresh breeze, a warm sun, and a sky flecked with light clouds. The leaves on the trees were at their best, the four horses were in excellent condition. What young fellow of two-and-twenty would have felt otherwise than happy at starting on a holiday away from the restraints of town, and in such weather?

"There is only one thing wanting," he said, as they finally cleared the houses, and were bowling along the smooth highroad between hedges bright with the flowers of early summer.

"What is that?" asked the Professor.

"Constance," he replied, boldly; "she ought to be with us to complete my happiness."

The Professor laughed.

"A most unmanly remark," she said. "How can you reconcile it with the precepts of morality? Have you not been taught the wickedness of expressing, even of allowing yourself to feel an inclination for any young lady?"

"It is your fault, my dear Professor. You have taught me so much, that I have left off thinking of unmanliness and immodesty and the copy-book texts."

"I have taught you," she replied, gravely, "things enough to hang myself and send you to the Tower for life. But remember – remember – that you have been taught these things with a purpose."

"What purpose?" he asked.

"I began by making you discontented. I allowed you to discover that everything is not so certain as boys are taught to believe. I put you in the way of reading, and I opened your mind to all sorts of subjects generally concealed from young men."

"You certainly did, and you are a most crafty as well as a most beneficent Professor."

"You have gradually come to understand that your own intellect, the average intellect of Man, is really equal to the consideration of all questions, even those generally reserved and set apart for women."

"Is it not time, therefore, to let me know this mysterious purpose?"

Professor Ingleby gazed upon him in silence for a while.

"The purpose is not mine. It is that of a wiser and greater being than myself, whose will I carry out and whom I obey."

"Wiser than *you*, Professor? Who is she? Do you mean the Perfect Woman herself?"

"No," she replied; "the being whom I obey and reverence is none other than – my own husband."

Lord Chester started.

"Your husband?" he cried. "*You obey your husband*? This is most wonderful."

"My husband. Yes, Lord Chester, you may now compose that sermon which shall show how Man is the Lord and Master of all created things, including – Woman. I told you I would help you in your sermon. Listen."

All that day they drove through the fair garden, which we call England. Along the road they passed the rustics hay-making in the fields; the country women were talking at their doors; the country doctor was plodding along her daily round; the parson was jogging along the wayside, umbrella in hand, to call upon her old people; the country police in blue bonnets, carrying their dreaded pocket-books, were loitering in couples about cross-roads; the farmer drove her cart to market, or rode her cob about the fields; little girls and boys carried dinner to their fathers. Here and there they passed a country - seat, a village with its street of cottages, or they clattered through a small sleepy town with its row of villas and its quiet streets, where the men sat working at the windows in hopes of getting a chat or seeing something to break the monotony of the day.

The travellers saw, but noted nothing. For the Professor was teaching her pupil things calculated to startle even the Duchess, and at which Constance would have trembled – things which made his cheek to glow, his eyes to glisten, his mouth to quiver, his hands to clench; – things not to be spoken, not to be whispered, not to be thought, this Professor openly, boldly, and without shame, told the young man.

"I might have guessed it," he said. "I had already half guessed it. And this – this is the reason why we are kept in subjection! – this is the LIE they have palmed upon us!"

"Hush! calm yourself. The thing was not done in a day. The system was not invented by conscious hypocrites and deceivers ; it grew, and with it the new religion, the new morality, the new order of things. Blame no one, Lord Chester, but blame the system."

"You have told me too much now," he said; "tell me more."

She went on. Each word, each new fact, tore something from him that he would have believed part of his nature. Yet he had been prepared for this day by years of training, all designed by this crafty woman to arm him with strength to receive her disclosures.

"What you see," she said, as they drove through a village, "seems calm and happy. It is the calmness of repression. Those men in the fields, those working men sitting at the windows – they are all alike unhappy, and they know not why. It is because the natural order has been reversed; the sex which should command and create is compelled to work in blind obedience. You will see, as we go on, that we, who have usurped the power, have created nothing, improved nothing, carried on nothing. It is for you, Lord Chester, to restore the old order."

"If I can – if I can find words," he stammered.

"I have trusted you," the Professor went on, "from the very first. *Bon sang ne peut mentir.* Yet it was wise not to hurry matters. Your life, and my own life too, if that matters much, hang upon the success of my design. Nothing could have happened more opportunely than the Duchess's proposal. Why, on the one hand, a sweet, charming, delightful girl; and on the other, a repulsive, bad - tempered old woman. While your blood is aflame with love and disgust, Lord Chester, I tell you this great secret. We have three months before us. We must use it, so that in less than two we shall be able to strike, and to strike hard. You are in my hands. We have, first, much to see and to learn."

Their first halt was Windsor. Here, after ordering dinner, the Professor took her pupil to visit Eton. It was half-holiday, and the girls were out of school. Some were at the Debating Society's rooms, where a political discussion was going on; some were strolling by the river under the grand old elms; some were reading novels in the shade; some were lying on the bank talking and laughing. It was a pleasant picture of happy school life.

"Look at these buildings," said the Professor, taking up a position of vantage. "They were built by one of your ancestors, beautified by another, repaired and enlarged by another. This is the noblest of the old endowments – for boys."

The Earl looked round him in wonder.

"What would boys do with such a splendid place?" he asked.

"Have my lessons borne so little fruit that you should ask that question?" The Professor looked disappointed. "My dear boy, they played in the playing-fields, they swam and rowed in the river, they studied in the school, they worshipped in the chapel. When it was resolved to divide the endowments, women naturally got the first choice, and they chose Eton. Afterwards the boys' public schools fell gradually into decay, and bit by bit they were either closed or became appropriated by girls. There was once a famous school at a place called Rugby. That died. The Lady of the Manor, I believe, gradually absorbed the revenues. Harrow and Marlborough fell in, after a few years, for girls. You see, when once mothers realised the dangers of public school life for boys, they naturally left off sending them."

"Yes – I see – the danger that –"

"That they would become masterful, Lord Chester, like yourself; that they would use their strength to recover their old supremacy; that they would discover" – here she sank her voice, although they were not within earshot of any one – "that they would discover how strength of brain goes with strength of muscle."

She led the young man back across the river to the Windsor side. On the way they passed an open gate; over the gate was written "Select school for young gentlemen." Within was a gymnasium, where a dozen boys were exercising on parallel bars, swinging with ropes, and playing with clubs.

"As for your education," said the Professor, "we have discovered that the best chance for the world is for a boy to be taught three things. He must learn religion – *i.e.*, submission, and the culture of Perfect Womanhood; he must learn a trade of some kind, unless he belongs to the aristocracy, so as not to be necessarily dependent; and he must be made healthy, strong, and active. History will credit us with one thing, at least; we have improved the race."

It wanted an hour of dinner. The Professor, who was never tired, led her pupil over such portions of the old castle as could still be visited – the great tower and one or two of the terraces.

"This was once yours," she said. "This is the castle of your ancestors. Courage, my lord; you shall win it back."

It was in a dream that the young man spent the rest of the evening. The Professor had ordered a simple yet dainty dinner, consisting of a Thames trout, a Chateaubriand, quails, and an omelette, with some Camembert cheese, but her young charge did scanty justice to it. After dinner, when the coffee had been brought, and the door was safely shut, the Professor continued the course of lectures on ancient history, by which she had already upset the mind of her pupil, and filled his brain with dreams of a revolution more stupendous than was ever suspected by the watchful bureau of police.

Their next day's drive brought them to Oxford. It was vacation, and the colleges were empty. Only here and there a solitary figure of some lonely Fellow or Lecturer lingering after the rest had gone flitted across the lawns. The solitude of the place pleased the Professor. She could ramble with her pupil about the venerable courts and talk at her ease.

"Here," she said, "in the old days was once the seat of learning and wisdom."

"What is it now?" asked her disciple, surprised. "Is not Oxford still the seat of learning?"

"You must read – alas! you would not understand them – the old books before you can answer your own question. What is their political economy, their moral philosophy, their social science – of which they make so great a boast – compared with the noble scholarship, the science, the speculation of former days? How can I make you understand? There was a time when everything was advanced – by men. Science must advance or fall back. We took from men their education, and science has been forgotten. We cannot now read the old books; we do not understand the old discoveries; we cannot use the tools which they invented, the men of old. Mathematics, chemistry, physical science, geology – all these exist no longer, or else exist in such an elementary form as our ancestors would have been ashamed to acknowledge. Astronomy, which widened the heart, is neglected; medicine has become a thing of books; mechanics are forgotten –"

"But why?"

"Because women, who can receive, cannot create; because at no time has any woman enriched the world with a new idea, a new truth, a new discovery, a new invention; because we have undertaken the impossible."

The Professor was silent. Never before had Lord Chester seen her so deeply moved.

"Oh, Sacred Learning!" she cried, "we have sinned against thee! We poor women in our conceit think that everything may be learned from books: we worship the Ideal Woman, and we are content with the rags of learning which remain from the work of Man. Yes, we are contented with these scraps. We will accept nothing that is not absolutely certain. Therefore we blasphemously and ignorantly say that the last word has been said upon everything, and that no more remains to be learned."

"Mankind is surrounded," the Professor went on as if talking to herself, "by a high wall of black ignorance and mystery. The wall is for ever receding or closing in upon us. The men of the past pushed it back more and more, and widened continually the boundaries of thought, so that the foremost among them were godlike for knowledge and for a love of knowledge. We women of the present are continually contracting the wall, so that soon we shall know nothing, unless – unless you come to our help."

"How can I help to restore knowledge," asked the young man, "being myself so ignorant?"

"By giving back the university to the sex which can enlarge our bounds."

Always the same thing – always coming back to the one subject.

There was a university sermon in the after noon, being the feast of St Cecilia; they looked in, but the church was empty. In vacation time one hardly expects more than two or three resident lecturers with their husbands and boys, and a sprinkling of young men from the town. The sermon was dull – perhaps Lord Chester's mind was out of sympathy with the subject; it treated on the old well-worn lines of Woman as the Musician.

"I will show you at Cambridge," said the Professor when they came out, "some of the music of the past. What are the feeble strains, the oft-repeated phrases of modern music, compared with the grand old music conceived and written by men? Women have never composed great music."

They left Oxford the next day and proceeded north.

"I think," said the Professor as they were driving smoothly along the road, "that they did wrong in not trying to maintain the old railways. True there were many accidents, and sometimes great loss of life; yet it must have been a convenience to get from London to Liverpool in five hours. To be sure the art of making engines is dead: such arts could not survive when their new system of separate labour was introduced."

They passed the old tracks of the railways from time to time, now long canals grass-grown, and now high embankments covered with trees and bushes. There were black holes, too, in the hillsides through which the iron road had once run.

"The country in the nineteenth century," said the Professor, "was populous and wealthy; but it would be at first terrible for one of us to see and to live in. From end to end there were great factories driven by steam-engines, in which men worked in gangs, and from which a perpetual black cloud of smoke rose to the sky; trains ran shrieking along the iron roads with more clouds of smoke and steam. The results of the work were grand; but the workmen were uncared for, and killed by the long hours and the foul atmosphere. I talk like a woman" – she checked herself with a smile, – "and I want to talk so that you shall feel like a man – of the ancient type.

"There is one point of difference between man's and woman's legislation which I would have you bear in mind. Man looks to the end, woman thinks of the means. If man wanted a great thing done, he cared little about the sufferings of those who did that thing. A great railway had to be built; those who made it perished of fever and exposure. What matter? The railway remained. A great injustice had to be removed; to remove it cost a war, with death to thousands. Man cared little for the deaths, but much for the result. Man was like Nature, which takes infinite pains to construct an insect of marvellous beauty, and then allows it to be crushed in thousands almost as soon as born. Woman, on the other hand, considers the means."

They came, after three days' posting, to Manchester. They found it a beautiful city, situated on a clear sparkling stream, in the midst of delightful rural scenery, and regularly built after the modern manner in straight streets at right angles to each other: the air was peculiarly bright and bracing. "I wanted very much," said the Professor, "to show you this place. You see how pretty and quiet a place it is; yet in the old times it had a population of half a million. It was perpetually black with smoke; there were hundreds of vast factories where the men worked from six in the morning until six at night. Their houses were huts – dirty, crowded nests of fever; their sole amusements were to smoke tobacco and to drink beer and spirits; they died at thirty worn out; they were of sickly and stunted appearance; they were habitual wife-beaters; they neglected their children; they had no education, no religion, no hopes, no wishes for anything but plentiful pipe and beer. See it now! The population reduced to twenty thousand; the factories swept away; the machinery destroyed; the men working separately each in his own house, making cotton for home consumption. Let us walk through the streets."

These were broad, clean, and well kept. Very few persons were about. A few women lounged about the Court, or gathered together on the steps of the Town Hall, where one was giving her opinions violently on politics generally; some stood at the doorways talking to their neighbours; in the houses one could hear the steady click-click of the loom or spinning-jenny, as the man within, or the man and his sons, sat at their continuous and solitary labour.

"This is beautiful to think of, is it not?"

"I do not know what to say," he replied. "You ask me, after all that you have taught me, to admire a system in which men are slaves. Yet all looks well from the outside."

"It began," the Professor went on, without answering him directly, "with the famous law of the 'Clack' Parliament – that in which there were three times as many women as men – which enacted that wives should receive the wages of their husbands on Monday morning, and that unmarried men, unless they could be represented by mothers or sisters, or other female relations of whom they were the support, should be paid in kind, and be housed separately in barracks provided for the purpose, where discipline could be maintained. It was difficult at first to carry this legislation into effect: the men rebelled; but the law was enforced at last. That was the death-blow to the male supremacy. Woman, for the first time, got possession of the purse. What was done in Manchester was followed in other places. Young man, the spot you stand on is holy, or the reverse, whichever you please, because it is the birthplace of woman's sovereignty.

"Presently it began to be whispered abroad that the hours were too long, the work too hard, and the association of men together in such large numbers was dangerous. Then, little by little, wives withdrew their husbands from the works, mothers their sons, and set them up with spinning-jennies and looms at home. Hand-made cotton was protected; the machine-made was neglected. Soon the machines were silent and the factories closed; in course of time they were pulled down. Then other improvements followed. The population was enormously diminished, partly by the new laws which forbade the marriage of unhealthy or deformed men, and only allowed women to choose husbands when they had themselves obtained a certificate of good health and good conduct. Formerly the men married at nineteen; by the new laws they were compelled to wait until four-and-twenty; then, further, to wait until they were asked; and lastly, if they were asked, to obtain a certificate of soundness and freedom from any complaint which might be transmitted to children. Therefore, as few of the Manchester workmen were quite free from some form of disease, the population rapidly decreased."

"But," said Lord Chester, "is that wrong? A man ought to be healthy."

That was, indeed, the creed in which he had been brought up.

"I am telling you the history of the place," replied the Professor. "Marriage being thus almost impossible, the Manchester women emigrated and the work-men stayed where they were, and gradually the weakly ones died out. As for the present Manchester man, you shall see him on Sunday when he goes to church."

They stayed in this pleasant and countrified town for some days. On Sunday they went to the cathedral, and attended the service, which was conducted by the Bishop herself and her principal clergy. As the Bishop preached, Lord Chester looked about him, and watched the men. They were mostly a tall and handsome race, though, in the middle-aged men, the labour at the spindles had bowed their shoulders and contracted their chests. Their faces, however, like those of the London congregation, were listless and apathetic; they paid little heed to the sermon, yet devoutly knelt, bowed, and stood up at the right places. They seemed neither to feel nor to take any interest in life. Some of the women looked as if they interpreted the law of marital obedience in the strictest, even its harshest manner possible.

Lord Chester looked with a certain special curiosity at a regiment of young unmarried workmen. He had often enough before watched such a regiment passing to and from church, but never with such interest. For in these boys he had now learned to recognise the masters of the future.

They were mostly quite young, and naturally presented a more animated appearance than their married elders. Those of them who came from the country, or had no parents, were kept in a barrack under strict rule and discipline, having prescribed hours for gymnastics, exercises, and recreation, as well as for labour.

They were not all boys. Among them marched those whom unkind Nature or accident had set apart as condemned to celibacy. These were the consumptive, the asthmatic, the crippled, the humpbacked, the deformed; those who had inherited diseases of lung, brain, or blood; the unfortunates who could not marry, and who were, therefore, cared for with what was officially known as kindness. These poor creatures presented the appearance of the most hopeless misery. At other times Lord Chester would have passed them by without a thought. He knew now how different would have been their lot under a government which did not call itself maternal. Neither boys nor incurables received pay, and the surplus of their work was devoted to the great Mothers' Sustentation Fund, or, as it was called for short, the Mothers' Tax. This was intended to supplement the wages earned by the husband at home in case of insufficiency. But the wives were exhorted and admonished to take care of their husbands, and keep them constantly at work.

"They do take care of them," said the Professor. "They make them clean up house, cook meals, and look after the children, as well as carry on their trade; while they themselves wrangle over politics in the street or in some of the squabble-halls, which are always open. The men never go out except on Sundays; they have no friends; they have no recreation."

"But formerly they were even worse off, according to your own showing."

"No; because if they were slaves to their wheels, they were slaves who worked in gangs, and they sometimes rose from the ranks. These men are solitary slaves who can never rise."

"Is there nothing good at all?" cried the young man. "Would you make a revolution, and upset everything? As for religion –"

"Say nothing," said the Professor, "about religion till I have shown you the old one. Yes; there was once something grander than anything you can imagine. We women, who have belittled everything, have even spoiled our religion."

They passed a couple of young men wending their way to the gymnasium with racquets in their hands.

"They are the sons of the doctor or lawyer, I suppose," said the Professor, looking after them. "Fine young fellows! But what are we to do with them? The law says that every boy, except the son of a peeress, shall learn a trade. No doubt these boys have learned a trade, but they do not practice it. They stay at home idle, or they spend their days in athletics. Some time or other they will marry a woman in their own rank, and then the rest of their lives will be devoted to managing the house and looking after the children, while their wives go to office and earn the family income."

"What would you do with them?"

"Nay, Lord Chester; what will *you* do for them? That is the question."

The next day they left Manchester, and proceeded on their journey. At Liverpool they saw seven miles of splendid old docks, lining the banks of the river; but there were no ships. The trade of the old days had long since left the place: it was a small town now with a few fishing smacks. The Professor enlarged upon the history of the past.

"But were the men happy?"

"I do not know. That is nowhere stated I imagine there used to be happiness of a kind for men in forming part of a busy hive. At least the other plan – our plan – does not seem to produce much solid happiness...."

Gradually Lord Chester was being led to think less of the individual and more of his work. But it took time to eradicate his early impressions.

At Liverpool they visited the convict-prison – the largest prison in England. It was that prison specially devoted to the worst class of criminals – those undergoing life sentences for wife-beating. They found a place surrounded by a high wall and a deep ditch; they were admitted, on the Professor showing a pass, through a door at which a dozen female warders were sitting on duty. One of them was told off to conduct them round the prison. The convicts, coarsely clad in sackcloth, were engaged in perpetually doing unnecessary and profitless work – some dug holes which others filled up again; some carried heavy weights up ladders and down again, – there was the combined cruelty of monotony, of uselessness, and of excessive toil. In this prison – because physical force is necessary for men of violence – they had men as well as women for warders. These were stationed at intervals, and were armed with loaded guns and bayonets. It was well known that there was always great difficulty in persuading men to take this place, or to keep them when there. Mostly they were criminals of less degree, who purchased their liberty by becoming, for a term of years, convict-warders.

"No punishment too bad for wife-beaters," said the Professor when they came away. "What punishment is there for women who make slaves of their husbands, lock them up, kill them with work? or for old women who marry young men against their will?"

"You must clear out that den," she went on, after a pause. "A good many men are imprisoned there on the sole unsupported charge of their wives – innocent, no doubt; and if not innocent, then they have been punished enough."

Lord Chester was being led gradually to regard himself, not as an intending rebel, but as a great reformer. Always the Professor spoke of the future as certain, and of his project, yet vague without a definite plan, as of a thing actually accomplished.

They left the dreary and deserted Liverpool, with its wretched convict-prison. They drove first across the country, which had once been covered with manufacturing towns, now all reduced to villages; they stopped at little country inns in places where there yet lingered traditions of former populousness; they passed sometimes gaunt ruins of vast brick buildings which had been factories; the roads were quiet and little used; the men they met were chiefly rustics going to or returning from their work; there was no activity, no traffic, no noise upon these silent highways.

"How can we ever restore the busy past?" asked Lord Chester.

"First release your men: let them work together; let them be taught; the old creative energy will waken again in the brains of men, and life will once more go forward. It will be for you to guide the movement when you have started it."

As their journey drew to a conclusion, the Professor gave utterance, one by one, to several maxims of great value and importance: –

"Give men love," she said; "we women have killed love."

"There is no love without imagination. Now the imagination cannot put forth its flowers but for the sake of young and beautiful women."

"No true work without emulation; we have killed emulation."

"No progress without ambition; we have killed ambition."

"It is better to advance the knowledge of the world one inch than to win the long-jump with two-and-twenty feet."

"Better vice than repression. A drunken man may be a lesson to keep his fellows sober."

"Nothing great without suffering."

"Strong arm, strong brain."

"When women begin to invent they will justify their supremacy."

"The Higher Intelligence is a phrase that must be transferred, not lost sight of."

"Men who are happy laugh – they must laugh. Women, who have never felt the necessity of laughter, have killed it in men."

"The sun is masculine – he creates. The moon is feminine – she only reflects."

And so, with many other parables, dark sayings, and direct teachings, the wise woman brought her disciple to her own house at Cambridge.

CHAPTER VII.
ON THE TRUMPINGTON ROAD.

PROFESSOR INGLEBY lived on the Trumpington Road, about a mile and a quarter from the Senate House. Her residence was a large and handsome house shut in by a high wall, with extensive grounds, and surrounded by high trees, so that no one could see the garden from the main road. The house was a certain mystery to the girls who on Sundays took their constitutional to Trumpington and back. Some said that the Professor was ashamed of her husband, which was the reason why he was never seen, not even at Church; others said that she kept him in such rigid discipline that she refused the poor man permission even to walk outside the grounds of the house. Her two daughters, who regularly came to church with their mother, were pretty girls, but had a submissive gentle look quite strange among the turbulent young spirits of the University. They were never seen in society; and for some reason unknown to anybody except herself, the Professor refused to enter them at any college. Meantime no one was invited to the house: when one or two ladies tried to break through the reserve so strangely maintained by the most learned Professor in the University, and left their cards, the visit was formally returned by the Professor herself, accompanied by one of her girls. But things went no further, and invitations were neither accepted nor returned. It is therefore not surprising that this learned woman, who seemed guided by none of the motives which influence most women – who was not ambitious, who refused rank, who desired not money – gradually came to bear a mythical character. She was represented as an ogre: the undergraduates, always fond of making up stories, amused themselves by inventing legends about her home life and her autocratic rule. Some, however, said that the house was haunted, her husband off his head, and her daughters weak in their intellect. There was, therefore, some astonishment when it was announced officially that the Professor was bringing Lord Chester to stay at her own house – "in perfect seclusion," added the paper, to the disgust of all Cambridge, who would have liked to make much of this interesting young peer. However, long vacation had begun when he came up, so that the few left were either the reading undergraduates or the dons.

"Here," said the Professor, as she ushered her guest into a spacious Hall, with doors opening into other rooms on either hand, "you will find yourself in a house of the past. Nothing in my husband's house, or hardly anything, that is not two hundred years old at least; nothing which does not belong to the former dynasty: we use as little as possible that is new."

Lord Chester looked about him: the Hall was hung with pictures, and these were of a kind new to him, for they represented scenes in which man was not only the executive hand, but also the directing head, usurping to himself the functions of the Higher Intelligence. Thus Man was sitting on the Judicial

Bench; Man was preaching in the Church; Man was holding debate in Parliament; Man was writing books; Man was studying. Where, then, was Woman? She was represented as spinning, sewing, nursing the baby, engaged in domestic pursuits, being wooed by young lovers, young herself, sitting among the children.

"You like our pictures?" asked the Professor. "They were painted during the Subjection of Woman two hundred years ago. Men in those days worked for women; women gave men their love and sympathy: without love, which is a stimulus, labour is painful to man; without sympathy, which supports, labour is intolerable to him; with or without, labour – necessary work with head or hand for the daily bread – is almost always intolerable to woman. Therefore, since the Great Revolution, there has been no good work done by man, and no work at all by women."

She opened a door, holding the handle for a moment, as if with reverence for what was within.

"Here is our library," she whispered. "Come, let me present you to my husband. I warn you, beforehand, that our manners are like our furniture – old-fashioned."

It was a large room, filled with books of ancient aspect: at a table sat, among his papers, a venerable old man, the like of whom Lord Chester had never seen before. It must be owned that the existing *régime* did not produce successful results in old men. They were too often frivolous or petulant; they were sometimes querulous; they complained of the want of respect with which they were treated, and yet generally neither said nor did anything worthy of respect.

But this was a dignified old man: thin white locks hung round his square forehead, beneath which were eyes still clear and full of kindliness; and his mobile lips parted with a peculiarly sweet smile when he greeted his guest. For the first time in his life, Lord Chester looked, with wonder, upon a man who bore in his face and his carriage the air of Authority.

The room was his study: the walls were hidden with books; the table was covered with papers. Strange, indeed, to see an old man in such a place, engaged in such pursuits!

"Be welcome," he said, "to my poor house. Your lordship has, I learn, been the pupil of my wife."

"An apt and ready pupil," she interposed, with meaning.

"I rejoice to hear it. You will now, if you please, be my pupil – for a short time only. You have much to learn, and but a brief space to learn it in before we proceed upon the Mission of which you know. Will you leave Lord Chester with me, my dear?"

The Professor left them alone.

"Sit down, my lord. I would first ask you a few questions."

He questioned the young man with great care; ascertained that he knew already, having been taught in these late days by the Professor, the most important points of ancient history; that he was fully acquainted with his own pedigree, and *what it meant;* that he was filled with indignation and shame at the condition of his country; that he was ready to throw off the restraints and prejudices of Religion, and eager to become the Leader of the "Great Revolt," if he only knew how to begin.

"But," said Lord Chester, stammering and confused, "I shall want help – direction – even words. If the Professor –" he looked about in confusion.

"I will find you the help you want. Look to me, and to those who work with me, for guidance. This is a man's movement, and must be guided by men alone. Sufficient for the moment that we have in your lordship our true leader, that you will consent to be guided until you know enough to lead, and that you will be with us – to the very death, if that must be."

"To the very death," replied Lord Chester, holding out his hand.

"It is well that you should first know," the old man went on, "who I am, and to what hands you intrust your future. Learn, then, that by secret laying on of hands the ancient Episcopal Order hath been carried on, and continues unto this day. Though there are now but two or three Bishops remaining of the old Church, I am one – the Bishop of London. This library contains the theology of our Church – the works of the Fathers. The Old Faith shall be taught to you – the faith of your wise fathers."

Lord Chester stared; for the Professor had told him nothing of this.

"You may judge of all things," said the Bishop, "by their fruits. You have seen the fruits of the New Religion: you have gone through the length and the breadth of the land, and have found whither the superstition of the Perfect Woman leads. I shall teach you the nobler Creed, the higher Faith, – that" – here his voice lowered, and his eyes were raised – "that, my son, of the Perfect Man – the Divine Man."

"And now," he went on, after a pause, ringing the bell, "I want to introduce to you some of your future officers and followers."

There appeared in answer to this summons a small band of half-a-dozen young men. Among them, to Lord Chester's amazement, were two friends of his own, the very last men whom he would have expected to meet. They were Algy Dunquerque, the young fellow we have already mentioned, and a certain Jack Kennion, as good a rider, cricketer, and racquet-player as any in the country. These two men in the plot? Had he been walking and living among conspirators?

The two entered, but they said nothing. Yet the look of satisfaction on their faces spoke volumes.

"Gentlemen," said the Bishop, "I desire to present you to the Earl of Chester. In this house and among ourselves he is already what he will shortly be to the whole world – his Royal Highness the Earl of Chester, heir to the crown – nay – actual King of England. The day long dreamed of among us, my children – the day for which we have worked and planned – has arrived. Before us stands the Chief, willing and ready to lead the Cause in person."

They bowed profoundly. Then each one advanced in turn, took his hand, and murmured words of allegiance.

The first was a tall thin young man of four-and-twenty, with eager eyes, pale face, and high narrow forehead, named Clarence Veysey. "If you are what we hope and pray," he said, looking him full in the face with searching gaze, "we are your servants to the death. If you are not, God help England and the Holy Faith!"

The next who stepped forward was Jack Kennion. He was a young man of his own age, of great muscular development, with square head, curly locks, and laughing eyes. He held out his hand and laughed. "As for me," he said, "I have no doubt as to what you are. We have waited for you a long time, but we have you at last."

The next was Algy Dunquerque.

"I told you," he said, laughing, "that I was ready to follow you. But I did not hope or expect to be called upon so soon. Something, of course, I knew, because I am a pupil of the Bishop, and knew how long Professor Ingleby has been working upon your mind. At last, then! "He heaved a mighty sigh of satisfaction, and then began to laugh. "Ho, ho! Think of the flutter among the petticoats! Think of the debates in the House! Think of the excommunications!"

One after the other shook hands, and then the Bishop spoke, as if interpreting the thought of all.

"This day," he said, "is the beginning of new things. We shall recall the grandeurs of the past, which no living man can remember. Time was when we were a mighty country, the first in the world: we had the true Religion, two thousand years old; a grand State Church; we had an ancient dynasty and a constitutional monarchy; we had a stately aristocracy always open to new families; we had an immense commerce; we had flourishing factories; we had great and loyal colonies; we had a dense and contented population; we had enormous wealth; science in every branch was advancing; there was personal freedom; every man could raise himself from the lowest to the highest rank; there was no post too high for the ambition of a clever lad. In those days Man was in command.

"Let us," he continued, after a pause, "think how all this has been changed. We have lost our reigning family, and have neither king nor queen; we have thrown away our old hereditary aristocracy, and replaced it by a false and pretentious House, in which the old titles have descended through a line of women, and the new ones have been created for the noisiest of the first female legislators; we have abolished our House of Commons, and given all the power to the Peeresses; we have lost the old worship, and invented a creed which has not even the merit of commanding the respect of those who are most interested in keeping it up. Does any educated woman now believe in the Perfect Woman, except as a means of keeping men down?

"As for our trade, it is gone; as for our greatness, it is gone; as for our industries, they are gone; as for our arts, they have perished: we stand alone, the contempt of the world, to whom we are no longer a Power. Our men are kept in ignorance; they are forbidden to rise, by their own work, from one class to another; class and caste distinctions are deepened, and differences in rank are multiplied; there is no more science; electricity, steam, heat, and air are the servants of man no longer; men cannot learn; they are even forbidden to meet together; they have lost the art of self-government; they are cowed; they are cursed with a false religion; they have no longer any hopes or any aims.

"Fortunately," he continued, "they have left man something: he has retained his strength; they have even legislated with the view of keeping him healthy and strong. In your strength, my sons, shall you prosper. But you will have to revive the old spirit. That will be the most difficult – the only difficult – task. Take Lord Chester away now, my children, and show him our relics of the past."

In the room next to the library was a collection of strange and wonderful things, all new and unintelligible to Lord Chester. Jack Kennion acted as exhibitor.

"These," he said, "are chiefly models of the old machinery. I study them daily, in the hope of restoring the mechanical skill of the past. These engines with multitudinous wheels which are so intricate to look at, and yet so simple in their action, formerly served to keep great factories at work, and found occupation for hundreds and thousands of men; these black round boxes were steam machines which dragged long trains full of people about the country at the rate of sixty miles an hour; these glittering things in brass were made to illustrate knowledge which has long since died out, unless I can recover it by the aid of the old books; these complicated things were weapons among us when science ruled everything; all these books treat of the forgotten knowledge; these paintings on the wall show the life of the very world as it was when men ruled it; these maps showed the former greatness of the country: everything here proves from what a height we have fallen. And to think that it is only here – in this one house of all England – that we can feel what we once were, – what we *will* be – yes, we *will* be – again!"

His eyes were lit with fire, his cheeks aflame, as he spoke.

During the talk of this afternoon, Lord Chester discovered that the education of every one of these young men had been conducted with a view to his future work in or after the Revolution. Thus Algernon Dunquerque was learned in the old arts of drilling and ordering masses of men. Jack Kennion had studied mechanics and mathematics; another had learned ancient law and history; another had been trained to speak, – and so on. Clarence Veysey, for his part, had been taught by the Bishop the Mysteries of the Old Religion, and was an ordained Priest. These things the new recruit made out from the eager talk of his friends, who seemed all of them anxious to instruct him at once in everything they knew.

It was a relief at last, when the first bell rang, to be alone for a few minutes, if only to get his ideas cleared a little. What had he learned since he left London? What was before him?

Anyhow, change, action, freedom.

He found the Professor and her daughter in the drawing-room. The girls received him with smiles of welcome. The elder, Grace – a girl whose sweetness of face was new to Lord Chester, accustomed to the hard lines which a life of combat so early brings upon a woman's eyes and brow – had, which was the first thing he noticed in her, large, clear grey eyes of singular purity. The other, Faith, was smaller, slighter, and perhaps more lovely, though in a different way, a less spiritual fashion. Both, in the outer world, would have been considered painfully shy. Lord Chester was beginning to consider shyness as a virtue in women. At all events, it was a quality rarely experienced outside.

He was already prepared for many changes, and for customs new to him. Yet he was hardly ready for the complete reversal of social rules as he experienced at this dinner. For the subjects of talk were started by the men, who almost monopolised the conversation; while the ladies merely threw in a word here and there, which served as a stimulus, and showed appreciation rather than a desire to join in the argument. And such talk! He had been accustomed to hear the ladies talk almost uninterruptedly of politics – that is, of personal matters, squabbles in the House, disputes about precedence, intrigues for title and higher rank – and dress. Nothing else, as a rule, occupied the dinner-table. The men, who rarely spoke, were occasionally questioned about some cricket-match, some long race, or some other kind of athletics. This was due to politeness only, however; for, the question put and answered, the questioner showed how little interest she took in the subject by instantly returning to the subject previously in discussion. But at this table, – the Professor's – no, the Bishop's table, – the men talked of art, and in terms which Lord Chester could not understand. Nevertheless, he gathered that the so-called art of the Academicians was a thing absolutely beneath contempt. They talked of science, especially the square-headed youth Jack Kennion, to whom they deferred as to an authority; and he spoke of subjects, forms, and laws of which Lord Chester was absolutely ignorant: they talked of history, and all, including the Bishop's daughters – strange, how easily the new proselyte fell into the way of considering bow the highest education is best fitted for men! – showed as intimate an acquaintance with the past as the Professor herself. They talked of religion; and here all deferred to the Bishop, who, while he spoke with authority, invited discussion. Strangest thing of all! – every man spoke as if his own opinion were worth considering. There was not the slightest deference to authority. The great and standard work of Cornelia Nipper on Political Economy, in which she summed up all that has been said, and left, as was taught at Cambridge, nothing more to be said; the Encyclopædia of Science, written by Isabella Bunter, in which she showed the absurdity of pushing knowledge into worthless regions; the sermons and dogmas of the illustrious and Reverend Violet Swandown, considered by the orthodox as containing guidance and comfort for the soul under all possible circumstances, – these works were openly scoffed at and derided.

Lord Chester said little; the conversation was for the most part beyond him. At his side sat the Bishop's elder daughter, Grace – a young lady of twenty-one or twenty-two, of a type strange to him. She had a singularly quiet, graceful manner; she listened with intelligent pleasure, and showed her appreciation by smiles rather than by words; when she spoke, it was in low tones, yet without hesitation; she was almost extravagantly deferent to her father, but towards her mother showed the affection of a loved and trusted companion. It was too much the custom in society for girls to show no regard whatever for the opinions or the wishes of their fathers.

The younger daughter, Faith, talked less; but Lord Chester noticed that as she sat next to Algy Dunquerque, that young man frequently ceased to join in the general conversation, and exchanged whispers with her; and they were whispers which made her eyes to soften and her cheek to glow. Good; in the new state of things the men would do the wooing for themselves. He thought of Constance, and wished she had been there.

When the ladies retired, the Bishop began to talk of the Great Cause.

"Your training," he said to Lord Chester, "has been, by my directions, that of a Prince rather than a private gentleman. That is to say, you have been taught a great many things, but you have not become a specialist. These friends of ours," – he pointed to his group of disciples, – "are, each in his own line, better than yourself, and better than you will ever try to become. A Prince should be a patron of art, learning, and science and literature; but it does not become him to be an artist, a scholar, a philosopher, or a poet. You must be contented to sit outside the circle, so to speak. Now let us speak of our chances."

He proceeded to discuss the best way of raising the country. His plan was a simultaneous revolt in half-a-dozen country districts; an appeal to the rustics; the union of forces; the seizure of towns; continual preaching and exhortation for the men; repression for the women; the destruction of their sacred pictures and figures; but no violence – above all, no violence. The Bishop was an ecclesiastic, and he was a recluse. He therefore did not understand what men are like when the passion of fighting is roused in them. He dreamed of a bloodless Revolution; he pictured the men voluntarily confessing the wisdom and the truth of the Old Religion. The event proved that all human institutions rest on force, and cannot be upset without the employment of force. To be sure, women cannot fight; but they had on their side the aid of superstition, and the strong arms of the men whom they led in superstitious chains.

Up-stairs one of the girls played and sang old songs: the words were strange; words and air went direct to the heart. Lord Chester listened disturbed and anxious, yet exultant.

The Professor pressed his hand.

"It is death or success," she whispered. "Be of good cheer; in either event, you shall be counted noble among the men to come."

When Grace Ingleby wished him good-night, she held his hand in hers with the firm grasp of a sister.

"You are one of us," she said, frankly. "In this house we are all brothers and sisters in hope and in Religion. And if they found us out," she added, with a laugh, "we should be brothers and sisters in death. Courage, my lord! There is all to gain."

Faith Ingleby, the younger sister, who had less ardour for the Cause than for the men who were pledged to it, whispered low, as he took her hand –

"We know all about Lady Carlyon; and we pray daily for her, and for you. Mother says she is worthy to become – to be raised – to be –"

"What?" he asked, reddening; for the girl hesitated and looked at him with a kind of awe.

"Queen of England."

"Don't anticipate, Faith," said Algy. "Considering, however, what we have come out of, it strikes me that we have nothing to lose, whatever we may gain. Come, Chester, we want to have a quiet talk together as soon as the Bishop goes to bed."

They talked for nearly the whole night. There was so much to say; one subject after another was started; there were so many chances to consider, – that it was four o'clock when they parted. Algy found, somewhere or other, a bottle of champagne.

"Come," he cried, "a stirrup-cup! I drink to the day when the 'King shall enjoy his own again.'"

"Algy!" said Lord Chester. "To think that you have deceived me!"

"To think," he replied, laughing, "that we have dreamed of this day so long! What would our Revolution be worth unless we were to have our hereditary and rightful king for leader! Yet, I confess, it was hard to see you drawn daily closer to us, and not to hold out hands to drag you in – long ago. Yes, the Professor was right. She is always right. She glories in her obedience to the Bishop, but – whisper, – we all know very well that the Bishop does nothing without consulting her first, and nothing that she does not agree with. Don't be too sure, dear boy, about the Supremacy of Man."

CHAPTER VIII.

THE BISHOP.

AT seven in the morning, Lord Chester was roused from an extremely disagreeable dream. He was, in this vision, being led off to execution, in company with the Bishop, Constance, the Professor, and Grace Ingleby. The Duchess of Dunstanburgh headed the procession, carrying the ropes in her own illustrious hand. Her face was terrible in its sternness. The Chancellor was there, pointing skinny fingers, and saying "Yah!" Before him, within five minutes' walk, stood five tall and comely gallows, with running tackle beautifully arranged; also, in case there should be any preference expressed by the criminals for fa.ncy methods of execution, there were stakes and fagots, guillotines, wheels to be broken upon, men with masks, and other accessories of public execution.

It was therefore a relief, on opening his eyes, to discover that he was as yet only a peaceful guest of Professor Ingleby, and that the Great Revolt had not yet begun. "At all events," he said, cheerfully, "I shall have the excitement of the attempt, if I am to be hanged or beheaded for it. And most certainly it will be less disagreeable to be hanged than to marry the Duchess. Perhaps even there may be, if one is lucky, an opportunity of telling her so. A last dying speech of that kind would be popular."

Shaking off gloomy thoughts, therefore, he dressed hastily, and descended to the Hall, where most of the party of the preceding night were collected, waiting for him. The tinkling of a bell which had awakened him now began again. Algy Dunquerque told him it was the bell for chapel.

"But," he added, "don't be afraid. It is not the kind of service we are accustomed to. There is no homily on obedience; and, thank goodness, there is no Perfect Woman here!"

The chapel was a long room, fitted simply with a few benches, a table at the east end, a brass eagle for lectern, and some books. The Professor and the girls were already in their places, and in a few moments 'the Bishop himself appeared, in lawn-sleeves and surplice.

For the first time Lord Chester witnessed the spectacle of a man conducting the services. It gave a little shock and a momentary sense of shame, which he shook off as unworthy. A greater shock was the simple service of the Ancient Faith which followed.

To begin with, there were no flowers, no incense girls, no anthems, no pictures of Sainted Women, no figures of the Holy Mother, no veiled Perfect Woman on an altar crowned with roses; and there were no genuflections, no symbolical robes, no mystic whisperings, no change of dress, no pretence at mysterious powers. All was perfectly simple – a few prayers, a lesson from a great book, a hymn, and then a short address.

The Ancient Faith had long since become a thing dim and misty, and well-nigh forgotten save to a few students. Most knew of it only as an obsolete form of religion which belonged to the semi-barbarism of Man's supremacy: it had been superseded by the fuller revelation of the Perfect Woman, – imposed, so to speak, upon the world for the elevation of women into their proper place, and for the guidance of subject man. It was carefully taught, with catechism, articles, doctrines, and history, to children as soon as they could run about. It was now a settled Faith, venerable by reason of its endowments and dignities rather than its age, supported by all the women of England, defended on historical and intellectual grounds by thousands of pens, by weekly sermons, by domestic prayers, by maternal admonitions, by the terrors of the after world, by the hopes of that which is present with us. A great theological literature had grown up around the Faith. It was the only recognised and tolerated religion; it was not only the religion of the State, but also the very basis of the political constitution. For as the Perfect Woman was the goddess whom they worshipped, the Peeresses who ruled were rulers by divine right, and the Commons – before that House had been abolished – were members of their House by divine permission: every member officially described herself a member by divine permission. To dispute about the authority of the ecclesiastical Decrees, which came direct from the Upper House, was blasphemy, a criminal offence, and punishable by death; and to deny the authority of the Decrees was to incur certain death. It is not, therefore, surprising to hear that there was neither infidelity nor nonconformity in the whole country. On the other hand, because there must be some outlet for private and independent opinion, there were many interpretations of the law, and opinions as many and as various as those who disputed concerning the right interpretation. Under the rule of woman, there could be no doubt, no compromise, no dispute, on essentials. The principles of religion, like those of moral, social, and political economy, were fixed and unalterable; they were of absolute certainty. As to the Articles of Religion, as to the Great Dogma of the Revealed Perfect Woman, there could be no doubt, no discussion.

And now, after a most religious training, Lord Chester – a man who ought to have accepted and obeyed in meekness – was actually assisting, in a spirit half curious, half converted, at a service in which the Perfect Woman was entirely left out. What next? and next?

Ever since Lord Chester had become awakened to the degradation of man and the possibility of his restoration, his mind had been continually exercised by the absolute impossibility of reconciling his new Cause with his Religion. How could the Grand Revolt be carried out in the teeth of the most sacred commandments? How could he remain a faithful servant of the Church, and yet rebel against the first law of the Church? How could he continue to worship the Perfect Woman when he was thrusting woman out of her place? We may suppose

Cromwell, by way of parallel, trying to reconcile the divine right of kings with the execution of Charles the First.

Here, however, though as yet he understood it not, there was a service which absolutely ignored the Perfect Woman. The prayers were addressed direct to the Eternal Father as the Father. The language was plain and simple. The words of the hymn which they sang were strong and simple, ringing true as if from the heart, like the hammer on the anvil.

The Bishop closed his book, bowed his head for a few moments in silent prayer, then rose and addressed his congregation; and as he spoke, the young men clasped hands, and the girls sobbed.

"Beloved," he began, "at this moment it would be strange indeed if our hearts were not moved within us – if our prayers and praises were not spontaneous. Let us remember that we are the descendants of those who handed down the lamp in secrecy from one to the other, always with prayer that they might live to see the Day of Restoration. The Day of Attempt, indeed, is nigh at hand. We pray with all our hearts that we may bring the Return of the Light of the World. Then may those who witness the glorious sight cry aloud to depart in peace, because there will be nothing more for them to pray for. What better thing could there be for us, my children, than to die in this attempt?

"You who have learned the story of the past; you who worship with me in the great and simple Faith of your ancestors; you who know how man did wondrous deeds in the days of old, and how he fell and became a slave, who was created to be master; you who are ready to begin the upward struggle; you who are the apostles of the old Order, – children of the Promise, go forth in your strength and conquer."

Then he gave them the Benediction, and the service was concluded.

Half an hour afterwards, when the emotions of this act of worship were somewhat calmed, they met at breakfast. The girls' eyes were red, and the young men were grave; but the conversation flowed in the accustomed grooves.

After breakfast, Lord Chester was intrusted to the care of the pale and austere young man who had been first presented to him.

"Clarence Veysey," said the Bishop, "is my secretary, my private chaplain, and my pupil. He is himself in full priest's orders, and will instruct you in the rudiments of our Faith. "We do not substitute one authority for another, Lord Chester. You will be exhorted to try and examine for yourself the doctrines before you accept them. Yet you will understand that what you are taught stood the test of question, doubt, and attack for more than two thousand years before it was violently torn from mankind. Go, my son, receive instruction with docility; but do not fear to question and to doubt."

"I am indeed a priest," said Clarence Veysey, taking him into the library. "I have been judged worthy of the laying on of hands."

"And do not your friends know or suspect?"

"No," he replied. "It is, in fact" – here he blushed and hesitated – "a position of great difficulty. I must, perforce, until we are ripe for action, act a deceptive part. The necessity for concealment is a terrible thing. Yet, what help? One remembers him who bowed himself in the House of Rimmon."

"The concealment," said Lord Chester, unfeelingly, because he knew nothing about Naaman, "would be part of the fun."

"The fun?" this young priest gasped. "But, of course – you do not know. We are in deadly earnest, and he calls it – fun: we strive for the return of the world to the Faith, and he calls it – fun!"

"I beg your pardon," said Lord Chester. "I seem – I hardly know why – to have offended you. I really think it must be very good fun to have this pretty secret all to yourself when you are at home."

"Oh! he is very – very ignorant," cried Clarence.

"Well –" Lord Chester did not mind being instructed by the old Bishop or by the Professor. But the superiority of this smooth-cheeked youth of his own age galled him. Nevertheless, he saw that the young priest was deeply in earnest, and he restrained himself.

"Teach me, then," he said.

"As for the deception," said Clarence, "it is horrible. One falsehood leads to another. I pretend weakness – even disease and pain – to escape being married to some one; because what can a man of my position – of the middle class – do to earn my bread? Then I have simulated sinful paroxysms of bad temper. This keeps women away: so long as I am believed to I be ill-tempered and sickly, of course no one will offer to marry me. A reputation for ill-temper is, fortunately, the best safeguard possible for a young man who would possess his soul in freedom. I try to persuade myself that necessary deception is harmless deception; and if we succeed –" he paused and sighed. "Come, my lord, let me teach you something of the true Faith."

They spent the whole morning together, while Clarence Veysey unfolded the mysteries of the Ancient Faith, and showed how divine a thing it was, and how fitted for every possible phase or emergency of life. His earnestness, the sincerity and honesty of his belief, deeply moved Lord Chester.

"But how," asked the neophyte, "came this wonderful religion to be lost?"

"It was thrown away, not lost," replied the priest. "Even before the women began to encroach upon the power of men, it was thrown away. Had the Ancient Faith survived, we should have been spared the coming struggle. It was thrown away. Men themselves threw it away – some wilfully, others through weakness – receiving forms and the pretensions of priests instead of the substance; so that they surrendered their liberty, put the priest between themselves and the Father, practised the servile rite of confession, and went on to substitute the image of the Mother and Child upon their altars, in place of the Divine Manhood, whose image had been in their fathers' hearts. Why, when after many years it was resolved to place on every altar the Veiled Figure of the Perfect Woman, the very thought of the Divine Man had been wellnigh forgotten.

"But not lost," he went on in a kind of rapture – "not lost. He lingers still among us – here in this most sacred house. He is spoken of in rustic speech; He lingers in rustic traditions; many a custom still survives, the origin of which is now forgotten, which speaks to us who knew of the dear old Faith."

He spoke more of this old Faith, – the only solution, he declared, ever offered, of the problem of life, – the ever-living Divine Brother, always compassionate, always helping, always lifting higher the souls of those who believe.

"See!" cried the enthusiast, falling on his knees, "He is here. O Christ – Lord – Redeemer, Thou art with us – yea, always and always!"

When he brought Lord Chester again into the presence of the Bishop, they both had tears in their eyes.

"He comes, my lord," said Clarence, a sober exultation in his voice – "he comes as a catechumen, seeking instruction and baptism."

Needless here to relate by what arguments, what teaching, Lord Chester became a convert to the new Faith; nor how he was baptised, nor with what ardour he entered into the doctrines of a religion the entrance to which seemed like the bursting of prison – doors, the breaking of fetters, the sudden rush of light. His new friends became, in a deeper sense, his brothers and his sisters. They were of the same religion; they worshipped God through the revelation of the Divine Man.

Then followed a quiet time of study, talk, and preparation, during which Lord Chester remained in perfect seclusion, and went into no kind of society. Professor Ingleby reported to Lady Boltons that her ward went nowhere, desired no other companionship, amused himself with reading, made no reference whatever to the Duchess or Lady Carlyon, and appeared to be perfectly happy, in his "quietest and most delightful manner." The letter was forwarded by Lady Boltons to the Chancellor, and by her to the Duchess, who graciously expressed her approbation of the young man's conduct. There was thus not the least suspicion. On Sunday, which was a day of great danger, because the young men were growing impatient of restraint, Lord Chester went to church with the Professor and her daughters.

Here, while the organ pealed among the venerable aisles of the University Church, while the clouds of incense rolled about before the Veiled Statue on the altar, while the hymn was lifted, while the preacher in shrill tones defended a knotty point in theology, while the dons and heads of houses slumbered in their places, while the few undergraduates remaining up for the Long leaned over the gallery and looked about among the men below for some handsome face to admire, Lord Chester sat motionless, gazing straight before him, obedient to the form, with his thoughts far away.

The strangeness of the new life passed away quickly; the outside life, the repression and pretence, were forgotten, or only remembered with indignation. These young men were free; they laughed – a thing almost unknown under a system when a jest was considered as necessarily either rude or scoffing, certainly ill-bred – they laughed continually; they made up stories; they related things which they had read. Algy Dunquerque, who was an actor, made a little comedy of the Chancellor and the Duchess; and another of the trial and execution of the rebels, showing the fortitude of Clarence Veysey and the unwillingness of himself; and another on the arguments for the Perfect Government. They sat up late; they drank wine and sang songs; they talked of love and courtship; above all, they read the old books.

Think of their joy, when they found on the shelves Shakespeare, Rabelais, Fielding, Smollett, and Dickens! Think of their laughter when they read aloud those rude and boisterous writers, who respected nothing, not even marriage, and had never heard of any Perfect Woman at all! Think, too, of their delight when the words of wisdom went home to them; when they reflected on the great and wise Pantagruel, followed the voyagers among the islands of Humanity, or watched over the career of Hamlet, the maddened Prince of Denmark! These were for their leisure hours, but serious business occupied the greater part of the day.

Continually, also, the young men held counsel together, and discussed their plans. It was known that the Rising would take place at the earliest possible opportunity. But two difficulties presented themselves. What would constitute a favourable opportunity? and what would be the best way to take advantage of it?

Algy Dunquerque insisted, for his part, that they should ride through the country, calling on the men to rise and follow. What, however, if the men refused to rise and follow?

Jack Kennion thought they should organise a small body first, drill and arm them, and then seize upon a place and hold it. Clarence Veysey thought that he was himself able, book in hand, to persuade the whole of the country.

For men to rise against women seems, since the event, a ridiculously easy thing. As a matter of fact, it was an extremely difficult thing. For the men had been so kept apart that they did not know how to act together, and so kept in subjection that they were cowed. The prestige of the ruling sex was a factor of the very highest importance. It was established, not only by law, but by religion. How ask men to rebel when their eternal interests demanded submission? Men, again, had no longer any hope of change. While the present seems unalterable, no reform can be even attempted. Life was dull and monotonous; but how could it be otherwise? Men had ceased to ask if a change was possible. And the fighting spirit had left them; they were strong, of course, but their strength was that of the patient ox.

If there was to be fighting, the material on the side of the Government consisted first of the Horse Guards – three regiments, beautifully mounted and accoutred in splendid uniforms – every man a tall handsome fellow six feet high. These soldiers formed the escort at all great Functions. They never left London; they enjoyed a very fair social consideration; some of them were married to ladies of good family, and all were married well; they were commanded from the War Office by a department of a hundred secretaries, clerks, and copying-women.

Would they fight for the Government? or would they come over? At present no one could tell.

In addition to these regiments, the nation, which had no real standing army, maintained a force of constabulary for prison-warders. It has been already stated that the prisons were crowded with desperadoes and violent persons convicted of wife-beating, boxing their wives' ears, pulling their hair, and otherwise ill-treating them against the religion and law. They were coerced and kept in order by some fifteen or twenty thousand of the constabulary, who were drilled and trained, commanded by men chosen from their own ranks as sergeants, and armed with loaded rifles. It is true that the men were recruited from the lowest class – many of them being thieves, common rogues, and jailbirds, some of them having even volunteered as an exchange from prison; their pay was low, their fare poor; no woman of respectability would marry one of them; they were rude, fierce, and ill-disciplined; they frequently ill-treated the prisoners; and their superior officers – women who commanded from the rooms of a department – had no control whatever over them. They would probably fight, if only for the contempt and hatred in which they were held by men.

Where, for their own part, could they look for soldiers?

There were the rustics. They were strong, healthy, accustomed to work together, outspoken, never more than half convinced of the superiority of women, practising the duty of obedience no more than they were obliged, fain to go courting on their own account, the despair of preachers, who were constantly taunted with the ill success of their efforts. Why, it was common – in some cases it was the rule – to find the woman in the cottage that most contemptible thing – a man-pecked wife. What was the good of paying wages to this wife, when her husband took from her what he wanted for himself? What was the good of making laws that men should not be abroad alone after dark, when in most of the English villages the men stood loitering and talking together in the streets till bed-time? What was the use of prohibiting all intoxicating drinks, when in every village there were some women who made beer and sold it to all the men who could pay for it, and though perfectly well known, were never denounced?

"They are ready to our hand," said Lord Chester. "The only question is, how to raise them, and how to arm them when they are raised."

CHAPTER IX.

THE GREAT CONSPIRACY.

ONE morning, after six weeks of this pleasant life, Lord Chester, who had made excellent use of his time, and was now as completely a man as his companions, was summoned to the Bishop's study, and there received a communication of the greatest importance.

The Professor was the only other person present.

"I have thought it prudent, Lord Chester," said the Bishop gravely, "to acquaint you with the fact that the time is now approaching when the great Attempt will be made. Are you still of the same mind? May we look for your devotion – even if we fail?"

"You may, my lord." The young man held out his hand, which the aged Bishop clasped.

"It is good," he said, "to see the devotion of youth ready to renounce life and its joys; to incur the perils of death and dishonour. This seems hard even in old age, when life has given all it has to give. But in young men – Yet, my son, remember that the martyr does not change a lower life for a higher."

"I give you my life, if so it must be," Lord Chester repeated.

"We take what is offered cheerfully. You must know then, my lord, that the ground has been artfully prepared for us. This conspiracy, which you have hitherto thought confined to one old man's house and half-a-dozen young men living with him, is in reality spread over the whole country. We have organisations, great or small, in nearly every town of England. Some of them have as yet only advanced to the stage of discontent; others have been pushed on to learn that the evil condition of men is due chiefly to the government of women; others have learned that the sex which rules ought to obey; others, that the worship of the Perfect Woman is a vain superstition: none have gone so far as you and your friends, who have learned more – the faith in the Perfect Man. That is because you are to be the leaders, you yourself to be the Chief.

"Now, my lord, the thing having so far advanced, the danger is, that one or other of our secret societies may be discovered. True, they do not know the ramifications or extent of the conspiracy. They cannot, therefore, do us any injury by treachery or unlucky disclosures; yet the punishment of the members would be so severe as to strike terror into the rest of our members. Therefore, it is desirable to begin as soon as possible."

"To-day!" cried the young Chief.

"No – not to-day, nor to-morrow. The difficulty is, to find some pretext – some reasonable pretext – under cover of which we might rise."

"Can we not invent something?"

"There are the convicts. We might raise a force, and liberate those of the prisoners who are victims of the harsh laws of violence and the refusal to take a husband's evidence when accused by a wife. Then the country would be with us. But I shrink from commencing this great rebellion with bloodshed."

He paused and reflected for a time.

"Then there is the labour cry. We might send our little force into the towns, and call on the workmen to rise for freedom. But suppose they would not rise? Then – more bloodshed.

"Or we might preach the Faith throughout the land, as Clarence Veysey wants to do. But I incline not to the belief in wholesale miracles, and the age of faith is past, and the number of our preachers is very small."

"You will be helped," said the Professor, "in a quarter where you least suspect. I, too, with my girls, have done my little."

She proceeded to open a packet of papers, which she laid before the young Chief.

"What are these?" he asked.

"They are called Tracts for the Times," she replied. "They are addressed to the Women: of England."

She took them up and read them carefully one by one.

"Who wrote these?"

"The girls and I together. We posted them wherever we could get addresses – to all the undergraduates, to all the students of hospitals, Inns of Court, and institutions of every kind; to quiet country vicarages; to rich people and poor people, – wherever there was a chance, we directed a tract."

"You have done well," said the Bishop.

"They have been found out, and a reward is offered for the printers. As they were printed in the cellars of this house, the reward is not likely to be claimed. They were all posted here, which makes the Government the more uneasy. They believe in the spread of what they call irreligion among the undergraduates. Unfortunately, the undergraduates are as yet only discontented, because all avenues are choked."

The Bishop took up one of the tracts again, and read it thoughtfully. It was headed, "Tracts for the Times: For Young Women," and was the first number. The second title was "Work and Women."

The writer, in brief telling paragraphs, very different from the long-winded, verbose style everywhere prevalent, called upon women seriously to consider their own position, and the state that things had been brought to by the Government of the Peeresses. Every profession was crowded: the shameful spectacle of women begging for employment, even the most ill-paid, was everywhere seen; the law in both branches was filled with briefless and clientless members; there were more doctors than patients; there were more teachers than pupils; there were artists without number who produced acres of painted canvas every year and found no patrons; the Church had too many curates; while architects, journalists, novelists, poets, orators, swarmed, and were all alike ravenous for work at any rate of pay, even the lowest. The happiest were the few who could win their way by competitive examination into the Civil Service; and even there, the Government having logically applied the sound political axioms of supply and demand to the hire of their servants, they could hardly live upon their miser: able pay, and must give up all hopes of. marriage. There was a time, the tract went on, when men had to do all the work, including the work of the professions. In those days all kinds of work were considered respectable, so that there was not this universal run upon the professions. And in those days, said the writer, the axiom of open competition in professional charges was not acted up to, insomuch that physicians, barristers, and solicitors charged a sum agreed upon by themselves – and that an adequate sum – for services rendered; while the pay of the Services was given in consideration to the amount required for comfortable living. The only way out of the difficulty, concluded the author, was to limit the number of those who entered the professions, to regulate the charges on a liberal scale, and to increase the pay of the Services. As for the rest, if women must work, they must do the things which women can do well – sew, make dresses, cook, and, in fact, perform all those services which were thought menial, unless, indeed, they preferred the hard work of men in the fields and at the looms.

The second tract treated of the Idleness of Men.

By the wisdom of their ancestors, it had been ordained that every man should be taught a handicraft, by means of which to earn his own living. This wholesome rule had been allowed to fall into abeyance; for while some sort of carpenter's work was nominally and officially taught in boys' schools, it had long been considered a mark of social inferiority for man to do any work at all. "We educate our men," the tract went on, "in the practice of every gymnastic and athletic feat; we turn them out strong, active, able to do and endure, and then we find nothing for them to do. Is it their fault that they become vacuous, ill-tempered, discontented, the bane of the house which their virtues ought to make a happy home? What else can we expect? Whence the early falling off into fat cheeks and flabby limbs? whence the love of the table – that vice which stains our manhood? whence the apathy at Church services? – whence should they come but from the forced idleness, the lack of interest in life?"

The tract went on to call for a reform in this as. in other matters. Let the men be set to work; let men of all classes have to work, Why should women do all, as well as think for all? "It must be considered, again, that every man cannot be married; indeed, under the present state of things few women can think of marriage till they have arrived at middle age, and therefore most men must remain single. Why should we doom them to a long life of forced inaction? Happier far the rustic who ploughs the field, or the cobbler who patches the village boots." Then there followed an artful and specious reference to old times: "Under the former *régime*, men worked, and women, in the freedom of the house, thought. The nominal ruler was the Hand; the actual, the Head. In those days, the flower of woman's life was not wasted in study and competition. The maidens were wooed while they were young and beautiful; their lovers worked for them, surrounded them with pleasant things, lapped them in warmth, brought them all that they could desire, made their lives a restful dream of love. It has come to this, O women of the New Faith, that you have thrown away the love of men, and with it the whole joy of creation! You worship the Woman; your mothers, happier in their generation, were contented each to be worshipped by a man."

"That is very good," said the Bishop.

Then the Professor produced another and a more dangerous manifesto, addressed to the young men of England. It was dark and mysterious: it bade them be on the watch for a great and glorious change; they were to remember the days when men were rulers; they were to distrust their teachers, and especially the priestesses; they were to look with loathing upon the inaction to which they were condemned; they were told to ask themselves for what end their limbs were strong if they were to do nothing all their lives; and they were taught how, in the old days, the men did all the work, and were rewarded by marrying young and lovely women. This tract had been circulated from hand to hand, none of the agents in its distribution knowing anything of the plot.

There were others, all turning upon the evils of the times, and all recalling the old days when women sat at home.

"We want," said the Bishop, "a pretext, – we want a spark which shall set fire to this mass of discontent."

That very night there was a stormy debate in the House of Peeresses. The Duchess of Dunstanburgh, whose Ministry was kept in power by nothing but the stern will of their leader, because it had never commanded the confidence or even the respect of the House, came down with a bundle of papers in her hand. They were these very tracts. She read them through, one by one. She informed the House that these tracts had been circulated wholesale: from ever town in the country she received intelligence that they had been taken from some girl's hands, – in many cases from the innocent hands of young men. She said that it had been ascertained so far that the tracts were posted from Cambridge; it was believed they were the work of certain mischievous and infidel undergraduates. She had taken the unusual course of instituting a college visitation, so far without effect. Meantime she assured the House that if the author of these tracts could be discovered, no punishment would be too severe to meet the offence.

The Countess of Carlyon rose to reply. She said that no one regretted more than herself the tone of these tracts. At the same time there was, without doubt, ample cause for discontent. The professions were crammed; thousands of learned young women were asking themselves where they were to look for even daily bread. In the homes, the young men, seeing the misery, were, for their part, asking why they should not work, if work of any kind were to be got. To sit at home, and starve in gentility, was a hard thing to do, even by the most patient and religious young man; while for a girl to see the days go by barren and unprofitable, while her beauty withered, – to have no hope of marriage; to see the man she might have loved taken from her – here the Countess faced the Duchess with indignant eyes – taken from her by one old enough to be his grandmother, – surely here was cause enough for discontent! She urged the appointment of a commission for the consideration of grievances; and she urged, further, that the evidence of men, old and young, should be received – especially on two important points: first, whether they really *liked* a life of inaction; and secondly, whether they really *liked* marrying their grandmothers.

The scene which followed this motion was truly deplorable. The following of Lady Carlyon consisted of all the younger members of the House – a minority, but full of life and vigour; on the opposite side were the old and middle-aged Peeresses, who had been brought up in the doctrine of woman's divine right of authority, and of man's divine rule of obedience. The elders had a tremendous majority, of course; but not the less, the fact that such a motion could be made was disquieting. The debate was not reported, but it got abroad; and while the tracts circulated more widely than ever, no more were seized, because they were all kept hidden, and circulated underhand.

From end to end of the country, the talk was of nothing but of the old times. Was it true, the girls asked, that formerly the women ruled at home, while the men did all the work? If that was so, would no one find a compromise by which they could restore that part, at least, of the former *régime?* Oh, to end these weary struggles, – these studies, which led to examinations; these examinations, which led to diplomas; these diplomas, which led to nothing; these agonising endeavours to trample upon each other, to push themselves into notoriety, to snatch the scraps of work from each other's hands! Oh, to rest, to lie still, to watch the men work I Oh – but this they whispered with clasping of hands – oh, to be worshipped by a lover young and loyal! What did the tract say? Happy women of old, when there was no Perfect Woman, but each was the goddess of one man!

CHAPTER X.

THE FIRST SPARK.

In the early autumn the Cambridge party broke up. Clarence Veysey was the first to go. His sisters wanted him at home, they said.

"They are good girls," he sighed, "and less unsexed than most of their sex. Thanks to my reputation for ill health, they do not interfere with my pursuits, and I can read and meditate. Writing is, of course, dangerous."

Lord Chester had not been long at the Professor's before he discovered two of those open secrets which are known by everybody. They were naturally affairs of the heart. It was pleasant to find that the young priest, the ardent apostle of the old Faith, was in love, and with Grace Ingleby. The courtship was cold, yet serious: he loved her with the selfish affection of men who have but one absorbing interest in life, and yet want a wife in whom to confide, and from whom to receive undivided care and worship. This he would find in Grace Ingleby, – one of those fond and faithful women who are born full of natural religion, to whom love, faith, and enthusiasm are as the air which they breathe.

The other passion was of a less spiritual kind. Algy Dunquerque, in fact, was in love with Faith Ingleby, – head over ears in love, madly in love, – and she with him. He would break off the most absorbing conversation – even a speculative discussion as to how they would carry themselves, and what they would say, when riding in the cart to execution – in order to walk about under the trees with the girl.

"The fact is," he explained, "that if it were not for Faith and for you, I doubt if I should have been secured at all for the Revolution. One more good head would have been saved."

Another complication made his case serious, and added fresh reasons for despatch in the work before them. His mother addressed him, while he was at Cambridge, a long and serious letter – that kind of letter which *must* be attended to.

After compliments of the usual kind to the Professor and to Lord Chester, – it was for the sake of this young man's friendship, and its possible social advantages, that Algy, as well as Jack Kennion, was permitted to stay so long from home, – Lady Dunquerque opened upon business of a startling nature. She reminded her son that he was now two-and-twenty years of age, a time when many young men of position are already established. "I have been willing," she said, "to give you a long run of freedom, – partly, I confess, because of your friendship for Lord Chester, who, though in many respects not quite the model for quiet and home-loving boys" – here Algy read the passage over again, and nodded his head in approbation – "will be quite certainly the Duke of Dunstanburgh, and in that position will be the first gentleman of England. But an event has occurred, an event of such good fortune, that I am compelled to recall you without delay. You have frequently met the great lawyer Frederica Roe, Q.C. You will, I am sure, be pleased to learn" – here Algy took the hand of Faith Ingleby, and held it, reading aloud – "that she has asked for your hand."

"I am greatly pleased," said Algy. "Bless the dear creature! She dresses in parchment, Faith, my angel: if you prick her, she bleeds ink; if she talks, it is Acts of Parliament; and when she coughs, it is a special pleading. Her complexion is yellow, her eyes are invisible, she has gone bald, and she is five-and-fifty. What good fortune! What blessed luck!" Then he went on with his letter.

"Of course I hastened to accept. She will be raised to the Peerage whenever a vacancy occurs on the Bench. I confess, my dear son, that this match, so much beyond our reasonable expectations, so much higher than our fortune and position entitled us to hope for on your behalf – a match in all respects, and from every point of view, so advantageous – pleases your father and myself extremely. The disparity of age is not greater than many young men have to encounter, and it is proved by numberless examples to be no bar to real happiness. I say this because, in the society of Lord Chester, you may have imbibed – although I rely upon your religious principles – some of those pernicious doctrines which are, falsely perhaps, attributed to him. However, we hope to see you return to us as you left us, submissive, docile, and obedient. And your friendship with Lord Chester may ultimately prove of the greatest advantage to you." "I hope it will," said Jack, laughing, as he read this passage. "Your father begs me to add that Frederica, who is only a few years older than himself, is in reality, though somewhat imperious and brusque in manner, a most kind-hearted woman, and likely to prove the most affectionate and indulgent of wives."

"What do you think of that, brothers mine?" he asked, folding up the letter. They looked at each other.

"Oh, begin at once!" cried Faith, clasping her hands. "They will marry you all, the horrid creatures, before you have struck the first blow. Do you hear, Algy? begin at once."

"It is serious," said Jack. "If pity is any good to you, Algy, you have it. A crabbed old lawyer – a soured, peevish, argumentative Q.C." He shuddered. "It is already Vacation; she is sure to want to push on the marriage without delay. What are we to do?"

He looked at Lord Chester for a reply.

"My own case," said the young Chief, "comes before the House in October. The first blow, so far as I am concerned, must be struck before then."

"For heaven's sake," cried Algy, "strike it before this old lawyer swallows me up! I feel like a piece of parchment already. A little delay I can manage; a tooth-ache, a cold, a sore throat – anything would do – but that would only delay the thing a week."

The little party was broken up. Jack Kennion alone remained. He had obtained permission to accompany Lord Chester to his Chester Towers, his country seat. The Professor and the girls were to go too – an arrangement sanctioned by Lady Boltons, happily ordered abroad to drink the waters.

Three weeks passed. Letter after letter came from Algy. His *fiancée* was pressing on the marriage; he had resorted to every expedient to postpone it; he knew not what he could do next; the day had to be named; wedding presents were coming in; and the learned lawyer proved more odious than could be imagined.

Lord Chester was not idle.

He was sitting one afternoon at this time, Algernon's last despairing letter in his pocket, on a hillside four or five miles from the Castle. Beside him stood a young gamekeeper, Harry Gilpin, stalwart and brawny: there was no shooting to be done, but he carried his gun.

"It is our only chance, Harry," said Lord Chester, in low earnest tones. "We must do it. Things are intolerable."

"If there's any chance in it; but it is a poor chance at best."

"What, Harry I would you not follow me?"

"I'll follow your lordship wherever you lead. I'll go for your lordship wherever you point. Don't think I'm afeard for myself. I'm but a poor creature – easy to find plenty as good as me; and if so be I must end my days in a convict-prison, why, I'd rather do it for you, my lord, than for lying accusations."

"Good, Harry." Lord Chester held out his hand. "We understand each other. Death rather than a convict – prison. We strike for freedom. Tell me next about the discontent."

"All the country-side is discontented, along o' the old women. It's this way, my lord. We get on right well, let us marry our own gells. When the gells gets shoved out o' the way, and we be told by the Passon to marry this old woman, an' that, why ... 'tis nature."

"It is, Harry, and my case as well as yours. Then if all are discontented, we may get all to join us."

"Nay, my lord; many are but soft creatures, and mortal afraid of the women. We shall get some, but we must make them desperate afore they'll fight."

"You keepers can shoot. How many can we reckon on?"

Harry laughed.

"When your lordship lifts up your little finger," he replied, "there's not a keeper for miles and miles round that won't run to join you, nor a stable-boy, nor a groom, nor a gardener. Ay! a hundred and fifty men, counting boys, will come in, once pass the word. A Chester has lived in these parts longer than men can remember."

"Do they remember, Harry, that a Chester once ruled this country?"

"Ay ... so some say ... in the days when .. but there! it is an old story."

"But the girls, Harry, who have lost their lovers, – your own girl, what will she do?"

"They whimper a bit; they have a row with the old woman; and then the Passon steps in and talks about religion, and they give in."

"What! If they saw a chance, if they thought they could get their sweethearts back again, would they not rejoice?"

Harry hesitated.

"Some would, some wouldn't. You see, my lord, it's their religion stands in the way; and their religion means everything. What they say is, that if they married their sweethearts, these being young and proper men, and masterful, they would perhaps get put upon; whereas, they love to rule their husbands. But some would ... yes, some would."

Lord Chester rose, and began slowly to return home across the fields.

A hundred and fifty, and all true and loyal men! As the occupation of most of them prevented their going to church, and kept them apart from the rest, in a kind of loneliness, they were comparatively uninfluenced by religion; and though their wives drew the pay, the keepers understood little about obedience, and indeed had everything their own way. A hundred and fifty men! – a little army. Never before had he felt so grateful for the preservation of game.

"You said, Harry, a hundred and fifty men!"

"A hundred and fifty men, my lord, of all ages, by to-morrow morning, if you want them, and no doubt a hundred and fifty more the day after. Why, there are seventy men on the Duchess's estate alone, counting the rangers, the gardeners, the keepers, stable-boys, and all."

Three hundred men!

Lord Chester was silent. He-had communicated enough of the plot. Harry knew that his master, like himself, was threatened with an elderly wife. He also knew that his master proposed an insurrection against the marriage of young men against their wills. Further, Harry did not inquire.

Now, while the leader of the Revolt was considering what steps to take, – nothing is harder in revolutions than to make a creditable and startling commencement, – accident put in his way a most excellent beginning. There was a hard-working young blacksmith in the village – a brawny, powerful man of thirty or thereabouts. No better blacksmith was there within thirty miles: his anvil rang from morning until night; he was as handsome in a rough fashion as any man need be; and he ought to have been happy. But he was not, for he was married to a termagant. Not only did this wife of his take all his money, which was legitimate, but she abused him with the foulest reproaches, accusing him perpetually of wife-beating, of infidelity, of drunkenness, and of all the vices to which male flesh is liable, threatening him in her violent moods with imprisonment.

That morning there had been a more than usually violent quarrel. The scolding of the beldam in her house was heard over the whole village, so that the men trembled and grew pale, thus admonished of what an angry woman can say. During the forenoon there was peace, the blacksmith working quietly at his forge. In the dinner-hour the row began again, worse than ever. At two o'clock the poor man came out with hanging head and dejected face to his work. One or two of the elder women admonished him against exasperating his wife; but he replied nothing. Children, for whom the unlucky smith had ever a kind word and a story, came as usual, and stayed outside waiting. But there was no word of kindness for them that day. Men passed down the village street and spoke to him; but he made no reply. Then the village cobbler, a widower, and independent, and so old and crusty of temper that no one was likely to marry him, came forth from his shop and spoke to him.

"How goes it, Tom?"

"Bad," said Tom. "Couldn't be worse. And I wish I was dead – dead and buried and out of it."

The cobbler shook his head and retired.

Then there came slowly down the street, carrying a basket with vegetables, a young woman of five-and-twenty, and she stopped in front of the forge, and said softly, "Poor Tom! I heard her this morning."

Tom looked up and shook his head. His eyes, which were soft and gentle, were full of tears.

And then ... then ... the wife rushed upon the scene. Her eyes were red, her lips were quivering, her whole frame shook with passion. For she was no longer simply in a common, vulgar, everyday rage; she was in a rage of jealousy. She seized the younger woman by the arm, dragged her into the middle of the road, and threw herself before her husband in a fine attitude. "Stand back!" she cried. "You ... you ... Susan! He is my man, not yours – not yours."

"Poor fellow!" said Susan. She was a young person with black hair and resolute eyes, and it was well known that she had regarded Tom as her sweetheart. "Poor fellow! It was a bad job indeed for him when he became your man."

A war of words between an elderly woman, who may be taunted with her years, her jealousy, her lack of children, teeth, and comeliness, and a young woman, who may be charged with many sins, is at best a painful thing to witness, and a shameful thing to describe. Suffice it to say, that the elder lady was completely discomfited, and that long after she was extinguished the girl continued to pour upon her the vials of her wrath. The whole village meanwhile – all the women, and such of the men as were too old for work – crowded round, taking part in the contest. Finally, the wife, stung by words whose bitterness was imbittered by their truth, cried aloud, taking the bystanders to witness, that the husband for whose sake, she said, she had endured patiently the falsehoods and accusations of yonder hussy, was nothing better than a beater, a striker, a kicker, a trampler, and a cuffer of his wife.

"I've borne it long," she cried, "but I will bear it no longer. To prison he shall go. If I *am* an old woman, and like to die, you shall never have him – do you hear? To prison he shall go, and for life."

At these words a dead silence fell on all.

The blacksmith stood still, saying not a word, leaning on his hammer. Then his wife spoke again, but slowly.

"Last night," she said, "he dragged me round the room by the hair of my head; this morning he knocked me down with his fist; and last Sunday, after church, he kicked me off my chair; yesterday fortnight he beat me with a poker – "

"Lies I *lies!!* LIES!!!" cried Susan. "Tom, say they are lies."

Tom shook his head, but spoke never a word.

"Tom!" she cried again, "they will take you to prison; say they are lies."

Then he spoke.

"I would rather go to prison."

"Don't believe her," Susan cried. "Don't believe her. Why, she's got no hair to be pulled. ... Don't. ... Oh! oh! oh!"

She burst into an agony of weeping.

The women clamoured round the group, – some for justice, because wife-beating is an awful sin; some for mercy, because this woman was in her fits of wrath a most notorious liar, and not a soul believed her accusations.

It was in the midst of this altercation that there arrived on the scene, from opposite points, Lord Chester with Harry, and two of the rural police.

"Take him into custody," gasped the blacksmith's wife. "Take him to prison. Oh, the wretch! oh, the wife-beater! oh, I am beaten to a jelly – I am bruised black and blue!"

Lord Chester stepped before the unhappy blacksmith.

"Stay!" he said to the policewomen. "Not so fast. Tom, what do you say?" he asked the blacksmith.

"I never laid hand on her," said the unhappy man. "But all's one for that. I suppose I'll have to go to prison, my lord. Anyhow, there can't be no prison worse than this life. I'm glad and happy to be rid of her."

"Stay again," said his lordship. The people gathered closer in wonder. The masterful young lord looked as if he meant to interfere. "Some of you," he said, "take this woman away, and look for any marks of violence. No," as the elder women pressed forward, "not you who have got young husbands of your own, and would like to get rid of them yourselves perhaps. Some of you girls take her."

But she refused to go, while the old women murmured amongst each other.

"Must obey orders, my lord," said one of the police. "Here's a case for the magistrates. Woman says her husband struck, beat, and kicked her. Magistrates will hear the case, my lord."

She pulled out her handcuffs.

Then Lord Chester saw that the moment had arrived.

"Harry," he said, "stand by."

He laid his hand on the blacksmith's shoulder.

"No one shall harm him," he said. "Tom, come with me."

"My lord! ... my lord," cried the police-women. "What shall we do? It's obstructing law – it's threatening the executive: what will the justices say? It's a most dreadful offence."

"Come, Tom," he said.

The crowd parted right and left with awestruck eyes.

As Lord Chester carried off his rescued prisoner, the Vicar came running out with dismay upon her face.

"My lord! my lord!" she cried. "What dreadful thing is this? And you, Tom, – you, after all your promises! In *my* parish, too!"

"Hold your foolish tongue!" said Lord Chester, roughly. "Why not in your parish? In every parish, thanks to you and your accursed religion, the young men are torn from the girls, and there is misery. Stand aside. ... You, Susan, will you come with me and your old sweetheart?"

The Vicar gasped. She turned white with terror. "Foolish tongue! Accursed religion!" Had she heard a right?

The police-constables looked stupidly at one another.

"Please, my lord," said one, "we must report your lordship."

"Go and report," replied the rebel.

It was now half-past five in the afternoon, and the labourers were returning from the fields The village street was crowded with men, most of them young men.

The men began whispering together, and the women were all delivering orations at once.

The Chief pointed to some of the men and called them by name.

"You, John Deer; you, Nick Trulliber; you – and you – and you, – come with me. You have old wives too; unless you want to be sent to prison for life for wife-beating, come with me and fight for your liberty."

They hesitated; they trembled; they looked at the vicar, at their wives: they would have been lost but for the presence of mind of the cobbler.

He was, as I have said, an elderly man, bowed down by his work and by years. But he sprang to the front and shouted to the men –

"Come, unless you are cowards and deserve the hulks. Why, it's slavery, it's misery; it's unnatural pains and penalties. Come out of it, you poor, wretched chaps, that ought to be married to them as is young and comely. Come away, all you young fellows that want young wives. Hooray! his lordship's going to deliver us all. Three cheers for Lord Chester! We'll fight for our liberty."

He brandished his bradawl, seized one of the men, and the rest followed. There was a general scream from the women of rage and terror; for all the men followed, like sheep, in a body. Not a single man of the village under sixty years of age or over sixteen slept in his wife's house that night.

"I always knew, my lord," said the cobbler, "that it was stuff an' nonsense, them and their submission. Yah! some day there was bound to be a row. Don't let 'em go back, my lord. I'll stick by your lordship."

("It is a very odd thing," said the Professor, when she heard the story, "that cobblers have always been atheists.")

What next?

Lord Chester had now got his men – a band forty-seven strong, nearly all farm-labourers – within the iron gates of his park, and these were closed and locked. They were as fine a body of men, both young and old together, as could be collected anywhere. But they understood as yet nothing of what was going to be done, and they slouched along wondering stupidly, yet excited at the risk they were running.

Lord Chester made them a speech.

"Remember," he said, "that the prisons of England are full of men charged with wife-beating. They never had an opportunity of defending themselves; they are tortured day and night. You may, all of you – any of you – be charged with this offence. Your word is not taken; you are carried off to hopeless imprisonment. Is that a pleasant thing for you?"

They murmured; but Tom the blacksmith waved his hammer, and Harry the keeper his gun, and the cobbler his bradawl, and these three shouted.

"Who asked you," cried Lord Chester, "if you wanted to marry an old woman? Did any of you choose her for yourselves? Why, when there were girls in the village, sweet and young and pretty, longing for your love, is it likely you would take an old woman?"

Then the girl they called Susan, who had followed with Tom, sprang to the front.

"Look at me, all of you," she cried. "Tom and me was courtin' since we were children – wasn't we, Tom." Tom nodded assent. "And she comes and takes him from me. And the Passon said it was all right, because a man must obey, and sweetheartin' was nonsense. How long are you going to stand it? If I was a man, and strong, would I let the women have their own way? How long will you stand it, I say?"

Here the men lifted up their voices and growled. Liberty begins with a growl; rage begins with a growl; fighting begins with a growl, – it is a healthy symptom for those who promote mischief.

"Are they pretty, your old women?" the orator went on. "Are they good-tempered? Are they pleasant to live with?"

There was another growl.

"Men," cried Lord Chester, "we have borne enough. Wake up! We will end all this. We will marry the women we love – the pretty sweethearts who love us – the young girls who will make us happy. Who will follow me?"

Harry the keeper stepped to the front with a shout Tom the blacksmith followed with a shout, brandishing his hammer. The cobbler pushed and shoved the men. Susan threw her arms round Tom's neck and kissed him, crying, "Go and fight, Tom; follow his lordship. Come, all you that are not cowards."

Two things happened then which determined the event and rallied the waverers, who, to tell the truth, were already beginning to expect their wives and sisters upon the scene.

The first was the appearance of Jack Kennion, followed by two men bearing a great cask of beer. Then tankards passed from lip to lip, and the courage which is said to belong to Holland rather than to England mounted in their hearts.

"Drink about, lads," cried Jack. "Here! give me the mug. Hurrah for Lord Chester! Drink about. Hurrah!"

They drank – they shouted. And while they shouted, they became aware of a tall and beautiful girl who came from the house and stood beside Lord Chester. Her lips were parted; her long hair flowed upon her shoulders; the tears stood in her beautiful eyes. She tried to speak, but for a moment could not.

"Oh, men!" she cried at last, – "Men of England! I thank kind Heaven for this day, which is the beginning of your freedom. Oh, be brave! think not of your own wrongs only. Think of the thousands of men lingering in prison; think of all who are shut in houses, working all day for their unloved wives; think of the young girls who have lost their lovers; think of your strength and your courage, and fight – to the death, if needs be!"

"We will fight," cried the cobbler, "to the death!"

Then Grace Ingleby, for it was she, went from man to man and from group to group, praising them, telling them that it was no small thing they had done – that no common or cowardly man would have dared to do it; commending their courage, admiring their strength, and informing them carefully that this their act could never be forgiven, so that if they did not succeed they would assuredly all be hanged; and imploring them to lose no time in drilling and learning the use of weapons.

The Professor, meantime, was writing letters. She wrote to her husband, begging him to remain quiet while the news was spreading abroad, when he had better get across country by night and join the insurgents. She wrote to all the disciples, telling them to escape and make their way to Lord Chester; and assisted by the girls of the household, who all espoused the cause of the men, she took down the guns, swords, and weapons from the walls, and brought them out for use.

After supper – they cooked plentiful chops for the hungry men, with more beer – Jack called the men out for first drill. It was hard work; but then drill cannot at first be anything but hard work. The men were armed with pikes, guns, clubs, anything; and before nightfall, they had received their first lesson in the art of standing shoulder by shoulder.

They slept that night in tents made of sheets spread out on sticks – a rough shelter, but enough. But the chiefs sat till late, thinking and talking.

Early in the morning, at daybreak, Lord Chester dropped asleep, worn out. When he awoke, Grace stood over him with smiling face.

"Come, my lord," she said, "I have something to show you."

He stood upon the terrace. The night before, he had seen a group of fellows in smock-frocks shoving each other about in a vain attempt to stand in rank and file. Now, the lawns were crowded with men of a different kind, who had come in during the night.

First and foremost, there were a hundred bronzed and weather-beaten men armed with guns – they were Harry's friends, the keepers, rangers, and foresters; among them stood a score of boys who had been sent round to summon them; and behind the keepers stood the rustics.

Oh, wonderful conversion! They had been already put into some sort of uniform which was found among the lumber of the Castle. The jackets were rusty of colour and moth-eaten, but they made the men look soldierlike; every man had round his arm a scarlet ribbon; some had scarlet coats, but not many. At sight of their Chief they all shouted together and brandished their weapons.

The Revolt of Man had begun!

CHAPTER XI.
A MARRIAGE MARRED.

THERE was great excitement in the village of Much cum Milton – a little place about thirty miles from Chester Towers – because Lady Dunquerque's only son, Algernon, was to be married that day to the great lawyer, Frederica Roe. Apart from the natural joy with which such an event is welcomed in a monotonous country village, Algernon was deservedly popular. No better rider, no better shot, no stouter, handsomer lad was to be found in the country-side; nor was it to his discredit that he was the personal friend of young Lord Chester, whose Case was on everybody's lips; nor, among young people, was it to his discredit that he was suspected of being on Lady Carlyon's side. The village girls smiled and looked meaningly at each other when he passed: there were reports that the young man had more than once shown a certain disposition to freedoms; but these, for the sake of his father's feelings, were not spread abroad; and indeed, in country districts, things which would have ruined a young man's reputation in town – such as kissing a dairymaid or a dressmaker – were rather regarded with favour by the girls thus outraged.

The only drawback to the general joy was the thought that the bride was over fifty years of age. Even making great allowances for the safety which experience gives, it is not often that a young man who has attracted the affections of a woman thirty years his senior, is found to study how to preserve those affections; and even considering the position offered by a woman safe of the next vacancy among the judges, a difference of thirty years did seem to these village girls, who knew little of the ways of the great world, a bar to true love. Their opinion, however, was not asked, and the festivities were not outwardly marred by them.

Early in the morning the village choir assembled on the lawn beneath the bridegroom's chamber, and sang the well-known wedding-hymn beginning –

"Break, happy day! Rise, happy sun!
　　Breathe softer, airs of Paradise!
The days of hope and doubt are done;
　　To higher heights of love we rise.

Ah! trembling heart of trusting youth,
　　Fly to the home of peace and rest;
From woman's hands receive the truth,
　　In woman's arms be fully blessed.

O sweet exchange! O guerdon strange
　　For love and guidance of a wife,
To yield the will, and follow still
　　In holy meekness all your life."

The bridegroom-elect within his room made no sign; the window-blind was not disturbed. As a matter of fact, Algy was half-dressed, and was sitting in a chair looking horribly ill at ease.

They began to ring the bells at six; by eight the whole village population was out upon the green, and the final preparations were made. Of course there were Venetian masts, with gay-coloured flags flying. The tables were spread in a great marquee for the feast which, at midday, was to be given to the whole village. There were to be sports and athletics for the young men on the green; there was to be dancing in the evening; there was a band already beginning to discourse sweet music; there was a circus, which was to perform twice, and both times for nothing; there were ginger-bread booths, and rifle-galleries, and gypsies to tell fortunes; they had set up the perambulating theatre for the drama of Punch and Judy, in which the reprobate Punch, who dares to threaten his wife with violence, and disobeys her orders, is hanged upon the stage – a moral lesson of the greatest value to boys; and there was a conjuring-woman's tent. The church was gaily dressed with flowers, and all the boys of the village were told off to strew roses, though the season was late, under the feet of bride and bridegroom.

At the Hall, an early breakfast was spread; but the young bridegroom, the hero of the day, was late.

"Poor boy," said his sister, "no doubt he is anxious and excited with so much happiness before him."

It was a well-bred family, and the disparity of age was not allowed to be even hinted at. The marriage was to be considered a love-match on both sides: that was the social fiction, though everybody knew what was said and thought. Lady Dunquerque had got the boy off her hands very well: there was an excellent establishment, and a good position, with a better one to follow; as for love – here girls looked at each other and smiled. Love was become a thing no longer possible, except for heiresses, of whom there are never too many. Fifty years of age and more; a harsh voice, a hard face, a hard manner, an unsympathetic, exact woman, wrinkled and grey-haired, – how, in the name of outraged Cupid, could such a woman be loved by such a lad? But these things were not even spoken, – they were only conveyed to each other by looks, and smiles, and nods, and little movements of the hands.

"I think; Robert," said Lady Dunquerque, "that you had better *go* up and call Algernon." Sir Robert obediently rose and departed.

When he came down again, his face, usually as placid as the face of a sheep, was troubled.

"Algernon will not take any breakfast," he said.

"Nonsense! the boy must take breakfast. Is he dressed?" Lady Dunquerque was evidently not disposed to surrender her authority over her son till he had actually passed into the hands of his wife.

"Yes, yes, – he is nearly dressed," stammered her husband.

"Well, then, go and tell him to come to breakfast at once, without any nonsense."

Sir Robert went once more. Again he came back with the intelligence that the boy refused to come down.

Thereupon Lady Dunquerque herself went up to his room. The two girls looked at each other with apprehension. Algy was hot-headed: he had already, though not before his mother, made use of very strong language about his bride; could he be meditating some disobedience? Horrible! And the guests all invited, and the day arrived, and the boy's wedding outfit actually ready!

"What did he say, papa?" one of them asked.

"I cannot tell you, my dear. I wash my hands of it. Your mother must bring him to reason. I have done my best." Sir Robert answered in a nervous trembling manner not usual with him.

"Does he ... does he ... express any unwillingness?" asked his daughter.

"My dear, he says nothing shall make him marry the lady. That is all. The day arrived and everything! No power on earth, he says, shall make him marry the lady. That is all What will come to us if her ladyship cannot make him hear reason, I dare not think."

Just then Lady Dunquerque returned. Her husband, trembling visibly, dared not lift his eyes.

"My dear girls," she said, with the calmness of despair, "we are disgraced for ever. The boy refuses to move. He disregards threats, entreaties, everything. I have appealed to his obedience, to his religion, to his honour, – all is of no avail. Go yourselves, if you can. Now, Sir Robert, if you have anything to advise, let me hear it,"

"I can advise nothing," said her husband, quite overwhelmed with this misfortune. "Who could have thought that a –"

"Yes – yes, – it is of no use lamenting. What are we to do? Heavens! there are the church bells again!"

Meantime his sisters were with Algernon. They found him sitting grim and determined. Never before had they seen that expression of determination upon a man's face. He absolutely terrified them.

"You are come to try your powers, I suppose?" he said. "Well; have your say. But remember, no power on earth shall make me marry that detestable old woman."

"Algernon!" cried his younger sister. "Is it possible that you ... you ... our own brother, should use these words?"

"A great deal more is possible. I, for one, protest against this abominable sale of men in marriage. I am put up in the market; this rich old lawyer, with a skin of parchment, blood of ink, heart of brown paper, buys me: I will not be bought. Go, tell my mother that she may do her worst. I will not marry the woman."

"If you will not think of yourself," said his elder sister, coldly, "pray think of us. Our guests are invited, – they are already assembling in the church; listen – there are the bells!"

"I should like," said Algy, laughing, – "I should like to see the face of Frederica Roe in half an hour's time."

The two girls looked at each other in dismay. What was to be done? what could be said?

"You two little hypocrites!" he went on, "you and your goody talk about the day of happiness! and the humbugging hymn! and your sham and mockery of the Perfect Woman! and your reign of the Intellect! Wait a little, my sisters; I promise you a pleasing change in the monotony of your lives."

"Sister," said the younger, "he blasphemes. We must leave him. Oh, unhappy boy! what fate are you preparing for yourself?"

"Come," answered the elder. "Come away, my dear. Algernon, if you disgrace us this day, you shall be no more brother of mine; I renounce you."

They left him. Presently his father came back.

"Algernon," he said, feebly, "have you come to your right mind?"

"I have," he replied – "I have. That is the reason why I am here, and why I am staying here."

"Then I can do nothing for you. Poor boy! my heart bleeds for you."

"My poor father," said his son, speaking in a parable, "my heart has bled for you a long time. Patience! – wait a little."

"The last wedding-present has arrived," said Sir Robert. "What we are to do I cannot, dare not, think. Your mother must break the news to Frederica."

"Whose is the wedding-present?"

"It is from Lord Chester – the most magnificent hunter, saddled, and all; with a note."

Algernon sprang to his feet and rushed to the window. On the carriage-drive he saw a little stable-boy leading a horse. He knew the boy as one of Lord Chester's – a sharp, trusty lad. What was the horse saddled for?

"Give me the letter," he said, almost fiercely, to his father.

Sir Robert handed him the note, which Lady Dunquerque had opened and read: –

"Congratulations, dear Algy; the happy day has dawned. – Yours most sincerely,
CHESTER."

"Among other disasters, you will lose this friend, Algy," moaned his father. "No one can ever speak to you again; no one can –"

"Tell my mother, sir, that I am ready," he interrupted, with a most extraordinary change of manner. "I will be with her as soon as I can complete my toilette. One must be smart upon one's wedding-day. Go, dear father, tell her I am coming down-stairs, and beg her not to make a row – I mean, not to allude to the late distressing scene."

He pushed his father out of the room.

Two minutes later he stood in the breakfast-room, actually laughing as if nothing had happened.

"I am glad, my son," said his mother, "that you have returned to your senses."

"Yes," he replied, gaily, as if it had been a question of some simple act of petulance; "it is a good thing, isn't it? Have you seen Lord Chester's gift, sisters?"

The girls looked at each other in a kind of stupor. What *could* men be like that they should so lightly pass from one extreme to the other?

"Tell the boy," he ordered the footman, "to lead the horse to the Green; I should like all the lads to see it. Tell them it is Lord Chester's gift, with his congratulations on the dawn of the happy day – tell them to remember the dawn of the happy day."

He seemed to talk nonsense in his excitement. But Sir Robert, overjoyed at this sudden return to obedience, shed tears.

"Now," said Lady Dunquerque, "we have no time to lose. Girls, you can go on with your father. Algernon, of course, accompanies me."

When they were left alone, his mother began a lecture, short but sharp, on the duty of marital obedience.

"I say no more," she concluded, "on the lamentable display of temper of this morning. Under the circumstances, I pass it over on condition that you look your brightest and best all day, and that you show yourself alive to the happiness of the position I have gained for you."

"I think," he replied, "that in the future, if not to-day, you will congratulate yourself on my line of action."

A strange thing for the young man to say. Afterwards they remembered it, and understood it.

Meantime the churchyard was full of the village people, and the church was crammed with the guests in wedding-favours; on the Green the band was discoursing sweet music; in the centre, an object of the deepest admiration for the village lads, stood Lord Chester's gift, led by his boy.

At a quarter to eleven punctually, the carriage containing the bride and principal bridesmaid, a lady also of the Inner Bar, about her own age, arrived. The bride was beautifully dressed in a rich white satin. She was met in the porch by the other bridesmaids, including the groom's sisters. All were in great spirits, and even the harsh face of the bride looked smiling and kind. The sisters, reassured on the score of their brother, were rejoicing in the sunshine of the day, the crowds, and the general joy. Sir Robert and the other elderly gentlemen were standing in meditation, or devoutly kneeling before the chancel.

Hush! silence! Hats off in the churchyard! There are the wheels of the bridegroom's carriage. Here come the Vicar and the choir ready to strike up the Processional Hymn. Clash, clang the bells! one more, and altogether, if it brings down the steeple! Now the lads make a lane outside. Off hats! Cheer with a will, boys! Hurrah for the bridegroom! He sits beside his mother, his head back, his eyes flashing; he laughs a greeting to the crowd.

"Capital, Algernon!" says his mother. "Now subdue your joy; we are at the lych-gate."

The carriage stopped. Algernon sprang out, and assisted his mother to alight. Then the procession, already formed, began slowly to move up the aisle singing the hymn, and the organ rolled among the old low arches of the little village church; and the Vicar walked last, carrying her hymn-book in her hand, singing lustily, and thinking, poor woman, that the marriage procession was advancing behind her.

Well, it was not; and when she turned round, having reached the altar, she stared blankly, because there was no marriage procession, but a general looking at each other, and whispering.

What happened was this.

After helping Lady Dunquerque out of the carriage, Algernon quietly left her, and without the slightest appearance of hurry, calmly walked across the Green and mounted Lord Chester's gift.

Then he rode to the churchyard gate, and took off his hat to his bride, and shouted, so that all could hear him, even in the church, "Very sorry, old lady, but you must look for another husband." Then he turned his horse and cantered quickly away through the crowd, laughing and waving his hand.

Half an hour later, Frederica Roe, after a stormy scene with Lady Dunquerque, which ended in the latter thanking Providence for having delivered her headstrong boy, even at the last moment, from so awful a temper, returned with her best-maid to town. There was laughter that evening when the news reached the Club. Cruel things, too, were said by the Juniors. There would have been more cruel things but for the circumstances which followed.

It was naturally a day of Rebuke at the village. The circus, the gypsies, the conjurors, and the acrobats, were all packed off about their business; there was no feast; the children were sent back to school; the wedding-guests dispersed in dismay; and Lady Dunquerque, with rage and despair in her heart, sat amid her terror-stricken household, none daring to say a word to soothe and comfort her. Later on, her husband suggested the consolations of religion, but these failed.

The summons reached Clarence Veysey on the next day. The boy who brought him the letter had ridden fifty miles.

He was waiting at home in great despondency. The perpetual acting, the deception, tortured his earnest soul; he lacked companionship; he wanted the conversation of Grace Ingleby; his sisters wearied him with their talk, and their aims – aims which he was about to make impossible for them. The boy, who was the son of one of Lord Chester's keepers, came to the house by the garden entrance, and found Clarence walking on the lawn. He tore open the note, which was as follows: –

"Come at once; we have begun. C."

Then Clarence waited for nothing, but started to walk to Chester Towers. He walked for four-and-twenty hours; when he arrived he was faint with hunger and fatigue, but he was there. The Rebellion had begun, and he was with the rebels.

CHAPTER XII.

IN THE CAMP AT CHESTER TOWERS.

THE first days were spent in drill, in exhortation, in feasting, and in singing. Grace Ingleby fitted new words to old tunes, and the men sang them marching across the Park. A detachment of keepers was placed at the gates to receive new recruits, and to keep out the women who crowded round them all day long – some laughing, some crying, some threatening. The women of the Castle, being offered their choice whether to remain in the service of the Earl or to go at once, divided themselves into two parties – the elder women deciding to go, and the younger to remain; "for," as they said, "if the men ride all over the country, as Mrs Ingleby says they will, what can we women do to keep them down?" And then they blamed the unequal marriages, and irreligious things were said about the Duchess of Dunstanburgh. Those who stayed were employed in making rosettes and ribbons in scarlet silk, and in getting out of the old lumber-rooms all the finery which could be found to serve for the men's uniforms.

"First rule," said Jack the prudent, "keep the men's spirits up – with beer, and singing, and feasting; next, make them proud of their gallant show."

Every hour raised the spirits of the men, every moment new recruits came in, who were greeted with shouts, beer, and exhortation, chiefly from the cobbler, who now wore a glittering helmet, and carried a ten-foot pike.

In the course of the next two or three days all the Bishop's disciples came in: Clarence Veysey, dusty and wayworn, yet full of ardour; Algy Dunquerque rode in gallantly, laughing at his escape. The others came in one after the other, eager for employment, and were at once set to work. No time this for love-making; but Grace exchanged a few words with Clarence and Faith ran about among the men, telling them all that Captain Dunquerque was her sweetheart, asking who were the girls they loved, and how they wooed them, and so delightfully turning everything upside down, that she was better than all the barrels of beer.

Lord Chester was the Chief, but Captain Dunquerque was the favourite. It was he who kept everybody in good spirits – who organised races in the evening, set the men to box, to wrestle, to fight with single stick, with prizes and cheering for the winners; so that the lads for the first time in their lives felt the fierce joy of battle and the pride of victory. It was Captain Dunquerque who had a word for every man, forgetting none of their names; who praised them and encouraged them, was all day long in the camp, never tired, never lost his temper – as some of the keepers did who were promoted to be sergeants; who was generous with the beer; who promised to every man money, independent work, and a pretty wife – after the Cause was won. So that Algy Dunquerque, the first commander-in-chief under the new *régime*, began his popularity as the soldiers' general from the very first.

On the evening of his arrival, Clarence preached to the men – a faithful discourse, which yet only revealed half the Truth. We must destroy before we can build up.

He bade them remember that they were, as men, the workers of the world – nothing could be done except by them; and then he told them some of the wonders which had been accomplished by their forefathers in the days when men had been acknowledged . to be the. thinkers and creators as well as the workers, and he told them, in such simple language as he could command, how, since women had taken over the reins, everything had gone backwards. Lastly, he bade them remember what they were, what their lives had been, how slavish and how sad, and what their lives would still continue to be Unless they freed themselves.

"Time was – the good old time – when every man could raise himself, when there was a ladder from the lowest station to the highest. Now, as you are born, so you must die. No rising for you – no hope for you. Work and slave – and die. That is your lot. They invented a religion to keep you down. They told you that it is the will of Heaven that you should obey women. It is a LIE." The preacher shouted the words. "It is a LIE. There is no such religion; and I am here to teach you the Truth, when you have proved that you are fit to receive it."

The preacher was received with an indifference which was discouraging. In fact, the men had been preached at so long, that they had ceased to pay any attention to sermons. Nor could even Clarence's earnestness surpass that of the Preaching Order, the Holy Sisterhood, which trained its members in the art of inspiring Hope, Terror, and Faith.

The address finished, the men betook them once more to singing, while the beer went round, about their camp fires. Here was a glorious change! Even the gamekeepers – a race not easily moved – congratulated each other on the recovery of their freedom. That night a proclamation was made in camp that every man would receive his pay himself – the same as that earned in the fields – in full. Men looked at each other and wondered. Those who only half believed in the Cause were reassured. To be paid, instead of seeing your wife paid, proved, as nothing else could, the strength and reality of the Rebellion. Another proclamation was made, repealing all prohibitions for men to assemble, remain out of doors after sunset, and form societies. This was even more warmly received than the former proclamation, because many of the men did not know what to do with their money when they got it; whereas they had all of them learned this grand pleasure of companionship, drink, and song.

On that night and the next, two councils were held, big with importance to the Realm of England. The first of these was at Chester Towers, under the presidency of Lord Chester. There were present the Bishop – whose impatience made him set out on the first receipt of the news – Clarence Veysey, Algernon Dunquerque, Jack Kennion, and the rest of the Disciples. The Professor and the girls were in the room, but they did not speak.

They sat until late considering many things. Had they known more of man's real nature, there would have been no hesitation, and a bold forward march might have saved many difficulties. The Bishop and Clarence Veysey, who believed the Truth by itself a sufficient weapon, wanted to await the arrival of all Englishmen in the Park, and meantime to be preaching perpetually. Algernon was for movement. The Chief at last decided on a compromise. They would advance, but slowly; and would send out, meanwhile, scouts and small parties to bring in recruits. The danger of the Revolt, provided it were sufficiently widespread, lay chiefly in the imagination. It was difficult even for the leaders, who had been so long and so carefully trained by the Bishop and his wife to shake off the awe inspired by the feminine oppression and their early training. Every woman seemed still their natural ruler. Yet the Reign of Woman rested on no more solid basis than this awe. Its only defence lay in the regiments of Horse Guards and its Convict Wardens; while, to make the latter available, the prisoners would have to be discharged.

The other council of war was held in the House of Peeresses, called together hastily. There had been grave disquiet all day long; and though nothing definite was known, it was whispered that there was an outbreak of the Men. A Cabinet Council was called at noon, the Home Department was agitated, the secretaries went about with pale faces, there was continual ringing of bells and scurrying of clerks, the Archbishop of Canterbury was sent for hurriedly, crowds of women gathered about the lobbies of the House, and it was presently known everywhere that the thing most dreaded of all things had happened – a Rising. Outside the House it was not yet known where this had occurred, nor under what leaders: within, the doors were closed, and in the midst of a silence most profound and most unusual, the Duchess of Dunstanburgh rose, with papers in her hand.

She briefly announced that a rebellion had broken out in Norfolk. A score or so of poor peasants belonging to one small village had risen in revolt. They were headed by Lord Chester. It was nothing – a mere lamentable outbreak, which would be put down at once by the strong hand of law.

Then she sat down. All faces were turned immediately to her Grace's young rival. Lady Carlyon rose and asked if her Grace had any more details to give the House. She implored the Government to put the House in possession of all the facts, however painful they might be. The Duchess replied that the news of this insurrection, about which there could unfortunately be no doubt, reached her that morning only. It arrived in the shape of a Report drawn up by the Vicar of Chester Towers, and sworn before two justices of the peace. The rising, if it was worthy to be called by such a name, was begun by the forcible rescue from the hands of the law of a certain blacksmith – a scoundrel guilty of wife-beating in its most revolting forms. He was torn from the hands of the police by Lord Chester and a gamekeeper. The misguided young man then called upon the men of the village to rise and follow him. He led them to his own Castle. He was joined by a body of gamekeepers, and men connected with manly sports of other kinds. By the last advices, he had gone the desperate length of defying the Government, and was now drilling and arming his troops. The Duchess assured the House again that there was nothing to fear except a probable loss of life, which was lamentable, but must be faced; that the Government had ordered two thousand of the Convict Wardens to be held in readiness, and that meanwhile they had sent two Sisters of the Holy Preaching Order with twenty constables to disperse the mob. As for the ringleaders, they appeared to be, besides Lord Chester himself, Professor Ingleby of Cambridge, her husband her two daughters, and a band of some half-dozen young gentlemen. The House might rest assured that signal justice would be done upon these mad and wicked people, and that no favour should be shown to rank or sex. As for herself, the House knew the relations which existed between herself and Lord Chester –

Lady Carlyon sprang to her feet, and asked what relations these were. The Duchess went on to say that there was no occasion to dilate upon what was perfectly well known. She would, however, assure the House that this unhappy man had cut himself off altogether from her sympathy. She gave up, without a sigh, hopes that had once been dear to her, and left a miscreant so godless, so abandoned, to his fate.

Lady Carlyon begged the House to suspend its judgment until the facts were clearly known. At present all that appeared certain was, that a body of men had locked themselves within the gates of Lord Chester's Park. She would ask her Grace whether any grievances had been stated.

The Duchess replied that at the right moment the alleged grievances, if there were any, would be laid before the House.

Lady Carlyon asked again whether one of the grievances was not the custom – falsely alleged to be based upon religion – which compelled young men to marry women who were unsuitable and distasteful to them by reason of age, temper, or other incompatibility?

This was the signal for the most frightful scene of disorder ever witnessed in the House; for all Peeresses with husbands younger than themselves screamed on one side, and the young Peeresses on the other. After a little quiet had been obtained, Lady Carlyon was heard again, and accused the Duchess of Dunstanburgh of being herself the sole cause of the Insurrection. "It is time," she said, "to use plainness of speech. Let us recognise the truth that a young man cannot but abhor and loathe so unnatural a union as that of twenty years with forty, fifty, sixty. For my own part, I do not wonder that a man so high-spirited as Lord Chester should have been driven to madness. All in this House know well, without any pretences as to the honour of Peeresses, that a majority in favour of the Duchess was certain. Can any one believe that the judgment of the House would have been given for the happiness of the young man? Can any one believe that he could have contemplated the proposed union without repugnance? We know well what the end of the rising may be; and of this am I well assured, that the blood of this unhappy boy, and the blood of all those who perish with him, are upon the head of the Duchess of Dunstanburgh."

Then began another terrible scene, in which all the invective, the recrimination, the accusations, the insinuations, of which the language is capable, seemed gathered together and hurled at each other: there was no longer a Government and an Opposition; there was the wrath of the young, who had seen, or looked to see, the men they might have loved torn from them by the old; there was the fury of the old, calling upon Religion, Law, Piety, and Order.

Constance withdrew in the height of the battle having said all she had to say. It was a clear and bright morning; the sun was already rising; there were little groups of women hanging about the lobbies still, waiting for news. One of them stepped forward and saluted Constance. She was a young journalist of great promise, and had often written leaders at Constance's suggestion.

"Has your ladyship any more news?" she asked.

"I know nothing but what I have heard from ... from the Duchess." It was by an effort that Constance pronounced her name. "I know no more."

"We have heard more," the journalist went on. "We have heard from Norfolk, by a girl who galloped headlong into town with the intelligence, and is now at the War Office, that, yesterday morning at nine o'clock, Lord Chester rode out of his Park, followed by his army, carrying banners, and armed with guns, pikes, and swords. They are said to number at present some two or three hundred only."

Constance was too weary and worn with the night's excitement to receive this dreadful news. She burst into passionate tears.

"Edward," she cried, "you rush upon certain death!" Then she recovered herself. "Stay! let me think. We must do something to allay the excitement. The Government will issue orders to keep the men at home – that is their first thought. We must do more: we must agitate for a reform. There is one concession that must be made. Go at once and write the strongest leader you ever wrote in all your life: treat the rebellion as of the slightest possible importance; do not weigh heavily upon the unhappy Chief; talk as little as possible about misguided lads; say that, without doubt, the men will disperse; urge an amnesty; and then strike boldly and unmistakably for the great grievance of men and women both. Raise the Cry of 'The Young for the Young!' And keep harping on this theme from day to day."

It was, however, too late for newspaper articles: a wild excitement ran through the streets of London; the men were kept indoors; workmen who had to go abroad were ordered not to stop on their way, not to speak with each other, nor to buy newspapers. Special constables were sworn in by the hundred. Later on, when it became known that the insurgent forces were really on their southward march, a proclamation was issued, ordering a general day of humiliation, with services in all the churches, and prayers for the safety of Religion and the Realm. The Archbishop of Canterbury herself performed the service at Westminster Abbey, and the Bishop of London at St Paul's.

Meantime, spite of law and orders, the country-people flocked from all sides to see the gallant show of Lord Chester's little army. Captain Dunquerque led the van, which consisted of fifty stalwart keepers. At the head of the main body rode the Chief, clad in scarlet, with glittering helmet; with him were the officers of his Staff, also gallantly dressed and splendidly mounted. Next came, marching in fours, his army of three hundred sturdy countrymen, armed with rifle and bayonet; after them marched the younger men, some mere lads, carrying guns of all descriptions, pikes, and even sticks, – not one among these that did not carry a cockade: their banner, borne by two of the strongest, was of red silk, with the words, "We will be free!" An immense crowd of women looked on as they started: some of them cursed and screamed; but the girls laughed. Then other men of the villages broke away from their wives and sisters, and marched beside the soldiers, trying to keep in step, snatching their cockades, and shouting with them. Last of all came a little band of twenty-five, mounted, who served to keep the crowd from pressing too closely, and guarded a carriage and four, in which were the Bishop, the Professor, and the two girls. They sat up to their knees in scarlet cockades and rosettes, which the girls were making up and the Professor was distributing.

In this order they marched. After the first few hours, it was found that, besides a great number of recruits, the army had been joined by at least a hundred village girls, who walked with them and refused to go back. They followed their sweethearts. "Let us keep them," said the Professor: "they will be useful to us."

At the next halting-place she had all these girls drawn up before her, and made them a speech. She told them that if they desired a hand in the great work, they might do their part: they would be allowed to join the army on condition of marching apart from the men; of not interfering with them in any way; of doing what they were told to do, and of carrying a banner. To this they readily consented, being, in fact, to one woman, enraged with the existing order of things, and caring very little about being the mistress if they could not have their own lovers. And in the end, they proved most valuable and useful allies.

Whenever they passed a house, Lord Chester sent half-a-dozen men to seize upon whatever arms they could find, and all the ammunition, if there was any. They had orders, also, to bring out the men, whom the officers inspected; and if there were any young fellow among them, they offered him a place in their ranks. A good many guns were got in this way, but very few men, – the young men of the middle class being singularly spiritless. They had not the healthy outdoor life, with riding, shooting, and athletics, that men of Lord Chester's rank enjoyed; nor had they the outdoor work and companionship which hardened the nerves of the farm-labourers. Mostly, therefore, they gazed with wonder and terror at the spectacle; and on being brought out and harangued, meekly replied that they would rather stay at home, and retired amid the jeers of the soldiers.

Several pleasant surprises were experienced. At one house, the squire, a jolly fox-hunting old fellow, turned out with his four sons, all well mounted, and brought with him a dozen good rifles, with a large supply of ammunition. The old fellow remarked that he was sixty-five years of age, and had been wishing all his life, and so had his father and his grandfather before him, to put an end to the intolerable upside-down condition of things. "And mind, my lady," he shouted to his wife and daughters, who were standing by, filled with rage and consternation, "you and the girls, when we get back again, will sing another tune, or I will know the reason why!" Nor was this the only instance.

When they marched through a village, the trumpets blew, the drums beat, the soldiers shouted and sang; then the men were brought out, and invited to join; the place was searched for arms, and the company of women ran about congratulating the girls of the place on the approaching abolition of Forced Marriages.

The first day's march covered twenty miles. The army had passed through five villages and one small town; they had seized on about two hundred guns of all kinds, and a considerable quantity of ammunition; they had increased their ranks by two hundred and fifty strong and lusty fellows. The evening was not allowed to be wasted in singing and shouting. Drill was renewed, and the newcomers taught the first elements of marching in step and line. For the first time, too, they attempted a sham fight, with sad blunders, as may be imagined.

"They are good material," said the Professor, "but your army has yet to be formed."

"If only," murmured Clarence, "they would listen to my preaching."

"They have had too much preaching all their lives," said the Bishop. "We will conquer first, and preach afterwards. Let us pray that there may be no bloodshed."

The second day's march was like the first; but the little army was now swelling beyond all expectations. At the close of the second day it numbered a thousand, and commissariat difficulties began. Here the company of women proved useful. They were all country girls, able to ride and drive; they "borrowed" the carts of the farmhouses, and, escorted by soldiers, drove about the country requisitioning provisions. It became necessary to have waggons: these also were borrowed, and in a short time the army dragged at its heels an immense train of waggons loaded with ammunition, provisions, and stores of all kinds. For everything that was taken., an order for its value was left behind, stamped with the signature of "Chester."

At the close of the second day's march, being then near Bury St Edmunds, they were two thousand strong; at the end of the third, being on Newmarket Heath, they were five thousand; and here, because the place was open and the position good, a halt of three days was resolved upon, in which the men might be drilled, taught to act together, and divided into corps, also, sham fights would be fought, and the men, some of whom were little more than boys, could grow accustomed to the discharge of guns and the use of their weapons. The camp was protected by sentinels, and the cavalry scoured the country for recruits and information. As yet no sign had been made by the Government. But on Sunday morning, being the third day of the halt, the scouts brought in a deputation from the House of Peeresses, consisting of two Sisters of the Holy Preaching Order, and a guard of twenty-five policewomen. Lord Chester and his staff rode out to meet them.

"What is your message?" he asked.

"The terms offered by the House to the insurgents," replied one of the Sisters, "are, first, laying down of arms, and dispersion of the men; secondly, the immediate submission of the leaders."

"And what then?" asked Lord Chester.

"Justice," replied the Sister, sternly. "Now stand aside and let us address the men."

Lord Chester laughed.

"Go call a dozen of the women's company," he ordered. "Now," when they came, "take these two Sisters, and march them through the camp with drum and fife. These are the women who are trained to terrify the men with lying threats, false fears, and vain superstitions. As for you policewomen, you can go back and tell the House that I will myself inform them of my terms."

The officers of law looked at each other. They saw before them spread out the white tents of the camp, the splendid army, the glittering weapons, the brilliant uniforms, the flags, the noise and tumult of the camp, and they were afraid. Presently they beheld, with consternation, the most singular procession ever formed. First went the drums and fifes; then came, handcuffed, the two Holy Preaching Sisters – they were clad in their sacred white robes, to touch which was sacrilege; behind them ran and danced the troop of village girls, shouting, pointing, singing their new songs about Love and Freedom; and the soldiers came forth from their tents clapping their hands and applauding. But the Bishop sent word that they were to be stripped of their white robes and turned out of the camp. It was in ragged flannel petticoats that the poor Sisters regained their friends, and in woful plight of mind as well as of body.

The three days' halt finished, Lord Chester gave the word to advance. And now his army, he thought, was large enough to meet any number of Convict Wardens who might be sent against him. He had eight thousand men, hastily drilled, but full of ardour; he had a picked corps of five hundred guards, consisting of his faithful gamekeepers and the men who had been always with gentlemen about their sports. These were good shots, and pretty sure to be steady even under fire. He had five hundred cavalry, mostly mounted well, and consisting of farmers' sons, officered by the fox-hunting squire, his four sons, and a few other gentlemen who had come in. The difficulty now was to admit all who crowded to the camp. For the news had spread over all England, and the roads were crowded with young fellows flying from their homes, defying the rural police, to join Lord Chester's camp.

The time was come for a bold stroke. It was resolved to leave Jack Kennion – greatly to his discontent, but there was no help – behind, to receive recruits, and form an army of reserve. Lord Chester himself, with the main body and Algy Dunquerque, was to press on. The boldest stroke of all was the surprise of London, and this it was decided to attempt. For by this time the ardour of the troops was beyond the most sanguine hopes of the leaders: the submissiveness of three generations had disappeared in a week; the meek and docile lads whose wives received the pay, and ordered them to go and sit at home when there was no work to do, were changed into hardy, reckless, and enthusiastic soldiers. Turenne himself had not a more dare-devil lot. They were nearly all young; they had never before been free for a single day; they rejoiced in their new companionship; they gloried in the sham fights, the wrestling, the single-stick – all the games with which the fighting spirit was awakened in them. As for the march, it was splendid: they sang as they went; if they did not sing, they laughed – the joy of laughter was previously unknown to these lads. The ruling sex did not laugh among themselves, nor did they understand the masculine yearning for mirth. In the upper classes jesting was ill-bred, and in the lower it was irreligious. Irreligious! Why, in this short time the whole army had thrown off their religion.

All over the country the men were rising and rushing to join Lord Chester. The great conspiracy was not alone answerable for this sudden impulse; nor, indeed, had the conspirators been successful in the towns, where the spirit of the men had been effectually crushed by long isolation. Here, however, the leaflets distributed among the girls bore good fruit. Not a household in the country but was now fiercely divided between those who welcomed the rebellion and those who hated and dreaded the success of the men: on the one side, orthodoxy, age, conservatism; on the other, youth, and the dream of an easy life, rendered easier by the work and devotion of a lover. So that, though the towns remained outwardly quiet, they were ready for the occupation of the rebels.

The army presented now an appearance very different from the ragged regiment which sallied forth from the gates of the Park. They were dressed in uniform: the guards wore a dark-green tunic – only proved shots were admitted into their body; the cavalry were in scarlet, the line were in scarlet; the artillery wore dark-green. All the men were armed with rifles. Of course, the uniforms were not in all cases complete, yet every day improved them; for among the volunteers were tailors, cobblers, and handicraftsmen of all kinds, whose services were given in their own trades. The great banner, with the words "We will be free!" was carried after the Chief, and in the rear marched the company of a hundred girls, also in a kind of uniform, carrying their banner, "Give us back our sweethearts!"

The line of march was kept as much as possible away from the towns, because it was thought advisable not to irritate the municipalities until the time came when they could be gently upset; also, the material of the men in the towns was not of the sturdy kind with which they hoped to win their battles.

Nothing more was heard of the House of Peeresses. What, then, were they doing? They were holding meetings in the morning, and wrangling. No one knew what to propose. They had sent executive officers of the law to the camp; these had been contemptuously told to go back. They had summoned the leaders to lay down their arms; they had been informed that Lord Chester would dictate his own terms. They had sent Preaching Sisters, – the most eloquent, the most persuasive, the most sacred: they had been stripped of their sacred robes, tied to a cart-tail, and driven through the camp by women, amid the derision of women – actually women! What more could they do?

The army was reported as marching southwards by rapid marches, headed by Lord Chester. They passed Bury St Edmunds and Cambridge, without, however, entering the town. They recruited as they went; so that beside the regularly drilled men, now veterans of a fortnight or so, it was reported that the line of march was followed for miles by runaway boys, apprentices, grooms, artisans, and labourers, shouting for Lord Chester and for liberty. All these things, and worse, were hourly reported to the distracted House.

"And what are we doing?" shrieked the Duchess of Dunstanburgh. "What are we doing but talk? Are we, then, fallen so low, that at the first movement of an enemy we have nothing but tears and recrimination? Is this a time to accuse me – ME – of forcing the rebel chief into rebellion? Is it not a time to act? When the rebellion is subdued, when the Chief is hanged, and his miserable followers flogged – yes, flogged at the very altars they have derided – let us resume the strife of tongues. In the name of our sex, in the name of our religion, let us Act."

They looked at each other, but no one proposed the only step left to them. Lady Carlyon was no longer among them. She would attend no more sittings. The clamour of tongues humiliated her. She sat alone in her house in Park Lane, thinking sadly of what might happen.

"On me," said the Duchess solemnly, "devolves the duty, the painful duty, of reminding the House that there is but one way to meet rebellion. All human institutions, even when, like our own, they are of Divine origin, are based upon – Force. Law is an idle sound without – Force. Duty, religion, obedience, rest ultimately upon – Force. These men have dared to band themselves together against law, order, and religion. We must remember that they represent a very small, a really insignificant, section of the men of this country. It is cheering, at this moment of gloom and distress, to receive by every post letters from every municipality in the country expressing the loyalty of the towns. Order reigns everywhere, except where this turbulent boy is leading his troops – to destruction. I use this word with the utmost reluctance; but I must use this word. I say – destruction. Among the ranks of that army are men known to many in this House. My own gamekeepers, many of my own tenants' sons and husbands, are in that rabble-rout of raw, undisciplined, and imperfectly armed rustics. Yet I say – destruction. We have now but one thing to do. Call out our prison - guards, and let loose these fierce and angry hounds upon the foe. I wait for the approval of the House."

All lifted their hands, but in silence; for they were sadly conscious that they were sending the gallant, if mistaken, fellows to death, and bringing sorrow upon innocent homes. The House separated, and for a while there was no more recrimination. The Duchess called a Cabinet Council, and that night messengers sped in all directions to bring together the Convict Guards – not only the two thousand first ordered to be in readiness, but as many as could be spared. It was resolved to replace them by men chosen from the prisoners, whose cases, in return for their service, should have favourable consideration. By forced marches, and by seizing on every possible means of conveyance, it was reckoned that they could muster some ten thousand, – all strong, desperate villains, capable of anything, and a match for twice that number of raw village lads.

They came up in dribblets – here a hundred and there a hundred – from the various prisons throughout the country: they were men of rough and coarse appearance; they wore an ugly yellow uniform; they bore themselves as if they were ashamed of their calling, which certainly was the most repulsive of any; they showed neither ardour for the work before them nor any kind of fear.

They were received by clerks of the Prison Department, who sent them off to camp in Hyde Park, where rations of some kind were prepared for them. The clerks showed them scant courtesy, which, indeed, they seemed to take as a matter of course; and once established in their camp, they gave no trouble, keeping quite to themselves, and patiently waiting orders.

Three days were thus expended. The excitement of the town was frightful. Business was suspended, prayers were offered at all the churches every morning, the men were most carefully kept from associating together, constables patrolled in parties of four all night long, and continually the post-girls came galloping along the roads bringing the news. "They are coming, they are coming!" Oh, what was the Government about? Could they do nothing, then? What was the use of the Convict Wardens, unless they were to be sent out to arrest the leaders, and shoot all who refused to disband and disperse? But there were not wanting ominous whispers among the crowds of wild talkers. What, it was asked, would happen if the men did come? They would take the power into their own hands. Very good. It could not be in worse hands than Lady Dunstanburgh's. They would turn the women out of the Professions. Very well, said the younger women. They only starved in the Professions; and if the men were in power, they would have to find homes and food at least for their sisters and wives. Let them come.

In three days Lord Chester was at Bishop Stortford. Next, he was reported to be encamped in Epping Forest. His cavalry had seized the arsenal at Enfield, which with carelessness incredible had been left in charge of two aged women. This gave him a dozen pieces of ordnance. He was on the march from Epping; he was but a few miles from London; contradictory rumours and reports of all kinds flew wildly about; he was going to massacre, pillage, and plunder everything; he was afraid to advance farther; he would destroy all the churches; he was restrained at the last moment by respect for the faith in which he had been brought up; his men had mutinied; his men clamoured to be led on London. All these reports, and more, were whispered from one to the other. What was quite certain was, that the Convict Wardens were all arrived, and were under orders to march early in the morning. And it was also certain, because girls who had ventured on the north roads had seen them, that the rebels were encamped on Hampstead Heath, and it was said that they were in high spirits – singing, dancing, and drinking. No one knew how many they were – thousands upon thousands, and all armed

There was little sleep in London during that night. The married women remained at home to calm the excitement of the men, now getting beyond their control. The unmarried women flocked by thousands to Hyde Park to look at the tents of the Convict Wardens, now called the Army of Avengers. In every tent eight men; more than a thousand tents; ten thousand men; the fiercest, bravest, most experienced of men. What a lesson, what a terrible lesson, would the rebels learn next morning!

CHAPTER XIII.

THE NIGHT BEFORE THE BATTLE.

It was evening when the rebel leader stood upon the heights of Hampstead and looked before him, by the light of the setting sun, upon the hazy and indistinct mass of the great city which he was come to conquer. Behind him his ten thousand men, with twice ten thousand followers, were erecting their tents and setting up the camp with a mighty bustle, noise, and clamour. Yet there was no confusion. Thanks to the administrative capacity of Algy Dunquerque, all was done in order. The Professor, who had left her carriage, stood beside Lord Chester. He was dismounted, and, with the aid of a glass, was trying to make out familiar towers in the golden mist that rested upon the great city.

"So far, my lord, we have sped well," she said, softly.

He started at her voice.

"Well indeed, my dear Professor," he replied. "I would to-morrow were over."

"Fear not; your men will answer to your call."

"I do not fear. They are brave fellows. Yet – to think that their blood must be spilt!"

"There spoke Lord Chester of the past, not the gallant Prince of the present. Why, what if a few hundreds of dead men strew this field to-morrow, provided the Eight prevails? Of what good is a man's life to him, if he does not give it for the sacred cause? To give a life – why, it is to lend a thing; to hasten the slow course of time; to make the soul take at a single leap the immortality which comes to others so slowly. Fear not for the blood of martyrs, my lord."

"You always cheer and comfort me, Professor."

"It is because I am a woman," she replied. "Let me fulfil the highest function of my sex."

They were interrupted by an aide-de-camp, who came galloping across the Heath.

"From Captain Dunquerque, my lord," he began. "The Convict Wardens are encamped in force in Hyde Park; they number ten thousand, and have got thirty guns; they march to-morrow morning."

"Very good," said the Chief; and the young officer fell back.

"Ten thousand strong!" said the Professor. "Then they have left the prisons almost without a guard. When these are dispersed, where will they find a new army? They are delivered into your hands."

Hampstead Heath may be approached by two or three roads: there is the direct road up Haverstock Hill; or there is the way by the Gospel Oak and the Vale of Health; or, again, there is the road from the north, or that from Highgate. But the way by which the Convict Wardens would march from Hyde Park was most certainly that of Haverstock Hill; and they would emerge upon the Heath by the narrow road known as Holly Hill, Heath Street, and the Grove, – probably by all three. Or they might attempt the upper part of the Heath by the Vale of Health.

The plan of battle was agreed to with very little debate, because it was simple.

The cannon; loaded with grape-shot and masked by bushes, were drawn up to command these three streets.

Behind the cannon the Guards were to lie, ready to spring to their feet and send in a volley after the first discharge of grape-shot.

The cavalry were to be posted among the trees, on the spot called after a once famous tavern which formerly stood there – Jack Straw's Castle; the infantry, now divided into five battalions, each two thousand strong, were to lie in their places behind the Guards. These simple arrangements made, the Chief rode into the camp to encourage the men.

They needed little encouragement: the men were in excellent spirits; the news that they would have to fight those enemies of mankind, the Convict Wardens, filled them with joy. Not one among them all but had some friend, some relation, immured within the gloomy prisons, for disobedience, mutiny, or violence; some had themselves experienced the rigours of imprisonment, and the tender mercies of the ruffians who were allowed to maintain discipline with rod and lash, rifle and bayonet. These were the men who were coming out to shoot them down! Very good; they should see.

Lord Chester and his Staff rode about the camp, making speeches, cheering the men, drinking with them, and encouraging them. Their liberties, he told them, were in their own hand: one victory, and the cause was won. Then he inspired them with contempt as well as hatred for their opponents. They were men who could shoot down a flying prisoner, but had never stood face to face with a foe: they were coming out, expecting to find a meek herd, who would fly at the first shot; in their place they would meet an army of Englishmen. The men shouted and cheered: their spirit was up. And later on about ten o'clock, a strange thing happened. No one ever knew how it began, or who set it going; but from man to man the word was passed. Then all the army rose to their feet, and shouted for joy; then the company of girls came, and shed tears among them, but for joy; and some, including the girl they had called Susan, fell upon the necks of their old sweethearts, and kissed them, bidding them be brave, and fight like men; and those who were old men wept, because this good thing had come too late for them.

For the word was – DIVORCE!

The young men, they said, were to abandon the wives they had been forced to marry. With Victory they were to win Love!

It was about ten o'clock when Lord Chester sought the Bishop's tent. He had just concluded an Evening Service, and was sitting with his wife, his daughters, and Clarence Veysey.

With the Chief came Algernon Dunquerque.

"We are here," said Lord Chester, "for a few words – it may be of farewell. My Lord Bishop, are you contented with your pupils?"

"I give you all," he said, solemnly, "my blessing. Go on and prosper. But as we may fail, and so die, because victory is not of man, let those who have aught to say to each other say it now."

Algernon spoke first, though all looked at each other.

"I love your daughter Faith. Give us your consent, my Lord Bishop, before we go out to fight."

The Bishop took the girl by the hand, and gave her to the young man, saying, "Blessed be thou, O my daughter!"

Then Clarence Veysey spoke likewise, and asked for Grace; and with such words did the father give her to him.

"Now," said Algernon, "there needs no more. If we fall, we fall together."

"Yes," said Grace, quietly, "we should not survive the Cause,"

"I hope," said Lord Chester, smiling gravely. "that one of you will live at least long enough to take my last message to Lady Carlyon. You will tell her, Grace, or you, my dear Professor, that my last thought was for her." But as he spoke the curtain of the tent was pulled aside, and Constance herself stood before them.

She was pale, and tears were in her eyes. She wore a riding-habit; but it was covered with dust.

"Edward!" she cried. "Fly ... fly ... while there is time! All of you fly!"

"What is it, Constance? How came you here?"

"I came because I can bear it no longer. I came to warn you, and to help your escape, if that may be. The Duchess has issued a warrant for my arrest, – for High Treason: that is nothing," with a proud gesture. "They will say I ran away from the warrant: that is false. Edward, your life is gone unless you are twenty miles from London to-morrow!"

"Come, Constance," said the Professor, "you are hot and tired. Rest a little; drink some water; take breath. We are prepared, I think, for all that you can tell us."

"Oh no! ... no! ... you cannot be. Listen! They have ten thousand Convict Wardens in Hyde Park ..."

"We know this," said Algernon.

"Who will attack you to-morrow."

"We know this too."

"Their orders are to shoot down all without parley; all – do you hear? – who are found with arms. The Chiefs are to be taken to the Tower!" she shuddered.

"We know all this, Constance," said Lord Chester.

"You know it! and you can look unconcerned?"

"Not unconcerned entirely, but resigned perhaps, and even hopeful."

"Edward, what can you do?"

"If they have orders to shoot all who do not fly, my men, for their part, have orders not to fly, but to shoot all who stand in their way."

"Your men? Poor farm - labourers! what can they do?"

"Wait till morning, Constance, and you shall see. Is there anything else you can tell me?"

"Yes. After the Wardens have dispersed the rebels, the Horse Guards are to be ordered out to ride them down."

"Oh!" said Lord Chester. "Well ... after we are dispersed, we will consider the question of the riding down. Then we need not expect the Horse Guards to-morrow morning?"

"No; they will come afterwards."

"Thank you, Constance; you have given me one piece of intelligence. I confess I was uncertain about the Guards. And now, dear child," – he called her, the late Home Secretary, "dear child," – "as this is a solemn night, and we have much to think of and to do ... one word before we part. Constance, you have by this act of yours cast in your lot with us, because you thought to save my life. Everything is risked upon to-morrow's victory. If we fail we die. Are you ready to die with me?"

She made no reply. The old feeling, the overwhelming force of the man, made her cheek white and her heart faint. She held out her hands.

He took her – before all those witnesses – in his arms, and kissed her on the forehead. "Stay with us, my darling," he whispered; "cast in your lot with mine."

She had no power to resist, none to refuse. She was conquered; Man was stronger than Woman.

"Children," said the Bishop, solemnly, "you shall not die, but live."

Constance started. She knew not this kind of language, which was borrowed from the Books of the Ancient Faith.

"There are many things," said the Bishop, "of which you know not yet, Lady Carlyon. After to-morrow we will instruct you. Meantime it is late; the Chief has business; I would be alone. Go you with my daughters and rest, if you can, until the morning."

The very atmospnere seemed strange to Constance: the young men in authority, the women submissive; this old man speaking as if he were a, learned divine, reverend, grave, and *accustomed to be heard*; and, outside, the voices of men singing, of arms clashing, of music playing, – all the noise of a camp before it settles into rest for the night.

"Can they," Constance whispered to Grace Ingleby, looking round her outside the tent – "will they *dare* to fight these terrible and cruel Convict Wardens?"

"Oh, Lady Carlyon!" Grace replied, "you do not know, you cannot guess, what wonderful things Lord Chester has done with the men in the last fortnight. From poor, obedient slaves, he has made them men indeed."

"Men!" Constance saw that she could not understand the word in the sense to which she had been accustomed.

"Surely you know," Grace went on, "that our object is more than we have ventured to proclaim. We began with the cry of 'Youth for the Young.' That touched a grievance which was more felt, perhaps, in country districts, where men retained some of their independence, than in towns. But we meant very much more. We shall abolish the Established Church, and the Supremacy of Woman. Man will reign once more, and will worship, after the manner of his ancestors, the real living Divine Man, instead of the shadowy Perfect Woman."

"Oh!" Constance heard and trembled. "And we – what shall we do?"

"We shall take our own place – we shall be the housewives; we shall be loving and faithful servants to men, and they will be our servants in return, Love knows no mastery. Yet man must rule outside the house."

"Oh!" Constance could say no more.

"Believe me, this is the true place of woman; she is the giver of happiness and love; she is the mother and the wife. As for us, we have reigned and tried to rule. How much we have failed, no one knows better than yourself."

Grace guided her companion to a great marquee, where the company of girls, sobered now, and rather tearful, because their sweethearts were to go a-fighting in earnest on the morrow, were making lint and bandages.

"I must go on with my work," said Grace. Her sister Faith was already in her place, tearing, cutting, and shaping. "Do you lie down; here is a pile of lint – make that your bed, and sleep if you can."

Constance lay down; but she could not sleep. She already heard in imagination the tramp of the cruel Convict Wardens; she saw her lover and his companions shot down; she was herself a prisoner; then, with a cry, she sprang to her feet

"Give me some work to do," she said to Grace; "I cannot sleep."

They made a place for her, Grace and Faith between them, saying nothing.

By this time the girls were all silent, and some were crying; for the day was dawning – the day when these terrible preparations of lint would be used for poor wounded men.

When, about half-past five, the first rays of the September sun poured into the marquee upon the group of women, Grace sprang to her feet, crying aloud in a kind of ecstasy.

"The day has come – the day is here! Oh, what can we do but pray!"

She threw herself upon her knees and prayed aloud, while all wept and sobbed.

Constance knelt with the rest, but the prayer touched her not. She was only sad, while Grace sorrowed with faith and hope.

Then Faith Ingleby raised her sweet strong voice, and, with her, the girls sang together a hymn which was unknown to Constance. It began –

> "Awake, my soul, and with the sun
> Thy daily course of duty run."

This act of worship and submission done, they returned to their work. Outside, the camp began gradually to awaken. Before six o'clock the fires were lit, and the men's breakfast was getting ready; by seven o'clock everything was done – tents struck, arms piled, men accoutred.

Constance went out to look at the strange sight of the rebel army. Her heart beat when she looked upon the novel scene.

Regiments were forming, companies marching into place, flags flying, drums beating, and trumpets calling. And the soldiers! – saw one ever such men before? They were marching, heads erect and flashing eyes; the look of submission gone – for ever. Yes; these men might be shot down, but they could never be reduced to their old condition.

"There is the Chief," said Faith Ingleby.

He stood without his tent, his Staff about him, looking round him. Authority was on his brow; he was indeed, Constance felt with sinking heart, that hitherto incredible thing – a Man in command.

"We girls have no business here," said Faith; "let us get back to our tent."

But as she spoke, Lord Chester saw them; and leaving his Staff, he walked across the Heath, bearing his sword in his hand, followed by Algernon Dunquerque.

"Constance," he said, gravely, "buckle my sword for me before the battle."

She did it, trembling and tearful. Then while Faith Ingleby did the same office for Algernon, he took her in his arms and kissed her lips in the sight of all the army. Every man took it as a lesson for himself. He was to fight for love as well as liberty. A deafening shout rent the air.

Then Lord Chester sprang upon his horse and rode to the front.

Everything was now in readiness. The cannon, masked by bushes, were protected by the pond in front; on either side were the Guards ready to lie down; behind them, the regiments, massed at present, but prepared for open order; and in the trees could be seen the gleaming helmets and swords of the cavalry.

"Let us go to my father," said Faith; "he and Clarence will pray for us."

"Algy," said Lord Chester, cheerfully, "what are you thinking of?"

"I was thinking how sorry Jack Kennion will be to have missed this day."

And then there happened the most remarkable, the most surprising thing in the whole of this surprising campaign. There was a movement among the men in front, followed by loud laughing and shouting; and then a party of girls, some of the Company of women which followed the army, came flying across the Heath breathless, because they had run all the way from Marble Arch to convey their news.

"They have run away, my lord!" they cried all together.

"Who have run away?"

"The Army of Avengers – the Convict Wardens. They have all run away, and there is not one left."

"Run away? What does it mean? Why did they run away?"

Then the girls looked at each other and laughed, but were a little ashamed, because they were not quite sure how the Chief would take it.

"It seemed such a pity," said one of them, presently, "that any of our own brave fellows should be killed."

"Such a dreadful pity," they murmured.

"And by such cruel men."

"Such cruel, horrible men," they echoed.

"So that we ... we stole into the camp when they were asleep and we frightened them; and they all ran away, leaving their arms behind them."

Lord Chester looked at Captain Dunquerque.

"Woman's wit," he said. "Would you and I have thought of such a trick? Go, girls, tell the Bishop."

But Algy looked sad.

"And after all this drilling," he said, with a sigh, "and all our shouting, there is to be no fighting!"

CHAPTER XIV.

THE ARMY OF AVENGERS.

THE awful nature of the crisis, and the strangeness of the sight, kept the streets in the neighbourhood of the Camp in Hyde Park full of women, young and old. They roamed about among the tents, looking at the sullen faces of the men, examining their arms, and gazing upon them curiously, as if they were wild beasts. Not one among them expressed the least friendliness or kind feeling. The men were regarded by those who paid them, as well as by the rebels, with undisguised loathing.

About midnight the crowd lessened; at two o'clock, though there were still a few stragglers, most of the curious and anxious politicians had gone home to bed; at three, some of them still remained; at four – the darkest and deadest time of an autumn night – all were gone home, every special constable even, and the Camp was left in silence, the men in their tents, and asleep.

There still remained, however, a little crowd of some two or three dozen girls; they were collected together about the Marble Arch. They had formed, during the evening, part of the crowd; but now that this was dispersed, they seemed to gather together, and to talk in whispers. Presently, as if some resolution was arrived at, they all poured into the Park, and entered the sleeping Camp.

The men were lying down, mostly asleep; but they were not undressed, so as to be ready for their early march. No sentries were on duty, nor was there any watch kept.

Presently the girls found, in the darkness, a cart containing drums. They seized them and began drumming with all their might. Then they separated, and ran about from tent to tent; they pulled and haled the sleepers, startled by the drums, into terrified wakefulness; they cried, as soon as their men were wide awake, "Wake up all! – wake up! – run for your lives! – the rebels will be on us in ten minutes! They are a hundred thousand strong: run for your lives! – they have sworn to hang every Convict Warden who is not shot. Oh, run, run, run!" Then they ran to the next tent, and similarly exhorted its sleepers. Consider the effect of this nocturnal alarm. The men slept eight in a tent. There were about thirty girls, and somewhat more than a thousand tents. It is creditable to the girls that the thirty made so much noise that they seemed like three thousand to the startled soldiers. To be awakened suddenly in the dead of night, to be told that their enemies were upon them, to hear cries and screams of warning, with the beating of drums, produced exactly the consequences that were expected. The men, who had no experience of collective action, who had no officers, who had no heart for their work, were bewildered; they ran about here and there, asking where was the enemy: then shots were heard, for the girls found the rifles and fired random shots in the air; and then a panic followed, and they fled – fled in wild terror, running in every direction, leaving their guns behind them in the tents, so that in a quarter of an hour there was not one single man of all the Army of Avengers left in the Camp.

The orders were that the march should begin about six o'clock in the morning – that is, as soon after sunrise as was possible.

It was also ordered that the Army of Avengers should be followed by the Head of the Police Department, Lady Princetown, with her assistant secretaries, clerks, and officers, and that they should be supplied with tumbrils for the conveyance to prison of any who might escape the vengeance prepared for them and be taken prisoners.

At a quarter past six o'clock an orderly clerk proceeded to the Camp. To her great joy the Camp was empty; she did not observe the guns lying about, but as there were no men visible, she concluded that the Army was already on the march. She returned and reported the fact.

Then the order of the Police Procession was rapidly arranged; and it too followed, as they thought, the march of the Avengers.

By this time a good many women were in the streets or at the windows of the houses. Most of the streets were draped with black hangings, in token of general shame and woe that man should be found so inexpressibly guilty. The church bells tolled a knell; a service of humiliation was going on in all of them, but men were not allowed to participate. It was felt that it was safer for them to be at home. Consequently, the strange spectacle of a whole, city awake and ready for the day's work, without a single man visible, was, for one morning only, seen in London.

The Police Procession formed in Whitehall, and slowly moved north. It was headed by Lady Princetown, riding, with her two assistant secretaries; after them came the chief clerks and senior clerks of the Department, followed by the messengers, police constables, and servants, who walked; after them followed, with a horrible grumbling and grinding of wheels, the six great black tumbrils intended for the prisoners.

The march was through Regent Street, Oxford Street, the Tottenham Court Road, Chalk Farm, and so up Haverstock Hill. Everywhere the streets were lined with women, who looked after the dreadful signs of punishment with pity and terror, even though they acknowledged the justice and necessity of the step.

These men, they told each other, had torn down Religion, scoffed at things holy, and proclaimed divorce where the husband had been forced to marry; they pretended that theirs was the right to rule; they were going to destroy every social institution. Should such wretches be allowed to live?

Yet, always, the whisper, the suspicion, the doubt, the question, put not in words, but by looks and gestures, – "What have we women done that we should deserve to rule? and which among us does not know that the Religion of the Perfect Woman was only invented by ourselves for the better suppression of man? Who believes it? What have we done with Love?"

And the sight, the actual sight, of those officers of law going forth to bring in the prisoners, was a dreadful thing to witness.

Meantime, what were the Army of Avengers doing?

Slaughtering, shooting down, bayoneting, no doubt. No farther off than the heights of Hampstead their terrible work was going on. It spoke well for the zeal of these devoted soldiers that they had marched so early in the morning that no one had seen them go by. Very odd, that no one at all had seen them. Would Lord Chester escape? And what – oh what! – would be done with Lady Carlyon, Professor Ingleby and her two daughters, and the crowd of girls who had flocked to London with the rebels? Hanging – mere hanging – was far too good for them. Let them be tortured.

The Procession reached the top of Haverstock Hill. Hampstead Hill alone remained. In a short time the relentless Lady Princetown would be on the field of action. Strange, not only that no sign of the Army had been seen, but that no firing had been heard! Could Lord Chester have fled with all his men?

Now just before the Police Procession reached the Heath, they were astonished by a clattering of mounted soldiers, richly dressed and gallantly armed, who rode down the narrow streets of the town and surrounded them. They were a detachment of cavalry headed by Captain Dunquerque, who saluted Lady Princetown laughing. All the men laughed too.

"I have the honour," he said, "to invite your ladyship to take a seat in a tumbril. You are my prisoner."

"Where – where – where is the Army?"

"You mean the Convict Wardens? They fled before daylight. Come, my lads, time presses."

They were actually in the hands of the enemy!

In a few moments the whole of the Chiefs of the great Police Department were being driven in the rumbling black tumbrils, followed by the Lancers, towards the rebel camp. They looked at each in sheer despair.

"As for you women," said Captain Dunquerque, addressing the clerks and constables, "you can go free. Disperse! Vanish!"

He left them staring at each other. Presently a few turned and hurried down the Hill to spread the news. But the greater part followed timidly, but spurred by curiosity, into the Camp.

Here, what marvels met their eyes!

Men, such as they had never dreamed of, bravely dressed, and bearing themselves with a gallant masterfulness which frightened those who saw it for the first time. Presently a trumpet blew and the men fell in. Then the astonished women saw that wonderful thing, the evolutions of an army. The regiments were drawn up in a great hollow square. At one corner stood the fatal black tumbril with Lady Princetown and her *aides* sitting dolefully and in amazement. Bands

of music stood in the centre. Presently Lord Chester, the Chief, rode in with his
Staff, and the bands broke out in triumphal strains.

"Men of England!" he cried, "our enemies have fled. There is no longer any
opposition. We march on London immediately."

The shouts of the soldiers rent the air. When silence was possible, the Bishop,
venerable in lawn-sleeves and cassock, spoke –

"I proclaim Edward, sometime called Earl of Chester, lawful hereditary King
of Great Britain and Ireland. God save the King!"

Then the officers of the Staff did homage, bending the knee and kissing the
hand of their Sovereign. And the bands struck up again, playing the old and
wellnigh forgotten air "God save the King!" And the soldiers shouted again.
And Lady Princetown saw, indeed, that the supremacy of women was gone.

Then the march on London was resumed.

After the advance-cavalry came the Guards, preceding and following the
King. Before him was borne the Royal Standard, made long ago for such an occasion by Grace and Faith Ingleby. The bands played and the soldiers sang "God
save the King" along the streets. The houses were crowded with women's faces
– some anxious, some sad, some angry, some rejoicing, but all frightened; and
the wrath of those who were wrathful waxed fiercer when the company of girls
followed the soldiers, dressed in "loyal" ribbons and such finery as they could
command, and singing, like the men, "God save the King."

The House of Peeresses was sitting in permanence. Some of the ladies had
been sitting all night; a few had fallen asleep; a few more had come to the House
early, unable to keep away. They all looked anxious and haggard.

At nine o'clock the first of the fugitives from the Police Procession arrived,
and brought the dreadful news that the Army of Avengers had dispersed without
striking a blow, that Lady Princetown was a prisoner, and that the rebels would
probably march on London without delay.

Then the Duchess of Dunstanburgh informed the terror-stricken House that
she had ordered out the three regiments of Guards. They were to be hurled, she
said, at the rebels; they would serve to harass and keep them in check while a new
army was gathered together. She exhorted the Peeresses to remain calm and collected, and, above all, to be assured that there was not the slightest reason for alarm.

Alas! the barracks were empty!

What, then, had become of the Guards?

At the first news of the dispersion of the Avengers, the wives of the Guardsmen, acting with one common consent, made for the barracks and dragged away
the soldiers, every woman her own husband to her own home, where she defied
the clerks of the War Office, who rushed about trying to get the men together.

For greater safety the women hid away the boots – those splendid boots without which the Horse Guards would be but as common men. Of the three thousand, there remained only two orphan drummer-boys and a sergeant, a widower without sisters. To hurl this remnant against Lord Chester was manifestly too absurd even for the clerks of the War Office. Besides, they refused to go.

On the top of this dreadful news, the House was informed by the Chancellor that the officers sent to carry out the arrest of Lady Carlyon reported that her ladyship had fled, and was now in Lord Chester's camp with the rebels.

What next?

"The next thing, ladies," said a middle-aged Peeress who had been conspicuous all her life for nothing in the world except an entire want of interest in political questions, "is that our reign is over. Man has taken the power in his own hands. For my own part, I am only astonished that he has waited so long. It needed nothing but the courage of one young fellow to light the fire with a single spark. I propose that a vote of thanks be passed to her Grace the Duchess of Dunstanburgh, whose attempt to marry a man young enough to be her great-grandson has been the cause of this House's overthrow."

She sat down, and the Duchess sprang to her feet, crying out that the House was insulted, and that these traitorous words should be taken down.

"We shall all be taken down ourselves," replied the noble lady who had spoken, "before many hours. Can we not devise some means of dying gracefully? At least let us spare ourselves the indignity of being hustled down the steps of Westminster Hall, as the unlucky Department of Police has been this morning hustled on Hampstead Heath."

Several proposals were made. It was proposed to send a deputation of religion. But the Preaching Sisters had been rejected with scorn, when the army was still small and hesitating. What would happen, now that they were victorious? It was proposed that they should send a thousand girls, young, beautiful, and richly dressed, to make overtures of peace, and charm the men back to their allegiance. The young Lady Dunlop – aged eighteen – icily replied, that they would not get ten girls to go on such an errand.

It was proposed, again, that they should send a messenger offering to treat preliminaries on Hampstead Hill. The messenger was despatched – she was the Clerk of the House – but she never came back.

Then the dreadful news arrived that the conqueror had assumed the title of King, and was marching with all his forces to Westminster, in order to take over the reins of power.

At this intelligence, which left nothing more to be expected but complete overthrow, the Peeresses cowered.

"As everything is gone," said the middle-aged lady who had first expressed her opinion, "and as the streets will be extremely uncomfortable until these men settle down, I shall go home and stay there. And I should recommend your lady-ships to do the same, and to keep your daughters at home till they can learn to behave – as they have tried to make the men behave. My dears, submission belongs to the sex who do none of the work."

She got up and went away, followed by about half the House. About a hundred Peeresses were left.

"I," said the Duchess of Dunstanburgh, "shall remain with the Chancellor till I am carried out."

"I," said the Chancellor, "shall remain to protest against the invasion of armed men and the trampling upon law."

"And I," said young Lady Dunlop, loud enough to be heard all over the House, "shall remain to see Lord Chester – I mean, his Majesty the King. He is a handsome fellow, and of course Constance will be his Queen."

"Ladies," said the Duchess, dignified and austere to the last, "it is at least our duty to make a final stand for religion."

Lady Dunlop scoffed. "Religion!" she cried. "Have we not had enough of that nonsense? Which of us believes any more in the Church? Even men have ceased to believe – especially since they were called upon to marry their grand-mothers. The Perfect Woman! Why, we are ourselves the best educated, the best bred, the best born – and look at us! As for me, I shall go over to Lord Chester's religion, and in future worship the Perfect Man, if he likes to order it so."

The Duchess made no reply. She had received so many insults; such dreadful things had been said; her cherished faiths, prejudices, and traditions had been so rudely attacked, – that all her forces were wanted to maintain her dignity. She sat now motionless, expectant, haggard. The game was played out. She had lost. She would have no more power.

It was then about half-past three in the afternoon. They waited in silence, these noble ladies, like the Senators of Rome when the Gaul was in the streets – without a word. Before long the tramp of feet and the clatter of arms were heard in Westminster Hall.

The very servants and officers, the clerks, of the House, had run away; there was not a woman in the place except themselves: the House looked deserted already.

There hung behind the Chancellor a heavy curtain, rich with gold and lace; no one in that House had ever seen the curtain drawn. Yet it was known that behind it stood the image in marble of the only Sovereign acknowledged by the House – the Perfect Woman.

When the trampling of feet was heard in Westminster Hall, the Duchess of Dunstanburgh rose and slowly walked – she seemed ten years older – towards this curtain: when the doors of the House were thrown open violently, she stood beside the Chancellor, her hand upon the curtain.

Tan-ta-ra-ta-ra! A flourish of trumpets, and the trumpeters stood aside.

The Guards came after, marching up the floor of the House. They formed a lane. Then came the Bishop in his robes, preceded by his chaplain, the Rev. Clarence Veysey, surpliced, carrying a Book upon a velvet cushion; then the officers of the Staff with drawn swords; last, in splendid dress and flowing robes, the King himself.

As he entered, the Duchess drew aside the curtain and revealed, standing in pure white marble, with undraped limbs, wonderful beyond expression, the Heaven-descended figure of the Perfect Woman.

"Behold!" she cried. "Revere the Divine Effigy of your Gooddess."

The young priest in surplice and cassock sprang upon the platform on which the figure stood and hurled it upon the floor. It fell upon the marble pavement with a crash.

"So fell the great God Dagon," he cried.

Then no more remained. The ladies rose with a shriek, and in a moment the House was empty. It is not too much to say that the Duchess scuttled.

And while the King took his place upon the throne, the bands struck up again, the soldiers shouted, volleys of guns were fired for joy, and the bells were rung.

Strange to say, the dense crowd which gathered about the army of victory outside the Hall consisted almost wholly of women.

CONCLUSION.

THE Great Revolution was thus accomplished. No woman was insulted: there was no pillage, no licence, no ill treatment of anybody, no revenge. The long reign of woman, if it had not destroyed the natural ferocity and fighting energy of men, had at least taught them respect for the weaker sex.

The next steps, are they not written in the Books of the Chronicles of the country?

A few things remain to be noted.

Thus because the streets were crowded with women come out to see, to lament, sometimes to curse, a proclamation was made ordering all women to keep within doors for the present, except such as were sent out to exercise children, and such as received permission for special purposes: they were forbidden the right of public meeting; the newspapers were stopped; religious worship of the old kind was prohibited.

These apparently harsh and arbitrary measures, rendered necessary by the refractory and mutinous conduct of the lower classes of women; who resented their deposition, were difficult to enforce, and required that every street should be garrisoned. To do this, thirty thousand additional men were needed: these were sent up by Jack Kennion, who had recruited double that number. As the women refused to obey, and it was impossible to use violence towards them, the men were ordered to turn the hose upon them. This had the desired effect; and a few draggled petticoats, lamentable in themselves, proved sufficient to clear the streets.

Then the word was given to bring out all the men and parade them in districts. Indeed, before this order, there were healthy and encouraging signs on all sides that the spirit of revolt was spreading even in the most secluded homes.

The men who formed the first army were entirely country born and bred. They had been accustomed to work together, and freedom became natural to them from the first. The men whom the Order of Council brought out of the houses of London were chiefly the men of the middle class – the most conventional, the worst educated, the least valuable of any. They lacked the physical advantages of the higher classes and of the lower; they were mostly, in spite of the laws for the Promotion of Health and Strength of Man, a puny, sickly race; they had been taught a trade, for instance, which it was not considered genteel to practise; they were not allowed to work at any occupation which brought in money, because it was foolishly considered ungentlemanly to work for money, or to invade, as it was called, woman's Province of Thought. Yet they had no money and no *dot*; they had very little hope of marrying; and mostly they lounged at home, peevish, unhappy, ignorantly craving for the life of occupation.

Yet when the day of deliverance came, they were almost forcibly dragged out of the house, showing the utmost reluctance to go, and clinging like children to their sisters and mothers.

"Alas!" cried the women, "you will find yourselves among monsters and murderers, who have destroyed Religion and Government. Poor boys! What will be your fate?"

They were brought in companies of a hundred each before the officers of the Staff. At first they were turned out to camp in Hyde Park and other open places, where the best among them, finding themselves encouraged to cheerfulness, and in no way threatened or ill treated by these monsters, began to fraternise, to make friends, to practise gymnastics, to entertain rivalries, and in fact to enter into the body corporate. To such as these, who were quickly picked out from the ignoble herd, this new life appeared by no means disagreeable. They even began to listen to the words of the new Preachers, and the doctrines of the new Religion; they turned an obedient ear to the exhortations of those who exposed the inefficacy of the old Government. Finally, they were promoted to work of all kinds in the public departments, or were enlisted in the Army. It presently became the joy of these young fellows to go home and show their new ideas, their new manners, their new uniforms, and their new religion, to the sisters whose rule they acknowledged no longer.

There came next the feeble youths who had not the courage to shake off the old chains, or the brains to adopt the new teaching. These poor creatures could not even fraternise; they knew not how to make friends. It was thought that their best chance was to be kept continually in barracks, there to work at the trade they had been taught, to eat at a common table, to live in common rooms, and to be made strong by physical exercise. Out of this poor material, however, very little good stuff could be made. In the long-run, they were chiefly turned into copying-clerks, the lowest and the meanest of all handicrafts.

Allusion has been made to the barracks in which were confined the unmarried men who had no friends to keep them. Among these were the poor creatures afflicted with some impediment to marriage, such as hump-back, crooked back, consumptive tendencies, threatenings of heart disease, cerebral affections, asthma, gout, and so forth. They were employed in houses of business at a very small rate of pay, receiving in return for their labour nothing for themselves but free board and lodging in the barracks. It is curious to relate that these poor fellows proved in the reorganisation of civic matters the most useful allies: they had lived so long together that they knew how to act together; they were so cheap as servants, and so good, that they had been intrusted with most important offices: in short, when the Government seemed about to fall to pieces by the threatened closing of all the mercantile houses, these honest fellows stepped to the front, took the reins, directed the banks, received the new men – clerks, taught and assigned their duties, and, in fine, carried on the trade of the country.

The question of religion was the greatest d fficulty. Where were the preachers? There were but two or three in whom trust could be placed; and these, though they did their best, could not be everywhere at once. Therefore, for a while, the Religion of the Perfect Woman having been abolished, there seemed as if nothing else would take its place.

The Government for the present consisted of the titular King, who was not yet crowned, and the Council of State. There were no ministers, no departments, no Houses of Parliament. As regards the Lower House, it would have been unwise to elect it until the constituencies had learned, by experience in local matters, something of the Art of Government. But the Upper? Consider that for two hundred years the title had descended through the mother to the eldest daughter. This being reversed, it became necessary to seek out the rightful heirs to the old titles by the male line. No titles were to be acknowledged except those which dated back to the old kings. These, which had been bestowed in obedience to the old laws, were to be claimed by their rightful owners. Now, it is easy to see that while a title held the female branches of the House together, because each would hope that the intervening claimants would drop out, the male branches would not be so careful to preserve their genealogies, and so a great many titles would be lost. This, indeed, proved to be the case; and out of the six hundred Peers who enjoyed their rank under Victoria of the nineteenth century, scarcely fifty were recovered. Many of these, too, were persons of quite humble rank, who had to be instructed in the simplest things before they were fit to wear a coronet.

All later titles were swept away together; nor was any woman allowed a title save by marriage, unless she was the daughter of a Duke, a Marquis, or an Earl, when she might bear a courtesy-title. Of course, the late Peeresses found themselves not only deprived of their power, but even of their very names; and it was the most cruel of all the misfortunes which befell the old Duchess of Dunstanburgh, that she found herself reduced from her splendid position to plain and simple Mrs Pendlebury, which had been the name of her third husband. All her estates went from her, and she retired to a first-floor lodging at Brighton, where she lived on the allowance made her by the Relief Commission appointed by Government for such cases as hers.

As regards public opinion on this and other changes, there was none, because Society was as yet not re-established; and the new daily papers were only feeling their way slowly to the expression of opinion. It remains to be told how these changes were received by the sex thus rudely set aside and deposed.

It cannot be denied that among the elders there was disaffection amounting to blind hatred. Yet what could they do? They could no longer combine; they had no papers; they had no club; they had no halls; they had no theatres for meeting; they had no discussion-forums, – as of old. Even, they had no churches; and although in the past days they seldom went into a church, regarding religion as a thing belonging to men, they now made it their greatest grievance, that religion had been abolished. In private houses the worship of the Perfect Woman was long continued by those who had been brought up in that faith, and in days when it was actually believed in and accepted.

As for the younger women, they, too, differed. The lower orders, for a long time, regretted their ancient liberty, when they could leave the husband to work in the house, children and all, and talk together the livelong day. But in time they came round. The middle-aged women, especially those of the professional classes, no doubt suffered greatly by being deprived of the work which was to them their chief pleasure. Some compensation was made to them by a system of partnership, in which practice in their own houses and private consultations were allowed some of them for life. As for the very young, it took a short time indeed to reconcile them to the change.

No more reading for professions! Hurrah! Did any girl ever really *like* reading law? No more drudgery in an office! Very well. Who would not prefer liberty and seeing the men work?

They gave in with astonishing readiness to the new state of things. They ceased to grumble directly they realised what the change meant for them.

First, no anxiety about study, examinations, and a profession. Next, no responsibilities. Next, unlimited time to look after dress and matters of real importance. Then, no longer having to take things gravely on account of the weaker sex, – the men, who now took things merrily – even too merrily. Lastly, whereas no one was formerly allowed to marry unless she could support a husband and family, and then one had to go through all sorts of humiliating conferences with parents and guardians, – under the new *régime* every man seemed making love with all his might to every girl. Could anything be more delightful? Was it not infinitely better to be wooed and made love to when one was young, than to woo for one's self when one had already passed her best?

Then was born again that sweet feminine gift of coquetry: girls once more pretended to be cruel, whimsical, giddy, careless, and mischievous; the hard and anxious look vanished from their faces, and was replaced by sweet, soft smiles; flirtation was revived under another name – many names. A maiden loved to have half a dozen – yea, she did not mind half a hundred – dangling after her, or kneeling at her feet; men were taught that they must woo, not be wooed, and that a woman's love is not a thing to be had for the mere asking: and dancing was revived – real honest dancing of sweetheart and maid. There was laughter once more in the land; and all the songs were rewritten; and such pieces were enacted upon the stage as would but a month ago have taken everybody's breath away. And there was a general burning of silly books and bad pictures; and they began to open churches for the new Worship, and always more and more the image of the Divine Man filled woman's heart.

Finally, these things having been settled in the best way possible, it was resolved to hold the Coronation of the King at Westminster Abbey.

"Constance," he said, holding her in his arms, "you believe that I have always loved you, do you not?"

"I pray your Majesty," she said, humbly, "to forgive my errors of the past."

"My dear, what is there to forgive?"

"Nay, now I know. There is the Perfect Woman; but she lives in the shadow of the Divine Man: she has her place in the Order of the World; but it is not the highest place. We reigned for a hundred years and more, and everything fell to pieces; you return, and all begins to advance again. It is as if the foot of woman destroyed the flowers which spring up beneath the foot of man. King, if I am to become your wife, I shall also become your most faithful subject."

"You are my Queen," he said; "together we will reign: it may be for the good of our people. We have little strength of ourselves, but we seek it – love –"

"We seek it," she replied, lifting her eyes to Heaven, "of the Divine Man."

On the day of the Coronation, by Royal Order all classes of the people were bidden to the ceremony; as many as could be admitted were invited to the Abbey. Along the line of march they had raised seats one above the other, covered with awnings. An innumerable crowd of people gathered at early morning, and took their places, waiting patiently for eleven, the hour of the procession.

At ten the Peers began to arrive – the newly recognised Peers – the men who had been brought up in ignorance of their origin and rank. They were uneasy in their robes and coronets; they had been carefully instructed in their part of the ceremony, but they were nervous. However, the people outside did not know this, and they cheered lustily.

Long before half-past ten there was not a vacant place in the Abbey; the venerable church was crowded with ladies, who were anxious to make the Coronation the point of a new departure; Society, it was said, would begin again with a King. No doubt, many ladies whispered, women were, after all, poor administrators; their nature was too tender, too much disposed to pity, which produced weakness. Men, who received these confessions, laughed courteously, but remembered the crowded prisons, and the prisoners, and the Convict Wardens.

At eleven o'clock the procession started from Buckingham Palace. The ancient ceremonials were copied as closely as possible. After the bands came the mounted Guards; then followed heralds; then came the Venerable Bishop of London, who was to crown the King, in a carriage; then officers of State on horseback; then the King's faithful Guards, those sturdy gamekeepers who stood by him at the beginning; and last of all, save for a regiment of cavalry which brought up the rear, the King himself on horseback – gallant, young, handsome, his face lit with the sunshine of success; and riding beside him – at sight of whom a shout went up that rent the air – no other than the beautiful Lady Carlyon herself.

It appeared, when they arrived at the Abbey, that the Coronation was to be preceded by another and an unexpected ceremony. For the organ pealed forth the "Wedding-March;" there were waiting at the gates a dozen bridesmaids in white and silver; the choristers were ready with a wedding-hymn; and the Bishop, with the Very Rev. Clarence Veysey, newly appointed Dean of the Abbey, was within the altar-rails to make this illustrious pair man and wife.

Then followed, without a pause, the Coronation service, with the braying of trumpets, the proclamation of heralds, the King's solemn oath, the crowning of King and Queen, and the homage of the Peers. And amid the shouts of the people, while cannon fired *feux de joie*, and the bells rang, and the bands played "God save the King," Edward the Seventh rode back to his Palace, bringing home with him the sweetheart of his childhood.

Now there is so much grace and virtue in a real love-match that it goes straight to the heart of all who witness it. And since such fruits as these manifestly followed with Man's administration, not a maiden among them all but cried and waved her handkerchief, and sang "God save the King!"

LESBIA NEWMAN

Besant received laudatory notices for his *Revolt of Man*, because his reviewers had enjoyed a comedy that returned women to their proper, subservient place in society. That was one long-established position in the struggle for the rights of women; however, in the yin-and-yang mode of future fiction the counter-battery fire was not long in coming. The total rejection of Besant's negative proposition appeared in the vehement assertions of *Lesbia Newman* by Henry Robert Dalton. He addressed himself to 'mature and earnest minds' with the single purpose of urging 'uncompromising advocacy of the rights of women, and of their training for the exercise of their rights'.[1]

Their struggle for equality had moved forward by slow stages for close on half a century – from the Married Women's Property Act of 1870, which gave women the control of their own property and earnings, to the Representation of the People Act of 1918 which gave the franchise to married women, women householders and women graduates aged over thirty. Although men, especially men as legislators, are first in the queue of suspects up for questioning about the long delay in giving women their rights, the main opposition came from the centre – from a society obliged to adapt to a population that had gone from 20 million in 1821 to 37 million in 1900. The Victorians had to rethink and reconstruct their society, reform by reform; by factory acts, army acts, and education acts; by commissions on sewage, water supply, and urban dwellings. They dealt rapidly and effectively with the practical problems of their time. The solution of 'the woman question', however, could not come with comparable celerity for reasons central to the cultural convictions and religious beliefs of the age.

It was a patriarchal society. The man, as husband and father, was head of the household. The woman's place was subordinate, as Besant demonstrates in *The Revolt of Man* when the men have regained their rightful place in society:

Then was born again that sweet feminine gift of coquetry: girls once more pretended to be cruel, whimsical, giddy, careless, and mischievous; the hard and anxious look vanished from their faces, and was replaced by sweet, soft smiles; flirtation was revived under another name – many names.[2]

Those who maintained the contrary position, like the author of *Lesbia Newman*, argued that justice required men to change their mental attitudes and abandon their preconceptions. In the words of Henry Dalton, 'men must feel women to be in all things *without exception* their equals...and that in order to feel them their equals, they must learn to make them so'. Only exceptional men could meet that challenge. They had to look beyond the circumstances of their times, and they had to take on the large majority that found their lively sense of male achievements admirably encoded in Carlyle's 'Lectures on Heroes'. In his grand Olympian style as a latter-day prophet, Carlyle revealed the great part-truth:

> Universal History, the history of what man has accomplished in this world, is at bottom the History of the Great Men who have worked here...They were the leaders of men, these great ones; the modellers, patterns, and in a wide sense creators of whatsoever the general mass of men contrived to do or to attain; all things that we see standing accomplished in the world are properly the outer material result, the practical realisation and embodiment of Thoughts that dwelt in the Great Men sent into the world.[3]

Great Men? That thought was anathema to Henry Robert Dalton. He cracker-jacks his way through the near future in *Lesbia Newman* in order to demonstrate that, once men have welcomed women as their equals, all will be well with the world. The result is a rarity in future fiction, since Dalton races through his account of coming things in a state of rising euphoria. He begins with talk about women's rights and then, as the reader will discover, he raises his sights to open fire on selected targets. He solves 'the Irish Question' with a future war, invents a most extravagant new theology for the Catholic Church, and ends with his scheme for a more perfect society. The frequent equestrian metaphors come straight from an author who gallops off into the future, taking his fences as he finds them. His model was the all-talking narrative that Thomas Love Peacock had employed with great effect. The wordplay of *Nightmare Abbey* and *Crotchet Castle* reappears in the codification of Dalton's characters: Fenrake the Gardener, Athelstan Locksta-ble, Julius Dandidimmons, 'a young loafer without brains', General Polishoff, and the narrator whose name reveals the man: Mr Bristley is Dalton's totally rational man, bristling his way through conversations, knocking the world into the best of all possible shapes. Women can do no wrong in Mr Bristley's book: that is, women like his Lesbia who are untainted by 'weakervesselism'.[4] Although she represents Dalton's ideal woman, Lesbia Newman has been created in the image of man, She does everything a man can do, but does it better. 'Manly games,' says Dalton with a nod to the reader, 'came natural to her, football and cricket both claimed her attention in their respective seasons; and she was not hampered with skirts'.[5] Dalton pursues the logic of his invention too: Lesbia riding astride in her knick-erbockers, Lesbia 'knocking about with the gloves' like any good sport, and future

Lesbias marching off to war. War? Dalton writes: 'If women are to descend into the arena of life, they must do so without reserve.'[6]

Notes
1. See vol. 4, p.131.
2. See p. 125.
3. Thomas Carlyle, 'Lectures on Heroes. Lecture I', *Complete Works* (London:Chapman & Hall, 1890), I, p. 185.
4. One can only guess at Dalton's intention in naming 'Lesbia Newman'. One possible decoding is to suggest that the context and the time of writing point to the *mea Lesbia*, the total female of Catullus and object of great poetry. Dalton may well have liked the mischievous association of the female with the male, since the great English cardinal and leader of the Tractarian movement, John Henry Newman, was in his last year of life at the time of publication. The Catholic elements in the story support that conjecture; and they are strengthened by the contemporary estimate of Newman's personal achievement in helping to renew the Old Faith in England. Today it is unusual to find an American university without its Newman Centre.
5. See p. 177.
6. See p. 165.

A desperate charge of the French cavalry cleared the ground, bearing down the tall flagstaff as an avalanche would a reed, and with a horrid smash sacrificing many horses, as well as the limbs of their riders, against the squat round lighthouse, Roche's Tower.

PREFACE.

LESBIA NEWMAN
A NOVEL
BY
HENRY ROBERT S. DALTON
LONDON
GEORGE REDWAY
YORK STREET, COVENT GARDEN
1889

SHOULD coming events not tally in every minute particular with the forecast incidental to the following pages, the reader will perhaps make allowance. Historians are not always quite agreed even as to the past; in writing the history of the future, the difficulties are obvious. It is curious, nevertheless, that although the rough copy of this work was written about five years ago, political affairs seem to be tending in the direction of its partial realisation.

But the characters are all fictitious, and therefore reflect upon no one. They are but 'shadows passing through the gloom' toward that light and hope of the world which cannot be reached by secular reforms alone, however thorough. For to raise woman and, at the same time, to depress the religious sentiment in mankind, is contradictory. Her elevation is the essence of religion itself, and will presumably be the better accomplished, the greater the prestige of the community which shall be called to the work. The fact that there exists one of ancient renown, already in some measure committed to, and pre-eminently fitted for, it, is patent indeed, but is not conclusive in favour of that one. The prize is open to all – *detur digniori*.

The author has done his best to make the book readable, but it is addressed to mature and earnest minds which care for something more than mere frothy sensation and amusement; the story being simply a vehicle, of no account in itself, but only in the single purpose it conveys, namely, uncompromising advocacy of the rights of women, and of their training for exercise of their rights. All else is beside the mark.

CHAPTER I.

THE INMATES OF DULHAM VICARAGE.

'REALLY, my dear brother, I can't at all agree with you; I don't think you are doing your duty either by society or by your niece herself. A girl who is brought up so differently from other girls can only end in being a martyr, besides causing a great deal of annoyance and discomfort to those about her.'

'Well, Jane,' replied the person addressed, 'since we can't agree, we had better agree to differ; in any case, I shall just go on as I have done with Lesbia; that is *my* duty to society, and it must be held to outweigh individual prejudices. As for making a martyr of my niece, would that be anything new? Are not all women, more or less, made, or make themselves, martyrs to hollow idols? If my influence should result in making one of Lesbia, it shall at all events be for something worth the martyrdom. She shall not be a martyr to 'weakervesselism,' as you and others are.'

'Hallo! what's that about martyrs?' exclaimed a young girl of about thirteen or fourteen, bursting into the room as the last speaker finished his sentence. 'A dispute over me, as usual, I suppose. Never mind; you stick to your colours, Uncle Spines, and I won't mind being martyred by people I despise. And happily the world is not made up entirely of old fogies.'

'Thank you, Lesbia,' said her mother; 'you are very complimentary.'

'Oh, I don't mean you, mamma, of course. I mean the people who preach maidenly femininity and womanly nimminy-pimminity, and all that stuff.'

'But I'm afraid I must plead guilty to liking that stuff myself.'

'So much the worse, mamma, dear; you insist that the cap shall fit you, which I did not intend.'

'Perhaps you will think differently when you are older, Lesbie,' said her mother sorrowfully.

'Not very likely, Jane,' put in the uncle. 'Not so long as she and I are within reach of each other.'

'That's right, uncle,' said the girl; 'you are the only sensible man I know.'

'I may be the only one you know, Lesbie, because your experience of the world is not wide as yet; but you would over-rate me and under-rate others if you imagined that there are not at this day plenty of men who share my views on the education of girls, and would do as well by you as I can.'

'Now to change the subject,' said the young girl; 'how about that machine; when's it coming?'

'What, the bicycle? It's come, and I told Fenrake to have it all ready by eleven this morning. It's about that now, I think.'

'That's all right; then I'll run up and get on my 'bikes'; the road looks quite dried up.'

No sooner was she gone than the old gardener knocked at the door.

The foregoing conversation took place in the library of a small but comfortable country parsonage in one of the eastern counties, situated, with a southern aspect, on an eminence a little removed from the highroad which, emerging from a broad avenue of fine elms on the right of the parsonage, passed the bottom of its garden into the hamlet of Dulham on the left. The view from the library window on that fine June morning, the brighter for a night's rain, extended over a wide range of flat grass land, bounded by gentle undulations in the distance; and the east breeze was bringing brine from the sea coast, distant about twenty miles.

The occupants of the room were the Reverend Spinosa Theodore Bristley, B.D., Vicar of Dulham, near Frogmore, Eastshire, a spare, tall, intellectual-looking man of about forty, with sharp features, a high open forehead, and thick glossy black hair; his widowed sister, Mrs Newman, and her daughter Lesbia. Mr Bristley had been married some years, but his wife had borne no children; she was a mild-mannered, amiable person, with no great natural gifts, and hardly as intelligent in conversation as might have been expected from one living with a man of her husband's stamp. Her sister-in-law, Mrs Newman, was of a different style, but not enough so to prevent the two women agreeing upon the point of bitter opposition to the scheme upon which the vicar – a very original character – was bent, that of bringing up a girl to take her proper place in the world, untrammelled by the habits of studied littleness, fashion-serving, mischief-making, mean rivalry and general unsoundness, which society – at least, so said this eccentric parson – considers essentials of the perfect lady. Hence a chronic feud existed upon that one subject in the otherwise harmonious family, the girl being already old enough and quick enough to perceive that her female relatives wanted to bolster up the moribund old slavery of women, while her uncle was determined to give her freedom and power. He was never tired of disseminating the doctrine that if girls were brought up more like boys, in what is called manliness, and boys more like girls, in refinement and delicacy of mind, they would, as grown women and men, lead happier and nobler lives; society would be less injured by brutality in men and by the really greater though more plausible evil of "weakervesselism" in women. However, as financial and other practical considerations had brought about the arrangement whereby Mrs Newman kept house with her brother and his wife, and as all parties were too sensible to suppose that perfect union is to be looked for anywhere, they made the best of their dogmatical differences and on the whole got on comfortably together.

About Mr Bristley's religious views, whether as clergyman or otherwise, all his professional brethren and their friends and belongings agreed that the less said the better. But he made up by works of charity, which, having some private fortune, he was well able to do; and his wife was constant in her ministrations to the sick and poor in the village. She was, in fact, out on her usual rounds on the morning when this story opens, and she appeared in the library about an hour after her niece had left it.

'Upon my word, Theo, the neighbours will think we're all crazy here. There's that girl careering up and down the public road astride of a high bicycle, with old Fenrake running by her side and trying to keep her from tipping over, which I saw her do twice. She is covered with mud – I only hope not with bruises too. And such a costume too – dark blue knickers, stockings, and short jacket to match, and billycock hat; in short, every vestige of her sex carefully rubbed out – it really passes belief, my dearest – '

'Why, that's all right; it's her bathing-dress; what better could she wear to begin learning in? You wouldn't have a young lady mount a bicycle in flowing robes, would you, Kit?'

'No, I wouldn't have a young lady mount a bicycle at all. But it seems to be your mission in life, Theo, to outrage its proprieties.'

'On the whole, I am disposed to agree with that remark,' returned Mr Bristley coolly.

Before his wife could reply, Lesbia presented herself at the door, in her muddy costume, with a healthy glow on her face and her eyes sparkling.

'Well, how did you get on?' asked her uncle.

'Oh, capitally; I rode about twenty yards by myself several times before tipping down. I haven't learnt a proper dismount yet. I got one cropper, but not what you may call the real orthodox straight dive over the head.'

'Enough to shake you though, I'm afraid. Feel any headache?'

'Nothing to signify. I shall get used to it after a few more.

'And, pray,' inquired her mother ceremoniously, 'did the – the public volunteer any observations?'

'They were quite welcome to,' answered the girl; 'but I saw no public except three gentlemen – of the Frogmore club, it seems – who happened to pass on high bicycles just as I got my cropper. They called out 'Bravo!' and dismounted.[1] One of them picked up my prostrate machine, and we had some general chat about bicycles and roads and makers and prices before they went on.' She paused, and added, – 'They want me to join the club and ride about with the members, half-a-dozen or so at a time. What do you say, Uncle Spines?'

'And didn't they sing in chorus, 'For she's a jolly good fellow?'' asked her mother, in the same manner as before.

'They didn't sing it, but I have no doubt they thought it,' retorted Lesbia. 'If they didn't, I do.'

'Capital idea to ride with them, eh, Kitty?' said Mr Bristley, appealing maliciously to his wife.

'You don't mean it, Theo?'

'Mean it? Decidedly I do. Why shouldn't she? She'll be safer with them than alone, and it'll give a famous blow to the proprieties, which you say is my mission.'

'Well, anyhow, I suppose you're going to put on your dress for luncheon, Miss Bravo,' said her mother. 'If so, you've not too much time.'

CHAPTER II.

FIDGFUMBLASQUIDIOT.

THE Vicar of Dulham agreed with his wife and sister in one thing at all events, they preferred old-fashioned domestics fished out of odd rustic corners to the ladyising and gentlemanising persons whom the town registry offices of to-day mostly supply. One we have already seen – the old gardener and general outdoor man Fenrake; his wife, a few years younger, was cook and housekeeper, and both were thoroughly efficient in their places. As much cannot be said for Mrs Fenrake's niece Fidgfumblasquidiot Grewel, who had been taken into the vicarage at the same time. Some four-and-twenty years before the opening of this story, Mr Bristley, then newly installed at Dulham, had represented to the village-girl's mother – a plump, blue-eyed, flaxen-haired, silly little woman, whose idol was royalty and 'haristocracy' – that Fidgfumblasquidiot was a very aristocratic name, and he had obtained Mrs Grewel's consent to have her christened by it one Sunday afternoon, while a titter ran through the congregation. 'Great thing, you know,' Mr Bristley explained after the service was over, 'for girls to have original names, and not to be all just Polly and Susey and Lizzie.' Honest, comely little Fidge – for she was of slight make – was specially Lesbia's attendant, and had lived with the family about eleven years in the capacity of a maid-of-no-work. Her mornings were spent in dawdling over her small jobs, and her entire afternoons in dawdling over the change of her gown. This latter operation generally lasted from about three to six P.M., but it must be said that when it was done she always looked very neat and even graceful.

To see Fidgfumblasquidiot dust a room was a study worth coming down early for on a cold morning. After a prolonged struggle with the handle of the door, she would come rolling in like a fishing-smack broadside on to a ground swell, a habit which had originated with her in the wearing of tight boots. Having rolled up to the china shelf or the mantelpiece, she would begin to swing a feather brush, held by the very top of the handle between her finger and thumb, lightly over two or three objects without touching them, muttering 'Oh?' interrogatively all the while to herself, and glancing now over one shoulder now over the other, as if she fancied a ghost were about to pounce upon her. This done, she would consider that the room was dusted, and still muttering 'Oh?' and glancing wildly about with her clear expressive eyes, she would roll lightly away into another apartment, and go through a similar dusting. All her other housemaid's work was conducted on these principles, until the welcome afternoon arrived when she could retire to her bedroom for the three hours' toilet. But she was trusty in all ways, and strongly attached to Lesbia, who liked her in return because Fidge had no taste for gossiping and flirtation, and what little she said could be relied upon, although she was not an intellectual companion.

'What an irreclaimable blockhead that girl is!' said Lesbia, when she rejoined the party downstairs, her little maid having brought some nitric acid to mark linen, instead of the marking-ink she had been told to fetch.

'Not quite irreclaimable, perhaps, Lesbie,' answered her uncle. 'Give a girl, even a half-wit like that, a chance to associate with persons such as – a – '

'Ahem! such as the Vicar of Dulham near Frogmore, and his still more remarkable niece,' interposed Mrs Bristley. 'Don't be modest, Theo.'

'I never am, Kitty,' was the reply, 'and I endorse your suggestion. My belief is, that if I were to superintend the training of a half-witted girl from childhood, she would pass the average mark. But with such treatment as most girls still undergo, the wonder is they don't all turn out Fidgfumblasquidiots.'

CHAPTER III.
BILL AND JOE.

THE incident in the road was soon followed by improving the acquaintance, and by our heroine's admission into the Frogmore bicycle club. Mr Lyttelhurst, its promoter, who had picked up the fallen machine on the occasion mentioned, was a married solicitor of repute, living in the town. Within a fortnight afterwards, during which the young girl practised alone and tumbled about for an hour or two every day, an arrangement was made that Mr Lyttelhurst should call at Dulham with some of the other members, and take her for a short ride of some dozen miles.

Her uncle, of course, came out to see them go off, and the two elder ladies, who disapproved of the whole proceeding, peeped nevertheless from a bedroom window above. Lesbia, a little nervous at first, soon began to enjoy the ride, the men having chosen the most level among their regular routes, so that she had no occasion to dismount, and already she was able to run 'legs over' down some easy slopes that occurred now and then. Their road took them right through Frogmore, the main street of which was macadam, in fairly good order. Lesbia kept her place steadily and carefully amid the traffic, which happened to be pretty thick, it being market day.

'Capital, Miss Newman!' exclaimed the man who had ridden next in rear of her through the town; 'you got throught it all like an old Londoner. Half-an-hour in a town is worth half a day in the country for steadying you.'

'Yes; you can't sleep on your machine like an albatross on the wing, when an omnibus is skinning you on one side and a coal waggon on the other,' replied Lesbia. 'Which way are we going? I don't know this side of Frogmore so well.'

'Northward for the present,' said Mr Lyttelhurst, who had dropped back to her side for a moment. 'We shall pass through Wisprill, and then by Poplars Weir, where we shall find means of ferrying over the river, and so approach Dulham again from the north side.'

'How far shall we have ridden altogether?' she asked.

'Nearly seventeen miles. That will be about enough for your first day.'

The road soon became continuously level as it ran along the side of a sparsely-wooded shallow vale, in the middle of which the gleam of water could be seen at intervals; further on, its course was marked by a series of clumps of poplars. The pace now increased, and in about three-quarters of an hour after clearing Frogmore, they passed through the little hamlet of Wisprill, and turned direct on the river where it was at its broadest, near the cascade of Poplars Weir. By so doing, they left the main road, which followed the stream, and made for one on the other side, which turned southwards toward Dulham. There was no bridge at or near this part, nothing but a huge antiquated covered barge, long disused for traffic, which lay fastened to the rail of the weir cascade. It was the summer abode of two watermen of the old stamp, who, when they could get nothing better to do, picked up coppers by ferrying people, and now and then a horse, over from one road to the other. For this purpose they had a couple of roomy but heavy punts, both of which, with their owners, happened to be on the opposite side when our bicyclists arrived and dismounted. Mr Lyttelhurst hailed them, and the two men, who were dozing in their respective punts, started to their feet and pushed off in such haste that as they shoved away with their backs to each other, (he lumbering punts collided in midstream and both bargees were thrown off their feet, one so forcibly that he not only let go his pole into the water, but went partly in after it. Recovering himself and his pole with a struggle, he turned to his comrade a visage flaming with wrath, and out of the fulness of his heart spake unto him wingèd words.

'Come, you fellows, I say, stop that now, can't you?' called out one of the bicyclists. 'We're waiting to cross; you can have it out between you afterwards. Please look sharp!'

The two bargees, by no means in a hurry now, began to punt on slowly towards their fares, still keeping their scornful countenances half turned to each other, and resuming the dialogue, during which Lesbia kept her little red silk pocket-handkerchief pressed upon her mouth, choking with laughter. Some of her companions were at first inclined to feel annoyed on her account; but so far from looking uncomfortable and keeping in the background, the young girl was first to wheel her bicycle into the nearer of the two punts as they at last touched the bank. She then held out a shilling to each of the controversialists, saying, –

'There, boys, that's to drink to your next bit of friendly chat. You've given me a good shillings'-worth each, I can tell you.'

The two hulking men took the money with a look of wonder at the girl, somewhat shared, to tell the truth, by her companions.

'Thankee, my lord,' said one of the bargees, completely quieted down.

'Yes, my lord, we'll drink your 'ealth and a pleasant ride to you,' said the other. 'Oi saay, Bill, oi vote we go and take the pledge in a gallon apiece at the White Cow, ah?'

'Roight, Joe, oi'll pledge yer,' answered his partner.

And having got twopence from each of the other fares, making a nice little catch in all, the illustrious pair went off together to their beer, as good friends as if not a word had passed between them.

'What a queer child she is!' observed the man next him, in an undertone to Mr Lyttelhurst, as the group advanced to a spot suitable for re-mounting.

'Very!' was the reply. Then aloud to Lesbia: – 'I am glad, Miss Newman, that at all events you were not annoyed by the bad language of those two roughs.'

'Annoyed!' she exclaimed. 'Bless you, I was delighted. Quite a treat to come across such refined sarcasm – the real Attic salt, you know. The only pity is we hadn't a shorthand reporter to take it down word for word. But I'm thirsty with laughing. Is there any pub near?'

'Yes, there's the White Cow, where Messrs Bill and Joe are gone. But you needn't follow them into the bar; the landlady will give you tea or beer or what you fancy in her private room.'

The ride home was pleasant; a light breeze at their backs and a smooth though narrow road helped the pace materially. The young men now felt that Lesbia Newman was a companion for them with whom they could be as much at ease as with each other, not a mere blush-and-simper sample of young-lady-stuff, keeping them in continual *gêne*. In little over an hour they reached Dulham, and as her friends declined to stop at the vicarage again that day, Lesbia entered the drawing-room just as her relatives were finishing afternoon tea.

'Well, Lesbie, what sort of a ride, how far, and how did you perform?'

'Jolly ride; about seventeen miles, Uncle Spines. I did as well as the rest, and we had a rare bit of fun at Poplars Weir. We were ferried over the water by Demosthenes and Cicero in person.'

'Eh? How?'

Lesbia then gave extracts from the bargee record, which much amused. the vicar, and much scandalised her mother and aunt.

'This is your system of training girls, Theo, it seems!' said his sister. 'To send her out skylarking astride of a bicycle with a pack of roystering boys to hear bad language.'

'I must tell Mr Lyttelhurst that you consider him a roystering boy,' said the vicar, smiling.

'But about the profane swearing, Theo,' said his wife.

'Oh, I assure you, Aunt Kate,' said Lesbia suavely, 'that the profane swearing was merely supplementary and ornamental – I should have just liked you and mamma to have heard the epithets those two bestowed on each other.'

'Thank you kindly, Lesbia,' said her mother; 'I'd rather not'

'After all said and done,' observed the vicar, 'hard words break no bones. But when spoken before girls, they do break something else which it is most desirable should be broken.'

'You mean their womanly delicacy,' said Mrs Newman.

'No, not quite that,' he replied. 'Not if you mean that delicacy which ought to be common to both sexes. But if you mean the prudish affectation which young ladies of the received pattern are taught to cultivate, then I say let it be annihilated at all costs – broken to atoms.'

CHAPTER IV.

AN AFTERNOON AT RUDDYMERE.

Shortly after the occurrences of the previous chapter our four of Dulham vicarage were invited to a large garden party at the country seat of the Marquis of Humnoddie, a few miles distant. The Ruddymere people, like other county families of the neighbourhood, often drove over on a Sunday to hear Mr Bristley's afternoon lectures, which were always on subjects suited to a cultivated audience. This common point of interest led to a genuine friendship, among the privileges of which Lady Humnoddie, who treated most matters as a joke, reckoned that of chaffing Lesbia about her advanced ideas.

Among the guests was a first cousin of the marchioness, Mr Athelstan Lockstable, a young man who, though not exactly silly, had a curious habit in society, that of dropping the thread of a remark he was in course of uttering, and so losing the bearings of the conversation around him, whilst he ransacked his memory, by the aid of expletives, to find the dropped thread, which he then suddenly sprang upon the company at the very moment most *malapropos*, regardless of the personality and the prejudices of anyone whom he could button-hole for the purpose, and overwhelm with a fresh batch of expletives expressive of bis satisfaction at having caught his lost idea.

Lesbia's bicycling costume having been perfected by the good taste of her uncle, was now very presentable; accordingly she rode her machine – a new 50-inch one – to Ruddymere, while the others drove in the pony-chaise.

'Well, dear,' said the hostess, taking the young girl's hands in each of her own, 'you do look sweetly manly today. I've heard of your doings on the bicycle; got it here, I suppose? Yes; and how are your friends of Frogmore? But, I say, don't you mind people noticing you wherever you go?'

'Not a bit, Lady Humnoddie; I'm getting quite a hardened, brazen character. But I get some encouragement too.'

'Mostly from men, I suppose?'

'No; I'm corresponding with the Reformed Dress Society, which is composed of ladies. I want to propose the institution of a girls' bicycle club.'

'Capital idea! but I suppose you'd reject tricycles with lofty contempt. I'm really thinking of a tandem for Hilda and Friga. My girls are both bitten by the mania. I wish they weren't, but it can't be helped. But, I say, Lesbie, is it your uncle's fad or your own?'

'His in the first place; mine now.'

'Ah, I guessed as much. Mr Bristley is well known to be a heretic and a sinner.'

This was said in a voice intended to reach the person concerned, who was in an adjoining group.

'I plead guilty to being a sinner, Lady Humnoddie,' said he, coming forward, 'otherwise I should be a better man than St Paul, who called himself the chief of sinners – and very accurately, considering the twaddle he always talked whenever he opened his mouth on the subject of women. But a heretic, no. I take a professional pride in keeping whole and undefiled the Catholic Faith, else without doubt I should perish everlastingly!'

Two of the other parsons of the neighbourhood, who were standing and talking with their backs to the group which the vicar of Dulham had joined, turned round and chuckled at the pompous tone of this last sentence.

'Your 'Catholic' faith, Bristley,' said one of them, who was an old friend of the Dulham family,' is a very whole one, we all know, and I suppose undefiled. It consists, if I mistake not, of uncompromising woman-worship. Well, why not? I'm devoted to the ladies myself. Eh, Lesbia?'

'You! I'm afraid, Mr Smeeth,' answered Lesbia, 'that your precious devotion is mollycoddle.'

'Pon my sawl – aw – that's too bad, Miss Newman,' put in Athelstan Lockstable, who had just joined them. 'When all these ages poets have been singing the praises of Lawve, you know, and – '

'Yes,' she cut him short, 'poets have been singing, and marriage bells have been ringing, and novel-writers have been scribbling, and nightingales have been dribbling, and troubadours have been sighing, and chaperones have been plying – it's all quite too utterly awfully chawming, you know. But, for all that, the master passion's rarely anything more noble that what I call mollycoddle.'

'You're a funny girl, Lesbie,' said Lady Humnoddie, 'a very funny girl altogether.'

'Perhaps so,' answered Lesbia; 'but though you'll say I'm young to judge, I don't imagine I shall ever be much addicted to mollycoddle.'

'But come, Lesbia, what *is* mollycoddle, after all? Do you apply that name to every kind of love?' asked Mr Smeeth.

'Oh! by no means. I do not call either tried affection or real woman-worship by that name. Mollycoddle is the feeling experienced by empty-headed young women and emptier-headed young men, when they flirt and spoon and go a courting, like that maiden all forlorn that waked the cock that lived under the thorn, that tossed the cow with the crumpled horn, that ate the dog, that swept the cat, that kissed the rat, that worried the house that Jack built.'

'Dash my wig, Miss Newman, you're quite one of the – eh – ah – um – what the deuce, eh? what the devil, you know, eh? why, those old Greek whaddy-call-'ems, demmy, why demmy, I'll be – .' And Mr Lockstable subsided into a brown study.

'So you've been to Rome, I understand, Lady Humnoddie,' said Mrs Bristley, who had been taking tea on another part of the lawn and had come over just too late to hear Mr Lockstable's commentary on his own text. 'Were you disappointed in the Easter ceremonies, or not? I asked because my husband said he was a good deal disillusioned when he went about six years ago. I remember he called Holy Week at Rome stale, flat, and unprofitable.'

'No, you don't say so? I'm surprised at that, Mr Bristley,' turning to him. 'I thought it very novel and amusing. Didn't you think the Pope's choir sang well, and weren't you interested in the vespers of those nuns at the Monte Carlo – I mean Trinità del Monte, up the steps there, you know, not far from the Piazza di San Pietro? I forget what order they belong to – not Benedictines, is it? the something – a – '

'Amazons, demmy! why demmy, Amazons!' shouted Mr Lockstable, facing his cousin, with a resounding slap on his thigh. 'Amazons! demmy, Amazons. There you are!'

Everyone stared.

'An order of nuns called demi-Amazons!' exclaimed Lady Humnoddie.

'Aw, no – not an order of nuns,' leisurely explained Mr Lockstable. 'I was thinking of those strong-minded Greek charmers who were something after Miss Newman's style, eh? But I say, if there ain't Arthur Guineabush and his cousin Miss Dimpleton at the end of the lawn! I shall cut it, *nem con*. I don't want to be overwhelmed with any more of that young lady's pious platitudes, – had enough of them and to spare on Sunday.'

'And she had enough of you probably,' observed Lesbia, laughing at him. 'You very markedly sat upon her piety, – squashed it quite into a 'platitude.''

Mr Lockstable slipped off, muttering as he went, – 'Dash my wig, sir, dash – my – wig, sir.'

CHAPTER V.

AN EDIFYING SUNDAY.

To account for the remarks of Mr Smeeth and of our heroine, it, is necessary to shift the scene back to the previous Sunday afternoon, and the parish of Dulham. Mr Smeeth was the incumbent of the little village of Flatton, and having no afternoon service of his own, had made an appointment with Athelstan Lockstable to walk over and hear Mr Bristley's discourse, which was greatly in vogue in the county on account of its polemical character. To hear the articles of the dominant creed pulled to pieces by innuendo was an intellectual pastime calculated almost to make an English Sunday lively, especially as, in a place like Dulham, church services were almost wholly useless for the purpose of displaying new mantles and head dress. Consequently Mr Bristley became so popular a preacher, that in order to save himself the need of replying to the many letters and postcards he received inquiring whether he would preach on such and such a Sunday, he hit upon the device of hoisting a white flag in his garden when he was not absent from home, which bore on it his crest and motto in black and red, a bristling porcupine astride of a sword (we do not attempt heraldic terms), and underneath, a scroll in the original Greek, 'It is hard for thee to kick against the pricks.' When this flag was up, the neighbourhood knew there would be an afternoon lecture next Sunday.

Our two gentlemen took a footpath to Dulham lying across some wide flat pastures, divided, not by hedgerows but by wet ditches of considerable depth, everyone of which was filled with a thick crop of tall marsh reeds, that rustled gently as they bowed to the breeze.

'Nice grazing lands,' observed the parson. 'Very different from what I remember them some five-and-thirty years ago. None of these ditches cut, and half the place a swamp. Capital sport for the gun, plenty of snipe, ducks too, in hard frosts; but as for farm stock – bless you!'

'Ah, and even now these rushes thrive well in their close quarters,' said Mr Lockstable, the path leading them at the moment by a plank and rail across one of the largest cuttings. 'They look, to my fancy, as if they liked their new place better than spreading wild about pools and moss.'

'Curious now you should think of that!' exclaimed Mr Smeeth, halting. 'The very same idea struck Bristley when he and I passed this way not long ago, and it gave rise to one of his original speculative notions!'

'What was that?'

'He said that the case of the rushes in their ditches is an analogue of cosmic economy. Just as these rushes do better for being confined to a set place where they make no waste, so various excesses of human nature which, if allowed to run riot through society, are felt as intolerable, do, when grappled with and organised, become not only harmless but positively useful. Under this conception, the soul has been aptly called a garden, and thus perhaps a key may be supplied to the fable of the garden of Eden. Anyhow, under this view, the phenomenon of the existence of evil, which has been such a stumbling-block to many deep thinkers endeavouring to vindicate belief in a supreme being and divine justice, may be explained and described as *wasted and disproportioned good*. Put any evil, any kind of suffering, mental or bodily, in its proper place and its right proportions in relation to its environment, and it will at once cease to be felt as an evil – it will have its use. Of course the practical difficulty for us shortsighted and feeble mortals is to find the conditions required; but however long a time may elapse before we can do so, they do exist somewhere, and will eventually be found. It is very simple, meanwhile – any child may comprehend it – when we feel ourselves puzzled to account for the evil that is in the world, to have the answer ready that *evil is good misplaced*. Certainly, to explain is not to remove it: still mere explanation is a satisfaction to the intellect.'

'That's Bristley's idea, is it?' said Mr Lockstable. 'Well, it's clear enough, I will say. And though I don't go in for being a thinker myself, I've heard clever people say that evil is a mystery beyond them.'

'They make it more beyond them than it need be, by not going the right way to work. They begin to puzzle their heads as to the *cause* of evil, without having first inquired into its *nature*. But that's all wrong; before we ask *why* it is, we should first ask *what* it is. The what goes some way toward explaining the why.'

'No doubt.'

'Great truths show their forms behind this small one,' resumed Mr Smeeth. 'It is manifest that a divine universe or a universal deity – it matters not much which you say – must *include*, not merely *oppose*, the phenomenon of evil. To set up a god and a devil boxing at each other across a gulf, is childish. You may have – and we do have – antagonism between partial and relative good on the one hand and partial and relative evil on the other. But it is obvious that there cannot be antagonism between universal good and universal evil, or you would postulate two universes, which is a contradiction in terms, – as much a contradiction as it would be to say that two and two make more or less than four.'

'Frankly, Smeeth, you begin to make me a little groggy. Gods and devils are not much in my line; and of the two, I rather prefer the second. But there! the bell's stopped; we shall be late for the fun.'

And so they found it.

'All seats full, sir,' said the old sexton at the church porch, 'twenty minutes before service, and very little standing-room now. You're welcome to my corner, gentlemen, an you care to stand there!'

They managed, however, to edge far enough into the crowd to be within hearing, and what they heard was a discourse on the text 'Great is Diana of the Ephesians,' wherein the apostle was dexterously likened to 'an upstart individual from the Cannibal Islands,' who might be imagined to come into Dulham church where they were now assembled, and begin to denounce the Christian worship. No hard epithets were used, but the congregation nevertheless left their places when it was over, under the vague impression that the goddess was sacrilegiously wronged, and that the missionary of the Lord was an ill-conditioned cur. This was nothing unusual nor unexpected; it was the sort of thing they came to hear, or four-fifths of them would have stayed away.

The people streamed out; in due course the vicarage party appeared, and each shook hands with the two friends in the churchyard.

'How do you do, Miss Newman?' said Lockstable.

'What a pretty voluntary you played us out with! Was it an impromptu?'

'Partly; a few variations of an old hymn.' Then gliding up to him, she whispered, – "King of the Cannibal Islands,' didn't you recognise it?'

'Haw! haw! haw!' he roared, with a slap on his thigh. 'Dash my wig, Miss Newman, that's good, by Jove!'

'Let me introduce you to my friend Rose Dimpleton, Mr Lockstable,' said Lesbia, to create a diversion. 'She is fond of music.'

The new acquaintances bowed, but felt a little embarrassed what to say to each other, so, as soon as politeness allowed, Mr Lockstable again addressed Lesbia, –

'Well, and how's the bicycle? You've not been out on it to-day, I see,' observing that Lesbia was not in knicker costume, but dressed in a frock of rich material and peculiar cut, with a hat to match.

'No,' said she, 'I'm not got up for it to-day; in fact, I don't ride on Sundays just about here. Besides, my machine is laid up for the moment; some grit or rust has got into the bearings, and I don't quite know how to take them out; I should like to see a machinist, and I'm afraid there's hardly one in Frogmore; yet there should be, because the bicycling men – '

'Just so, there's a man they employ, a very clever one said to be; ironmonger and blacksmith combined, and good at repairing sewing-machines, bicycles, and what not. He's not been there long, – came last summer, I think.'

'Indeed! pray what's his address?'

'He lives in the High Street, third or fourth corner on the right after the railway bridge, and his name's eh – ah – um – let me see – stupid I am – what the deuce is the fellow's name?' And Mr Lockstable lapsed into silence and study.

The vicar, who had ceased talking to another acquaintance when his ear caught remarks which so much interested his niece as the subject of her disabled bicycle, looked down, biting his lip; while pious Miss Dimpleton turned a sharp frown upon Athelstan, which had no more effect in disturbing his reverie than if he had taken opium.

'And so you're to be confirmed next month, I understand, dear,' said Mrs Bristley, in a soothing tone, wishing to relieve the young lady from the impression made by Mr Lockstable's invocations.

'Yes, I hope so; I'm very late, I know; I ought to have been confirmed three years ago, only I could never feel prepared for it. That reminds me – while I think of it – since Mr Bristley is so kind, and papa likes me to talk to him sometimes, there are a few questions about the New Testament history in which I am shamefully ignorant, and if it would not be intruding upon his time – '

'Certainly, certainly, my dear Miss Dimpleton,' said the vicar, coming forward. 'Pray ask me whatever you like; I shall be most happy to be of use to you. Does anything occur to you which I can answer now, or would you rather come and see me at another time?'

'Thanks, very much, perhaps that would the best, though indeed, while I think of it, there was just one question I should like to ask, and if – '

'Ask it, by all means,' said the vicar.

'Well then,' she said timidly, 'which of the Apostles was it who – '

'BUMMINGBY!' roared Mr Lockstable, with a vivid stare into her face and a slap on his thigh that was heard by the furthest of the departing congregation. 'Bummingby, of course, of course! Who *should* it be but Bummingby? Bummingby, Bummingby, of course! *That's* your chappie, my beauty!' still at Rose Dimpleton, with another but gentler slap on his thigh.

Poor Miss Dinipleton became white and then crimson, and stood rooted to the spot. The two clergymen turned their backs and covered their faces with both hands in suppressed convulsions; while Lesbia leant against a tree and screamed unrestrainedly. The other ladies choked in their pocket-handkerchiefs; several of the hindermost of the vanishing congregation turned round with a smile at Lesbie's boisterous merriment. Even Fidgfumblasquidiot, who with her mother was among the last, looked back over her shoulder for ghosts, and then laughed outright.

'Are you clean out of your mind, Lockstable?' asked the vicar, as soon as he could speak. 'The name of an apostle – *Bitmminghby!*'

'Aw no – not an apostle,' drawled Mr Lockstable, with the utmost composure; 'not an apostle, bless you! The ironmonger at Frogmore, who can furbish up Miss Newman's bicycle.

'Oh, I understand,' said the vicar, with a bow. 'The explanation was needed, and is satisfactory.'

'You have nearly killed poor Miss Dimpleton,' said Mr Smeeth.

'Now, Lesbie, hold up, can't you – you'll hurt yourself if you go on like that,' remonstrated her uncle, though with difficulty commanding his own countenance.

The young girl made no answer, but still clung to the tree with her mouth wide open, and her eyes invisible.

'Sorry to have spoken out of season, Miss Dimpleton, apologised Athelstan; 'but, fact is, we were at cross purposes. You were thinking about the Bible, I was thinking about the bicycle; that's how the mistake arose.'

'And pray, sir, which do you consider is the more fitting subject to think about when just out of church on Sunday? she asked sternly.

'Why, fact is, I can't ride a bicycle, myself; I suppose the Bible is,' he said timidly; 'but, fact is, I'm not much of a Bible man either – at least – what the mischief – excuse me, I've such an infernal habit of speaking out my thoughts – what I mean is – only I'm demd if I can ever make myself clear – '

Lesbia, perceiving his discomfiture, and having laughed herself out, came to the rescue.

'Really I'm much obliged for your information, Mr Lockstable. I shall most certainly get Mr Bummingby to overhaul my machine. There is no fear of my forgetting his name. Now, Rose, are you inclined for a walk with us?'

CHAPTER VI.
A LUNCHEON OUT.

On taking her bicycle to Frogmore, Lesbia found that the capacities of Mr Bummingby the ironmonger had not been overstated; he soon found out what was amiss, set it right, and showed her how to do so for herself another time. While they were standing in the shop-door, Lesbia suddenly exclaimed: –

'What a glorious white bulldog! I wonder where that gentleman lives he's following.'

'It's the new master of the hounds, miss,' replied Mr Bummingby.

'What's his name?'

'Sir Richard Robins.'

'The dog's?'

'No, the gentleman's, miss. The dog's name is Whiting. They say as Sir Richard's refused fifty pounds for that dog.'

Lesbia could think of nothing the rest of that day but the white bulldog. Her uncle had some time since promised her a dog of her own, when she should make up her mind as to the sort, and she had made it up now,

'I should like one just like Whiting, Uncle Spines, a monster, all tusks and wrinkles, with his shoulders a yard apart and his nostrils flat between his eyes; ears uncut, of course.'

'I much approve your choice, dear; a good bull is the dog for you. But I think it would be better to try and bring up a pup of good stock than to buy a full-grown animal; the bulls are very faithful and affectionate, and if you brought one up, you could form his character.'

'I think the best way to form his character will be to provide that he shall hear sermons by the vicar of Dulham,' replied his niece. 'I have a saving faith that if he ever afterwards were to meet a gospel missionary, he'd take him by the – '

'By the manner of his conversation to be an angel Lesbie, to be an angel. Well, if I'm not mistaken, there are some people, connections of Robins, of the name of Guineabush, who have taken a house on the other side of Frogmore – I met them the last time we were at Ruddymere – who have some pups of the same breed. I have a great mind to write and ask if they will sell us one.'

No sooner said than done; the next day, the vicar received a friendly reply from Blackthorne Lodge, the residence of Mr Arthur Guineabush and his wife, saying that they would gladly show our friends the pups if they would look in and stay luncheon on the following Friday. The invitation was gladly accepted, and about one P.M., Lesbia and her uncle arrived in the pony-carriage. Mrs Guineabush, guessing Lesbia's impatience to see the pups, proposed that they should follow the pony-carriage to the stable.

'Here are the pups,' said the host. 'They are the truly-begotten children of Whiting himself, the idol of your admiration.'

'Oh, what sweet little monsters!' exclaimed Lesbia, with rapture. 'And one's all white, like its father! May I take it up?'

As the young girl stroked and kissed the square block of skin and bone which did duty for a head to the little creature, Mrs Guineabush whispered to her husband, –

'Couldn't you let her have it, Arthur? she seems to have taken such a violent fancy to it.'

'Well, Miss Newman,' said he, 'forasmuch as this pup will certainly be swallowed alive by you if I attempt to keep him in my possession, I therefore ask you and say, 'Wilt thou take this pup, to have and to hold, for better, for worse, for richer, for poorer, in sickness, in health – joking apart, will you make him your constant companion all his life, and never part with him, even to your dearest friend?'

'All this I steadfastly promise,' responded Lesbia, but doubtful whether it was really meant.

'Then I pronounce that you be mistress and dog together, in the name of the Three Graces.'

'A gift! Really that is too good of you, Mr Guineabush,' answered Lesbia, delighted. 'It sha'n't be for want of care on my part, if anything ever happens to the little darling.'

'You don't need me to tell you, by the way,' said Mr Guineabush, 'that a bull-dog can never keep up with a bicycle. You have considered that point, I suppose?'

'Certainly; for the matter of that, I don't think a dog of any kind should habitually go out with a bicycle; they endanger both yourself and other bicyclists. He will be my companion when I'm not riding.'

They now went in to luncheon. As they crossed the flower-garden to the front door, the guests were startled at hearing a gruff voice call from an upper window, –

'Kiss my claw! Kiss my claw!'

'That absurd parrot!' said Mrs Guineabush, while the others tittered. 'He's really a clever bird, Miss Newman – I suppose I may call you Lesbia now. Some of the things he says are so *àpropos* of the conversation around him, that I really believe he understands both what he hears and what he says. Will you sit there, facing the window, dear?' – as they entered the dining-room. 'I should like to know your opinion about parrots, Mr Bristley. Is it possible, after all, that they understand human language?'

'I believe they do,' he replied, 'to the same extent as a very young child does, that is, not grammatically or analytically, but connecting certain sounds with certain things.'

'Exactly; that's what I think,' said Mrs Guineabush. 'It seems to me there's a great deal of twaddle talked about animal instinct and human reason: don't you think so? It's only our conceited ignorance that makes us draw such wide distinctions between ourselves and the lower animals.'

'I quite agree with you,' he answered. 'Reason is nothing more than *the analysed ingredients of instinct*. Every act of instinct can be described as an act of rapid reasoning. For example, if I withdraw my hand in haste when about to touch a stinging-nettle, I do not deliberately argue, "when I have before touched plants of that class, I have been stung: what has occurred before will occur again, given exactly similar conditions: *ergo*, if I touch that nettle I shall be stung." I say that I do not go and spell out all that to myself; but the act of withdrawing my hand in haste is equivalent to that argument gone through in a second of time.'

'I see,' said Mr Guineabush, who had followed attentively. 'Then according to that, Mr Bristley, you make instinct a superior quality to reason, in the sense, at least, that the whole is superior to its parts or processes.'

'Undoubtedly,' he replied.

'Rather a triumph for us women,' observed Mrs Guineabush, glancing at Lesbia; 'we are always said to be more instinctive, men more rational.'

'That's nothing new, Mrs Guineabush,' said she.

'Every department of philosophy whatever,' said her uncle, 'if honestly gone into, must result in the triumph you refer to, Mrs Guineabush.'

'You have the reputation of being a champion of our sex, Mr Bristley,' she replied.

'And an honest one, I hope, Mrs Guineabush. I fear that species is not so plentiful as it should be. There's lots of strutting 'gallantry' in the world, but it is better to be a straightforward woman-hater, than to be a champion of that sort.

We want the men who are ready to give back to women all the privileges they themselves have usurped. The others may keep their blarney to themselves.'

'But, Mr Bristley,' pursued the hostess, who was not a frivolous person, 'since you set so much store by the powers of instinct, do you believe that the lower animals have immortal souls?'

'Before directly replying to your question, Mrs Guineabush, I must take exception to the word *have*. It is not a question of 'having' a soul as you may 'have' blue eyes or a striped shirt or the headache; it is not that I *have* a soul, but that I *am* a soul. It is a body that you *have*, a soul that you *are*.'

'But at any rate,' objected Mrs Guineabush, 'the soul is dependent upon the body.'

'As the body is upon its food and clothing,' rejoined the vicar. 'But 'is not the life more than meat, and the body than raiment'? Are you and I who talk together nothing more than the flesh and vegetables we have eaten and the animal and vegetable tissues we have worn as clothes? Would it not be ridiculous to say that such and such a book is the work of the food and drink and suits of clothes which made up its author? But it is equally foolish to say that it emanated from the author's brain. It did not emanate from his brain, except in the sense in which it emanated from his pen. The pen and the brain alike are mere instruments guided by the soul, which is the man himself. He *has* a pen, he *has* a brain, he *has* a body, of which the brain and the hand are parts; but he *is* a soul.'

'Yes, that's clear,' said Lesbia. 'But, uncle, how do you regard disease of the body, especially of the brain, which hampers the soul's action so much and so often?'

'As I regard the walls of a gaol or the fetters which paralyse a prisoner's action so much and so often,' was the reply. 'Is the prisoner no longer a man, because he is a man in irons? Is the soul no longer a soul, because its machine has got out of order and hampers it?'

'But again,' said Lesbia, 'the body is temporary; it had a beginning we know and will have an end we know. May not the soul begin and end with it?'

'This coat and trousers I am wearing,' he replied, 'had not only an ascertainable beginning and ending, but also can be, and every day are, put off and exchanged for other garments. But do I not still remain your Uncle Bristley, parson of Dulham, whether I am in coat, dressing-gown, or night-shirt? Why then shall I not be still the same person, when I shall have put off my suit of bones and muscles, etc., my earthly body?'

'There seems to me a difference nevertheless,' said Mrs Guineabush – 'kindly pass the mustard, will you? – that the body grows and decays. Are we to say the same of the soul?'

'That question is more subtle, Mrs Guineabush,' replied Mr Bristley, 'but the answer is this: – The growth of the soul – that is, of the real person, need by no means end with the growth nor even with the death of the earthly body. Why should it? Do I not continue to live, even though I may have worn a shirt threadbare? I will go further, and say that it need not even have begun with the birth of the natural body. This body is but a vesture, soon made, soon destroyed, but I am not my body; I need neither begin with it nor end with it. I may have lived many previous lives, I may live many more hereafter. Still through all my potential changes, I am the same soul.'

'Try this nutty brown sherry, Mr Bristley,' said the host passing it to him. 'It's old, but not so old as the doctrine of transmigration, in which you seem to be landing us.'

'Thanks. The doctrine is old enough certainly, if that be a fault,' he replied, 'but on what other theory can you account for the diversified lower forms of life? That parrot upstairs, those puppies in the stable, how are we to account for their forms and their nature? It is the part of man not merely to see the world, but to *account* for it to himself. The transmigration theory does, to my mind, account for the zoological world. The animals are souls like ourselves, all tending upward to or downward from the architype mankind. Some are in process of degradation, others in process of elevation, each according to the use or abuse of his preceding probation in the flesh, has earned his own reward or punishment in kind and degree. This is natural law in the spiritual world, the only kind of supernatural we need trouble ourselves about.'

'I thought,' said Mrs Guineabush, 'that Darwin had sufficiently explained the origin of species by natural selection.'

'By all means,' replied Mr Bristley. 'But who or what, after all, is the selecting nature? Nature, in the abstract, is but a name for Design in the universe, and the laws of nature are the sequences which form essential parts of that design. But we cannot conceive of Design without a Designer, which means a designing soul or mind. Thus we arrive at the great first principle which is the basis of philosophy, that soul or mind is the reality of existence, inert matter or body its image and instrument merely.'

'Then, uncle,' said Lesbia, 'since you make every living being a soul, not a body, you exclude and deny the rule of the laws of matter – those of chemistry and physiology, for instance.'

'Laws of matter, my dear girl! Matter has no laws; how can it have any? We know nothing of matter; we cannot demonstrate its existence but as the matter of our cognisance, the medium of our consciousness. Matter is immeasurably divisible and augmentable and removable; it is, if you please, the medium of everything, but it is the substance of nothing. In the last resort, it is simply the mode or modes of thought and feeling, and however much you may alter the modes and shift them about, you can never get behind that of which they are the modes. You can never get behind the fact that the laws of nature, chemistry, physiology, what you please, are the laws of our perceptions. The world of thought and sensation is the real world; the matter of which it is composed is a mere condition, not a reality. Science is simply self analysis; mathematics, for instance, do but illustrate the structure of the mind. Its structure limits its view of the world to two classes of operations – analysis, wherein the universe appears as diverse; synthesis, wherein the diversity of the world appears as the universe. But in all other cases alike there is but the one reality, the Mind; Matter has no existence but as the matter *of* mind. Is that clear to you now?'

'I gather the idea,' said his niece, 'but it is a slippery one to hold, because it contravenes one's habits.'

'Man is put in these earthly conditions in order to contravene his habits and form better ones,' replied her uncle.

After some desultory conversation on other topics the company left the luncheon table, and as they entered the drawing-room a basket-carriage, drawn by a small Shetland, drove up to the hall door. It was occupied by two young ladies, one of whom Lesbia recognised as her friend Kose Dimpleton, the other was a stranger, an American, whom the sequel of this story will show in closer acquaintance with our heroine than anyone else, for the simple reason that she was better capable of understanding her. The acquaintance between Miss Letitia Blemmyketts and Rose Dimpleton was certainly not one of intellectual affinity; it arose merely from the fact that both young ladies were devoted to painting on china, and had already made some little profits by their respective talents, and on this occasion they had brought a jar to exhibit to the Guineabushes, whom they had met at one of Lady Humnoddie's garden parties, the American being indebted to that lady for her introduction into such county society as the neighbourhood afforded. Miss Dimpleton lived at Wisprill, near Frogmore, of which her father was clergyman, while Miss Blemmyketts, the daughter of a wealthy merchant of New York, had for some time past taken up her residence at Breakdown Villa, Pasteboard Row, New Scampings, an outskirt of the town of Frogmore which had lately sprung up, handy for the railway station.

No sooner were they introduced than our heroine found she had met something of a kindred spirit in the American, who, however, was several years her elder. Mrs Guineabush having the quickness to observe this, proposed to the two girls to take a saunter down the shrubbery together, which they both were wishing at the moment. It will suffice to give the last bit of their conversation as they returned, a reply of Letitia's to a question of Lesbia's as to the use of making oneself a martyr to advanced ideas.

'How then,' said the American, 'did any notions in the world ever get a start? How were the to-day triumphs of civilisation won? My dear girl, the reformers of the world have never gained their ends by, Shall I succeed? but by *I will* succeed. It's the set purpose and resolve before which the inert mass of social stagnation sooner or later gives away. Besides, if you don't martyr yourself to a good cause, you'll only be martyred by a bad one, I guess the trials of life are not to be given the slip by just hiding your light in order not to be eccentric. Won't you be hunted down by small worries and ignoble sufferings after you have turned tail and cut your mission? Why, the young lady who hasn't the courage to stick up for women's rights, is just the one to be made spiteful and miserable for weeks because Count Alamode took her sister down to the ball-supper instead of herself.'

"'A Daniel come to judgment!'" exclaimed Lesbia, regarding her new friend with genuine and sympathetic admiration.

'Well, act on the judgment, dear,' answered the other. 'Now I guess we mustn't keep Rose and the little beast waiting any longer.'

The Vicar and his niece took their leave soon after the others, and during the drive home, which was rather windy and cold, she was in high spirits. She had got just such a bull pup as her fancy pictured; she had been much interested by the conversation at luncheon; above all, she had met for the first time with one of her own sex who could understand her views and back up her endeavours. All this combined to make her feel happy that afternoon; but most of our pleasures in this world have their drawback of one kind or another, beforehand or afterwards; and this happy day was not to end without its *contretemps*.

A trifling one occurred, even on the way home. As they passed out of Frogmore under the railway bridge, the Happygolucky Express from London to Northeasterton thundered over it at sixty miles an hour; and the old pony, usually imperturbable, took fright and made a dash which grazed the enamelled panel of the carriage against the brick wall.

'Jib, you old fool!' scolded Mr Bristley, lashing him up, 'what do you see to shy at on the way, that makes you, behave like that ass of Balaam's, eh?'

CHAPTER VII.
MRS NEWMAN'S DREAM.

NOTWITHSTANDING the great difference which both circumstances and disposition made, even so early, in their ways of looking at the rights and duties of their sex, and the consequent want of communion between them on all the highest human interests, Lesbia was undoubtedly tenderly fond of her mother, and could not be at ease when anything, however slight, was amiss with her. And so when, on arriving home that afternoon, she hurried to her mother's room with the pup in her arms, she was startled to find Mrs Newman sitting on the sofa with her hands fallen by her sides, gazing abstractedly out of window, and looking very pale and unwell.

'I've got my prize, mamma – but gracious! what is the matter with you? – has anything happened?'

'No, Lesbia dear, nothing particular. Why?'

'Because you look so pale and ill! Why didn't you send a messenger to fetch us back at once?'

'There was no need, dearest. I have been a little out of sorts, it's true; but I feel better already: now that you are with me, and all right.'

'*And all right!* Why, mamma, what made you imagine I was not all right? You knew I was with Uncle Spines, and where we were gone.'

'Yes, it was silly of me to be nervous about nothing; but anyhow I feel *myself* all right, now that you are with me.' And Mrs Newman clasped her daughter in her arms even more affectionately than usual.

'I'll tell you what, mamma, this is quite strange. When I go out on my bicycle – which *is* risky, all riders know – you have none of these anxious fits; and now you have one when I simply go out to lunch, driven by my uncle with a steady old pony! Though it's true, he did make one little breach of good-manners to day. The fact is, I don't believe my safety has anything to do with it. What ails you is that you lead too dull a life, and therefore feel depressed and ready to fancy anything. I do wish you wouldn't stay at home so much. You know Uncle Spines is always urging you to accept invitations and go about with us wherever we go – why don't you do it? The fact of our not agreeing in opinion on certain social subjects, is no reason for our being so much apart. It's unnatural, and there's no good reason for it?'

'I know, darling, your uncle is kindness itself where my personal wants are concerned. But – well, perhaps you are right; at all events, I will consider what you say, and try to act on it more than I have done.'

'That's right, dearest mother, I do hope you will, for my sake as well as your own. But still,' she resumed, after a few moments' silence, 'I don't feel quite satisfied in my mind; I wish you would tell me exactly all you have been doing since we left this morning. Something unusual must have taken place to make you feel so much upset on this particular day. I feel convinced there is a reason for it; so don't put me off by saying you feel all right. You have been all wrong, and I want to know why.'

'What have you done with your prize, your precious pup, my darling?' asked Mrs Newman, attempting to change the subject.

'Oh, he's all right; I just popped him into my bed, where he'll be snug for the present; I couldn't have him here and attend to you. But, mamma dearest, you evade my question; I want to know what it is that has upset you.'

Mrs Newman hesitated a few seconds, then she said timidly: –

'No, Lesbie, I've no wish to put you off, you're always so tonder to me, but – well since you must have it, I've been dreaming; there! that's what it is.'

'Dreaming!' exclaimed Lesbia, with a laugh, much relieved. 'Bless you, darling mamma, is that all? I was afraid something real was the matter. Why, you don't mean to say that you condescend to bestow a second thought upon dreams? Why, if I had eaten a crab, shell and all, and had such a nightmare as might be expected, it wouldn't trouble my mind once it was over! Not unless I died of the indigestion.'

'No, it's weak of me, Lesbie, I admit; only some dreams affect one more than others. Never mind; it's past and gone now.'

'But how comes it, mamma, that we never heard a word about all this at breakfast? You seemed quite yourself then, and also when we drove from the hall door.'

'It wasn't last night, Lesbie, darling, it was to-day. About half an hour after you and Theo were gone – about half-past twelve – I felt strangely oppressed and drowsy, and longed for a midday nap – most unusual with me. So I lay down on this sofa and went off in a moment, and it was then that I had this dream.'

'Indeed!' and Lesbia looked at her mother with momentary solicitude. 'Indeed! Come then, dear mamma, tell me without delay what this dream was, and let me charm it away for you. Out with it in all its ghastly details! 'Avaunt, thou evil dream!' as Homer says. But seriously you must tell it me, dearest mamma. Not that it can really signify what you dreamt; still I want to know it.'

'Well, I will then, Lesbie, since you insist upon it. I daresay you'll think it very fantastic and pointless; however, here it is. I found myself at a garden party at Ruddymere Park, just such as you described to me last time you and Theo went. Strange to say, I was there, you were not!'

'That's just like a dream,' said Lesbia. 'Well, mamma?'

'Lord and Lady Humnoddie,' resumed Mrs Newman, 'were standing chatting and laughing with a few friends just in front of where I was. I didn't hear what they said, for a singular reason. My whole attention was absorbed – I couldn't help it – in gazing at that pretty green hill with large elms on its summit which you must have remarked, Lesbie, about a couple of miles away, I should think, to the north; you must have noticed it, for it's the only hill to speak of in this part of the county.'

'Yes, yes; I know it well; they call it Screechowl Hill. I was there not long ago with the Frogmore bicyclists; the highroad runs straight up over it, and we tried to ride it, but not one of us could get half way except Mr Lyttelhurst, who managed about three quarters, then had to jump off by the pedal. Well, mamma, now what did you dream about Screechowl Hill?'

'I stood looking at that hill,' continued Mrs Newman, 'I suppose because the weather seemed to be clouding over behind it, and already I felt the close sensation one gets when a storm is brewing. 'I'm afraid we're going to have a change,' I said to Lady Humnoddie, who came for a moment to my elbow. No answer. I repeated what I had said, and turned to her. She was gone. So were all the other people. I was left alone on the slope of the lawn; but I felt no surprise – none. A powerful attraction made me gaze at that hill again, and forget everything else. The clouds had now gathered about it so thickly as to hide the elm clump; still I looked, and looked, as if I were determined to see through the clouds. And as I looked I became conscious of a curious buzzing in my ears which was quite unaccountable. It got stronger, and soon became a deep vibrating hum like a bass organ pipe, which began to alarm me. I tried to turn and walk briskly away: I could not. Nor could I wrest my attention from that mysterious hill. It had changed, Lesbia, it had changed like a dissolving view: it no longer looked like itself.'

'Poor Screechowl Hill! it had followed your example, then, mamma dear!'

But though Lesbia thus affected to treat it gaily, a feeling of strong interest was coming over her.

'The clouds now shifted about,' pursued Mrs Newman, 'so that I had glimpses of the hillside between their openings, and I saw that it had changed; it had become much higher, much steeper, much nearer. There were no trees on it now, but on the top was an old white stone windmill without arms, or it may have been an old dilapidated lighthouse, I couldn't say which. With a great effort I turned to look on my left: I felt impelled to do so. And then, Lesbie, I was astounded to see that Lord Humnoddie's garden and park and house had all disappeared, and in their place was a great sheet of calm water stretching away out of sight under a white fog. It might have been a lake, but I think it was the sea, because there were gulls in great numbers flying about over it and calling to each other in a state of wild excitement. I now could look backwards and forwards, sometimes at the old lighthouse on the hill-top, sometimes at the smooth foggy sea, that deep humming sound in my ears increasing all the while, and gradually altering into another sound, a sound as if hundreds and hundreds of people were beating carpets on the land, both around that hill and upon it. Suddenly there came from the sea a straight short flash, followed by a clap – no, not a clap, a long peal of thunder, which echoed and bellowed among the hills, and did not die away as echoes do, but went tearing round and booming louder and louder, and the straight rod-like flashes of lightning – I suppose it *was* lightning – ' here Mrs Newman paused in her narrative with a scared look – 'came thick and fast out of that white fog, which had now spread over the land as well as the sea, so that the old lighthouse on the hilltop was hidden from sight. The noises, I tell you, Lesbia, went on worse and worse, and all the time, mixed with the dreadful thunder and the constant rattle like carpet-beating, there was the blowing of brass horns in short regular cadences repeated over and over again. At moments the great roar seemed beginning to subside, but it always broke out afresh; and I was getting already very frightened and giddy, when the white pall of cloud or smoke or whatever it was opened, and I saw the hillside clear, and everywhere about, all over the ground, there were streaks and patches of a horrid red, like blood! That finished me; I fell forward on my face and shut my eyes, and the noises slowly surged away into the far distance on my right. Presently I summoned courage to open my eyes and then to get up. The whole scene had changed like a dissolving view again, and the last part of my dream was beautiful; but I felt so shaken that I could not enjoy it. I saw another place with another atmosphere, under an exquisite rainbow, and there was a fine old building with towers – it may have been a cathedral – I don't exactly remember; but what I do remember is this, that I saw you, my darling – ' here Mrs Newman sobbed with emotion, 'in a procession of lovely young girls, not walking, but all borne aloft upon men's shoulders, seated on gorgeous thrones and with banners and images and emblems carried before and after, enter the building to grand music that sounded like parts of Mendelssohn's Priests' March in *Athalie*. I wanted to ask a bystander what it all meant, but before I could do so I awoke. Now, you know all, darling.'

Lesbia looked very grave, but she felt it her duty to say nothing but what might cheer her mother.

'Very well, mamma, dear, and what is there in all that to disturb you – on my account? Is not all well that ends well? Why, your dream makes out that I was not in the tumult and horrors of the first part, while I *was* in the beautiful procession of the second. What better could you desire – for me at least?'

'Yes, indeed, Lesbie, when one comes to reason about it. But I did not feel inclined to reason before I had told it you: I could do nothing but mope.'

'Come, we must have no more moping, dearest mamma; there's been a deal too much of that already. However, since this thing has weighed on your mind, should you object to uncle's hearing the story? You know he is sensible.'

'No, I shouldn't object; why should I?'

Lesbia soon fetched the Vicar. He listened with deep attention and without comment to his sister's repetition, and was silent for some seconds after she had concluded. At last he asked, –

'Have you told this dream to Kate?'

'No,' replied Mrs Newman; 'when I told her – rather crossly I'm afraid – that I wanted to go to sleep, she went out for a walk and has not yet come in. Perhaps she went to luncheon at the Smeeth's.'

'Well then,' said Mr Bristley, to whom it occurred that his question had not been quite judicious, 'at all events I'll give you the benefit of my opinion in a very few words. I don't believe in dreams; they're nothing but the action of the humours of the stomach upon the brain, throwing the residue of memory into confusion and causing phantasmagoria – there's a word for you! but what I do believe in is the injurious effect of a dull life upon the mind, and through it upon the body. I've often told you, Jane, that the secluded life you've been leading won't do, and now you see for yourself that I was right. It's a fine evening, and there's an hour and a half to dinner; come with us for a stroll round the fields, and then I'll get out a bottle of the dry champagne, which will brace you up and clear your head. You must try and forget all about this weird vision; I'll tell Kitty the substance of it myself, we can't have you recounting it a third time. Ah, here she is, so we shall have the party complete – that is, if you're not too tired for a little constitutional, Kitty?' – to his wife as she entered the room.

'Not for a short turn, Theo,' she replied; 'but I've only just come back from lunching at Flatton. I met Mr Smeeth on the path, and he insisted. What's ever the matter with you, Jenny? I thought your nap would have done you good, and you look more poorly than before!'

'Mamma's had a disturbing dream, Aunt Kate,' said Lesbia.

'Indeed!'

'Yes,' took up the vicar with alacrity; 'she dreamt she was out somewhere by the seaside in a bad thunderstorm, and some people were killed by the lightning; and altogether she was alarmed and shaken by it. That's all, and now the sooner it's forgotten the better. There are quite enough ills in real life, without fostering those of dreams also.'

'I quite agree with that,' replied his wife; 'come in! come in!'

There was a very gentle but continuous tapping at the door. Then the handle turned round and back again and was still. Then the attempt was renewed, and the handle turned round and back and round and back again.

'Come in, can't you, it's not bolted!' called out Mrs Newman.

'It's that priceless Fidge, of course,' said Lesbia. 'She and a door handle are natural enemies.'

A more agitated twist round and back and round again, then an unnecessary shove against the door, which flew open, and Fidgfumblasquidiot rolled lightly into the room, not looking at any of the company, but rather at ghosts who might be in the background.

'Well, Fidge, what has scattered you now?' asked her young mistress.

'Please 'm, it's that puppy's a been and got into your bed, and drawn a map!'

'Got in! a thing that can hardly crawl? I put him in myself, Fidge, but I won't let it happen again; he shall have a bed of his own, poor little pet.'

As Fidgfumblasquidiot withdrew, her aunt the housekeeper appeared at the door.

'Come in, Mrs Fenrake,' said the vicar; then observing that she looked anxiously at his sister, he added, – 'Mrs Newman has been troubled with dreams – indigestion I suppose, but she'll be better presently; we're going out for a turn.'

'Indeed, sir!' said the housekeeper; 'well, that's strange now; I was dreaming myself last night. I dreamt Fidge married a bishop. Well, sir, I was a-going to ast you as I might go for a few days to see my brother at Norwich. I've had a letter from his wife; she says, says she, as he's getting a invalid – quite breaking up. He can't work, says she, any later than four o'clock; then he goes out for three or four hours on his bicycle, and when he comes home he can't fancy nothink for his supper excep a little roast beef and plum-pudding, washed down with a quart o' Bass's strong Burton ale.'

'Poor man!' exclaimed Mr Bristley, 'what a wreck he must be, and what a lot of nursing he must want! I suppose the doctor insists upon that diet for him?'

'Well, no, sir; he don't see no doctor, says she; he says he must keep his money for medicine – that is, beer. He says it's the only thing for decline.'

'Really! He is in a decline, then?'

'Yessir, decline and fall of the sheer yellow leaf, he calls it.'

'Oh, I see. Very well, Mrs Fenrake, we'll spare you for a week, and I hope your presence will cheer the bicycling invalid.'

'Thank you kindly, sir,' answered the housekeeper; 'that's just what Lucy says, cheer the invalid as has always got the sore of dammyplease a-hanging over his 'ead. Though, says she, for the matter o' that, he's cheerful enough when he's got his beer down; then he looks quite resigned and ready to go, and says he don't hate nobody nor nothink in the world excep teetotallers and cold water.'

These little incidents gave a turn to their thoughts, and the four went out in good spirits. Mrs Newman that evening did as she was advised, and the next day felt decidedly better than she had been for some time. The topic of dreams was tabooed, none of the family, even in Mrs Newman's absence, feeling inclined to recur to it at present.

CHAPTER VIII.
MR LOCKSTABLE'S COURTSHIP.

Mr Bristley did not talk about his sister's dream, but it haunted him, and obscure hints which he let fall involuntarily betrayed the current of his thoughts.

'What shall we name the pup, now we have got him, Uncle Spines?' asked his niece one morning in the garden.

'What do you say to a Scriptural name?' he asked, in reply. 'How would it be to call him Mahcr-shalal-hash-baz?'

'A nice name to call up and down stairs!' said Lesbia, laughing. 'Mayors-shall-'olloa-hodge-podge – that's what people would turn it into. But what does it mean?'

'Spoil is nigh, pillage hasteneth.'

'No, no. I won't have my cub christened by such an ominous name, uncle. I've just thought of a good name for a white bulldog – Gossamer. It shortens well too. Goss! Goss!'

'Yes, that's a very good name, and, as you say, just suitable to a bull. Talking of dogs reminds me of another dependant of man, the horse. I want to see you start in the reformation of horseback for women, Lesbie. Having begun with the bicycle, this will come easy to you, and will be more easy for others to copy you in. It is not quite so novel, and has no element of danger.'

'Do you mean riding astride on horseback?'

'Just so. The lady's side-seat is the curse of the riding world. Foolish, awkward, uncomfortable, unsafe, there is not a good word to be said for it. It belongs to the age of tattooing and nose-rings.'

'I agree with you, Uncle Spines. I've often thought that circus girls riding astride are the only females who ever look well on horseback. But when and where shall I begin?'

'We'll take out the old pony and practise you a bit over gaps. When you get beyond him, I'll find you a proper mount. I shall consider that I spend money on an important social duty.'

The pony was a tough one who could bear a little knocking about, and in a few days Lesbia was quite at home in her new and more natural position on horseback. One afternoon, while she was practising backwards and forwards over a hedge and ditch on the glebe land, her uncle watching the performance, there appeared on the scene, from a gate which opened into the bottom of the field out of a lane, screened by a high bullfinch, three visitors, two ladies and a gentleman. They came just in time to see Lesbia get her third tumble, the edge of the ditch breaking under the pony's fore feet as he landed. The nimble young girl was up in a moment and mounted again as they came within distance to be recognised.

'Why, uncle!' she exclaimed, 'if here isn't Mr Lockstable under the protection of Letitia and Rose! How did you find us out?' she asked them as they approached.

'We called at the vicarage,' answered Athelstan, 'and that maid of yours, Fee-fofumsquintingpot, eh?'

'How absurd you are, Mr Lockstable!' Lesbia laughed; you never get that precious girl's name right. Fidgfumblasquidiot, can't you say?'

'Fiddlefumblehisidiot – no go – give it up.'

Lesbia shrieked.

'Yes, you'd better give it up; why don't you call her simply Fidge, as I do?'

'Well, Fidge, then; she told us you had the pony out for practice, and as we knew there are no hedges about here except in this direction, we struck right.'

'But how did you three get allied?' asked the vicar. 'Blemmyketts, Dimpleton, and Lockstable, an unlikely firm, eh? almost as unlikely as those people in that book you know – what's it called? – dear me – '

'Oh, ah, yes, indeed,' chimed in Mr Lockstable, 'what the deuce is the book called, and what the devil's the name of those people, you know, Miss Dimpleton, hang me, Miss Dimpleton – '

'I think the subject is not worth pursuing, Mr Lockstable,' said Rose, with a severe frown. But she might as well have frowned at a guide-post, for Athelstan was already rapt.

'Well, Lesbia, you soon pick up the bits, I will say,' observed Miss Blemmyketts, as she clasped her young friend's hand. 'And so glad to see you ride in that rational style. Some Philadelphian girls who were staying with us did it, but I guess they didn't tumble over fences as you do.'

'You've none of you told me yet, Miss Blemmyketts, how you three came to be in company,' said the vicar.

'Well, you see, Miss Dimpleton's our mutual friend, and Mr Lockstable happened to be making tracks here too, to see Lesbia's reformed riding, and we met him just as he reached the vicarage. That's how we came together, Mr Bristley, and not for nothing; but I hope Lesbia won't break her neck.'

'If I had considered that, Letty,' said Lesbia, 'I should never have learnt the bicycle. One thinks very little of falls from horseback, after one has been thrown over the head of a bike. Of course, one must be reasonably prudent on the machine, and trust the rest to luck.'

'Luck? I should prefer to place my trust higher than that, Lesbia,' said Rose Dimpleton, with a serious look at her.

'Quite right, Miss Dimpleton; we are all of us too thoughtless,' said the vicar. 'By the way, how are you progressing in your studies?'

'Thanks, my preparation goes on satisfactorily. But I should like to talk with you one day, Mr Bristley, since you are so kind as to ask me, about the Athanasian Creed.'

'With pleasure,' he replied. 'But you select a very difficult subject. I am quite inclined to believe that the compilation is that of a thinker, and that the spiritual constitution of man is its real theme. But it is a pity the thoughts are wrapped up in terms so far-fetched and obscure. The literal meaning is, of course, worthless.'

'Is it, Mr Bristley? I don't find it so obscure, but, of course, you know best. I should have thought it was manifest enough that the main theme of the Athanasian Creed is simply the greatest of the mysteries we are bound to receive, that of – '

'QUIRK, GAMMON & SNAP, bless your soul and body!' roared Mr Lockstable into her face, with the usual resounding slap on his thigh. 'Quirk, Gammon & Snap, *those* are your three chappies, eh?' still at Rose Dimpleton, and with a second slap that actually brushed the front of her black fur tippet as it descended.

'For shame!' cried the poor girl, flushing crimson, while the two other girls screamed, and Mr Bristley turned away before he could control himself sufficiently to say in a quiet tone, –

'With all deference to your theological acumen, of which I have the highest opinion, Mr Lockstable, I think you are making a slight confusion between the Athanasian Creed and *Ten Thousand a Year*. Unless I err – which is possible – the respectable trio you name belong to the novel, not to the Creed.'

'Aw – yes, that's correct, Bristley,' drawled the invocator. 'I wasn't thinking of creeds; in fact, I didn't quite hear what you were all saying. Miss Dimpleton, I apologise. Sorry to have been at cross purposes; but surely you didn't think I meant to imply that Mr Oily Gammon had anything to do with your creed? Should be awfully sorry.'

'You only put your foot in it more the further you go, Lockstable; you'd better not apologise,' laughed the vicar.

Rose Dimpleton gazed at him in stern silence.

'No; but really I hope you will forgive my awkwardness, Miss Dimpleton. On your own principles as a Christian, you should,' looking at her piteously.

Rose relented, smiling sweetly.

'So your principles are *not* those of a Christian, then? Well, say no more about it, Mr Lockstable. I see you can't help it, and I don't believe you mean any harm.'

'I don't indeed,' he replied; 'and in any case I should never mean any to you, I feel so uncomfortable when you are angry with me.'

'I'm not at all angry now,' she said gently.

'Tell you what,' Miss Blemmyketts half whispered to Lesbia, 'I guess friend Rose's forgiveness is getting a little more than Christian.'

'No?' exclaimed Athelstan. 'Not angry at all! Bravo! Then I feel all jolly again, as jolly, sir, as that fellow Eno, whom his daughter Lottie translated into a pillar of Fruit Salt – eh? But I'll not quote Scripture any more in your presence, Miss Dimpleton; I only make a mess of it.'

'Yes, you do,' said Rose, facing him with a boldness of look and tone which none present had ever known her exhibit before, and which took Athelstan Lockstable quite aback; a pleasant tremor ran through him, and he remained silent. Miss Blemmyketts nudged Lesbia, who nodded in reply, and even Mr Bristley involuntarily raised his eyebrows for the moment.

'I sorter kinder guess you're potted, my mannikin,' said Letitia, loudly enough only to be heard by Lesbia; but Lockstable met and understood the look Miss Blemmyketts fastened upon him, and he stood as one dazed with the suddenness of the prospect. He had never until now thought of Rose Dimpleton but as an acquaintance, but now there could be no doubt in his mind that she had taken a strong fancy to him, that the little collisions between them had broken the ice and ended in attraction. Why not, after all? She was a little young to marry, but they could wait a year or two if necessary. He had means to marry any girl who would have him, and he would choose her. Done; they would come to an understanding; the sooner the better. Miss Blemmyketts read everything that was passing in his mind, and good-naturedly gave him a lift.

'Lesbia,' she said, 'when you have done your practising, I should like to have a talk with you.'

'By all means,' she rejoined. 'I've knocked this poor beast about enough to-day; suppose we go back, uncle.'

On entering the house the two girls excused themselves, and retired to Lesbia's bedroom; the vicar did his part by saying, –

'I'm going to be unceremonious with you, Miss Dimpleton, I have business that may keep me half-an-hour or more; do you think now that if I were to leave you two alone together for that space, you could refrain from breaking each other's heads over some knotty point in theology?'

'I think we could, Mr Bristley,' Rose said.

There is no need to inflict upon the reader the common-places of a young couple who have just discovered that they are made for each other; such interviews generally are much in the same strain and have much the same ending. Lesbia and Letitia, meanwhile, had begun their *tête-à-tête*.

'Changed in the twinkling of a bedpost, isn't she?' said Letitia. 'Ah, these pious girls, when they do lay hold of their man, they grip like a grizzly b'ar, no getting out of the clutch; but I guess Lockstable will find his rose a sweet one. I like her, spite of her piety; she'll get over that when she begins married life.'

'My uncle would say, Letitia, that it is not desirable to get over piety. He would rather see it directed into its proper channel – woman-worship.'

'No doubt; but how long must we wait for that?'

'Not so long as many people suppose,' replied Lesbia. 'The pace is increasing, and if it increase up to a smash, all the better for the cause. But to come down from great matters to the small one we've been handling to-day, won't you join me in my reformed horseback initiative? You're a good rider, I suppose?'

'Yes, yes, as ladies go. I'll back you up by all means, and we'll go together. Blest pair of syrens, eh?'

We will suppose the curtain to drop upon the remainder of this interview and to rise again an hour afterwards upon the drawing-room, where enter our blest pair of syrens, followed by the vicar, to find Miss Dimpleton and Mr Lockstable sitting hand-in-hand upon the sofa in the bay-window, both looking radiant.

'I publish the banns of marriage,' gave out Mr Bristley in a nasal monotone, 'between divers sorts and conditions of persons here assembled. If any of you know any just cause or impediment why these parties, collectively, should not be joined together in holy matrimony, ye are now to declare it.'

'Then I declare,' said Lesbia, on the spur of the moment, 'that two of them are male-factors, and therefore ineligible to the agapemone.'

'Oh, indeed, that is the reason, is it? how very interesting!' said Mr Bristley.

Rose gave a keen glance at Lesbia and her friend, and the Vicar of Dulham looked like anything rather than a country parson as he bowed ceremoniously to his niece, gently rubbing his hands over each other.

'But, seriously,' he resumed, recovering his ordinary manner, 'I trust we may felicitate both you, Miss Dimpleton, and you, Mr Lockstable, on having at least explained away your occasional misunderstandings and become fast friends?'

'Yes, we're all right, thanks, Bristley,' answered Athelstan; 'in fact, one needn't beat round the bush. Miss Dimpleton has promised to think of no man but me when the time comes for her to choose a husband.'

'That is what I hoped, and I congratulate you heartily.'

'And I accept your good wishes with equal heartiness, Mr Bristley,' said Rose. 'But, Lesbia, dear, we've been very selfish, monopolising the drawing-room so long. How dull Letitia and you must have been, shut up together all this time, just that Mr Lockstable – I may call him Athelstan now – might discuss affairs with me!'

'Not a bit, my dear Rose, I asssure you,' answered Lesbia carelessly; 'we've been discussing the question of reformed horseback for women, and we've settled to work together in it as soon as circumstances permit.'

'That means as soon as you have a proper mount, Lesbie,' observed her uncle, smiling. 'Well, I'll do my best to bring about that concourse of atoms. Miss Blemmyketts, I presume, can mount herself.'

'Easily,' she replied. 'Binns of Frogmore lets out nags which will do for me. I'm pretty good at the old side scat, but I shall have to practise this new one, as Lesbia does.'

'Then I hope to see you make an appearance together in the hunting field before long,' said the vicar.

'Nothing I should like better,' said Miss Blemmyketts.

'But, uncle,' Lesbia objected, 'how about our dresses? These knickers and brown gaiters of mine do well enough for pony-practice, but if we're to appear at a meet, we ought to be dressed well.'

'Certainly, Lesbie,' returned her uncle. 'I would suggest the body to be of an ordinary cloth ladies' riding-habit. In place of the skirt, of course, tights – that is, knee-breeches of some strong stuff, say kersey or Bedford cord, buttoning, or better lacing, far enough below the knee not to ruck up and show a gap between them and the boot, which looks very untidy. Boots to be of thick patent leather and level at the top like a top-boot, not hollowed out behind like the military; I don't like that. Plated spurs, without rowels, which I consider both cruel and dangerous. For headgear, you'll do nothing better than a stiff black felt shooting-hat, very solid. The chimney pot, however low, is an abomination of the heathen, and the billycock is rather undress. Gloves, tan deerskin, better than dogskin. Hunting-crop without the thong, which is a nuisance, and there you are complete. Cost of the whole about seven pounds, I should say.'

'Very nice indeed, Uncle Spines; don't you think so Letty?'

'Very. I'll ask you to give the order for me too, Mr Bristley; you seem to understand it.'

'*Au revoir*, then, Letty,' said Lesbia, 'we'll drop you a line.'

The others took their leave at the same time, and at the bottom of the garden met Mrs Newman and Mrs Bristley coming in from a walk.

'Mamma,' said Lesbia, 'I expect shortly to have a new surprise for you.'

'I doubt that, Lesbie,' replied her mother. 'I am never surprised now at anything you may say or do. But you won't broach it at the clerical meeting to-morrow, I hope?'

'Oh, no; it's not important enough for that.'

CHAPTER IX.

MR BRISTLEY MOUNTS HIS HOBBY, AND BRINGS
THE DREAM UPON LESBIA.

WHEN the Vicar of Dulham held what he was pleased to call a clerical meeting at his home, it was well understood by all the guests that no parochial 'shop,' was to be talked, but instead of it, the politics and science of the great outside world were to form a sort of intellectual symposium, with the aid of good wines. A still more peculiar feature of these gatherings was the presence at table of the vicar's niece throughout the entire proceedings; the two holding firmly to the principle that whatever is fit to be said at all on any subject is fit to be said before women. This soon came to be understood by those who attended the meetings, and they chatted away just as if no female were present, the only slip of the tongue that had to be carefully avoided being any sort of commonplace implying inequalities or differences between the sexes; if such a slip were ever made, the hosts, of course, took it good-humouredly, but the unlucky person who had made it at once felt that he had committed a solecism.

On the present occasion, however, after other topics of the day had been well thrashed out, Mr Smeeth, the oldest acquaintance of the family, saw an opening to take the bull by the horns.

'But frankly, and in plain English, Bristley, am I to understand that the profession of arms ought, in your and Lesbia's opinion, to be thrown open to the ladies equally with the other callings?'

'Yes, decidedly, Mr Smeeth,' answered Lesbia at once. 'We can have no exceptions.'

'Of course not,' assented her uncle. 'To admit that there may be any one thing suitable for men, but not for women, would weaken our position. If a thing be good for either sex, it is good for both; if it be bad for either, it is bad for both. Of course this doctrine is bounded by the possibilities of nature. Physically, a man cannot bear children; spiritually, a man can have no sanctity, either inherent or delegated.'

'But he can lawfully pretend to have some, for a consideration,' said Mr Smeeth dryly, at which the others tittered.

'If his constituents please,' was the ready reply. 'If I refused pay to play the fool, I should be one.'

'Never mind that, uncle,' Lesbia checked him. 'What were you going to say about women and arms?'

'Why, I was going to say that preach as we will about the rights of morality to shape the conduct of the world, physical force will still remain in the background. Hence, so long as it is supposed that the female sex cannot compete with the male in the last resort, which is the resort to physical force, the rights we may concede to women will always appear as boons, as privileges existing upon sufferance. And previously to the march of modern science, this, no doubt, was actually the case. The bigger heavier animal, purposely trained in athletic habits from which the smaller though more highly organised animal was as purposely debarred, had an undeniable advantage over her with the club, the battle-axe, the bow, the cutlass. But those times are rapidly passing away. Fire-arms of precision, whereby you are picked off by an invisible enemy a mile or more distant, are beginning to take the place of the old hand-to-hand *mêlée*; mere gallantry and dash avails ever less and less against cool skill. Even in the works of peace, automatic machinery is every year more widely supplanting the brawny arm of the labourer or smith; in short, it is a patent fact that the steady and relentless progress of nineteenth century civilisation is neutralising, one by one, those physical advantages which men formerly possessed over women in the struggle for existence.'

'Your inference from which, I suppose,' said Mr Dimpleton, the father of Rose, who was among the clergy present, 'is that we ought to set on foot female regiments along with the others?'

'I think the military strength of every nation might be advantageously increased by enrolling as a volunteer corps such strong, and perhaps not very intellectual, young women as might take to the life from choice. Such a change would, in my belief, rather conduce to the maintenance of general peace. It would bring home to women the miseries of war, if they were liable to take part in it personally, and men might on their account also be less willing to engage in bloodshed. But whether this be so or not, as my niece observed just now, we can admit no distinctions. If women are to descend into the arena of life, they must do so without reserve.'

'Will public opinion in this country ever sanction such a revolutionary innovation, think you?' asked another parson.

'Public opinion may have to accommodate itself to that and other changes, whether sanctioning them or not,' returned Mr Bristley, in a somewhat defiant tone. 'Revolution, when it comes, does not ask leave of people's prejudices. And I have an undefined but very pronounced feeling that we want in England, and shall very shortly have, the new broom that sweeps clean. We are getting socially and politically demoralised, – losing tone; and the reason is not far to seek. Our actions as a nation are not up to our words. We talk of progress and free thought, but in morals and religion we progress not at all, and our thoughts, on those subjects, are not free. We are still wrapped up in our old insular bigotry, while we lack, whether for better or for worse, our old insular hardihood. Puff and pretentiousness take the place of solid earnestness in public relations, vulgarity in taste is becoming rampant – witness the stuff that is now most popular in literature, in the drama, and in music. Unavowed Nihilism seems to undermine social sincerity; and if we are less superstitious, we are more materialistic. Nevertheless, all this might pass muster, if only it could be regarded as a transitional state of things, incidental to the most important of all developments mankind has ever undergone or can undergo, the emancipation of the female half of the race. But that still hangs fire; the heart of the community is not in it, mainly, I suppose for the reason that the heart of the community is not to-day in anything that is not either sordid or frivolous. But this cannot last, on the face of it. We shall be called to account, depend upon it, for our national sins both of omission and commission, and I should not be surprised if the day of reckoning were much nearer than any one of us suspects. What's the matter, Lesbie; do you feel unwell?'

The young girl had turned ghastly pale, and some small beads of perspiration were starting from her forehead, while her eyes had a fixed stare. But the attack, whatever it was, passed quickly, and as her colour came back, she smiled at the company, saying, –

'Nothing, nothing, uncle; only a little dizziness; perhaps the port wine hasn't agreed with me; but I don't feel it now.'

'I never knew this port disagree with anyone: I don't think it can be that,' said Mr Bristley. 'Send it on, Smeeth, – no? Well, if nobody'll have any more, shall we go to coffee in the drawing-room?'

Shortly afterwards the vicar had an opportunity of speaking to his niece alone.

'It's unlucky, Lesbie dear, that you should have an attack of vertigo to-day. But just at your age little things of that sort needn't alarm one.'

'It was hardly what you'd call vertigo, Uncle Spines, – rather a sort of trance; perhaps I inherit the disposition from mamma. What happened exactly was this: Your last words, about a day of reckoning, had the effect of bringing before me a part of my mother's dream, as if I were dreaming it myself. I seemed to hear the notes of bugles mingled with heavy rolling thunder, and a curious dropping noise as if a cataract of loose stones kept slipping over a precipice. I didn't see anything horrid; all I saw was a desolate hill with a tower like a lighthouse on its top, and a volume of white smoke, such as would come from a number of weed-heaps burning on a mild moist day; then there came a rainbow over all, and the noise ceased. I suppose I must have been what the mesmerists call *en rapport* with the past state of my mother's mind when she had that awful vision. I wonder if she herself was thinking about it at the moment. I don't like to ask her, because I want her to forget all about it; and, after all, my bit of a phantasm was a trifle to hers, poor darling mamma!'

'Don't like these women's visions at all,' Mr Bristley muttered to himself, looking deeply concerned. 'Come, Lesbia,' he said, turning back toward the dining-room, 'it's plain you're getting out of sorts. Come and correct the port with a whitewash of Madeira, eh?'

'You're very practical, Uncle Spines,' she answered, with a merry laugh; 'but I won't exorcise the demon in that ignoble way. No, no, enough wine for to-day, thanks; it may have been only a little biliousness, and if so, I oughtn't to have taken any wine at all. If it comes again, I'll have some medicine; but I don't think it will, somehow.'

CHAPTER X

REFORMED HORSEBACK IN A RUN WITH THE FROGMORE.

IT was a dull grey morning in December; the two friends who were to start Reformed Horseback stood before the fire in the vicarage drawing-room, dressed exactly according to Mr Bristley's design already described. Lesbia showed to the better advantage, because her waist had never been pinched in by stays, nor her feet by shoes which jam the great and little toe together into a point like a well-cut cedar pencil, still less by those abominable stilt heels which torture the foot into the shape of an inverted U. Poor Letitia Blemmyketts had undergone all these barbarities, but nevertheless she contemplated the rounded robust figure of her athletic young friend with an admiration unmixed with any of that jealousy an inferior mind might have felt.

'I congratulate you on your figure, love,' she said. 'I see you have never been waspified, – wish I hadn't!'

'Never been what, Letty?'

'Waspified; your waist squeezed in like a wasp's by those cussed stays. The waspification of girls by tight lacing is the ruin of their bodies, as 'weakervesselism' is the ruin of their minds. Good-morning, Mr Bristley; you find me just spitefully envious of this young beauty of yours. I guess she could digest a boa-constrictor, and guess a boa constrictor couldn't digest me: my hips are too sharp.'

'That's not the part of you which is sharp, my dear Miss Blemmyketts,' said the vicar, as he shook hands with her. 'What have you to complain of? Probably the greater part of the people who will see you to-day will prefer your figure to Lesbia's.'

'Don't care a cuss for the approval of a pack of fools,' she answered bitterly. 'I can't have my own, because of my waspification. Cuss'd be the waspifiers and deformers of girls, I say. I should like to see them all wedded to the Iron Maiden of Nuremberg. That would tighten them up *à la mode* to their hearts' content, and also to the content of sensible people.'

'Please, sir, breakfast's ready,' said Fidge, putting in her head, after having fumbled a minute at the door handle.

Meanwhile the two hunters, a bay hired by Miss Blemmyketts and a dappled grey, almost white, mare, about fifteen and a half hands, which the vicar, who had been a hunting man in his college days and was a judge of horseflesh, had bought for his niece – were sent on to the meet in charge of a boy whom Mr Bristley employed occasionally; while the whole party, including the two elder ladies, who liked going now and then to a meet to see their acquaintances, were to start later in the pony-carriage. At ten o'clock they drove off, the two girls in the small back seat, while the three elders managed to crush into the roomy front.

It was still a cold grey morning, with the wind in the east, and the party were well wrapped up in skins and rugs. On their way they had to pass through the town of Frogmore, stopping a minute at Bummingby's for a parcel.

'How's the bicycle, ma'am?' inquired the ironmonger of Lesbia, as he put the packet in the carriage.

'Oh, she's all right, thank you, Mr Bummingby, – had no mishaps since I saw you last. But the season's about over for a few weeks; we're going to hunt this morning, you can see.'

'Well, that is a novelty, ma'am!' exclaimed the tradesman, as he surveyed with admiration all that was visible of the young ladies' costume.

On getting clear of the town, they shortly came in sight of some water on the left, and about two miles further passed near where a solitary group of poplars could be seen on its brink. From that time until they neared the meet, continual shouts of laughter from Miss Blemmyketts made the occupants of the front seat look round repeatedly.

'What *is* the joke, girls?' Mrs Newman at last inquired.

'It's this unfeminine daughter of yours doing irate bargee,' answered Letitia.

Lesbia had pointed out to her the place where she and the Frogmore bicyclists had been ferried over by Bill and Joe that summer afternoon, and was doing her best to reproduce the scene, language and all, for the American's benefit.

'Now, really, Lesbia,' her mother remonstrated, 'one would have thought you'd been ashamed of that affair, instead of dwelling on the recollection and making fun of it. Come, here's something better to engage your attention; look at the red coats! What a large field for such a nasty day!'

The meet was on a broad village green with a guide-post at cross roads; the servants and the dogs were moving about, waiting for the master, who was not always very punctual. Eleven was the nominal hour, it was now a quarter past. About a hundred and thirty riders of all sorts were present, including some dozen ladies. Several carriages were standing in the road, Lady Humnoddie's, with herself and her two daughters, being among them. As Mr Bristley's boy brought the nags to be mounted, it struck Lesbia for the first time how conspicuous she would be in her new style on her white steed.

'It's my belief, Uncle Spines,' she said, 'that if you could get my name painted in large black letters upon the sun, you wouldn't hesitate to do it. Why did you choose a white horse for me?'

'For the reason you state, Lesbie. When one is setting a new fashion, it is an object to be conspicuous.'

'But one ought to ride better than I do before coming forward in such a character.'

'I don't see that; you ride quite well enough; there's a deal of luck in hunting. Don't let your mare blow herself, and don't follow anyone in particular; choose your own place at the fences; you'll be quite as safe, and do yourself more credit.'

'I'll do my best, but I feel a little nervous,' she said.

'So do I,' added Miss Blemmyketts. 'Not a little; I'm all in a twitter.'

'Others here feel nervous too, depend upon it,' said Mr Bristley, 'those who really mean riding to the hounds.'

The two young girls now threw off their over garments, got out of the carriage, and mounted astride in public. This did not, however, attract very much attention, until Lady Humnoddie, who could not resist the temptation to quiz, called out to them, standing up in her barouche, –

'Here, reformers! come and show yourselves this way. I want to examine you.'

After this it ran rapidly through the meet that the two neat little riders in dark costumes were young ladies mounted astride; and now numbers of people rode near and past them, scrutinising as closely as good manners would permit, some making remarks as they moved off which were just audible to the girls' quick ears, such as 'New idea that; what do you think of it?' 'Not bad; I wonder it's not been done before.' 'I say, here's the nineteenth century come out strong at its close!' 'Ah, never saw that before; very neat though, I will say.' 'Just look; there's that eccentric parson Bristley brought out some girls astride!' 'H'm; I don't dislike it; they're devilish well got up, and they sit well.' 'Ha! that's original. Wants a little brass to start, but, after all, it's more natural than the lady's seat, and better for the horse, else why don't *we* ride side-saddle?'

From these and like observations our two girls gathered that their reception was on the whole favourable. Two or three of the more old-fashioned lady members of the hunt regarded the innovation with displeasure; but there was something in the demeanour of the two friends which made those who were inclined to be bitter against them think it well to reserve the expression of their opinions for occasions when the objects of them were not present. The master now arrived, and after excusing himself to those nearest for being late, started with the huntsman for cover at a steady trot.

'Take care of yourselves; don't be rash,' called out Mrs Bristley from the carriage, turning round to go home. The two girls replied by a wave of the hand, not very comfortably spared, as the nags were already pulling under them in the excitement of the move.

The route to the first cover usually drawn from that meet lay by a cart-track through a line of gates. It was a small square gorse, so called, but of late years it had grown more blackthorn than gorse, and was fenced in with hedge and ditch. Our two girls, partly, it must be said, from the eagerness of their horses, reached it among the first, and were much interested by watching the throw off.

'Go hark, hark, hark! yoi! my beauties, go hark, hark!' called the huntsman, cracking his thong, while his horse backed about in elegant curvetings.

'How funny that all the dogs have the same name!' remarked Miss Blemmyketts to her friend, as they drew up side by side. 'If they're all called Hark, how does he know one from another?'

A gentleman in red who came up at that moment, pretending to have his eyes fixed on the hounds leaping and scrambling into the thicket, but really with a view to study our two girls' costume, bent forward and said with a smile, –

'I think you are under a mistake; Hark is not the name of any dog, it's only a way of sending hounds in to thread the cover and turn out a fox if there is one.'

'Thank you, sir,' said Miss Blemmyketts; 'and do you think there is one in this little place?'

'I'm afraid not,' he replied; 'but we shall know in a minute or two. Ah, I thought so – blank,' he added, as a single short note on the horn came from the other side of the cover.

'What's blank, sir?' asked Miss Blemmyketts.

'Drawn blank; that is, there's no fox. Never mind, we shall find at Midham Leys, if we don't before.'

'Pray, is it far to Midham Leys?' inquired Lesbia.

'Why, yes, it's nearly three miles. You can just see the top of the wood over the rising ground. There are several little spinnies to be drawn on the way; if we don't find in them, we're sure, at all events, at the big wood. I've hunted twenty years over this country, and never knew Midham Leys drawn blank yet.'

The trot was resumed until they reached the first of the spinnies; it was tedious work the drawing blank of one little copse after another, but the popping over gaps out of the lane which it entailed, settled our two girls in their saddles and wore away their nervousness. They were among the first to enter the long straggling wood of Midham Leys when at last it was reached, between one and two o'clock. They entered through a narrow hand-gate, and after traversing some three hundred yards of wet deep slough called a ride, they were arrested by the halt of the column of horsemen of which they formed part; the master, who now pushed to the front, holding up his hand on reaching a wide circular space whence several rides diverged. Here our two girls, sitting at ease on their horses like the rest, chatted freely to each other, their somewhat naïve observations being listened to in silent amusement by their hunting neighbours. The same gentleman in red who had given them information before happened to be near them again.

'There!' he suddenly exclaimed; 'didn't a hound speak?'

'Speak, sir?' said Miss Blemmyketts, opening her eyes wide.

'Speak – that is, whimper.'

'Whimper, sir, why? has he got scratched by a bramble?'

'No,' replied the gentleman, after a second's pause, 'he wants to tell us that a fox is afoot.'

'In what sense is a fox a foot, sir? More than a foot long, sure-ly?' inquired Miss Blemmyketts.

'I mean,' explained the gentleman, biting his lips, 'that he has got scent of a fox and is trying to let the other hounds know it. There it is again, don't you hear? No doubt about it. They've found.'

'Tallyho, over!' holloaed the huntsman from lower down the wood. 'Over – over – over – over!'

'Just keep an eye down that next ride, gentlemen, will you,' said the master, turning his head.

The hounds were now in full cry through the wood, and our two girls, who heard the sound for the first time, began to feel the excitement.

'Yoi over – over – over!' called another, who was in front down that ride.

'Now, ladies,' said the good-natured one who had spoken to them before, 'you can help us too. Keep your eyes fixed down this third ride, and you'll most likely see the fox cross from right to left.'

'There he goes!' exclaimed Lesbia, raising herself in her stirrups and pointing with her crop.

'Right you are. Yoi over – yoi over – over – over – over – over!'

'Can't go on like this, I should think; he must break soon,' said a farmer in grey coat, gaiters, and white cords, close by Miss Blemmyketts.

'Poor creature, I hope not!' she exclaimed in a disappointed tone. 'Guess he'd hardly carry his tail so sprightly if he were going to break.'

This was too much for the politeness of her hearers, and laughter exploded on all sides. But the next moment there came the voice of the first whip from the end of the wood.

'Tally-ho, gone away! Gone away – away – away – away!'

Bridles shortened up, hats jammed on heads, heels dug into horses' flanks, a thundering, floundering, splashing, dashing, helter-skelter rush down the long ride after the tooting horn, not a few knees bruised in crowding out of the hand-gate – in this fashion, the open field was reached, the pack streaming over it in full chorus. Our two novices had a good place, but they had not got away scatheless. Miss Blemmyketts had her right eye closed by a huge clot of wet mud, kicked up from the quagmire by the horse next in front of her, and with difficulty she cleared her sight by hastily smearing the mud down over her cheek. Lesbia had a worse mishap; her mare stumbled in one of the deep grips of the ride, and as the girl was not prepared, she was thrown so much forward over the pommel that her face met the mare's head as she jerked it up in recovering, thereby giving her rider a nasty blow on the mouth, as well as making her nose bleed. Thus, the one with her face half-masked by dirt, the other with blood trickling over her chin, they settled into their stride across the open, and began to taste the not unmixed pleasures of fox-hunting.

The scent was good, the line of country mostly grass, the fences fair, and both girls did credit to the reformed style, Lesbia generally giving the lead to her friend. The run had lasted about twenty minutes without a check, the fox making straight up wind; our two girls were still in the first flight, and a few yards in rear of the master – who was a hard man to beat – when they crossed a large pasture which they had entered over a small double rail and ditch. The master here bore away to the left, toward a gap visible in the formidable stake-and-bind fence which bounded the field on its opposite side, and toward the middle part of which the hounds were running. This move was followed by the rest of the field, including Miss Blemmyketts, for reasons which they judged sufficient, after a cursory glance at the stake-and-bind; but Lesbia, whose courage was rather warmed than otherwise by her little misadventure at the start, determined to stick to the hounds as long as possible, and trust to the chapter of accidents for getting out of the pasture. Arrived at the gap, the master and huntsman found that it had been lately repaired, two sheep-hurdles having been bound together in it, end upwards, with wire, and supported by very sharp stakes, which again had been wattled at the bottom.

'What's to do now, Miller?' said the master; 'they've been playing the deuce here!'

'Yes, Sir Richard,' answered the huntsman. 'I'd better try and pull that hurdle down; it won't do as it is, I reckon.'

He was off his horse in a moment and tugging away at the vexatious obstacle, which was well anathematised by eager riders coming up one after another; but it was quite three minutes before they could get the place open enough to be passed without a certainty of staking the horses.

Meanwhile Lesbia, not in the line of the pack, but a good many yards on one side – a rule of riding her uncle had carefully impressed on her – was steering cheerfully for a place of a very different sort. It was a gap in the high top of the stake-and-bind, barred across by a quite new timber railing. She felt a little trepidation during the short breathing-time afforded while the hounds were climbing the high and difficult fence; but her mare was already pricking her ears and shortening under her in that peculiar bucking whereby a good hunter seems to convey to his rider, 'I can do it, if you'll let me.' A bold horse makes more than half the boldness of the rider; Lesbia took her decision at once, kept her shoulders down, elbows in, head erect and knees well closed on the saddle, as the mare charged the formidable place. A violent spring that tried her seat, a splintering crash under her, a deep swoop down, and she was striding away over the ridge and furrow, alongside of the pack, and alone, not having even slipped a stirrup.

'Criky!' exclaimed the master, whose attention had been diverted from his accursed hurdle by curiosity as to what Lesbia meant to do; 'that was an ugly one, and no mistake. Who's that lad, d'ye know, Miller?'

'It's not a lad, Sir Richard, it's a young lady,' gasped the huntsman as, very red and hot, he scrambled back and caught his bridle.

'A girl! the devil – you don't mean to say so! I never saw anything like it. We sha'n't catch her now; they're going like smoke.'

The huntsman then put his horse at the gap, knocking out two of the pointed stakes in his passage; the master followed, and Miss Blemmyketts was the first after him. They put on all the pace they could, but only to hear the distant music of the hounds, and now and then see over intervening hedges the head and shoulders of the solitary rider flying along with them.

Lesbia's initiation into hunting had not been all smooth, but she had now the very cream of the sport, and no longer felt any pain in her swollen upper lip and nose. The fox could not have taken a better line *of* country, mainly grass pastures with a plough, stubble, or turnip at intervals; and as she crossed them at a swinging gallop, with plenty of time to take a pull at every fence, now a trim quickset in and out of a road, now a succession of common hedges with double ditch, now a bullfinch twelve or fifteen feet high, which the strong mare cleft as if it were a paper-hoop, now and then a stile where the hedge was impracticable, and two or three locked five-barred gates, over which she rose with an easy lift, the young girl experienced a physical exhilaration beyond what she had known before, as also a feeling of triumph at having shown her new style of horseback to advantage by distancing the field.

Presently the ground began to rise, and on passing the crest and beginning to descend, a wide grass valley opened before her, along the middle of which was visible that ominous line of pollard willows which makes many a straight-going man reconsider his position. But Lesbia had no hesitation about her now, and as she sailed away by the chorusing pack, her only thought was whether she could jump or would have to swim. As the gleam of the brook came in sight, she pulled up for a few seconds to choose her place, then, sitting well down in the saddle, let the mare rush. A powerful effort, and some twenty feet of water swept away behind her, the edge of the bank breaking where she landed, and causing a struggle but no fall. Half the pack was still swimming the stream whilst she galloped, standing in stirrups, up the opposite slope almost abreast of the leading hound, who was pointing straight for a group of large and remarkable grass mounds with a hawthorn or two growing on their summits. It was an ancient tumulus, and had been the scene of antiquarian excavations some years before. Of late it had been abandoned to rabbits, and for that reason was a favourite earth for foxes. A regular passage inwards, large enough for a wheelbarrow, had been cut by the explorers, and a footpath led close by. It so happened that on this afternoon an Irish labourer who was employed in the neighbourhood every autumn, was passing the spot, when he heard the hounds, and presently saw them coming like smoke down the meadows, with the white steed stretched out in full gallop a few yards on their right rear. Having before seen a run end at these mounds, a happy thought struck him; he ran into the cutting and threw himself flat on his stomach near the entrance, with his head out, to watch the event. Sure enough, in another minute appears the beaten fox, making straight toward him. Up jumps Pat – 'Dhivel a bit, ye varrment! an it's skhulking into the earrth ye'd be afther – get along wid ye, ye halting spalpeen!' and first his hatchet then his hat whirled after the scared animal, who turned and went at random northwards, parallel with the brook, not knowing what he was about, his howling pursuers now in full view and gaining upon him every second.

Meanwhile, the master and the huntsman, seeing there was no saving the rest of the run unless by a chance of cutting in, took their course, followed by the rest, toward an eminence which commanded a view of the grass valley and the brook. Arrived there, they pulled up and looked in the direction of the cry.

'We're quite out of it,' said the master. 'Yonder they go right across the valley; Eastwold Mounds is his point: I thought it would be. Now then, how will that young Amazon tackle the brook? There! She's over! Capital, upon my word!'

'Well done, Lesbia!' ejaculated Miss Blemmyketts at his side. They all had seen the leap which, being at a bend in the brook, was taken broadside to the spectators.

'Eh? she's a friend of yours?' asked Sir Richard, turning with sudden interest on hearing the girl's voice from one mounted and dressed in the same style as our heroine.

'Yes, that's my intimate friend Lesbia Newman, sir,' said Letitia; 'we came out together; but she's too good a rider for me.'

'So she is for all of us, it would seem, Miss – I haven't the pleasure of knowing your name.'

'Miss Blemmyketts – Letitia Blemmyketts of Brooklyn, New York, sir.'

'Thank you; I took the liberty of asking, because I have heard of your friend Miss Newman through the Guinea-bushes of – there now! how odd! the fox must have got headed and missed his point; they're turning to the left, by Jove! Come along, we'll see the finish yet perhaps.'

Away they all cantered down the slope towards a hamlet, through which a stony by-road led over the brook by a bridge. The clatter of hoofs on the hard bottom and the glint of scarlet – for the sun shone out now – scurrying past the windows, brought out many a small brat to the cottage doors, shouting with glee, 'Oh, ma! 'ere are some fox-hunters!'

The houses past, they turned into the fields by a gate on the right and trotted up another rise, where they halted again. The cry was nearing rapidly, but the hedges between were too tall for anything to be seen yet.

'Here they are!' exclaimed Miss Blemmyketts, as at last the hounds came pouring over a gate into the furthest field visible from where they were.

'Hold hard, gentlemen, please,' said the master; 'no use riding to meet 'em; not a bit; let 'em come, let 'em come.'

The next moment the white mare topped the gate in first-rate form; then the cry ceased suddenly behind the near hedge, and Lesbia was seen to pull up and dismount in the middle of the same field.

'All right, they've run into him!' exclaimed the master. 'Try and save the fur, Miller; that young lady has won it well.'

'Yes, she has indeed, Sir Richard,' and the huntsman dashed off as hard as he could. The whips and several of the field trotted after him.

'Fifty-three minutes from breaking cover, or just an hour from find to finish,' said the master, taking out his watch as he jogged in the same direction by the side of the American girl. As he spoke the horn sounded several blasts, and the well-known Whoo – oop! mingled with the renewed chorus of the hounds.

'I congratulate you, Miss Newman, it's been the fastest thing this season, and you've had it all to yourself ever since you beat us at that ugly place,' said the master, dismounting to shake hands with our heroine. 'Devilish fine fencer that mare of yours, and very plucky of you both to go at that rail; I was afraid it wouldn't break. Fortune favours the brave. Now you must be blooded – I presume this is your first kill in the open?' So saying, he approached her again, with the dripping brush in his hand. 'Why there's blood upon your face already! How's that? No, don't wipe it off, it's an honourable scar.'

'Mare tripped at the start in the big wood, and threw up her head; it's nothing, Sir Richard, thanks,' answered Lesbia, all aglow.

'No, that's a small mishap; but you had a fine piece of luck at that rail, I can tell you. It was quite a relief to see you safe over; and even when you had broken it, I don't think anyone followed you. Now for the rite,' – and he drew the sanguinary stump down each of her cheeks. 'By the way, aren't you the young lady who had from the Guineabushes a bull pup by my dog?'

'Yes, they gave me a milk-white one, a beauty; I've named him Gossamer; I hope he'll be my pet for years to come.'

After more friendly chat about the run, Lesbia, in her war-paint, with the brush suspended to the cantle of her saddle, the mask and pads tied on the pommel, rode up to Miller and slipped a half sovereign into his hand – he had saved the fur for her with difficulty, as the dogs were savage – and then jogged home by the road with her friend, reaching Dulham, a distance of eleven miles, just before dusk.

The vicar had come out on foot a little way in hope to meet them.

'Who is this that cometh from Edom – why, Lesbie, you sanguinary barbarian! I wish you joy of your blushing honours: you bear them thick upon you, with a vengeance!'

'Yes, Uncle Spines, sanguinary barbarian is the right word. A small part of the blood is my own, however; I can't help wishing it were all so. They talk of hounds running for blood, but I have been running for it too.'

'Oh, that's all right, Lesbie, you needn't have any scruples of that sort; I can soon prove that to you. But what have you had to eat and drink all day?'

'The sandwiches and my sherry-flask supplied our wants.'

'Why didn't you stop at a pub and have a tankard, or three of Irish hot?' asked her uncle.

'I was afraid Letty would take too much, and get to using bad language.'

'I like that, you bargee!' laughed Letitia, striking at her with her crop. 'Guess I'd have to get up early, across the pond, to hear such language as yours in the pony-chase this morning.'

The American accompanied them to the vicarage to stay that night. As the family party sat at dessert, talking over the events of the day, the vicar remarked, –

'By the way, Lesbie, about your scruples against being accessory to the death of a fox, the answer to them is obvious. Foxes owe their lives and their enjoyments of life entirely to the practice of fox-hunting, for which they are preserved. Put a stop to that sport, and within a year foxes will be as scarce in England as wolves. A price will be set on their heads by farmers, game-keepers, and poultry breeders, and they will be shot, trapped, and poisoned out of hand. Is that a better fate than the prospect of being occasionally chased during the winter months and perhaps caught at last? If I were a fox, I should not think so. I should be only too glad to compound for my life and liberty on such easy terms. No; if you like to take up other grounds of objection against fox-hunting, they may be debateable. For instance, it might be questioned whether the sport be worth the destruction of edible animals which foxes prey on. Or farmers may change their mind and not care to have their fences broken and their fields trampled by the hunt, or they may conceive a grudge against the country gentry, and thence discourage the sport. Or various social causes, like those which have prevented the sport from taking root on the Continent, may operate against its continuance here. All these may be open questions, but I think it must be clear to you, Lesbie, that arguments against fox-hunting on the ground of cruelty to animals will not hold water.'

'I see,' his niece replied; 'you have relieved my conscience, Uncle Spines. I certainly should have been sorry not to go out again, now that I have made a good beginning.'

CHAPTER XI.
MORE COUNTRY LIFE.

LESBIA'S achievements described in the preceding chapter soon made her both known and popular in the county, at all events among the intelligent portions of its society. During the rest of that winter she and her friend made regular appearances in the hunting field, so often indeed that her uncle felt it incumbent upon him to send a subscription on her account. From hunting the young girl could easily have passed to shooting and fishing had she been so disposed; but though her uncle would have helped her, and she had no lack of invitations, she remained content with hunting, and did not care to launch into the other field sports. Manly games, however, came natural to her, football and cricket both claimed her attention in their respective seasons; and as she was not hampered with skirts, she could take her part in these on equal terms with men. Hardly an out-door or in-door exercise could be named in which she did not join with a capacity and a zest unknown to other girls, who had to compete with each other and with men, trammeled by the old and stupid fashion. She was getting 'as hard as nails ' in body and mind, – as indifferent to bruises and blows as to the taunts of 'weakervesselish' women, for whom she never took the trouble to conceal her contempt. Not that she was ever inconsiderate toward any one of either sex on account of weak health or other infirmity; it was only the prejudices of those who wished to keep her sex in the old grooves, which she snarled against and set her heel upon.

Playing one afternoon in the following summer at Ruddy-mere at lawn-tennis, a game in which her dress, of course, gave her a great advantage over other girls who had had much more practice, she happened to have as an opponent a Mr Julius Dandidimmons, a young loafer without any brains to speak of, who looked upon women generally as his inferiors by nature. On Lesbia's making some clever stroke, he remarked, –

'Well done, Miss Newman; you really play very well, for a lady.'

This riled Lesbia, but she said nothing, watched her opportunity, and when they happened to be both near the net, she returned the ball with her favourite stroke and caught him such a stinger in the face that he had to retire from the game, followed by Lesbia's apology.

'Dear me, Mr Dandidimmons, what a pity! Too smart *for a lady*, wasn't it? I'm afraid you napped that heavily on your whisker-bed, as St Thomas Aquinas hath it.'

'St Thomas Aquinas!' exclaimed Rose Dimpleton, who was in the four.

'Not St Thomas Aquinas?' asked Lesbia innocently; 'well then, the *Sporting Slap-up*, which was his organ, or some other equal authority.'

Several of the other ladies gathered round the wounded Julius; Lesbia presently came too, but only to punish him more under the guise of sympathy.

'I hate that Miss Newman,' he afterwards confided to some intimate friends; 'she's not a bit like a gurl, – quite unsexed, a regular hoyden, don't you know. I like gurls to be gurls, soft and feminine, don't you know – but, for gracious' sake, don't tell her I said so!'

Rowing in four and pair outriggers and sometimes in a skiff alone, was another of Lesbia's out-door exercises this summer. The river to which she had to go for this purpose was the same across which the memorable ferry had taken her with the bicyclists, and it was some members of that club who got up such boating as was to be had on its rather narrow water. It was better than none, however, and further up there was a wider reach, where racing was practicable. Lesbia rowed sometimes bow, other times stroke, and everyone admired the easy and powerful style she had acquired. One bright evening just before sunset, as she pulled down past the well-remembered group of poplars, two big rough-looking men on the bank saluted her respectfully. She did not recognise them at first, but they had recognised her, and a second glance showed her that they were none other than the identical bargees. Poor Bill and Joe! we shall meet with them once more in this story; but on a very different scene.

CHAPTER XII.
SEEING LETTIE OFF.

THE autumn came round, and would no doubt have passed in the same pleasant mode of life, had not Letitia Blemmyketts been wanted back by her people at home. Lesbia was the first person to whom the letter was read, then Lady Humnoddie, who had shown Letitia much hospitality. The next day Lesbia met Rose Dimpleton at a quiet luncheon at Letitia's lodging, the only other person present being the landlady Miss Skimpsalt. Here they discussed their plans how to make the most of the remaining short time, although pleasure-seeking on the eve of separation is rather a half-hearted affair, and the two girls really thought more of spending the time together than of going out.

'I guess you're more fortunate than we are, Rose,' said Letitia; 'we shall soon be parted for some time at least, while you'll have the pleasure of looking forward to become Mrs Lockstable.'

'Your parting will be worse than a divorce, I've no doubt,' answered Rose, looking at Lesbia, 'but depend upon it, Letitia won't leave you for long.'

'I hope not, Miss Dimpleton,' said Miss Skimpsalt. 'My little house will be void and desolate when she is gone.'

'Not for ever, I hope, Miss Skimpsalt,' said Letitia; 'but, Lesbie, you must get your uncle to step with you over the puddle one day to see me, and we'll all run up to the Falls for a tryst. But, listen now, to be practical, I've an idea to draw out the parting. Why shouldn't you and your uncle just go with me for a short trip as far as Queenstown?[2] You'd see something of the south of Ireland, and you could run back by Dublin and Holyhead. I guess it's no use asking you, Rose?'

'Thanks no, Letitia, I'm a shocking sailor. Folkestone to Boulogne's more than enough for me.'

Lesbia approved, and on reaching home at once mentioned the proposal to her uncle, who fell in with it readily. After some consultation, it was settled that his niece and he should accompany Miss Blemmyketts as far as the Irish coast, the two elder ladies not caring to face a sea passage merely for pleasure. Eventually the three went to London, and after staying a night at the Great Western Hotel, Paddington, ran down by the morning express on that line to Milford Haven, where they put up at the Railway Hotel, New Milford, the Cork steamer not leaving until the following evening. They had rather a rough passage by her, but none of our party suffered from sea-sickness or looked any the worse when they met in the saloon for breakfast; the vessel having been delayed in departure, the captain said it would be past noon before they could make Cork Harbour.

When they met on deck afterwards, there was some fog, and the Irish coast loomed dark through it, the great waves lashing up fiercely against rock-bound islets.

'What a forbidding country!' Lesbia said to her friend. 'It suggests to my mind that horrid name of the Dark and Bloody Land.'

'No,' answered Letitia; 'that name's our property, and I shall bring an action against you if you steal it. It was given to Kentucky. After all, I guess you mustn't judge of poor Ireland by the outside. Wait till you've been inside a bit.'

Presently they came in view of a headland, on the summit of which stood out conspicuously a rather low, round white lighthouse. This, for some unexplained reason, attracted Lesbia's attention strongly.

'Do you know that place?' she asked of Letitia, who was sitting on a camp-stool by her.

'Yes, that's Roche's Tower, and just below it is Roche's Point, the entrance to Cork Harbour. As soon as we get well round that point, we shall sight Queenstown, and then your little watering pilgrimage will be over, Lesbia. My voyage will continue without you, worse luck! I sha'n't enjoy it a bit, having left you behind. What on earth makes you stare so at that fumbling old lighthouse up there? You don't hear what I'm saying, Lesbia.'

'Roche's Tower did you say they call it?' asked Lesbia excitedly, unheeding her friend's reproach.

'Certainly, Roche's Tower. Why? Or rather why not? What's the matter with it?'

'*I've seen it before!*' Lesbia exclaimed, looking dazed.

'Indeed!' said Letitia. 'Didn't know you'd ever been this way.'

'I have not, that's the extraordinary part of it,' answered Lesbia; 'nevertheless, as sure as I stand here, *I've seen that place before*. I know perfectly well that steep gloomy hill in the fog, with the old lonely lighthouse on the top. Where and how I've seen it I can't divine, but seen it before *I have*, as sure as I stand here.'

'Guess you dreamt it, my Lesbia.'

'Good gracious, yes, that's it!' exclaimed the young girl, turning to her friend, with a wild look. 'It is so; you're right, Letitia, it's the Dream, my mother's dream, the very place she saw and described, and which afterwards reflected upon me one day at dinner, when we had a clerical meeting at Dulham. Here, uncle, I say! uncle! uncle!' calling to Mr Bristley, who was standing a few yards off at the bulwark.

'Well, Lesbie?'

'*Do you recognise that?*' she asked, very loudly, her outstretched arm pointing at the hill top and her figure posed in a graceful, eager attitude.

'Recognise what? No; I've never been here before.'

'It's the Hill of the Dream,' she said solemnly.

'The hill of – Oh, nonsense! Lesbia dear; how that bogey does haunt you!' he said, looking vexed and anxious. 'I had hoped the change of scene would have rid you of all that sort of thing.'

'I can't help being somewhat of a visionary, Uncle Spines,' replied Lesbia; 'and, after all, it's better to be that than a weaker vessel, eh?'

'A thousand times, Lesbie – no doubt of that.'

'I should think so indeed,' assented Letitia; 'and now to come down from dreaming dreams and seeing visions, to real life. There's Queenstown before us; that island before us in the harbour is Spike Island, where they used to keep convicts, but which is now a depôt of some sort; and those two forts frowning down upon us right and left are Forts Carlisle and Camden.'

While Lesbia was looking up at the two forts very attentively, a boat came alongside, the captain of the steamer having signalled one to land our party at Queenstown, while he steamed further up the harbour to Passage and thence with the tide to Cork. They accordingly landed at Queenstown, and took rooms at the principal hotel, on the quay. They spent that afternoon in walking about the place, and visiting the fine Catholic church; and the next morning, a berth having been previously engaged for Miss Blemmyketts in the fore state-rooms of a Cunard liner for New York which was to call that day, they went with other passengers and their luggage in the tender which conveys between the town and the steamships which, as a rule, lie off the mouth of the harbour near Roche's Point. There was an interval of about an hour between the arrival of the Queenstown tender and the departure of the steamship for the western ocean, and Lesbia was much interested in being shown over the great vessel, with its spacious saloons and cabins, long corridors and vast engines, and in walking up and down the long parade of deck open to passengers from stem to stern. But the inexorable moment of parting came, a bell was rung for visitors to quit, and after reiterated promises between the two girls to write often, our heroine went down the side after her uncle, and waved farewell as the great ship pounded forth on her outward way and the tender bore them back toward the quays of Queenstown.

The separation proved more of a wrench than Lesbia had anticipated. To say that they had been to each other as two sisters would be a common-place quite beside the mark; rather should they be likened to lovers in a state of society toward which the race is painfully struggling, but which it has not yet reached or even approached, a state in which the merely sensual nature will be depressed and the spiritual raised, or at any rate the lower will be brought into such complete harmony with the higher, that theologians of the future, so far from warning mankind against fleshly lusts as warring against the soul, will, on the contrary, strive rather to indicate the method whereby the flesh may most effectually be made the purified and ennobled soul's instrument.

Even while the great ship ploughed the broad Atlantic swell, leaving their little vessel to return across the calm basin, Lesbia felt that she had passed through the first act of her youthful life, and that greater issues were now to concern her than could be circumscribed by her country home. Her uncle partly comprehended her feelings, and said kindly, –

'It's *au revoir*, that's all, Lesbie. Depend upon it, you'll meet again, and before very long, humanly speaking. There's work for each of you to do in the great cause, and you can keep each other up to the mark by writing often.'

Lesbia felt her uncle's sympathy, but still went ashore with a heavy heart. Yet she was not wanting in moral courage any more than in physical, and her good sense soon bade her rouse herself against brooding over troubles more or less imaginary. 'Come,' she said to herself, 'I can surely be as strong-minded as my dear mother, who has made an effort and is quite cheerful now, and never says a word about the Dream.'

CHAPTER XIII.
THE BACKGROUND OF THE DREAM.

LESBIA, however, did not recover her spirits that day, and she asked her uncle to send a postcard home, announcing their safe arrival, as she did not feel up to writing a letter. As they sat together at their evening meal she said, breaking a long silence, –

'Uncle Spines, to-morrow's my birthday, and I want you to do something for my diversion; you must take me across the harbour to that village they call Whitegate; we can see it from here. From that place we can walk up to Roche's Tower, and see Roche's Point too, if we have time and think it worth the trouble. But up to the lighthouse I *must* go; it's been on my mind even more than parting from Lettie. I have felt something drawing me to that spot ever since I first saw it from the deck of the steamer as we came in from England, though I really don't know what there is to see when we get there, except perhaps a fine stretch of ocean coast.'

'I'm sure I don't know either, Lesbie,' replied her uncle; 'but since your heart's set upon it, we'll go the first thing to-morrow, weather permitting. It's to be hoped we shall have it clearer than to-day, because Roche's Tower in such a mist as we saw it this afternoon would be a dismal pilgrimage indeed. However, I should not grumble at that if only it led to your collaring the foul fiend and chucking him into the vasty deep once for all. We mustn't forget to take some lunch with us into Dreamland, because the stuff that dreams are made of doesn't suit my digestion, and I fancy there's nothing else to be had there.'

The next day, fortunately, was fine and clear on the whole, but a warm southerly wind brought short showers at intervals. The regular ferry having ceased for the year, they hired a small boat to take them over to the village of Whitegate, situated in a bay of Cork Harbour to the south-east of Queenstown, and partly hidden from it by an intervening islet. After the boatman had pulled up some distance, they got a side wind and were able to set sail, and bounding merrily along, past the various craft that dotted the wide basin, they landed in less than an hour on the road which runs along the face of the village as a sea-wall would do. As they walked away, Lesbia began to feel a vivid interest in every portion of the route, notwithstanding that behind the village there was nothing but the most ordinary and tame scenery of wood and down. The road leading from the village southwards divides into two, the main road following a partly wooded valley, the other, which keeps more the coast line, mounting the hill at once. It was this latter route our friends chose, and it soon led them out on the high bleak down, where, a pelting shower coming, they were glad to shelter for two or three minutes under the lee of a fragment of wall. They then walked on until stopped by the dyke on the inland side of Fort Carlisle already mentioned, the eastern portion of which they skirted.

'Strong place this,' Mr Bristley remarked, as they stood looking down into the great gulf of masonry.

'Yes, *whether in the hands of friend or enemy*,' replied Lesbia, in an incisive tone, which made her uncle look at her with momentary surprise.

'I wonder if we could get admittance to see the interior,' he then said.

'Not worth while to lose time, uncle; I want to get on to the lighthouse – Roche's Tower; I can see its nose peeping over there.'

They found, however, that the goal of their enterprise was further than it looked; there was a glen to be crossed by a narrow path leading down along the cliff past some hovels in the bottom, over a watercourse purling through large shingle, then up the opposite slippery ascent, until they scrambled over a low rough wall at the top, and found themselves on an undulating down without furze, where a few cows were grazing, with the little promontory of Roche's Point, its lighthouse and other buildings lying below them to the right, while the squat white column of Roche's Tower rose some distance in front, that is, to the south-east, on the very edge of the high down, looking upon the ocean. Reaching it at last, they found it had none of the imposing appearance it had worn when they saw it through the fog from the steamer's deck; it was merely a primitive round watch-tower or light-house some thirty-five feet high and perhaps fifteen thick, made of white stone or white-washed, with a tall signal-staff standing near on its right or western side. Fancies apart, a more common-looking group of objects could hardly be met with.

'Well, seer, and here you are at last,' said Mr Bristley, out of breath by the pace at which his niece had hurried him to the lighthouse, 'here you are at last on the hill of the dream, as you ordain it, and with the veritable tower itself in stern and stony reality before you! Why don't you apostrophise it, and say with Macbeth: –

> "Approach thou like the rugged Russian bear,
> The armed rhinoceros, or the Hyrcan tiger;
> Take any shape but that, and my firm nerves
> Shall never tremble."

Well, I must say it might very easily wear any shape but that, and be improved. I suppose it's because I'm a plain, prosaic, undreaming mortal, that I remain quite unimpressed by Roche's Tower. How odd of the spirits of the dream to select such a building! I should blow them up about it, if I were you, Lesbie. But really the coast view is wild and wide, and the ocean breeze is refreshing; so it's almost worth our trouble, after all. Look! there comes a homeward-bound American liner as big as Letitia's, or nearly. No doubt she's going to call here on her way to Liverpool: most of them do.'

The young girl paid no attention, but with an eager expression turned to gaze inland, that is, east and northwards.

'Let us go a little this way,' she said, leading on again until they reached the western descent of a valley of considerable but gradual depth, which extended from the cliff in a very straight line northwards. 'What is that mansion and place with a wood at its back and a thin plantation extending all along the valley? There, I mean, down below us, near the sea.'

'That, I believe,' answered Mr Bristley, 'is or was an Irish lord's estate; it's called Trabolgan on the map. Good house, I daresay, fine sea climate, and lots of solitude. Don't know that I should care to live there, though, somehow.'

'Good heavens! no, uncle; I should think not indeed! *The place is doomed!*'

Lesbia rapped out the last four words in that stern, loud, incisive tone which seemed to come from other lips than hers. The clergyman started, and a shade of alarm and annoyance passed over his face, which, however, he instantly suppressed.

'Come, come, Lesbie, have a drop of sherry and a sandwich. You've been fasting too long, I see; it's my fault: I ought to have thought of that before.'

The young girl shook her head as she took her uncle's hand affectionately.

'Not hungry, thanks, Uncle Spines. *I'm not through it yet.* When I am, I'll eat and drink, I promise you. Come along the ridge now; we'll get back to Whitegate by the valley road.'

And off she tramped at a pace that taxed her uncle's powers to keep up with her, along the crest of the hill northwards, that is, with her back to Roche's Tower and the ocean. After passing about half-a-mile of level and rather swampy pastures, separated by high rough walls with projecting stones fixed up either side to do duty for a stile at every point of crossing the footpath, they dropped over the fence into a lane which ran straight down into the valley at right angles to their previous course, that is, eastward. It not only ran into but crossed the valley, continuing straight up the wood-besprinkled slope opposite, in full view; here, however, it ceased to be a lane, for it was joined in the valley by the main road from Whitegate already mentioned, the road by which our friends had not come, but by which they were about to return. Thus – we must beg the reader's particular attention here – all the ways now visible to our heroine and her uncle formed together a

$$\text{A} \underset{\text{D}}{\overset{\text{B}}{\top}} \text{C} \quad ,$$

whereof the vertical shank B D ran north and south, forming the main road along the valley by which our friends were about to return to Whitegate; that is, they were about to proceed from the top of the shank, B, or the south, to the bottom D, or the north, descending c B the right or western arm of the

$$\text{A} \underset{\text{D}}{\overset{\text{B}}{\top}} \text{C}$$

which represented the lane just now mentioned, and having in their faces, while descending B A, the left or eastern arm running, as already said, up the opposite slope and vanishing over it. At the junction B of the three limbs of the

$$\text{A} \underset{\text{D}}{\overset{\text{B}}{\top}} \text{C}$$

– that is, of course, in the bottom of the valley – they came upon the lodge and iron gate of the carriage drive to Trabolgan, which drive was in fact a private continuation southwards, towards Roche's Tower, of the main road forming the shank B D of the

$$\text{A} \underset{\text{D}}{\overset{\text{B}}{\top}} \text{C}$$

. This road was therefore flush with the carriage-drive, and pursuing it north-wards, they turned their backs upon Trabolgan. These dry details of a very tame, uninteresting locality were sharply engraven on our heroine's memory, ready for the lurid light destined to be thrown upon them by after events.

When they had got about three hundred yards northward, with their backs to Trabolgan Lodge gate, along the main road to Whitegate, Lesbia halted suddenly.

'Here are a cottage or two, at last,' she said; 'it's really pleasant to see a human habitation, however lowly, in this howling wilderness. I should have been glad to go into that one, where you see a woman with her brats at the door, but no, uncle, I cannot; I feel something pulling me back. We must return to the lane – I am sorry for it, but we must – and then we must continue along the ridge until we sight Queenstown.'

Her uncle saw that her waywardness on this occasion must be humoured, and he turned back at once without reply. They retraced their steps to Trabolgan Lodge, and then re-ascended the lane, the right arm B C of the until they reached the crest of the hill; they then resumed their northward course, over pastures and wall-stiles as before, making again towards Whitegate, parallel to and above the valley road B D they had been partly pursuing. About half-an-hour brought them to the northern end of the ridge – a wooded shoulder, which their route in the morning had skirted, whence the view was open to Queenstown, prettily displayed on the frontage of a steep eminence across the great blue basin.

'We shall have to get down into the road again, I think,' observed Mr Bristley. 'It's evidently all wood from here right down to the Cove; there's no way through the wood that I can see; and look! there's another shower making for us. Hadn't we better use that little sheltered hollow just below as our refectory, eh? I'm not so spiritual as you are, Lesbia, and my inner man craveth for creature comforts.'

The girl only remarked in a dreamy manner, –

'How the gusts moan through the trees! Do you hear what the voice in the wind says?' looking at her uncle fixedly.

'Voice in the wind! No. What do you mean?'

'It keeps calling, *Close the ranks! Close the ranks*!'

Mr Bristley took to his pocket-handkerchief, and, under cover of using it, gulped down his uneasy feeling with one of his strong efforts. Then turning to his niece, with a cheerful laugh, –

'What nonsense, Lesbia! what an imagination you have! To me now the voice in the wind – since you mention it – does certainly seem to say, Sherry and sandwiches! Sherry and sandwiches!'

Her uncle's persistent good-humour at last produced upon her the effect he desired; she laughed in her turn, merrily and naturally.

'And what an imagination you have too, Uncle Spines! There's no fear you'll ever be haunted – you haven't self-respect enough. But sherry and sandwiches, by all means. It's over now, and I'm as hungry for creature comforts as you can be.'

Mr Bristley produced the packet and bottle with much relief at the change in the young girl's manner. Presently they reached the road again by a ravine which led directly down to it, and in about ten minutes afterwards found themselves again on the landing-place at Whitegate, where the same boat was awaiting them on the chance of a back fare. They took it, of course, and scudded swiftly back to Queenstown before a favourable breeze. The special interest of that place, however, was now exhausted, and the following day they proceeded by rail to Cork, and the next day to the lakes of Killarney.

CHAPTER XIV.
HOME NEWS, AND INTERVIEWING A NATIONALIST.

ABOUT ten days after their arrival at Killarney, Lesbia received from her mother a reply to a long letter of her own narrating the previous events. A few extracts from Mrs Newman's answer will suffice.

'MY DARLING LESBIA, – I was delighted to get your interesting letter at last, and to know that on the whole you are enjoying your trip, in spite of the parting from your Yankee friend, whom I do not dislike, although I should not care to resemble her. What a lovely place Killarney must be! I have seen many paintings of it, but nothing which comes up to your description. Now I must tell you, dearest, that a certain part of your letter startled me very much, and that is your description of your picnic from Queenstown to Roche's Tower. There is nothing extraordinary in your having seen an old lighthouse on a high hill by the sea, but then you go on to say that an absorbing and painful interest, which there was no reason for, took possession of you while you walked over the ground. It is this which forces me to connect the real place you have come upon with that terrible day-dream you remember my having more than a year ago. God forbid there should be anything in it, but if there is, what more natural than that you, my child, should feel by sympathy some of its effects upon me? I shudder as I recall that fearful scene; it is better not to think of it, and to be thankful that the great catastrophes of the future are not wielded by our feeble and clumsy hands.

'What a *volte-face*, as you say, this outcome of the general elections and the accession of the Bunglers to power! And our excellent friend Lord Humnoddie Prime Minister, too! I could not help telling his wife what you said about him. She took it good-naturedly, as she does everything, and said that, *entre nous*, her own opinion of her husband's capacity as helmsman of the ship of state is much the same as yours.'

(Here followed some talk about the gossips and squabbles of Dulham village and neighbourhood.)

'There was a great to-do here last Saturday evening with that poor mad woman Topsy Wriggles. I'm very glad they are going to remove her, because the demon of drink seems to get more and more hold on her. But it is curious that the madder and the more tipsy she gets, the more she falls to quoting scraps of Scripture in her fits. What a pity her propensity is! because she has evidently been well educated for a person in her station. I happened to be near the garden gate when she was in the thick of it, and could hear what she was saying, all the way from the public house. "Multitudes, multitudes in the valley of decision; for the day of the Lord is near in the valley of decision. The sun shall be turned into darkness, and the moon into blood, before the great and terrible day of the Lord come." This I must tell you, Lesbia, made me feel very uncomfortable. I'm glad she's going, and I hope she'll do better; we don't want any more such mad women here.'

(The rest of the letter was occupied with domestic affairs.)

Mr Bristley was standing at the edge of a terrace by the lake side, looking up with his binocular at Mangerton mountain, when his niece came to him and put her mother's letter into his hand.

'You see, Uncle Spines,' she said gravely, 'mamma has at once recognised the Background of the Dream in my description of our day at Roche's Tower.'

'Why, of course, my dear girl; what else could you expect? If Jane had never had the dream at all, the way you go on about your own fancies would have been enough to give it her.'

'Well, never mind, uncle, leave the dream alone; here's Mr O'Logan, the gentleman we talked with at the *table-d'hôte* yesterday; I should like to know more of his views on the political question.'

O'Logan was a prominent member of the National party,[3] who had come to the lake scenery for a few days for the benefit of his health, and happened to have his place next to our friends at the hotel dinner table. He raised his hat to Lesbia as he approached saunteringly, and the three were soon engaged in an animated discussion, of which we need only give that part which embodied this gentleman's views.

'No, sir,' he continued; 'you would be very wrong to imagine that the Irish people hate the English people. We do not, whatever a few ranters may be found to say. On the contrary, it's my belief, sir, that the sensible and reflecting among us are aware that Ireland has derived greater benefits on the whole from the English connection than she has sustained damage. But, in any case, it is absurd to pretend that the Irish of to-day owe a grudge to England on account of ancient history. Bosh! What do we care now what wrongs Cromwell or Arthur or Noah or Adam or the first gorilla may have inflicted on the former inhabitants of this island? Our grievances are practical, sir, not romantic; we do not want to discuss history, but to be let alone to manage our own affairs. And from this point of view, we say that it is time the English nation at large came to realise the fact that peoples, like individuals, outgrow the period of their tutelage. As the young man of eighteen cannot be expected to stand from his father the hectoring which he took as a matter of course when he was a boy of eight, so a nationality which feels that it has grown competent to take care of itself socially and politically, cannot longer acquiesce in being kept in leading-strings and debarred from following its bent and realising its own modes of life and thought. Political coercion, used against a people like the Irish, can only produce resentment, and, eventually, determined resistance. The first we have already seen bearing its fruits in boy-cotting and moonlighting outrages, not to speak of the dynamite scare; but it remains yet to be seen whether a stupid prejudice will be fostered to the extent of producing a resistance which would bring in sight disintegration of the Empire such as could not result from a grant even of quite unlimited Home Rule.'

'What do you allude to as determined resistance, Mr O'Logan?' asked Mr Bristley – 'civil war?'

'Civil war? No, sir, foreign war. Civil war would be nonsense between the soldiers of England and the sparse, untrained, almost unarmed Irish peasantry. What I mean, sir, is that where a powder magazine exists, it needs that everybody in the neighbourhood should be unremittingly careful how they carry fire of any sort about near it. If there be one person among the neighbours who is watching his opportunity with a box of cigar-lights, sooner or later he will explode the magazine, let his neighbours be as careful as they may. Europe is still such a magazine, notwithstanding the growing dislike of war and the endeavours which have lately been made by diplomacy to remove the danger of an outbreak. It needs unanimity on the part of all civilised peoples, to back up those endeavours successfully and keep the peace. We do not want – and I still hope that we shall never have – one people among them saying, What hast thou to do with peace, get thee behind me. But if that state of things should unfortunately come about, it needs no political genius to surmise that a single naval battle lost by the British fleet – and such a contingency is possible, however the naval estimates may be increased – would mean the landing of an allied army, in overwhelming force, on these shores, and the rising of three-fourths of the people to aid it with heart and hand. That is what I mean by resistance.'

'But what a terrible thing that such a spirit should exist between two peoples who ought to be one and indissoluble, and stand shoulder to shoulder against all troubles from within and from without!' said Lesbia sadly. 'Aid a foreign invader!'

'Well, Miss Newman,' he answered, 'I have not said that such a spirit does exist. I hope, as sincerely as you can, that there never will be any occasion for its existing. On our side, we are quite ready to listen to reasonable arguments and proposals, especially if they are put forward as matters of business untinged by political passion. Undoubtedly a large amount of English capital has been invested in Ireland, under the belief that commercial integrity and stability are as sure here as elsewhere. And stakes in the country, no matter by whom held, ought not to be confiscated; because once admit the principle of simple spoliation, and who can say where it will stop? That line of contention is all right, and it is for statesmen on both sides to put their heads together and see how our national aspirations can be realised, alike with the least possible injury to vested interests and with the least possible sacrifice on the other side in fairly compensating them. None of our recipes are infallible, but in the multitude of counsellors there is wisdom, and it surely cannot be but that a satisfactory solution of such a problem can be peacefully worked out. Still the contingency of a lack of sufficient wisdom to bring about the consultation should be faced; and I have only said that in that deplorable event, a struggle would mean something very different from the silly spectacle of an Irish mob armed with shillelaghs and fowling-pieces and a stray revolver or two, going out to be mown down by a few regiments from Aldershot. I feel certain that the most filibustering among our party will know how to be quiet and patient while the demand for Home Rule is under *bona fide* treatment; but I feel equally certain that any attempt to force upon Ireland continuance of the present form of connection, so far from maintaining the greatness of the Empire, will eventually knock the whole boiling into smithereens.'

'Yes,' said Lesbia; 'it happens unluckily that the Bungling party have got the reins at this critical time. I try not to be a partisan, but it does seem to me that while there's something to be said for Toriosity, and something for Radicality, there's nothing to be said for Whiggery-piggery: it possesses the faults of both, and the virtues of neither.'

The two men laughed.

'And you call that not being a partisan, Lesbie!' said her uncle.

At this moment a boatman came up to speak to our two about a row on the lake, which gave a turn to the conversation, and O'Logan nodded *au revoir*. About another week of bright, warm weather passed pleasantly enough, before they made their way home *viâ* Dublin and Holyhead.

CHAPTER XV.
LESBIA'S CORRESPONDENCE, AND THE PENUMBRA OF THE DREAM UPON LETITIA.

IT will readily be supposed that letters began to pass between the bosom friends without much delay. Some extracts from their communications may be more suggestive than the tittle-tattle which most young ladies still wrote to each other, even at the date of our story's outset.

No. 1. – Letitia to Lesbia, dated New York, Oct. 189 – .

'Well, as I was telling you, as we got into the "rolling forties" off Newfoundland, it blew pretty stiff from the north-west almost a head wind. This floored half the passengers, but I am a good sailor and did not mind it. I passed some of the time in the smoking-room – I smoke a good deal at sea, to the scandal of the old fogies of propriety. Among the men I used to meet there were three Irish Nationalists, who gave me an eye-opening about the dangerous state of feeling that is growing again in their country, and still more on this side of the water, since the change of Ministry in England. As girls like you and me, sweet Lesbia, have no national resentments, looking upon all our sex as belonging to one human family, I shall not be misunderstood by you if I say that there is reason to fear breakers ahead. The Irish ivy is overgrowing our walls, it is becoming yearly of more weight in our national councils, – at all events, our foreign policy; and the end can only be a rupture between Jonathan and Paddy on the one side and John Bull on the other, unless the three can manage to hit off some sensible arrangement to the satisfaction of all. I have a notion of my own that the question is not one of simple politics; its Celtic element is indispensable to the solidarity of the British race, and if that be alienated, the backbone of national power will have been taken out. But I am tired of politics: there has been little else talked in my hearing since you and I parted.

'A bad sign of the times is the extravagant taste displayed by the new fashions in ladies' dresses, which burlesque the form divine more than ever. And yet the same people who submit to be made such guys of in sacrifice to their only real deity, *La Mode*, are, or pretend to be, shocked at beautiful studies in the nude, whether in painting or sculpture. Upon the whole, I am driven to doubt whether it would not be better for society that all women should be openly licentious, than be thus strait-laced, prudish, and hypocritical. However, the point will perhaps be settled without your or my intervention; we can but wait and see, perhaps not wait very long.

No. 1. – Lesbia to Letitia, dated Dulham, Frogmore, Nov. 189 –

'My short and imperfect acquaintance with the political question, Letty, leads me to much the same conclusions as you draw. It is to be feared that the Bungling party, now in power, may land us in a catastrophe. But sufficient unto the day, etc. Now about the other matter. The perversion of women to which you refer is, I think, capable of explanation. It is a survival, one of the many useless survivals in the evolution of humanity. We have numerous instances of useless survivals in our own persons. There is, for example, the beard, which a large proportion of men in all ages have rid themselves of by shaving, and which women generally do not grow. Our hair and our nails require clipping; we use artificial soap and brushes and sponges; in short, civilised man has to eliminate by art the encumbrance of various survivals or inheritances from his lower physical history. Analogously, we have also moral survivals, which the progress of enlightenment calls upon us to exterminate. We cannot help having inherited them from our lower ancestry, be they apes or what not, but we can exterminate them by culture, and if we fail to do so, we fail to fulfil the mission of our race, – we are retrograding, tending downwards. The subjection of women and the habits of mind which that subjection engenders in women, is the most prominent and the most pernicious of all the moral survivals from a lower world. It is natural only in the sense in which it is natural for everyone to be dirty and ignorant. But the practical difficulty in emancipating our sex is that of rousing women themselves to be earnest in the work. It is the old story of the man in the Bastille; after he had passed a number of years immured in his cell, he felt uncomfortable out of it. And little can be done, I fear, with those of us who have reached middle life under the old bondage. It is the education of young girls that must be attacked, as my uncle has attacked it in my case, and as your friends have evidently in yours, Letty. That has certainly been done to some extent also in the best girls' schools and colleges which late years have brought into being. Still there is a deplorable backsliding and want of wholeness in the movement, as evinced by the fashions in dress against which we both declaim. The old social disease is very deep-seated, and may need some drastic remedy. A new broom sweeps clean, and it seems to me that the present atmosphere of society bears signs that some great event is at hand to do the work. What form it will take exactly none of us can tell, but the signs are in the sky.'

As the American girl read these last lines of her English friend's, she felt a swimming in the head quite unusual with her. Someone in the room at her house, where she was conning over Lesbia's letter, interrupted her reading to ask a question, but her memory and comprehension collapsed; she could only stare stupidly at the speaker. And as she gazed thus vacantly, the room and its furniture melted away before her, and there rose in its place the deck of the Milford steamer entering Cork Harbour, with herself and Lesbia and Mr Bristley upon it, looking up at Roche's Tower looming grim through the fog. The experience was as unpleasant as new to her, but it was over in a minute, and Lelitia sprang up and went out of the room, edifying her companion by the remark, 'Guess philosophy's a fine thing, but at times a blue pill's a finer, and I'll just put myself outside one.'

CHAPTER XVI.

THE CORRESPONDENCE CONTINUED.

No. 2. – LETITIA to LESBIA.

'SINCE writing my last, conversation with an unprejudiced friend – though she is not your equal in any way, Lesbie – has led me to consider the other side of the question. As regards Mrs Grundy's prudery, may it not be a matter of self-defence? I mean defence of female dignity. If all men could be trusted to be reverent toward nude beauty, if even men in general could be trusted not to be vulgar and vile, – not to make scurrilous obscene jests upon it, well and good. But you know that is not the case, and therefore the only way for women to act is to frown down all exhibition of the kind to common and coarse-minded people. The objection can be removed, no doubt, but only by training the youths of the rising generation to be something very different in their demeanour from what their forefathers were. Let them be licentious as they will upon one condition – asceticism is no virtue in men; but let them be so *with reverence toward all women*. If they can make their passions into a heart religion, let there be no restraint upon them, short of injuring others. But so long as they cannot, or do not, the women of society are right in keeping a straight-waistcoat upon them in the matter.

Akin to this is the marriage question. You may not be a marrying girl, Lesbie; you may be fit for the higher life – virginity *is* the higher life in women, I admit – but I am not, and I look to annexing a husband some day, to love, honour, and obey me. And most certainly I should never consent to my husband having any other wife beside me. I may spare him for a *few liaisons* and irregularities upon occasion, and I might claim a few myself; but I would have no one to be practically a rival wife, either upon the premises or elsewhere. And you will find, if you inquire, that women who cohabit with a man outside legal marriage have also this monogamic instinct. It is easy enough to see why. A harem of concubines is a drove of domestic animals, the toys of their owner. Look at King Solomon, the man of wisdom, who, notwithstanding his wisdom and his multitudinous wives and concubines, could declare that all things under the sun are vanity and vexation of spirit. He could not, then, have felt much more respect for his women than a huntsman feels for his hounds. It is a truth which happily the world is more alive to in these latter days, that formally to attach a plurality of women in any sense or manner to one man, is a direct negation of woman's dignity. The opposite – polyandry – would be far more natural, even upon physical grounds, and it would moreover have this advantage upon moral grounds, that a man has no dignity *of that sort* to lose. But I do not propose to enter upon further discussion of that question. The point I am now contending for is that the puritanical code of morality which you and I feel inclined to kick against, is no proof that women are puritanical and bigoted at heart; it is only a proof that the brutality of men has obliged women to resort to defensive measures.

'Men at large still refuse or neglect to do their duty by the female community, and their sin recoils upon their own heads in the shape of a distorted, pinched, uncomfortable, unsound society, making discontent, jealousy, and bitterness rife, and breeding mysterious physical as well as mental maladies. I guess this hits the blot, Lesbie, and I long to see prudery and bigotry on our part swept away, *mais que messieurs les assassins commencent!* Let men begin the reform by conceding to women their full rights in all matters; then these secondary symptoms of the social disease will disappear fast enough, that is my notion about it.'

No. 2. – Lesbia to Letitia.

'Granting, my dear Lettie, that the causes of society's hollowness be what you say, I cannot agree with you that it rests only with men to initiate the remedy. There must be something more than mere acting on the defensive which induces so many among our sex to hang back against their own development and elevation; I account for it by the slavish habits of mind which have been inculcated upon the female race, and which must be eradicated before anything material can be done to better the world. We want one like the Hebrew prophet to sound in our ears his warning: – "Rise up, ye women that are at ease, hear my voice, ye careless daughters. Many years shall ye be troubled, ye careless women," etc., etc.

'This reminds me that there is a part of the question we have hitherto left out of sight, the effects of a false system of religion. I do not mean by this that one sect or body is false as compared with the rest; I mean that a fundamental falsehood underlies and dominates them all. The subjection of woman in religion cannot but have a vast effect upon her social status, and this notwithstanding the fact that what may be called priestcraft rather than religion is losing its hold upon Western nations. The hold it still retains is mainly supported by female influence, and if that influence is perverted to the degradation of the sex to which it chiefly belongs, how can we wonder that many women who ought to know better hug their chains? Train up a girl in the way she ought *not* to go, and when she is old she will find it hard to turn into the right one. I do not deny that Christianity may be a trifle better than the other systems, for the reason that it upholds monogamy. But these old-world religions, one and all, are based upon the genuine original sin – that of deposing the female from her spiritual dignity and setting up the male in her place. Nothing but a radical change of front can cleanse Christianity or any other theological system from this congenital and inherent stain. There is one partial exception, I allow. The Roman Church has within her – more, however, in her practice than in her doctrine – the saving germ of Madonna-worship, which of course means practically woman-worship. Whether that germ will bud and blossom, and so the old hierarchy be saved from extinction along with the other creeds, remains yet to be seen. My uncle believes it will for myself I cannot say. In any case, I see cause for satisfaction in the rapid spread of secularism both in England and on the Continent. Before you can build up the true, you must clear away the false; and though it may be painful to many good kind souls to have their early beliefs undermined, yet that is but a temporary trial, an indispensable condition of attaining finally that which is really satisfying. It does not give pain to everyone, either. For instance, last Sunday I asked one of my Frogmore bicycling friends why he attended service at Dulham so often, as I knew he was not what is commonly called pious. 'Because, Miss Newman,' he replied, 'the thwack of your uncle's stick across the shoulders of fanatics who despised women is grateful and comforting to me as cool streams to the hunted hart, or as Epps's cocoa for breakfast to the person who hunts him.' And I believe, Lettie, that is really the secret of Uncles Spines' popularity as a preacher. He treats Christianity impartially, – always ready to do justice to the golden grain, but equally ready to burn the chaff with unquenchable fire. The chaff, however, which I desire to see burnt – whether it exists in the Bible, the Koran, or elsewhere – is the usurpation by man of woman's place in spiritual interests. That, to my mind, is the only theology worth discussing; all else is rubbish. This would be rubbish too, were it not that the relations of women to men and to each other in this world are falsified and spoilt by the false religious position. You, Lettie, lay all the blame on man's arrogance; I, for my part, hold that we are at least equally to blame, because if women generally were to insist upon a reversal of the relations of the sexes in religion, men, even those most opposed to the change, would have no alternative but to submit. Any religion in the world, deprived of the countenance of its women, would fall to pieces like a house of cards. The game, therefore, is really in our own hands.'

CHAPTER XVII.
THE SAME.

No. 3. – Letitia to Lesbia.

'Your reference to the theological aspect of the woman's rights question, Lesbie, seems to compel us into examining the origin of the difference of sex; since we cannot expect the world to take our word that the female portion of mankind is the superior, unsupported by proof. There is no help for it, then, we must go to the root of the question, or leave it alone.

'Well, I guess no one will dispute that the beauty of the race inheres mainly in its feminine portion. I do not speak of features merely, but all that constitutes grace, – the beauty of figure and movement, the sweetness of the voice, and the infinite variety of charm which woman generally possesses in contrast with man. That being so, what can there be in man which attracts woman downward toward him? I could understand the theory that the mutual love of human beings, in the angelic state of perfection which we profess to aspire to in professing religion, should require a bodily adaptation for union, but then it might be a similar one, not a different one, one sex, not two sexes. I do not understand why we are divided into two sexes or classes, whereof the one is, generally speaking, beautiful and refined, the other uncomely and coarse. The separation itself is to me unaccountable. How comes it that a genuine hermaphrodite in the flesh is as mythical a creature as the unicorn or griffin of armorial bearings? If the higher beings, the 'angels' of immortality, whose state we aspire to reach after the death of this body, combine the two sexes in one person, why is that perfection not copied in our earth-world? If, on the other hand, they do not so unite them – why do they not? I complain (as a philosopher) of arrangements in this earthly existence which introduce the ugly and coarse into the animal economy without necessity. Assuming, if you like, that parthenogenesis is a mere fable, and that the introduction of the zoosperm to the ovum is in all cases indispensable to reproduction, I ask why the zoosperm should not be engendered in woman by herself, or by other women. What is man needed for? And why, being needed as it seems, must he be a coarse and brutal being as compared with woman? And yet again, being as he is coarse and brutal, what is it that attracts woman toward him. To say that her taste is depraved, affords no answer. How came her taste to be depraved? Low qualities for low beings, but the architype of nature can have no business with depraved tastes, unless in the very wide sense that universal good includes all evil. Nor does the principle of evolution, which is the principle of cosmogony, explain this phenomenon. Evolution is the division of function-monopolising homogeneities into function-distributing heterogeneities; in other words, it is the principle of the division of labour. Good; but that does not imply the degradation or corruption of any of the distributed functions. Why should the spiritual hermaphrodite evolve the natural woman and man, the one beautiful or noble, the other by comparison base? That is where I collapse.'

No. 3. – Lesbia to Letitia.

'Do I rightly understand you to mean, Lettie, that women are attracted downwards to men in the sense that they actually prefer a hirsute brute of a man to an Apollo Belvedere, or would do so if they had the choice? If such be your intention, I flatly deny the fact. I say that it is just through lack of that very choice, that women are driven to make the best of a bad situation, and cling to that caricature of the male sex which the races of this planet produce. *Quand ou a pas ce que t'on aime, il faut aimer ce que t'on a.* You will find that whenever women idealise manhood, in fiction or otherwise, they invariably tend to invest their *beau ideal* with feminine virtues and attractions; they may put some fierce whiskers and a horsey swagger, etc., to their hero, but if there is anything about him worth admiring, or which his creators admire, it is glaringly feminine. Woman, say what you will, does invariably and instinctively tend to reproduce and to worship *her own beauty;* she does but tack on the masculine capacities to it, to meet certain earthly and temporary requirements. There are exceptions to this rule, no doubt, but those exceptions are the fruit of perversion, especially early perversion. What indeed may not be accomplished in the way of degradation by this means? By perverted training you may debase a woman as much as or more than a man; you may teach her to care for nothing in the world so much as the brandy-bottle; you may turn her inclinations to all that is corrupt and nauseous. The wonder is that we are not much more debased than is generally the case. Therefore it is not difficult to account for the fact that here and there we do meet with a woman whose tastes and sympathies are on the side of brutality in men, and who herd with men of that stamp, calling unmanly whatever is refined in men, while they call unwomanly whatever is self-helpful in woman. Would you believe it, Lettie, I have even heard women say that they rather like boys to be cruel? What can you expect of boys who are brought up by such females as that? It is not uncommon to hear shallow people say that boys are naturally cruel, mischievous, and coarse. This is a libel and slander from top to bottom. Boys are not *naturally* anything of the sort; they, like girls, are the victims of society's folly and perverseness. A different training is devised for each, and is suitable to neither; they are distorted in opposite directions, hence the evils you and I complain of when those girls and boys become grown-up women and men.

"'From the sole of the foot,'" says the same prophet I quoted before, "even unto the crown of the head, there is no soundness, but wounds and bruises and putrefying sores; they have not been closed nor bound up,'" etc., etc. But, I repeat, you must not put any of these things down to nature, unless, indeed, upon the principle *humanum est errare.* It is not in the nature of women to be servile, nor are they naturally attracted by what is base in men; it is not natural in men to usurp women's place, and by so doing make a burlesque of religion and defile the spiritual atmosphere. These moral obliquities are repugnant to the better nature in each sex, as disease is opposed to health. We must not acquiesce in them as natural, we must extirpate them as morbid.

'Nevertheless there is, after all, a sense in which you may correctly say that woman is attracted downwards towards man, but it is that sense in which we are all 'attracted downward' to our lower animal functions. If the digestion does not go on as it should, not only the stomach, but through it the thoughts and the temper become deranged; and therefore it may be said that we inevitably take an interest in the state of our own health, or feel attracted towards those conditions which go to constitute it. If, then, you will accept this position for the masculine portion or sex of your hermaphrodite; namely, that it is indispensable to the higher, the feminine portion, as the digestive organs are indispensable to the heart and brain, I will not quarrel with your statement about the downward attraction. It vouches for and explains itself in that relation; you need no longer be puzzled why the higher clings to the lower.

'You will hardly suspect Mr Bristley's niece of being a bibliolater, Lettie, therefore I need not fear being misunderstood when I express my belief that the reason why rationalists make light of and ridicule the wisdom contained in the Bible, is because they do not understand it. They will insist upon judging the book, or rather books, by the letter, whereas we are repeatedly told that the letter is exactly what it is *not* to be judged by: the letter killeth; the spirit, that is, the hidden meaning, giveth life. I am not going to treat you to a verbatim interpretation of any text, but it will aid our inquiry to outline what my uncle considers to be the esoteric purport of the myth of the Fall, which, taken in its literal sense, would, in common with all other biblical marvels, be a silly nursery tale. It will be difficult to make every term clear to you, but in speculations so deep, one must be content with faint sketches of the truth, seeing them for the present 'through a glass darkly.' The meaning of the myth we take to be briefly as follows, –

'Out of the divine Unity, the eternal Womanhood, called by Solomon *Wisdom*, come forth by Her act the diversified world of nature. By the production last of all of the earthly image of the Eternal Wisdom, namely, woman in the flesh, the reason and object of creation stood explained. The last product was the image of the first origin. Woman was the first and the last, Alpha and Omega, the beginning and the ending, beginning in the spiritual world, ending in the natural, and thence returning again to the spiritual. Thus the male of mankind is the last step short of the Divine image, the female is that image itself. The whole varied world which we call Nature was latent in that Divine Wisdom whereof woman is the image; therefore man himself was latent in Her as much as any lower part of nature. This view does away with the plausible theory of spiritual equality between the sexes. Man is neither a separate being equal (spiritually) with woman, nor is he co-essential with her to the perfect humanity, unless you call it co-essential to belong to her in the sense in which our legs and arms belong to us. Therefore in regarding Deity as the Spiritual Hermaphrodite, it is of the first importance to bear in mind that the two factors of hermaphrodism are not of equal dignity – the feminine factor being the divine, the masculine the earthly. The masculine or temporal side of humanity is in principle as much evolved from and involved back to the feminine or eternal side as is any lower organic or even inorganic form of existence. Hence it follows that to sunder the spiritual hermaphrodite, in other words, to evolve the phenomenon of two separate sexes, is to sunder the baser from the nobler part of the Divine Human Being. Reducing this theory to practice, it becomes manifestly the greatest of society's duties to repair the Fall by bringing about the elevation of womanhood, this being the true and demonstrable scheme of redemption, or the buying back by human labour the lost position of human divinity, the position where the masculine sex is but a power of the feminine, not something apart from and even antagonistic to it. The loss or fall thus described shows the nature of the Original Sin from which we need to be redeemed. It consists in reversing the proper relations of man and woman in spiritual interests, placing man above and woman below. Of this reversal the prophet speaks, "Surely your turning of things upside down shall be reckoned as the (case of the) potter's clay; for shall the clay say of him that formed it, He formed me not?" etc., etc. By this, the original sin, society has been doing the work opposite to that of re-constructing the spiritual hermaphrodite. It has been stirring in the direction of making the separation more pronounced, the discord greater; and this discord has been the parent of all the discords of the world.

'I think, Lettie, I have now shown you at least how my uncle would answer your inquiry as to the cause of the downward attraction of woman to man of which you speak. Both that and the degradation of man are explained by the Fall, that is, the disintegration of the hermaphrodite, which disintegration it is the mission and *raison d'être* of Religion properly so called, to repair.'

CHAPTER XVIII.
THE CORRESPONDENCE CONCLUDED.
No. 4. – Letitia to Lesbia.

ASSUREDLY, my dear girl, I do not take you, or your uncle either, for a bibliolater in the vulgar sense; but it is clear that Mr Bristley is a believer, after a sort, in the inspiration of the Bible, I hardly expected this, and I must say it is a belief I do not share. A man with a hobby and lots of talent can hew anything he pleases into the shape of his theory; but to my mind the authors of the Jewish sacred books were simply augurs, who pandered to the ignorant superstitions of a people sitting in darkness, solely with a view to keep them under their thumb. Still your uncle is not the only clever man of the present day who thinks otherwise. For instance, we have here in Brooklyn a noted preacher, Dr Josiah Mispath,* who delights in just such lucubrations as those you have treated me to. I read to him that part of your letter; he was much interested, and said he would like to meet you. In particular, he asked me to draw your attention to Isaiah xiv. 29. "Rejoice not thou, whole Palestina, because the rod of him that smote thee is broken: for out of the serpent's root shall come forth a cockatrice, and his fruit shall be a flying dragon." Dr Mispath says this is a passage containing more occult wonders than those you have found in Genesis. He sees in it an esoteric doctrine to the effect that the male sex of mankind is to be superseded by the female, not only in all the higher

*   Corrupted from *Mishpat.*

functions common to both, but virtually also in those physiological ones which hitherto have been his separate province. He finds also other parts of Hebrew Scripture, such as the song of Deborah and Barak, where this monster out of the deep is obscurely alluded to. Well, that will not happen in our time, Lesbie, or only very exceptionally; so I will confine my attention to more practical relations.

'And this leads me to say that, mythology apart, I have strong misgivings upon the whole subject, I mean upon the manner in which your philosophy handles the other sex. As I gather your drift, the love of woman for son or husband is a delusion and a snare, or at least it is love for an object essentially temporal – one which has not and cannot have the afflatus of eternal life. I understand you to say that as man rises in the spiritual world, he must put off from his soul all its masculine accoutrements, and incorporate the graces and virtues which are distinctively feminine. In doing so, he perforce discards his old identity altogether, he becomes – not the same person developed and improved, but a different person – a woman. No doubt the new and beautiful butterfly will retain some traces of its former self; still it will be no longer the dear ugly old grub upon whom so much tenderness used to be lavished. To argue home, I guess I have a good daughter's affection for my own father, although I do not meet in him that intellectual affinity you are fortunate enough to find in your Uncle Bristley. Again, as I told you before, I look to marrying some day, when I get an offer from a man whose mental calibre I need not despise. In that event, I shall probably grow deeply attached to my mate as the years roll by, and feel that my existence is indissolubly bound up with his, for better for worse, both on this side of the grave and beyond. Even without any progeny to cement the bond, such a feeling of union and such joint hopes of immortality between husband and wife are, happily, not uncommon. Well, but now, according to your theories, Lesbie, it seems there is to be no Beyond for my father or my husband! Or rather, the Beyond will change their sex, and in so doing, will change their identity! To show how thoroughly it will do so, suppose my future husband to be a gigantic bearded man with a deep bass voice. When, in the future life, he is transfigured into a woman, will he keep the same bass voice or one like it, his person being changed into that of a gigantic female beauty? I grant you, the effect of such a metamorphosis would be grand, but would it not give a sad wrench to my tender thoughts of 'auld lang syne?' Do we not – those of us who are true-hearted – bestow more sterling love on our old decrepit pets than on the most attractive newcomers? If your own fine bull pup Goss were to live to be an old infirm dog, would you part with him to the first sausage-man who might come round, in order to make way for a new fancy? No, Lesbie, I am very sure you would not. And yet you calmly tell womankind that we must prepare to do with our husbands and fathers what you would not consent to do with your dog, – discard them hereafter in favour of more attractive personalities! This can hardly be accurate.

'Believe me, I detest the loathsome idolatry upheld by the dollymopses, weaker vessels, or whatever you call them, who look upon wedlock as the end and aim of woman's existence. I hold with you that to worship any men or man whatever, setting them up in our place, is the very essence of spiritual corruption. But that does not compel me to deny any place at all to the male sex; it does not prove to me that the leaning of a mother toward her son *as* a son, of a wife towards her husband *as* a husband, are illusions belonging to the terrestrial conditions, and doomed to pass away along with those conditions. Rather it seems to me that just as the common religious instinct of the world is a guarantee for a future life, so the equally general attraction of women toward their male kith and kin is a guarantee for the permanence of the bi-sexual relation in that future life. If you may despise the guarantee in the one case, why not also in the other? Anyhow, Lesbie, I must hear a good deal further, before I can digest the notion that the male half of society is an optical illusion! For in sober truth, your doctrine almost comes to that.'

No. 4. – LESBIA to LETITIA.

'Decidedly, dear Lettie, I should like to know your friend Dr Mispath; it would be one of the many inducements to my crossing the ocean to see you, if ever that can be compassed. Meanwhile, I see the drift of what be says, and if it be true, if the writers of the Hebrew mystical books were controlled by spirits, not lying ones, superior to their own intelligence, the passage you refer to about the fiery dragon out of the serpent's root conveys at once a promise of Eden to those who are with our cause, and a warning of another place or state to those who are against it.

'But to come down from ethereal speculations of that kind to the more homely part of our subject, I quite admit the force of what you say in praise of faithful affection for old companions, be they human beings or lower animals, and I admit, moreover, that if as frail mortals we have been true-hearted in that way, assuredly we shall not be less, but rather more so, when we become immortals. So far you and I are agreed; but you must see, nevertheless, that your contention as regards fidelity to the individual cuts both ways. If it establishes on the one hand that true love is for old companions, not new charmers, it surely implies on the other hand that such love should endure through any conceivable change in the personal appearance of the loved one. It should endure even through a change for the worse; how much more, then, through a change for the better! And, as a matter of fact, it does endure through change. Does not every mother's son change his personality, to all intents and purposes, with his growth? What resemblance can a mother pretend there is between the boy of four who sat on her knee and the man of forty who brings her grandchildren to see her? The identity of the son is little more than nominal, yet the maternal affection, as a rule, endures. And so with husband and wife; does not your 'auld lang syne' represent a great change in both? 'We twa hae run aboot the braes,' etc.

etc., in what respect does their old age resemble that time? Their affection is for a personality which endures through change, not for an unchanged personality. I maintain, therefore, that the constancy of good women's love is a guarantee of its continuance, and of its increase too, for the quondam male partner who in the hereafter shall have cast his slough and returned into the Image of God, retaining only that which was pure in his former state.

'But it stands to reason, from the analogies of natural evolution, that such upward change can only be for those who have striven upwards sincerely. They, for instance of the contrary, who, by wilfully opposing the elevation of womanhood upon earth, have done what in them lies to mar the rehabilitation of the spiritual hermaphrodite sundered by the Fall – such, it is clear, have forfeited for the time their birthright of redemption; their portion is the second death, the degradation below humanity, in order that they may have a chance to do better when eventually they reach it again through the varieties and degrees of animal transformation which may be necessary in each case. I need not go further into that: you have heard my uncle talk about it more than once; and, after all, it is an open question after a certain point, that point being that we have to account for the existence of the lower world somehow. Swedenborg, who went deeply into the great questions of the other world, does not seem to have taken up the transmigration theory; that is rather surprising, because one would have expected that a philosopher who brought such a powerful understanding to bear upon human destiny, would not be content to leave unsolved the problem of animal origin. No doubt it may be said in reply that minds which range high, need not necessarily be able to range wide; but that is unsatisfactory to modern thought, which prefers rather to deal with patent facts than to invent ingenious theories. But what is more to your and my purpose, Lettie, I believe that neither class of mind, nor any class, will be able to see far behind the veil which separates us from the other world, until the intelligence of the one half of mankind shall be as free as the other, until the complete emancipation of our sex from the bondage which is partly traditional, partly self-imposed, shall give the world an impetus such as it has never yet had toward the better recognition of its temporal and eternal interests alike.'

(This closes such of the correspondence between our two girls, extending over several months, as it is worth while to give samples of. Great events, already dimly foreshadowed to each of them, arose to put an end for the time to their speculations.)

CHAPTER XIX.

ENGLISHWOMEN AND THE POLITICS OF THE DAY.

AT the date of our story, 189 – , there were still nominally three great political parties in England, the Jingoes, the Shillyshallies, and the Thoroughgoers. The power of the last-named had been long in abeyance, but was now coming to the front with such impetus that it promised shortly to sway the national legislature exclusively, so that there remained little chance for the other two parties to regain their footing except by coalition.

This change in the balance of power had considerably furthered the cause of women's rights. The Married Women's Property Act,[4] passed some dozen or fifteen years before, had been a move in the right direction, and latterly the suffrage had been extended to women possessing the same qualifications to vote as men. However, this plausible form of enfranchisement was in reality one-sided; it did not in practice bring the number of enfranchised females in the kingdom anywhere near that of enfranchised males, and the still surviving disabilities of women in other matters went far to neutralise the partial equality of the sexes in this one. Still it was the edge of the wedge inserted in the old fabric, and in the normal course of things the rest of the desired reforms should have followed rapidly. Already in some of the professions, notably in that of medicine, the female intruders were making their way, mostly by their own perseverance, but partly also by the encouragement they received from a few far-sighted and liberal men. But what told most of all was the improvement in young girls' education; for with the rise in their education went that lever of all improvement, their ambition. Nobler aspirations began to fill their enlarged minds. University examinations and university establishments had now, for a generation of pupils, been making havoc of the little needlework, little music, little French, little history, little geography, little theology, which formerly had been judged proper for the young lady brain, and – no insignificant matter – the newspaper press had long ago dropped the bantering (not to say scurrilous and ribald) tone in which in past days it had been accustomed to criticise all efforts of women to compete with men. Much, very much, still remained to be accomplished, but the progressive and self-respecting portion of the female community felt that if it was a minority, it was a minority which had a great future before it, and which felt its strength increasing steadily year by year.

But the year 189 – was destined to witness a disastrous reaction which threw out the calculations of the reformers. It may seem strange at first that the extension of the suffrage to women did not, after all, prove any safeguard against reaction, in fact, the contrary; but it is to be remembered that only a limited class, namely female householders, had as yet been included. A married woman, not a householder in her own right, might be as cultivated and experienced as you please, with the veriest dolt or brute for a husband; she had no voice in the making of the laws under which she lived; she bore her full share of burdens, but no share of privileges. The previous Parliament, though it had broken the ice, had not mustered courage to take the plain, straightforward course of giving a vote to every wife whose husband has a vote, and to every husband whose wife has one, in addition to the enfranchisement of spinster and widow householders. The consequence of such pusillanimity had been that the enfranchisement of women was restricted to a class who, as might have been foreseen, were likely to favour reaction; most of them had reached a time of life when their habits of thought were fixed, and these having been cast in the mould of the immemorial slavery and degradation of womanhood, there was no hope of much re-casting. So the prospect of having to throw off their slough at the bidding of their advanced and strong-minded sisters did not please these weakervessels and dollymopses, and they began to combine against the women's rights movement, both socially and politically. Unfortunately their advantage of numbers and of the power of the purse made it easy enough to work mischief against the interests of their own sex, and the new Parliament returned by the General Election of 189 – could be trusted to legislate so that the social piggery might slumber undisturbed on its old dirty straw. It proved, however, that this could not be done so as to clog only the obnoxious Women's Rights movement, leaving home and foreign policy in general to develop healthily.

As already remarked, the Jingoes and the Shillyshallies, although they had no political love for each other, saw that in these days they had no chance against the Thorough-goers, except by merging their differences. Accordingly it was agreed between them that the new Cabinet should form what was technically called a Bungling Coalition. Under these auspices the political atmosphere was growing close, stifled, charged with malarious elements requiring a storm to clear them away. The country, much to the surprise of resident foreigners who were not disposed to agree with their compatriots in regarding the British power as a *puissance finie*, was getting generally out of touch with an impatiently progressive age, hanging back and acting as a drag where formerly it had been the propeller. One serious result of this was a slackening of cordiality with the continental neighbours, especially with France, the rapidity of whose transition toward an enlightened Socialism made her the more susceptible of coldness and discouragement, so inconsistent with the former character of her old ally. Then again, in relation to the United States, untoward incidents connected with the fisheries disputes had recently occurred which, though in years past they would have been easily smoothed over, were now seized upon by the Irish-American faction in order to breed resentment between the old and the new portions of the Anglo-Saxon race. All this would have been difficult to bring about but for the Bungling Coalition which the influence of reactionary Englishwomen had done so much to set at the helm, and which thus continued to make such bad blood between the nation and its neighbours and natural allies that, what with little Ireland determined to trouble the waters if possible, and great Russia, also alienated, biding her time until they should be troubled, it needed no statesman of genius to foresee that any trivial dispute which in ordinary times would do no harm beyond agitating the money markets for a day or two, might now precipitate war.

But every dog has his day, and the Bungling Coalition had theirs. They spent it in snapping and snarling abroad, and in leaving their traces against every important institution at home. Venality began to appear in public concerns, while vulgarity was stamped on the surface of a society which had ceased to believe in its professed principles, and which cared little more to shape its own destiny than our three friends, in the trip previously narrated, would have cared to take personal charge of and navigate the steamer which carried them over the water to Queens-town.

Yet the unwitting lords of misrule who were guiding England thither were not exceptionally remiss nor stupid. They were not less conscientious than other men, but their official conscience was for place and power. The inherent badness of the ends for which they had been called to office left no worthier motives any scope; it paralysed their efforts for improvement, and destroyed their sense of proportion in government and legislation; in a word, it made them consummate Bunglers all round; and for this, as will afterwards appear, those responsible for the state of things over which they presided, had to bear the penalties equally.

CHAPTER XX.
FROM COUNTRY TO TOWN.

FRANCIS HAWKNORBUZZARD, Marquis of Humnoddie, our heroine's acquaintance of Ruddymere Park, was the man called to head the Bungling Coalition, a post for which his pliant and amiable disposition well fitted him. It happened just now that his wife was frequently evading the press of her social obligations in town by a run down for a day or two to Ruddymere, accompanied by her younger daughter Friga, who, unlike her sister, loved the country and hated London.

Thus it came about that Lady Friga and our heroine saw a good deal of each other in their respective homes, and further, that the more they saw, the better they liked each other. Not that Friga Hawknorbuzzard could pretend to the intellect of Letitia Blemmyketts, but she was nevertheless of a cultivated mind and a sweet, simple nature, which gave to her voluptuous style of beauty a very spiritual expression. And if she could not lead in the domain of speculative thought, she could follow; and this she was ready enough to do when her leader was such as Lesbia Newman. Hence the latter, without being unfaithful in thought to Letitia, found that the void made by the absence of her American love was in course of being filled up: the old tie was not weakened, but a new one was added to it. Her home was no longer dull to her, a zest being given to ordinary pursuits such as only the satisfaction of an emotional nature can give. It was therefore no welcome announcement which her new friend brought Lesbia one morning as she met her near the park gate.

'Lesbie, my pet, I was trotting over to you with bad news. My fidgety mother and your mischievous uncle have been plotting against our peace.'

'Uncle Spines! How, Fri?'

'She's been persuading him that he wastes his time and talents rusticating here, – wants him to go to town for the summer season and lecture to audiences worthy of him, while you will see something of that blessed sphere, London society.'

'I suspect your mother thinks more of London society converting me than of my uncle converting it. It will be a bore to give up our sweet nooks and bowers to suffocate in London; still, if we can do any useful work there, I suppose one ought to make the sacrifice.'

'You and your uncle may do useful work, but what can I do, Lesbie?' answered Friga, somewhat sulkily. 'Snubbing everybody right and left is about the only congenial occupation I have in London.'

'But it needs to be done with discrimination, Fri. Suppose you had snubbed me now?'

'That would have been a mistake, love; but I didn't meet you in London.'

'But you might have. There are as good fish in the sea as ever came out of it.'

'I doubt that, Lesbie; I don't believe there are any fish like you in the sea.'

'Bless you, yes, there are plenty, only they don't come out. But I wonder Uncle Spines has not told me of this project.'

Mr Bristley did so, however, the same day. Negotiations had been going on, unknown to Lesbia, for an exchange of duty with a clergyman of Kensington, Mr David Aluminium Mountjoy, who needed a spell of rusticating. The upshot was that shortly afterwards the whole Dulham party migrated to the West End. Here Mr Bristley at once commenced a course of lectures to a fashionable audience, in which he did not speak smooth things, but roundly denounced the reactionary and stagnant condition of the social atmosphere which had set in with the recent political changes. In one of the gloomiest of these discourses, while touching upon the religious question, he somewhat surprised his audience by expressing the opinion that amid the crash of falling idols the Roman Church may yet become a rallying point for the spiritually-minded gathered out of all sects, because she contains the germ of a higher form of worship than the world has yet known. However, this remark was soon forgotten by the bulk of his hearers, in the crowd of more interesting and practical subjects on which he afterwards dwelt, and but for one young lady, not personally known to him, who happened to be present, it is probable that no more would have been heard about it.

Three more Sundays had passed, the lecturer amplifying his discourse upon the same lines, when on the Thursday morning following the fourth lecture, whilst Lesbia was in her room, Fidgfumblasquidiot, who had been allowed to accompany her young mistress to London, having made several ineffectual attempts at the door handle, eventuall put her head in, saying, –

'Please'm, Lady Friga Hawknorbuzzard's here, waiting in the drawing-room to see you; she says she can't stop but just a minute to speak to you.'

Lesbia hurried down, with Gossamer, now growing into a fine dog, thumping the stairs behind her.

'Good-morning, Fri, darling, won't you come up to my room; we shall be more cosy than here?'

'No, Lesbie pet, not this morning; I've kept the hansom waiting because I've no time. Hilda has made up a party to a Crystal Palace concert which I don't care about – I'd much rather stay with you; but they want me to go. Down, Goss! you're not to mud me now, you ugly full moon with teeth!' as the bulldog reared up, wagging his rat's tail, almost as pleased to see Friga as his young mistress. 'Look here, Lesbie, mamma says you *must* all come to our tea to-morrow – it's Friday, my day, you know; at any rate, you and your uncle must come, be the weather what it may. Cardinal Power's coming, and he wishes to meet Mr Bristley.'

'The Cardinal wants to see Uncle Spines? How very odd! What's it about, Friga; have you any idea?'

'Yes; I think he's heard of the lectures and the allusions to his Church. But I must really be off; good-bye, dear; see you all to-morrow.'

Lesbie told her uncle as soon as he came in.

'Eh?' said Mr Bristley. 'The Legate wishes to try his hand on me? Very good, I'm quite willing to be converted to the true faith – upon certain conditions. All right; we'll be there in good time.'

CHAPTER XXI.

FRIVOLOUS AND IMPORTANT.

CARDINAL ARCHBISHOP POWER, Papal Legate in the year 189 – the hierarchy had succeeded in winning back this ancient privilege from the late Government – was a man fitly chosen for his responsible post. His rise in the Church was due to no truckling, but, on the contrary, to the possession of a powerful will and natural ascendency over common minds which marked him out to the shrewd Roman curia as a man well able to take care of its interests. His ruling motive was ambition, but not of a vulgar kind; mere place and title he set little store by, unless as they could help him to figure as one of the men who have made epochs in ecclesiastical history. For this end he was ready to discard prejudice of all kinds, and to seize his opportunity in whatever shape it might present itself. Having no political bias, he was on terms with the best London society, whatever party might be in office; particularly he had known and visited the Hawknorbuzzard family, who were not catholics, for some three years before the present juncture.

The afternoon gathering at the marquis's house in Belgravia next day was fairly large; about half-past four there were over a hundred people in the rooms. Lady Hilda was in her element, and, even more than her mother, seemed to be everywhere at once, but Friga thought it detestable, and whenever she could snatch half-a-minute from the incessant conversation she was obliged to keep up, drew Lesbia aside. Our heroine's mother and aunt had both come, partly out of curiosity to see the Cardinal, who had not yet arrived. As for her uncle, he was extensively interviewed by old and new acquaintances, and had his hands full. Lesbia's dress for such occasions was a compromise between frock and zouaves, with tunic above and stockings below carefully harmonised. She and her uncle had bestowed great pains upon it in consultation with the makers to the Rational Dress Society, and the result was a decided success; everyone who knew her, and some who did not, coming near to have a look, and go ng away with a gain of new ideas as to female fashion. As for the young girl herself, she was by this time so thoroughly inured to being peculiar, that it sat as naturally upon her as her clear healthy complexion. It is fair to mention, by the way, that the complexion, good or bad, of all ladies who had the *entrée* of this house sat naturally upon them; the hostess did not care to know the sort of people who make themselves up, no matter in what manner or in what region.

'How d'ye do, Miss Newman; rawther meet you here than at lawn tennis, aw,' suddenly drawled a dapper little young man, twirling his moustache with his right finger and thumb, while he thrust the left into his trousers pocket, and swung his way up to Lesbia on alternate heels.

'What? Oh, Mr Dandidimmons, to be sure!' she said, holding out her hand. 'How could I be such an oaf as not to recognise at once the Julius Cæsar of chivalry, the patron of ladies?'

Julius seemed a little dashed for the moment, but resumed with smiles and swaying and more vigorous manipulation of the moustache.

'Waal, you converted me, Miss Newman; you worked a revolution in my notions, aw, about gurls, aw. I'm now all for gurls pitching modesty and that sort of thing to the dogs, aw, and showing us what's what, aw, don't you know.'

'Are you indeed, Mr Dandidimmons?' said Lesbia suavely. 'I should like to put you to the proof. Suppose now you were to make me the prettiest and sugariest of sugary pretty speeches, something quite too transcendentally the thing, don't you know; and suppose, instead of hanging my head with the regulation coy-maidenly blush and simper – 'she gives a side glance and looks down,' don't you know – I were just to walk round the table and plant you a persuader, don't you know.'

It was over Mr Julius Dandidimmons' face that the maidenly blush now spread, while a peal of laughter rang from Lady Hilda and all the other girls near. Mrs Bristley's teacup stopped half-way to her mouth, and her stare was if she had run her nose against the dark portion of the moon.

'Upon my word, Lesbia!' said Mrs Newman, biting her lip, 'one would think you had been brought up entirely among stable-boys.'

'Better that than among weaker vessels, mamma,' she replied.

But Julius felt that he cut a foolish figure and must do something for prestige. Taking for granted that Lesbia would not be as good as her word, he swaggered up to he again.

'Haw, weally, Miss Newman, can only say, aw, shall be quite delighted, aw, to have a kick, cuff, or what you please, aw, from such a peculiarly sweet gurl as you.'

'Really, Mr Dandidimmons? Mind I've got a biceps as well as a boot – a pretty good one for a sweet gurl, else I've knocked about with the gloves for nothing.'

'Never mind,' he persisted; 'let's see what you'd do if I sugared you all over.' Without another word, hitting straight from the shoulder, Lesbia sent Dandidimmons sprawling upon the floor.

'Now there's a sweet gurl shown your chivalry what's what, aw; how do you like it?' laughed Lesbia.

The fallen hero made no answer, but lay quite still in the same position. The others still laughed, but Lesbia changed countenance, and, springing to the side of Julius Dandidimmons, snatched him up in her arms as if he had been a baby, carried him to a sofa which happened to be vacant at the time, laid him gently on his back, putting the cushion under his head, then sat down by him on a chair and took his hand in hers while she said tenderly, –

'I hope you don't feel badly hurt, Mr Dandidimmons? I never meant that, I assure you.'

Already the smart, sharp as it had been, was passing away, and the young man was occupied more with his mental than with his bodily sensations. He felt shaken in his self-esteem; it was giving place to a new feeling, one of respect for the girl, wholly different in kind from the sort of respect one might feel toward a man. His habits of thought about girls had sustained a double shock, first in the unconventional violence, then in the unconventional caressing; he was getting a glimpse of the truth that the frailty and timidity of women is a paste of imposture, manufactured by the slavery system of an undeveloped civilisation, and having nothing corresponding to it in the spiritual world. A comical way by such an incident as this, we allow, for Divine Order to reveal itself to the conscience; yet Julius Dandidimmons might have studied theology till it oozed out of his fingers, without learning what he was taught by the rudeness and rough treatment of this unspoilt girl. With an involuntary and genuine glance of devotion at her, he raised himself on his elbow and said timidly, –

'No, Miss Newman, I don't feel it now, and if I did, you have more than made up for it.'

'I'm thankful you're not the worse,' said Lesbia gently. 'But I see we understand each other better now, and I will always be your friend if you wish it; that is the most I am likely to say to any man.'

Julius understood the hint thus delicately and promptly conveyed on purpose to prevent him from commiting himself to a declaration which frivolous young ladies would have been only too ready to gratify their vanity by evoking. The next time he had occasion to speak of Lesbia Newman behind her back, he did not say he hated her, but expressed his opinion fearlessly that 'she's queer, but a noble gurl for all that.'

Meanwhile the hostess in another part of the rooms was saying to Lesbia's uncle, –

'I do hope nothing has prevented the Cardinal from coming; I thought he would have been here before now. *En attendant*, let me introduce you to another acquaintance of his, Miss Francesca Wilson; it was through her I heard of his wish to meet you.'

'Pray, Miss Wilson,' asked Mr Bristlcy, when they had been introduced, 'do you know why Cardinal Power is so good as to be interested on my account? I have not hitherto found myself sought out by Catholic prelates.'

'Yes, it's very simple, Mr Bristley,' she answered. 'Though I have known the cardinal for years, and we are firm friends, I may tell you at once that not even he has been able to induce me formally to enter the Church for whose ritual I have so great admiration. I prefer to keep my judgment free, and you would not be far wrong in calling me an extreme Rationalist. I cull the flowers of all religions as I find them by the wayside. You will not wonder, then, that I was attracted to your lectures, which well repaid my attendance.'

'I see that you and I have much in common, Miss Wilson. Still your interest in my lectures does not explain that of the cardinal.'

'That is explained,' she answered, 'by your frequent and mysterious allusions to a mission of the Church of Rome, which you have never described. It was I who mentioned this to Cardinal Power, and he can no more guess the riddle than I. But it has aroused his curiosity, and that is why he desires to see you. I wonder what makes him so late.'

At this moment the servant entered, announcing, 'His Eminence, Cardinal Power.'

'Better late than never, cardinal,' said the hostess, advancing; 'we almost gave you up.'

'Very sorry, Lady Humnoddie; I had to preside at a meeting and could not get away. But I hope,' he added, looking round, 'that I am still in time for a few words with the learned friend to whom you kindly promised to introduce me?'

'Certainly; here he is. Mr Bristley, thou man of sin or of wisdom or of something, come forth and come hither.'

'Lady Humnoddie evidently supposes me to be in a furnace of expectancy to meet your Eminence. And that might be justified by the result; who knows?'

'More likely on my side than on yours, Mr Bristley,' replied the cardinal; 'it is I who should expect much from the acquaintance. Miss Wilson, with whom you were speaking as I came in, has perhaps told you why.'

'Yes, I understand it is because of certain references to your Church, which have occurred in my lectures. Well, the reasons for making those references were very strong, but being also very grave, I hardly know how to state them in a way suitable to an occasion like this.'

'We will make a suitable occasion, with your kind permission,' said the cardinal, smiling, 'and an early one, for I confess you make me very curious. A special mission of the Catholic Church about which she remains wholly in the dark! I cannot conceive of it. Is it new? has it never been propounded before?'

'It is older than the beginning of the world. It is propounded by every fact in nature. But whether it has been formulated to you in words by others, I do not know, and care not to inquire. If it has not, it is because the time was not ripe, – you were unprepared to receive the higher dispensation. The important question is whether you will receive or reject it now.'

'Do you claim to be its depositary then?'

'Far be such a claim from an individual, and that individual a man!' replied the other gravely. 'I may claim to be one of its humbler apostles, at the most, one of the mere teachers of the divine wisdom. Consider, Cardinal Power, what is the relation, for example, of a good teacher of singing to his pupil. If nature has given the pupil a good voice, the teacher can show how the true tone of that voice should be produced and made the most of. But if the vocal organs be naturally bad, no teacher in the world can make them good. Analogously, if the heart of your Church be in a fit state for the higher dispensation, I can tell you what that dispensation is. But I cannot give you the grace to accept it.'

'More and more mysterious,' said the cardinal, half to himself, as, pressing his knuckles on his lips, he gazed for a few seconds abstractedly on the floor. 'Let me see,' he added, consulting a pocket-book. 'I am rather busy just now, Mr Bristley, but if to-morrow week, Saturday, at nine in the evening, would suit, I expect to be at home, and could spare two or three hours for discussion.'

'I shall be delighted, Cardinal Power,' he replied. 'But may I be allowed to introduce to your Eminence my niece Lesbia Newman, and may I further take the great liberty of asking permission to bring her with me? She is fully as capable of taking part in such a discussion as I am, and even more directly concerned in it.'

'So indeed!' said the cardinal, regarding our heroine with unusual interest. 'By all means come with your uncle, Miss Newman,' he added, smiling, 'and when he has defeated me, construct a golden bridge for a retreating foe.'

Cardinal Power was then summoned by the hostess to another introduction, and the groups dispersed.

Her friend Lady Friga approached Lesbia in another part of the rooms.

'I say, Lesbie, would you like to go with me to the Ladies' Gallery of the House of Commons next Wednesday? My father can give you an order; the Screaming Farce Bill is on, and they expect a shindy.'

'What, Parliament is still good for that, Fri? Yes, I should like very much to go with you.'

'Well, I'll drop you a line about Monday evening.'

CHAPTER XXII.

THE SCREAMING FARCE BILL.

From the *Daily Twaddler*, June 31st 189 –.

IMPERIAL PARLIAMENT,
HOUSE OF COMMONS.
Wednesday.

The Speaker took the chair at four o'clock.

After the despatch of some preliminary business –

Mr Jacobson, in moving the second reading of a Bill to substitute paid delegates for unpaid deputies, with a view to prevent the House of Commons from degenerating into a Screaming Farce, said that, in his opinion, the prevalent popular notion about this honourable House being a club pure and simple, a place for good-fellowship and jollification only, should be corrected, and it should be boldly made known that the national welfare and civilisation, not merely the personal entertainment of hon. members of the club, were the paramount objects of our parliamentary institutions. The question, however, was whether such innovation was practicable in the present shape of the constitution. If not, then the constitution ought to be altered. No romantic sentiments towards a historic assembly should obscure the main issue from the people of this country. Utility must be considered first, sentiment afterwards. They had to ask themselves plainly whether the House of Commons continued still to be what it was formerly, the most perfect legislative machine in the world, or whether, under present conditions, it was proving more and more a failure, and tending more to become what he was sure all parties alike would be sorry to see it – simply a Screaming Farce.

The O'Blunderbuss rose to order. He would support the Bill, as a good Loyalist who liked screaming farces in their proper places, but did not think that the Imperial Legislature was a proper place. How could Loyalists look to a Screaming Farce to maintain law and order in the sister island? There was already reason to fear that the moonlighters were getting the upper hand again, and it was scandalous that surrounding nations should be led to believe that the kingdom was destined to remain for ever under moonlight government.

A member of the Opposition, – That would be nothing new. (Laughter.)

The Speaker, – I must beg hon. members to observe that they are wasting the time of the House by these irrelevancies.

Mr Jacobson did not quite gather the drift of the hon. member for Belfast with respect to moonlight, but he still hoped that practical unanimity existed as to the objections against allowing this honourable assembly to degenerate into actors in a Screaming Farce. The disrepute would not attach to the legislature merely, the national character would be lowered in the eyes of surrounding nations, and not even the most magnificent feats of arms of precision against naked savages armed with spears would avail to restore our prestige. He did hope that the British nation, still, in some respects, the foremost in the world, had not come to such a pass, otherwise it would matter little what was said by anyone in these once august precincts. (Cheers.) Now to come to the remedy. He contended that there was no better way to impress on Parliament the stamp of earnestness than by instituting paid delegates in place of unpaid deputies. Our old deputy system was getting worn out – it was an anachronism. Formerly the two Houses of Parliament really represented the legislative intelligence of the country. Hodge and 'Arry were then content to vote at elections just as they were bid or bribed, and to leave politics in the hands of that oligarchy which they had been bred up to regard as a superior order of beings. Education was then an expensive luxury, and was tacitly looked upon as the privilege of a caste. Now all that was changed. The cheap press and the forcing school had made politics common property, and disposed nine people out of ten to have an opinion of their own on the questions of the day. Public opinion no longer meant, as it did once, the hooraying or hooting of an ignorant mob; it had become a subtle, sensitive, and, in the last resort, irresistible power. This being so, the representative deputy was out of place. He had comparatively *carte blanche*, his parliamentary action was at his own discretion, and he could at any time retort against reproaches from his constituents that he was not paid for his services, but, on the contrary, put to heavy expense to render them. The constituency was thus in a false position, feeling it awkward to call its deputy representative to account, except in extreme cases. Now the paid delegate would be differently situated altogether. His instructions upon every important question would be clear and concise, and if he took liberties, he would be liable to ejection from his seat with as little ceremony as a defaulting clerk. An assembly composed of such delegates would feel in no metaphysical way that it was trustee for the public time and money, and that it could be very shortly and sharply hauled up if it abused its trust. (Hear.)

Mr Giles Doherty rose to move an amendment, namely, that the word delegates should be held to include females. He was of opinion that the time was come when the talents of both sexes should be called, without partiality or favour, to rescue the legislative machine of this great empire from lapsing into the condition of a Screaming Farce. It was only a combination of superstition and arrogance on the part of men which had stood in the way of this being done before; and they were now paying the penalty by the degradation of that assembly, the membership of which they had been proud to associate with their names. The principle of the Bill, so far as it went, was right enough; he entirely concurred with the views of the hon. member in charge of it, so far as they went, but they did not go far enough. A reform of this kind must be drastic to be effective, and he did not for his part see the use of destroying the old jollification club of squires, if it were not to be replaced by a completely revolutionised body, which might reasonably be expected to accomplish the work the jolly squires had left undone. (Hear.)

Mr Normanton seconded the amendment. He would ask hon. gentlemen of all parties what good ever had been or ever would be done by continuing to withhold from legislation the benefit of feminine intelligence. It was nonsense to say that women were conservative or were this, that, or the other. Every political party, from the extreme Right to the extreme Left (to borrow the French mode), possessed its highly cultivated and intelligent women. More particularly, if the plan were about to be adopted of substituting paid delegates with plainly defined parliamentary duties for unpaid deputies almost irresponsible, the little experience which the country already possessed of employing women in public posts, certainly went to show that they discharged public duties quite as efficiently and as a rule more conscientiously than men in the same position. He did not like the term Screaming Farce as applied to this ancient and honourable house, and he rather wondered that a measure had been drafted containing so undignified an expression. But assuredly the very way to make the Lower Chamber merit such an appellation, would be to persevere in the old ruts after all the warnings we had had. (Hear.)

Mr Battleboy Bottleboy then moved the Previous Question, in accordance with his notice. He said that the principle of the Bill was objectionable throughout, but the amendment which had been sprung upon them made it doubly objectionable. As an old member, he felt sure that Englishmen at large were attached to the parliamentary system which had withstood so many shocks, and would regard as a sort of impiety any attempt to tamper with it. As for the idea of introducing petticoat rule into Parliament – (Oh!) – he should feel bound to oppose it tooth and nail, as the saying was. The admission of women into the House would never do; they would always be fussy and wanting things. (Laughter.)

A Radical member, – Things! What sort of things?

Mr Batlleboy Bottleboy, – Why, what they would call practical measures – redress of crying wrongs, stoppage of waste, effective sanitary provisions, free discussion of social evils, suppression of cruelty to children, animals, and all the defenceless, thorough investigation and reform of the poor-laws, and so forth, in short, all sorts of d – d nonsense. (Order.)

The Speaker, – I regret that it is my duty to call the hon. member for Lundy to order.

Mr Battleboy Bottleboy, – I withdraw the expression, Sir, but I am sure hon. gentlemen on both sides of the House must see that it would never do. If through the admission of petticoats – (Order) – through the admission of ladies, this House were to get into unprecedented habits – (Laughter) – it would lose caste, and then surrounding nations would begin to sneer at us and would decline to follow our example. For I conceive that this country has still a mission to fulfil, it is that of being jolly herself and teaching foreigners to be jolly. And if that mission is to be frustrated bythese – these most undesirable reforms, why, I would rather see Parliament both retain and deserve the name of a Screaming Farce, than be a party to the sacrilege. The very introduction of such a measure is a sign, I am afraid, that the country is going to the dogs. It may not be elegant to say so, but that is the truth. Although we have done well and wisely by seating a Bungling Coalition in power, yet revolutionary democracy continues to be a disturbing force in the land. (Ironical Opposition cheers.) The bonds of society are in danger of giving way, for open infidelity and blasphemy are tolerated, and licentiousness of all sorts is winked at and is spreading: we are coming under a moral plague. Still, as I said before, in spite of the forces of disintegration which are doing their fatal work, there remains one thing which this great country can do, and that is to be jolly herself and teach foreigners to be jolly. But this is dependent upon sticking up for our old customs and not allowing new-fangled considerations of utility to corrode and undermine our glorious constitution. I am quite aware that in the present temper of the House, moving the Previous Question is the emptiest of hollow forms; nevertheless, I am confident that when the ill-advised measure reaches another place, it will be summarily disposed of (Hear, from the Ministerial benches.)

Mr Giles Doherty said that if a majority of this House were against the Bill, there was, of course, an end of the matter; but as for the will of the country being set aside in another place, although he, for one, should be reluctant to see another place made to enlarge her borders and open her mouth without measure, yet he took leave to remind the House that the swamping of another place by the wholesale creation of new inmates was a measure within the scope of the existing constitution. He would prefer, however, to see the Upper Chamber dealt with by having its veto taken away; by this its political teeth would be drawn without injuring ils social utility, if it had any. (Radical cheers.)

The Speaker, – I must take occasion to remind hon. gentlemen that these informal attacks upon another estate of the realm are unparliamentary.

The Chancellor of the Exchequer said he felt sure of the assent of his colleagues in predicting that such a step as the wholesale creation of new peers would not be recommended by Her Majesty's present Government.

It being now the dinner hour, the sitting was suspended. When the debate was resumed.

Mr Battleboy Bottleboy, on rising again, was greeted with loud Ministerial cheers. The hon. gentleman was observed to take up an attitude of address with his thumbs inserted in the arm-pits of his waistcoat, his chin depressed, his countenance illumined with a beaming smile, his feet planted firmly about eighteen inches apart, as if for cavalry sword exercise, and the central portion of his person maintaining a regular horizontal oscillation, suggestive of an attempt to restore thereby a badly-fitting key to the door to which it belonged. He said, –

'M – m – m – mishter Speaker an – m – m – m – mluds-anjellum. I am quite sh – sh – shensible of the t – t – truth o' the osservation made by the hon. member for Eastshire respecting the proposed ammition of pettico – l – l – ladies to the p – p – p – privileges of a p – p – parliamentary career, and I'm q – quite ready to sh – shport by vote whatever p – p – pleasbesladies – hic! As the hon. jelium truly remarks, it would do away with the character of a Shcreaming Farsh which attaches to this – hic! ancient and honourable 'Ouse, and therefore I'm q – quiteweady.' (Laughter, cries of 'Speak up.' 'Explain.' 'You said the contrary before.') 'Quite true, m – m – mludsanjellum; hon. members are quite q – quitewight. But – fact is, ye see – I've ch – ch – ch – changememine – yes, completely ch – ch – changememine – hic!' (Uproar, Ministerial groans, Opposition cheers, much laughter.)

The Speaker, – I really must beg the hon. member for Lundy to bring his speech to a close; this is positively indecorous.'

Mr Battleboy Bottleboy, – Quite wight M – m – m – mishter Speaker – I 'umbly bow to your decision, Sir – hic! – always b – b – bow to the authority o' the chair, you know; but weally and truly, mludsanjellum, I – I – ('Speak up!' 'Sit down!' Great laughter.)

The Speaker, – I shall be obliged to name the hon. member if he will not desist. It is impossible that this can be allowed to go on.

Mr Battleboy Bottleboy, – I b – b – beg to deshist at once an – t – to – b – b – bow to the authority o' the chair – you know – but also I mus – b – b – begleave M – m – mishter Shpeakaw – hic! jush to shay in conclusion, that on sh – shecond thoughts I've ch – changemine back again, and now I'm quite in favour of this – hic! – honourable 'Ouse being and becoming a sh – sh – sh – hic! a sh – Shqueamingfarsh – hic! (More uproar, Ministerial cheers, Opposition groans, whistles, cat-calls, etc., amid which the hon. gentleman the member for Lundy resumed his seat with a heavy thud, and then rolled on to the knees of the hon. member on his left, and finally upon the floor.) It now became a question of applying the closure, when, taking advantage of a momentary lull,

Mr Giles Doherty rose to withdraw his amendment, fearing it might wreck the measure. Cries of 'Divide' then arose, and eventually the House divided upon the Bill in its unamended form, when there appeared

For the second reading	189
Against	278
Majority against	89

The Bill was therefore lost.

CHAPTER XXIII.

TOWARD THE FLAMINIAN GATE.

A QUARTER-PAST nine on the following Saturday evening found our heroine and her uncle at a supper tea in the Legate's back drawing-room in Westminster. The conversation at table was light; Lesbia, who, as we have seen before, had a talent for mimicry, entertained her host, a man of the world, whose guests felt no *gêne*, by reproducing the ludicrous parts of the Parliamentary debate at which she had been present since they last met. When they afterwards seated themselves in easy chairs in the larger room, another sort of debate began, the final results of which proved to be in no manner a screaming farce.

'Well now, Mr Bristley,' said the cardinal, 'we are in private conclave at last, so there need be no more reserve about this mystery. What is it, then; out with it.'

'It's Madonna-worship,' answered Lesbia promptly.

'Indeed!' said the cardinal. 'But I thought there was question of a special mission of Rome?'

'That *is* her special mission,' said Mr Bristley, with brevity like that of his niece.

'But surely – I was under the impression that non-catholics blamed us for exalting Our Lady too much,' objected the cardinal.

'They may,' retorted Mr Bristley. 'It is not my business to take up the heads of fools that pave hell. Excuse my warmth of expression, Cardinal Power, my point of view is remote from that of the non-catholics you speak of, remote, I fear, even from your own. Exalt Our Lady too much, say you? You cannot. My charge against you Catholics is, that you do not exalt Her nearly enough. I arraign you for being wilfully blind and deaf in the very visible presence of Deity itself to which you have been admitted, and if you were dumb also when in that presence, it would be better: there would be less sacrilege.'

Cardinal Power gazed at his new acquaintance for some seconds in unfeigned amazement.

'Not worship Her enough!' he at last repeated.

'Not nearly enough,' responded the other. 'This people flatter me with their lips, but their heart is far from me.' You come to Her with lachrymose hypocrisy, babbling about intercession. Intercession! Are you aware, Cardinal Power – you are *not* aware, or you would not do it – that to ask the Supreme Deity to *intercede*, is the very essence of blasphemy? Intercede with whom? It cannot be with those below Herself, for that would be nonsense. But who is above Her – who can be above the Supreme? That is why I said you Catholics were better dumb; because you could not blaspheme in that fashion.'

'Your Eminence will excuse my uncle's pithy language, I am sure,' said Lesbia gently; 'enthusiasts such as he are not Chrysostoms.'

'That's all right, Miss Newman,' answered the cardinal, who cared nothing for useless ceremony. 'But, Mr Bristley, is Our Lady, then, above the Trinity?'

'Why, of course,' he replied. 'The Trinity is but a metaphysical analysis of humanity, Our Lady is its synthesis. The synthesis is the living person, the analysis is but its anatomy. You yourself theoretically admit as much in styling Her the Mother of God; yet when it comes to practical application, you manage to misunderstand and pervert your own words, and to lapse into the worse than heathen idolatry in which Protestant Christianity is sunk. Thus you miss, nay, you trample upon, your mission, which is to lead the world out of the old idolatry toward the new light.'

'By throwing Christ and his religion overboard?' asked the cardinal.

'No, by interpreting them conformably to the light of nature,' replied the other. 'Your Church claims the right of interpretation: be it so. But why does she waste and throw away that right? or rather, why does she use it to league herself with devils and darkness?'

'How does she so?' asked the cardinal.

'My uncle calls all spirits that are not spirits of woman worship devils of darkness,' explained Lesbia, with a smile.

'But what exactly am I to understand by woman-worship?' inquired the cardinal.

'Woman-worship,' answered Lesbia, 'is at any rate the reverse of the man-worship which the religions of the world hitherto have set up.'

'Yes,' assented Mr Bristley, 'it is that certainly, but it implies a good deal more beside. It implies that carnal affections and even passions are to be impressed into the service of religion, instead of being suppressed as though they were its enemies.'

'I see,' said the cardinal; 'your religion of the future is to be based on hedonism – it is to be a religion of pleasure.'

'Of pleasure that is in keeping with and belongs to Divine Order, yes. Not otherwise.'

'Divine Order!'

'Certainly, Divine Order is the spiritual subjection of the masculine to the feminine in humanity. It is the reversal of this order which constitutes the sin and causes the miseries in the world.'

'Spiritual subjection; not temporal then?'

'Yes, temporal too, in all things that relate to the spiritual, in all the direct and indirect concerns of religion.'

'Is not that the doctrine of Comte the Positivist?'

'He said, I believe,' replied Mr Bristley, 'that the time is coming when man shall no more bow the knee except to woman; but I do not gather that his idea was that of a deep spiritual religion, it was rather that of a materialistic gallantry, chivalry, or what you like to call it, superficial, unpractical, and, in this work-a-day world, impossible. We do not want to put women into a glass case to be stared at, we simply to reverse the present relations of the sexes in all things religious, and to put women into the priestess's place, which is now usurped by man. Along with this will go, of course, the establishment of her equal rights in things temporal. That is what I understand by Divine Order: is it clear to you?'

'Clear enough,' replied the cardinal. 'But why is this great revolution to be the work of Rome, the least revolutionary of human – let us say human – institutions? Would not some new religious body undertake the work with freer hands? The ostensible character of our holy Church is to remain always the same; she changes not, or as little as possible. Built upon the foundation of Apostles and Prophets, our Lord himself being the chief corner-stone' – the prelate made as though he would cross himself or bow his head as he recited this, but concluded that it was not worth the trouble, which was just as well, since the effect would have been spoilt by an unmistakable wink which he directed at Lesbia – 'built upon that security, she changes as little as the moon, the faithful witness in heaven. Devout but infirm minds, troubled with doubt in these subversive days can turn to her as to a strong rock whereto they may always resort, a shield against aggressive Atheism, a tower of defence against all spiritual foes. Their responsibility is eased off their shoulders; they need not think; they have but to trust and obey. They receive the light yoke laid upon them by an infallible authority, and they need not fret themselves about its source. They repose in a palace of archaism, and can shut their eyes in comfort to what the infidel world calls the facts of science. A ready-made and regenerate conscience is supplied to them on easy terms. Why would you disturb this happy family?'

Both his visitors laughed at the undisguised irony which ran through this defence of Catholicism.

'Your Eminence reminds me of the Parliamentary debate we were talking about at tea,' said Lesbia. 'It would appear that the mission of the Church of Rome also is to be jolly herself and teach surrounding Churches to be jolly.'

'Evidently it comes to that,' said the cardinal, with such simplicity that the other two laughed again. 'The more so,' he resumed, 'because there is another consideration. The happy and holy family is flourishing. Propagandism thrives; more pence jingle into Peter's box; fine new churches, convents, and even monasteries are springing up; in short, the old thing pays. Why upset it?'

'That is plausible, Cardinal Power,' answered Mr Bristley, 'plausible, but not sound. In the first place, it is not a question of upsetting catholicism, but of strengthening it, – raising it above competition. Then you say it flourishes and extends; good, I am glad to hear it. But may not the same be said for every sect or church, for the Salvation Army, for the Jews themselves? The reason is not far to seek: this is an age of tolerance, and why should Roman Catholicism not be tolerated equally with other creeds? But it is not an age of tolerance merely, it is also an age of scepticism; and sects or schools of irreligion are free, equally with those of religion, to do their chosen work. The result, however, of that work is to stimulate the religious spirit, wherever it really exists; hence the prosperity of your creed (equally with that of other creeds) among the minority of baptised Catholics who are not sceptics. They see that unless they put their shoulder to the wheel their religion must decay and lapse; that is not their desire, therefore they show that zeal which strikes your imagination so much. But, after all said and done, you have shown me no more than this, Cardinal Power, that the religious body of which you are a dignitary, is as free as any other body to come and drink at the fountain among the crowd. You have not shown that you Catholics possess any special privilege in society; you have not shown that you are on the way to attain such; you have not even shown that you really care about it.'

The cardinal was listening attentively, and the urbane sneer which was his habitual expression had already faded from his countenance. As he made no move to reply, the other resumed: –

'Or, if you do care about it, then I am afraid you are making the fatal mistake of setting down to fancied penitence and reaction on the part of the modern world, what is really the manifestation of its æstheticism conjoined with its liberality. You think people are deferring to you as of old, when in fact they are but patronising you. Get rid of such a delusion, Cardinal Power. You cannot stand a second Reformation like the Lutheran; it would shatter you to pieces; do not provoke it. You have a grand opportunity, and unless you are the most insensate of men, you will not let it slip. Consider well. Competition is pervading every branch of secular industry; is it likely to leave out of sight the motive power of religious sentiment? Assuredly not; therefore that religious body will be the most favoured, will become the richest in all things that make this life worth living or the life to come worth preparing for, which shall succeed in attaining to the greatest popularity, not to the greatest orthodoxy. Dogma is an intellectual quicksand, but hedonism appeals to our common instincts, and only upon that basis can any temple of worship endure, now that the old sacerdotalism has passed away. You possess that basis in the cult of Our Lady, it only needs developing: the devotion toward Her which already exists among Catholics is ample evidence of the fact. Is not, then, that fact a plain call to the rulers of our Church, – a voice in the wilderness crying to them, 'Arise, shine, for thy light is come, and the glory of the Eternal is risen upon thee.'"

'You are an enthusiast, Mr Bristley,' said the cardinal, in a tremulous voice. For as he was about to reply, he looked up and his eyes met those of Lesbia.

Never before, not among the thousands of girls and women he was accustomed to meet in the exercise of his ministrations and in society, had he been transfixed by such a look as that. It penetrated to his inmost heart, as an illustration of the words, 'The glory of the Eternal is risen upon thee;' it was, in truth, looking out at and overwhelming him. But neither of the two spoke to the other, and the parson, who was too intent on his subject to notice the incident, was left to continue his attack.

'Enthusiast! Yes I am, Cardinal Power, an enthusiast in this cause, and with good reason. I see the goal to which all human religion has been striving through these long ages of agony. I see that goal within reach, within *your* reach; why do you not press forward to it? Have you no lofty ambition, no aspirations, no sense of corporate dignity, none of that initiative and enterprise without which the great Church of which you are a pillar could never have been founded? After all that she has achieved and suffered through these semi-barbarous centuries, are you content at last to vegetate in the shade, existing upon sufferance, the sufferance of your inferiors, regarded with respectful pity by the vigorous, racy young sects springing up around you, and with pity the reverse of respectful by the rapidly-growing army of Freethinkers? To take a parallel case, it seems to me that there are few more lamentable sights than that of a person possessing some special gift which might be the means of conferring benefit and pleasure upon thousands, but who, not from stress of ill-health or penury or other adverse fortune, but solely from lack of courage, hides that talent away in a napkin, and allows it to be lost to the world. Then, if this be so where only an individual is concerned, how far more strongly does it apply to a venerable society whose avowed mission is to lead mankind to the light? What shall we say of such a body if it wilfully throw up its mission and slink into self-inflicted obscurity and impotence, and that too at a time when there is ample evidence that the mission promises to be successful, and needs only a determined effort to bring it to a glorious issue?'

Again the prelate, looking up, met Lesbia's gaze, and again it shook him more than her uncle's trenchant words. The latter resumed: –

'What is the use of standing with folded hands, waiting for water to flow up hill or time to travel backwards? Your old priestly dominion is gone, you can no more recover it by dint of obstinacy than you can force us back into the pre-railway modes of life. The world is not what it was; it has cast off, for better or worse, its swaddling clothes, and that childish kind of faith which a claim to infallibility could sway is fading out of remembrance. You cannot resuscitate the past, but you can grasp the future; you can compel no one to come in to you, but you can allure the masses of mankind by a direct yet a religious appeal – religious in the highest sense of the word, – to the most universal and ineradicable of its affections and passions.'

'A splendid dream, Mr Bristley,' observed the cardinal, who by this time had recovered himself, 'but can it ever be realised? Have the masses got it in them to be trained up to such a lofty view and use of their natural inclinations? Can they ever, think you, be brought to comprehend your Divine Order? Will they ever ennoble their loves and desires very far above the amours of the beasts of the field or the dogs of the street? I doubt it.'

'Then to what purpose is religion – Catholic or other – professed and taught?' rejoined the other. 'Is it not altogether a gigantic waste of human time and energy? If religion cannot ennoble our passions, what *can* it do? It cumbers the earth. But whether it is to exist as an encumbrance or as a treasure, you may be sure of this, Cardinal Power, that if the rising generation accepts any religion at all, it will be one founded upon its desires and hopes, not upon its fears. Hell and purgatory are scouted; heaven may be believed in, *if it is made attractive.*'

'A heaven of black-eyed houris, like the Mussulman's,' observed the cardinal, smiling.

'No; because those do not keep Divine Order. But, anyhow, you must lead the rising generation how you can, not how you would like. It may be led; it will not be driven.'

'Then Divine Order, as you read it, bids the Church face right about, and proclaim that the very propensities in mankind which heretofore she has most striven to combat, must henceforward be relied upon as her main resource.'

'Subject to Divine Order, yes, Cardinal Power. You must do it, or your Church will perish, not by violence – we don't do that nowadays – but by neglect and inanition.'

'Then you simply throw up, reject, and scout the notion that there may be such things as eternal and immutable verities, of which the Catholic Church is the depositary, Mr Bristley?' said the prelate, with a sneer on his face which plainly showed his own opinion of that convenient doctrine.

'There is and can be but one such verity in the universe, Cardinal Power, and that is Divine Order. The Catholic Church the depositary of it, you say? That is just what we want to see her. However, I am not discussing verities with you,

Cardinal Power, but expediency. You have to take the plunge, in order that your Church may live, not because it is the truth. Secular education of the masses is already overtaking you, it is close on your heels, shortly it will tread upon them, then it will grip you by the throat and hurl you to the ground. You must agree with it quickly while you are in the way; wrestle with it and conquer it you cannot. Be wise in time; listen to the counsels of impartial bystanders. I am an impartial bystander, because I know that woman-worship must triumph before the world is much older, whether it be your Church or some other that is destined to be its champion. My reason for urging you to take it up, is that I see the many advantages you possess over other competitors, and what a crying pity it would be that you should turn tail and leave your inferiors to carry off the prize. I have said enough at the outset, I think, to show you that the apparent hold which Catholicism is regaining here and in other non-Romish countries, is nothing more than the hold which all sects, old and new, are gaining through the spread of tolerance, and of the freethought which you miscall infidelity. Working on your present lines, then, all you can hope for is to remain one tolerated and respected sect among many; but even this hope may not be fulfilled, because there are points on which you are professedly opposed to tolerance, and which, sooner or later, must involve you in a struggle with it to which there can only be one ending. If your dream is to make England and English countries Catholic again, it must be by re-casting Catholicism in the mould shaped by the spirit of the age; for to attempt the opposite course, that of bringing the English-speaking peoples under the Papal yoke, is only to court certain and probably swift destruction.'

'But I cherish no such illusions, Mr Bristley,' answered the cardinal, with a more gloomy expression than before. 'You are right, I must admit, in what you say about our hold on this country. I do not mind admitting it to such exceptional disputants as you two, although I should not say it from the pulpit; but it is unfortunately true that, after all our efforts, the bulk of the English people still look upon our doings and our ceremonial as if they were nothing but a money-making entertainment. Where we give them good music, they will come to our churches for that, and they look with a languid curiosity at what is going on at the high altar. A certain number of flies get caught in the paste on these occasions, no doubt' – his two listeners chuckled at hearing the chief priest thus express himself concerning the winning of souls to Christ's Church – 'but the multitude gets further away every year from genuine belief in our religion or in any other. People patronise it, as you have said, according to their tastes, but none, except, perhaps, a few washy girls in their teens, bow their wills to it as of old.'

'Then what do you propose to do, Cardinal Power?' inquired Lesbia, looking steadfastly at him again with her serious, searching eyes, 'To lie for ever stifled amid the rank heaps of tolerated creeds, one of a number of decaying sects destined to be shunted off and shot as rubbish by the secular board schools? How

are the mighty fallen! Mark my words. Never in the religious history of mankind will so tremendous a blunder have been committed, such an opportunity
thrown away, as you and your Church will have to answer for, if you deflect from
your mission now that it has been set plainly before you, and not only that, but
has even been in some degree begun to be realised by the actual devotion of
members of your Church to Our Lady throughout the world.'

As the cardinal hesitated for an answer, Mr Bristley said, –

'Now, Lesbie, I think we have trespassed long enough upon his Eminence's
good-nature: it is half-past eleven. He must be as tired of us as King Agrippa was
of St Paul.'

'Not at all,' answered the cardinal, as they rose from their chairs. 'Agrippa
may have been tired of Paul, but I am not of this young prophetess; on the contrary, I feel inclined to say to her, Almost thou persuadest me to be a – well no,
not a Christian, most decidedly.'

'And I hope that it will be not almost, but altogether,' she replied, holding
his proffered hand. 'I hope that you will come to see, Cardinal Power, how vast
a work of beneficence your exalted position might be used to achieve. Good-
night, and many thanks for your kindness.'

As they walked to the Underground Railway to catch the last train for
Kensington, Mr Bristley said, –

'We've done the best we could, eh, Lesbie? Time will show whether it has
been to any purpose. The conservatism of Rome has always been a hard nut to
crack by any fingers softer than General Cadorna's[5] in 1866.'

I think I have cast my seed,' she replied, 'but I do not look for any real movement, religious or social, until after – the crash.'

Her uncle did not reply, and little more was said between them until they
got out at their station. The two elder ladies were sitting up for them, and were
curious to hear, not about the subject of discussion, but about Cardinal Power
personally. But Lesbia and her uncle were not up to further conversation, and in
a few minutes all were in their bedrooms.

The short summer night turned into dawn, and the renewed rumble of a
vehicle here and there, the chirp of town sparrows in the sooty trees, a street cry
in the distance, as the grey glimmer grew on, showed that London was waking
up to its stiff, dismal Sunday; still in his solitary drawing-room, with the gas
burning faintly over his head, with his elbows resting upon the table and his face
buried in his hands, sat the Roman Catholic prelate, lost in thought. For three
hours he had hardly changed his attitude; at last he rose and moved slowly to the
door, muttering, – 'Madness, madness! the idea of getting bewitched like this by
a visionary young girl!'

But that did not end the matter.

CHAPTER XXIV.

GATHERING CLOUDS.

IT was a fine morning, and the Russians walked into Herat, Quetta, Candahar, and Cabul. It was done in the most gentlemanly way, so as to give the least possible shock to anyone's susceptibilities. A circular had been despatched a few days before to all the great Powers, to the effect that in view of possibly unsettled relations, it behoved every nation to take guarantees for the preservation of peace. In particular, an Envoy Extraordinary to England had instructions to concede and promise everything without stint.

The Russian guarantee came about in this way. The Ameer of Afghanistan, Lamplighterawshat Khan, had just waited to trouser his annual British subsidy at the regular time, and had then ceded the above-named places to the Czar, for a handsome consideration. It was very mean and ungrateful, this conduct on the part of Lamplighterawshat. He had been petted, patted, stroked, feasted, festooned by the British Government; he had reviewed Indian forces; yet no sooner did he get an opening, than he sold his benefactors to the highest bidder, for Russia bid him higher than the tribute paid to him by our Bungling Coalition in return for his countenance and support. The Indian Executive was paralysed, and did not see how to stir in the matter; the Home Government was at once applied to, and despatched peremptory orders to resist the encroachment by force; but a *few* hours afterwards equally peremptory orders were telegraphed to do nothing without having first received a satisfactory explanation.

On the Sunday morning which concludes the previous chapter, our party were sitting down to breakfast, when Lesbia opened the *Observer*, which she had got from a newsman at the street corner.

'Here's a shindy, all the fat's in the fire! the Russian bear is on the rampage again, the Eastern Question is up in full dance, India's threatened, and they've called a Cabinet Council for this afternoon.'

'On Sunday!' said her uncle; 'very unusual; they must think it a serious crisis. Very awkward, isn't it, with this new African embroglio in prospect, and the United States taking an unfriendly tone. I suppose because the wild boar out of the wood is worrying them into it.'

'Yes, those Irish are at the bottom of every mischief. What's to be the end of it?'

'I suppose we shall have to fight somebody,' said her uncle. 'It'll depress the money markets to-morrow.'

'Fight!' repeated Lesbia,

Singing] 'We don't want to fight, and, by Jingo! if we do,
We'll show our heels, we'll show our pace,
    We'll show our beauty too:
We've run away before, and so we shall again,
Shoulder to shoulder with the brave Egyptian.'

Really, Lesbia,' said Mrs Bristley, 'I wonder you don't apply for an engagement in a music-hall.'

'Well, Aunt Kate, if nothing better turns up, I shall try for that.'

'A nice kettle of fish indeed,' said Mr Bristley, pursuing his own thoughts. 'I'm afraid it is the little cloud, no bigger than a man's hand.'

'I must say,' remarked his niece, in a more serious vein, 'that much as I dote on sweet Friga, I do wish someone else than her excellent father were at the head of affairs. He's too pliable to steer a Bungling Coalition. They say, too, that he leaves foreign policy entirely to his relative the Foreign Secretary, who, in turn, leaves it to the Under Secretary, that Irishman Fitzgorin.'

'Well, what then, Lesbie?' asked her uncle.

'Why,' she replied, 'you know that –

'When a twister a twisting would twist him a twist,
While twisting one twist, three twists he must twist;
But if while twisting, one twist should untwist,
The twist untwisting untwists the twist.

Through him or through others, I am afraid our twist will be undone.'

'My belief has always been,' said Mr Bristley, 'that the better plan would be to cut Ireland adrift. Leaving them to shift for themselves would, in practice, draw them closer to us: such is human nature. "You shall," is always answered by "We won't;" but "Do as you please," often leads to calm reconsideration.'

'I believe so too, Uncle Spines,' answered Lesbia; 'but the Irish difficulty is only one among the many bad signs of the times. Does it not strike you that the social as well as the political atmosphere is lurid and gathering? A bubble is biggest before it bursts, and the society of the day gives me the idea of an inflated bubble. Bedridden superstitions seem to be regaining their hold; the ruling classes are lapsing into that condition where they learn nothing and forget nothing. Advances in the direction of pure taste unsullied by vulgarity cannot be made, even in such matters as female attire – not to any appreciable extent. There is little real initiative anywhere, and what there is, is soon snuffed out by smug, self-sufficient common-place; the ball of civilisation is refusing to be pushed further up hill, and gives signs of rolling back upon its supporters, I see all this as I did not see it before I came to town and had the benefit of conversation about London life with Friga, who has been accustomed, much against her will, to the throng of it. Altogether, I have a sense of being stifled by the moral atmosphere, and a presentiment that the present state of things cannot last long. We shall have an explosion – not dynamite – but revolution.'

'It may not suit your wild originality, Lesbie dear,' said her mother, 'that society should be coming to its senses, and that there should be a reaction in favour of womanliness of the old sort; but that is the light in which the circumstances which displease you appear to old fogies like your aunt and me.'

'Pray, mamma,' asked Lesbia, in a cold, hard tone, 'do you remember the Dream?'

The young girl put this unwonted question to her mother in a moment of uncontrollable irritation; and no sooner were the words out of her mouth than she regretted them. Mrs Newman turned deadly pale, and the newspaper, which she had taken up to glance at, fell on the carpet, as she rested both her hands on the table and gazed out of window.

'Ah, yes, indeed I do, Lesbie,' she said at last sadly. 'God knows in what shape the catastrophe is to come, but it cannot be for nothing that I listened in my trance to the tremendous thunder rolling and rattling, and saw that dreadful hillside spattered with blood. And to think that you should have seen a place in Ireland which answers to it exactly! I'm sure we may well pray, 'From battle, murder, and sudden death, good Lord, deliver us.''

'Yes; well, it can't be helped,' said Mr Bristley, rising, with a grave face; 'there's no use in crying over spilt milk, or spil – let's have a constitutional down the Hammersmith Road before service; what d'you say, ladies all? I don't see why I should have stagnation in my legs, whatever may happen in the body politic.'

CHAPTER XXV.
ANOTHER VICTIM OF JUGGERNAUT.

ATHOUGH Lady Humnoddie's regular receptions were on Fridays, she was glad to see any old friends who chose to come in to tea on Sundays; and this eventful week our heroine and her uncle found her alone about half-past five. The conversation, of course, turned upon the Cabinet Council.

'They won't do anything, bless you, Mr Bristley,' she said, in reply to a question of his; 'it'll all end in smoke, you'll see. We shall never fight for Afghanistan, – had enough of that hornet's nest; and, after all, Afghanistan is not India. If the Afghans like the Russians for masters, I don't see what we can do to prevent their having them.'

'What's up now, I wonder?' said Lesbia, going to the window. 'What a row the newsmen are making down the street! What can they have got hold of on Sunday afternoon? Surely not the result of the Cabinet Council already?'

'Throw, the sash wider open, Lesbie,' said the marchioness; 'some humbug, I suppose; but let's hear.'

The men came within hearing, selling copies of a new Sunday halfpenny sheet at every area railing.

'*Telltale, special! Telltale! Assassination of the Emperor of Russia by ladies of the Court! Full particulars! Telltale, special! Telltale!*'

'Good heavens, how horrible!' exclaimed Lady Humnoddie, ringing the bell. 'Get one of those papers, please;' and the servant re-appeared with one in half a minute, and handed it to her.

'Can it be true? the Emperor shot dead in the throng of a summer festive gathering, by two Nihilists, ladies in the Empress' suite! The assassins not yet arrested! What dreadful days we live in!'

'I am very grieved to hear it,' said Lesbia. 'Poor Czar! Pity the sorrows of a despotic monarch! And so useless to the cause of freedom! They'll only put up another in his place, perhaps a more tyrannical one.'

'There is no proof that any of the modern Czars have been personally tyrannical,' said Mr Bristley, recovering from his amazement at the tragic news; 'they have probably been the tools of an interested clique, and this is how they have to pay the penalty for a system into which they have been born and bred, and from which it is hard for them to escape. What a pity it is! Give me any respectable place in the world rather than that of a Russian emperor; but if I *were* one, I would infinitely rather take my chance of being murdered by my own rascally underlings than go about in perpetual fear of those who can pose before the world as the champions and martyrs of popular liberty. I would adopt Garibaldi's motto, 'Se cadro, cadro da fute, il mio novue resteia.' How much better, how much more satisfactory to heart and conscience, to incur personal danger in the cause of reforms, which would draw together prince and subjects, and win for my country the confidence and approbation of Europe, than to incur it by perseverance in courses which have the very opposite of those effects!'

'It's very sad,' said Lady Humnoddie; 'but as for that, I fancy the Panslavonic party in Russia hold that the territorial expansion of the country cannot reach its proper limits except under the autocracy.'

'Then how comes it,' asked Mr Bristley, facing her full, 'that constitutional and democratic England has accomplished *her* territorial expansion all round the globe? It has come to pass because the faculty of such expansion depends upon the character of a people, and not upon its form of government. But you mistake me if you imagine I am inveighing against the Russian autocracy. On the contrary, I believe there is very much to be said for it, or would be, if only the despotic monarch sat enthroned above a European constitution, instead of above a barbarous and corrupt bureaucracy. The imperial prerogative and veto might be the final appeal from the laws even of a thoroughly republican constitution; and a *good* despotism of this sort would have many and obvious advantages over a simple republic. But the links of a constitution are indispensable, in order to connect the monarch with his people. The Russians themselves, I believe, have a saying, 'Heaven is high, and the Czar is far off.' He ought not to be far off; and the practical way of bringing him near is to create a constitution whereby genuine, not manufactured, public opinion may reach his ear.'

'Meanwhile, I wonder how this will affect the foreign policy of Russia,' said Lady Humnoddie thoughtfully. 'Will it make for peace or war?'

'For war, I fear,' said Lesbia, to the surprise of both the others. 'Murder does not bring good, and perhaps the Conservative party in Russia may prefer the risks of war abroad to those of revolution at home.'

'Yes, if they can choose between them,' said the Marchioness. 'But they might get both.'

'So might we,' rejoined Lesbia.

CHAPTER XXVI.
COMPLICATIONS AND CONFLAGRATION.

Our heroine's prognostication was verified – a military dictatorship succeeded to power during the unlooked-for interregnum in Russia, and cast in its lot with the most aggressive section of the Panslavonic party. The old quarrel with Turkey was revived, on a pretext about arrears of an indemnity due from '77, and the upshot was that eighty thousand Russians, under General Polishoff, passed Kars, and marched upon Erzeroum. The terrified Sultan called upon Allah and his friends – that is, Turkish bondholders – all over Europe, to come to his aid in this extremity, and the Bungling Coalition, under pressure of influential capitalists, was weak enough to be drawn into an entanglement involving such national discredit that the sober judgment of the country succumbed for the time to the Jingo element, and an auxiliary expedition for the defence of Asia Minor was resolved upon.

The medley army of the Sultan had already scrambled together at the first alarm, and had been sent forward to the interior of Asia Minor, under Rhumbegar Pasha, chosen for the command simply because he was a palace favourite. He sustained a crushing defeat by the Russians, to the south-east of Erzeroum, and, hardly escaping with a few thousand men, retreated to Scutari, where he met the English force of fifteen thousand men, under Brigadier-General Burnfingal, hurrying to his support. On learning of Rhumbegar's defeat, however, the English commander did not think it prudent to risk an engagement with so small a force, and applied for reinforcements to the home Government. The country now awoke to the fact that a struggle as big as the Crimean War had begun, and the Opposition made the most of the discontent this discovery was likely to evoke. But this time the weight of public opinion leant to the side of the Bungling Coalition, and not only did the Ministry remain in power, but the supplies for a great war were voted, and an additional force of thirty thousand men, raising the force in Asia Minor to a total of forty-five thousand, was sent out, under the distinguished and popular commander General Lord Gurth Redhill, to supersede Burnfingal. Meanwhile, however, the latter had been venturing on a little glory on his own account. He pushed forward on the line of the beaten Turk's retreat, met the enemy, nearly three times his own strength, in a mountainous and unexplored district, and after a smart engagement of about two hours, was repulsed with a loss of four hundred and eleven men, three field pieces, and an ammunition waggon. This little reverse caused much irritation at home, and the general public looked with impatience for Lord Redhill to avenge it. But the Russians knew their advantages, and were not to be tempted into a pitched battle. By feints and stratagems of various kinds they gradually drew the British army on from point to point, until it was close to the great fortified position at Erzeroum, to which large Russian reinforcements were already on their way. To advance against such a force and such a fortress as the place had now been made, was out of the question; and had it not been for the rallying of Rhumbegar's demoralised troops, and their advance to the support of their English allies, the situation would have been very critical. As it was, all that Lord Gurth Redhill could hope to do at present was to hold his own; and even this he could not have done, had not a temporary diversion been effected by the fleet at Trebizonde, which made it necessary for the Russians to be prudent about leaving their right flank exposed to the advance of fresh troops landed at that port. Thus the expedition which was to be so glorious for our Jingoes, was at a deadlock.

The political grievances of Ireland not having been removed, but rather intensified by the stupid obstinacy of the Bungling Coalition, this troubling of the waters in the East was welcomed by the Nationalist party, now the vast majority of the Irish people. They saw in the thickening difficulties of the British Ministry a chance to extort the independence they could not hope to win by patience and persuasion, and the whole energy of the Irish Americans was thrown into getting up a quarrel, on some pretext or other, between the Governments of the United States and of England. Nor were the men of action in little Ireland itself behindhand with their special industry. Arson – a very difficult thing either to prevent or to prove – and, when practicable, dynamite, were the order of the day, or rather of the night; and those methods of procedure were by no means confined to the congenial climate of the distressful country. There moonlighting, boycotting, and plans of campaign, which had ducked their heads to Coercion Acts for a time, raised them again, and were as rampant as ever, the office having been given from over the ocean by those who wanted to carp at any possible error of the Bungling Coalition. They found this not so difficult as it might have been in another and, for with all their esteem for the old country, and their commercial reasons for keeping on terms, the Yankees could not forget that each 4th of July they celebrated an independence wrung by physical force from this same power from whom the Irish – or at least four-fifths of them – were now seeking in vain a friendly and partial separation.

The crisis schemed for came about; the dynamite scare in the British Islands increased and spread over town and country. The fact was that nitro-glycerine had of late been very largely used at Woolwich to try the new long pneumatic guns throwing dynamite shells, which the Americans, by whom they were invented, had some time since adopted for their navy, but which short-sighted trade interests had opposed in England, so that the Admiralty was only now in the stage of experiment with them. However, the explosive for these performances was kept in large quantities, a considerable fraction of which was secretly but regularly sold to the other patriots by Government officials who loved their country so long as it paid them well, but naturally did not allow flighty music-hall sentiments to interfere with the solid realities of personal profit. No doubt a large percentage of those who manipulated this business were Irish Americans, certainly those who conducted the explosions were so, that class generally being endued with more nerve than their congeners in the little island, many of whom were apt to be somewhat squeamish about scattering destruction in a mixed crowd of harmless people.

But anyhow, these gentlemen took their pleasure in their own way, and were not in any sense or manner the emissaries of the American Government or nation. But the party in power, owing perhaps to its fiasco in Asia Minor, was in a quarrelsome mood, and communications, in an overbearing tone, were addressed to Washington on the subject. The Washington Government replied shortly that it had nothing to do with the matter, and could not undertake duties which belonged to the police in England. Here the dispute should have ended, only that to drop it would not have suited the purpose of the agitators. The wire-pullers strained their resources to improve the occasion, and before long there was a brisk interchange of unfriendly despatches between the two countries, the sinister spell of the Irish question working upon each of them in its different way. And just when temper was at its highest on both sides, a fresh dispute about the Canadian Fisheries served to precipitate matters; Congress was hastily summoned, the action of the Foreign Minister was endorsed, and diplomatic relations with England were broken off with a suddenness and completeness implying a state of war. Our unfortunate Ministry would probably have stopped short of this madness, had they not reckoned without their host upon the allegiance and alliance of Canada. But here too they had been giving umbrage by their want of tact, and the upshot of their proceedings was that the Canadians engaged to observe neutrality, and left the Bunglers of England to face alone the struggle which they alone had provoked.

The costly and melancholy Soudan expedition, some dozen or fifteen years before, had pretty well disgusted the British public with their part in North African affairs.[6] Since Egypt was not to be theirs out and out, taxpayers began to grumble at having to pose as head-nurse there, bolstering up the Khedive, tying on the Khedive's bib, applying the Khedive's pap-bottle, blowing the Khedive's nose, wiping the Khedive's tears, and so forth. The road now lay open, so far as the English public cared, to a renewal of French ascendancy in Egypt; but

France, too, was no longer jealous or keen about it, and certainly the *entente cordiale* between the two neighbours would not have been disturbed on that account. But the same morbid condition of feeling which had already broken the peace in the East and in the West, gave rise to needless complications about matters in which British interests were even less concerned than in Egyptian affairs. For instance, the Bungling Coalition thought proper to interfere about a project which the French press had taken up with great enthusiasm, – that of converting a portion of African desert into a navigable salt lake, by letting in the ocean at a certain point where it had been ascertained that the sand lay considerably below the sea level, thus giving new scope to the commercial relations of the rest of the world with that continent. The scientific pros and cons having been thoroughly thrashed out by competent explorers, the objections made by the British Government were frivolous and vexatious. Perhaps that was the very reason why they were made, harmonious relations with the Republic having become more and more impaired ever since the accession to office of the Bungling Coalition. Any stick will do to beat a dog, and, given the disposition to quarrel, a pretext is not hard to find. With all their national defects – what nation is without? – the French of the day were, on the whole, struggling honestly through difficulties toward a higher standard of civilisation; they were weighted with some anarchy, some crime, much violent partisanship, yet, taken altogether, the people wished and strove to press forward rather than to lapse backwards or stagnate; while, on this side of the Channel, stagnation, rooted in the social, and evinced in the political sphere, had set in, and showed no signs of giving way under any milder stimulants than those which were now ready in the hand of Fate.

The unfriendliness of – we do not say England, but the dominant English party – thus showing itself in minor matters, provoked the French Chamber to re-open the question of an extended protectorate over the southern coast of the Mediterranean. The pulse of Italy was felt in regard to a French advance over her African possessions; and it was soon clear that she would not go to war about that territory merely, so long as her commercial and other interests were guaranteed. The views of the Russian Provisional Government were also ascertained, and found to be favourable, in fact, Russia and France would now become allies by the force of circumstances. The upshot was that Tripoli was annexed, in the face of impotent scolding on the part of the time-serving section of the London press. Impotent, at least, it was against France; but it incited and assisted the crowning of that structure of political folly which the Bungling Coalition had been unremittingly building. They managed to obtain the consent of their obsequious – though, in this instance, narrow – majority in Parliament to the sending out of an expedition of fifteen thousand men to Alexandria, an act which at once strained their treaty rights, was a direct slap in the face to France, and weakened the home force, which could not very safely be spared at all, and which, if it were spared, should have been sent to Asia Minor, where it was sorely needed, Red-hill and Burnfingal having their work cut out for them to maintain their feeble grasps upon the alarming and daily-increasing number of Tartars they had caught. The French Government, in a most conciliatory message, requested some explanation of the step; although exasperated, the French were fully alive to the serious and lamentable character of a rupture with their old friend and ally, and they were resolved to put up with a good deal rather than allow it to happen. But a reply was returned, carefully worded for the purpose by Fitzgorin of the Foreign Office, and carelessly signed by the Chief Secretary, which amounted to an open defiance and challenge. It was hopeless to go any further in conciliation of an opponent who seemed to quarrel for quarrelling's sake, and to demand more the more was conceded. The sensible and just minority of the English people took alarm and protested loudly; but motions of censure and sparely-attended indignation meetings were of no avail; the Opposition in Parliament had become a metaphysical expression; the besotted men in power had got the bit in their teeth, and rushed madly to their doom, dragging their aiders and abettors with them. Before long, a collision, provoked by the British troops on the Tripoli frontier, put an end to the French Ministry's earnest attempt to keep a peace which our constituted authorities had now broken with three of the great Powers of the world, under some infatuation, the source of which was not on the surface of politics, unless that be the place of those deep-seated internal dissensions which, where they have been left uncured, take the backbone out of a nation.

The outlook for England was now very formidable, and a flurried appeal was made by the Cabinet to Berlin and Vienna to throw their great weight into restoring the peace of the world. But the German Powers replied in a joint Note that the quarrel was none of theirs; that it was now their turn to reserve liberty of action, as England did, and had a right to do, in 1866 and 1870; that they had taken their full share of hard knocks at the dates referred to, and needed rest; and that they did not see the logic of keeping peace by plunging into a general war. They accordingly stood in firm neutrality, back to back, and drew a cordon round their frontiers.

CHAPTER XXVII.
APPROACHING THE REALITY.

THE summer was slipping away, and, in spite of wars and rumours of wars, London was emptying fast – we know that London gets empty at the end of the summer, just as the bed of the Atlantic does in dry weather. Mr Bristley's exchange of duty was up; and indeed Lesbia was not sorry at the prospect of getting away from town, where her health had slightly suffered from the close atmosphere, to which she was unaccustomed, and where fewer opportunities than she had looked for had offered for exerting her reforming influence over other young girls. Certainly her intimacy with Lady Friga Hawknorbuzzard had given her the *entrée* to refined society, and she had made the most of it. Her perseverance in dressing more rationally than those with whom she associated had begun to crack the wall of prevailing fashion among them, not only in the matter of costume itself, but, as a natural consequence, in the many habits with which fashion in dress is associated. Not a few women who at first made fun of her, had begun to envy her vigorous independence of character, and even to think of casting off some of their own fetters. Among the many un-young-ladylike things she did, her bicycling was, on the whole, that which attracted most attention when the sex of the rider was noticed, as, astride of a nickled fifty-two, she careered along the wood pavement of the principal thorough-fares, cool and collected as any of the habitual London riders. Her uncle was secretly as glad as her female relatives to see her come in safe and sound, but he took care to encourage her in showing herself off where the traffic was thick, as setting an example to other girls which tended to knock the bottom out of weakervesselism.

But, these little successes apart, she found, as he did, that the tone of society was adverse to them at present. Innovation was uphill work, it fell flat, met with but narrow sympathy and response. No wonder; for had it been otherwise, the grave political situation could hardly have come about – the common-sense of the nation would have prevented it, It was no time, then, for pioneers to make their mark; it was, rather, the jubilee of parasites, snobs, and swindlers, whom the apathy of the outside public allowed to have their own way, obstructing enlightened reformers, and fostering hollowness and pretentiousness everywhere.

The sitting of Parliament had been protracted into September on account of the crisis, the recess was to be for a few days only, and an autumn session to follow. The Premier, with his family, had decided to remain in town, that he might be within reach at this anxious time. So our heroine was about to return home deprived of her new bosom friend, when a diversion occurred. Among the acquaintances they had made at Lady Humnoddie's receptions in Belgravia, was that of a Mr and Mrs Whyte, who owned a comfortable villa situated almost on the sands of the ocean at Bude, in the north of Cornwall. These people took a great fancy to the original young girl, and they invited her to go back with them to Bude for a month or six weeks. Lesbia, who was always glad of a chance to get to the seaside in bathing season, accepted gladly, and it was arranged that they should start for Cornwall the day before the others went home to Dulham. In less than a week she was enjoying the salubrious air and the wide reaches of sand over which the Atlantic ebbs and flows at Bude, where to the west and the southwest there is no opposite shore short of America. She had taken her bicycle with her, but, as she found the roads in that part mostly narrow and hilly, much of her exercise while at Bude was taken on foot, either over the broad sands when the tide was out, or along the downs of the cliff stretching southwards. Mr Whyte was a good walker, and always ready to accompany her, and they conversed mostly on topics of local interest, for both were glad to forget London life, with its depressing influences of the troublous times.

Still these were not to be altogether shut out. Black care sits behind the horseman, and even one of Lesbia's strong character could not help feeling that at this period there was something or other hovering in the atmosphere of England which was not canny. Undefined and baseless apprehensions about their own private concerns were taking possession of people's minds, which became morbidly imaginative and irritable; with herself it took the form of an excessive anxiety about her mother's health, which made her write almost daily, although every letter she received from Dulham might have re-assured her on the subject. She astonished Mrs Whyte one day, with whom she was sauntering over the sands at low water, in a very abstracted mood, by suddenly halting, facing round to the ocean, and saying aloud to herself those words of Macbeth in the dagger scene, –

'There's no such thing;
It is the bloody business which informs
Thus to mine eyes.'

'What, my dear?' asked Mrs Whyte, looking at her with a puzzled expression.

'Nothing, nothing, Mrs Whyte, only a habit I have of quoting the poets to myself when I'm absent-minded. What a curious crow that is, there, flying away from us to the cliff'; it has red beak and legs!'

'Yes, that's a Cornish chough – you know that fine old glee,' The chough and crow to rest are gone.' I'm sorry to say there are very few of them left; loafing louts, with guns in their hands, are extirpating all our rare British birds. I heard some popping about last Sunday.'

The next day they all made an excursion southwards to see the old ruin of Dundayel or Tintagel Castle, on a jutting rock about twenty miles from Bude, along the cliff; a day or two afterwards they went to Hartland Point, the interesting headland which forms the north-west corner of Devon and divides the Bristol Channel from the ocean on that side. Short outings for the day like these were made by the Whytes in their pony-carriage, Lesbia accompanying it on her machine when the roads were fair; but Mr Whyte soon proposed a little tour inland, which was agreed to readily, and as the railway, which had been extended to Stratton, a country town at a short distance, would come into requisition, Lesbia decided wisely to leave her bicycle behind.

They accomplished a pleasant tour to all the well-known places of interest on the north Devon coast, and finished by turning inland to the Dartmoor hills, where Lesbia greatly liked the wild, desolate moors and tors, with their gigantic masses and druidical circles and cromlechs, varied here and there by wooded glens with brown mountain burns purling in their depths, from which they had many a basket of fresh caught trout for breakfast. Although the weather sometimes recalled Carrington's lines to Devon, –

'Thou hast a cloud for ever in thy skies,
A breeze, a shower, for ever on thy plains,'

yet they had many glorious days, and, in spite of her love of the sea-side, Lesbia was almost sorry when the excursion came to an end, and they reached Bude again, the second week in October.

The time was now about up during which she thought it well to accept the Whytes' hospitality; but as the 13th of October, her sixteenth birthday, was at hand, Mrs Whyte made her promise to stay over that day. Meanwhile, the excitement of seeing new places had decidedly done her good, it had shaken her out of those unusual fits of abstraction and melancholy, and she did not feel that nervous anxiety to get home to her mother which she had expected to do as the time came near.

Although Mr Whyte had not talked politics much to Lesbia since they left London, he was a keen newspaper reader when there was anything stirring. He took in the *Daily Twaddler* from a news-agent at the Stratton railway station, and if there was one thing which annoyed him more than another, it was when the paper did not come punctually. This vexation he happened to have on the afternoon of Saturday the 11th of October, and Lesbia at once offered to run into the country town on her machine to see about the delayed paper. But as this would have stood in the way of a little promenade they were to take to where the great swell of the spring tide was rolling in upon the rocks, Mr Whyte said No, he could very well wait till the next or even Monday morning – 'although,' he added 'it is provoking to have one's news stopped just when it's uncertain what may happen any day with this mad and wicked war against half the world.'

Sunday the 12th came, a calm day as to the weather, but a gloomy and fearsome one in the political atmosphere; for a report had reached Bude late on Saturday night, that the allied forces of the enemy were threatening a descent upon Ireland; and Sunday morning's gossip swelled the rumour to the dimensions of an actual landing and the repulse of a British corps of observation near Bantry Bay, the scene of Hoche's attempt in December 1796, The rumour was contradicted and re-affirmed and contradicted again; and thus, amid random conjectures and forebodings, the evening of Sunday the 12th passed unquietly away.

CHAPTER XXVIII.

'BUT IT SHALL NOT COME NIGH THEE.'

MONDAY the 13th of October 189 – rose a calm, lovely, sunny morning, with a light warm air from the W.N.W. breathing soft over the placid blue sea.

'Good-morning, Lesbia, and many happy returns of the day to you, dear,' said Mrs Whyte, meeting and kissing the young girl on her way downstairs, as she herself was coming in from the terrace garden about eight o'clock, or an hour before their usual breakfast time. 'Not having anything more costly to present you with in this out-of-the-way place, I've made up this simple autumnal bouquet, hoping you'll take the will for the deed.'

'Oh thanks, my dear Mrs Whyte, how very pretty! one or two rich colours like those please me better than common variety; I'll put it in water at once in my room. And then do you think I could get to Stratton and back on my bicycle, without keeping breakfast waiting for me? I should so like to get Mr Whyte his paper the first thing this morning, as I saw he was in a fidget for it yesterday. I think I could be back a few minutes past nine.'

'Well, since you're ready dressed for it, I suppose I must let you go; it's really very thoughtful of you; but don't ride as if you were racing. We shall none of us starve to death, even if you should be a quarter of an hour late.'

'Besides, after all, Mrs Whyte, you needn't wait. If I should be a little behind time, pray begin breakfast without me; I shall feel less hurried, if you will.'

'All right, we will then; take care of yourself,' said Mrs Whyte.

Lesbia ran upstairs again to deposit her flowers, then led out her machine; and Mrs Whyte watched her mount and rapidly disappear out of sight along the Stratton road.

Nine o'clock came, and, as Mrs Whyte had promised, she and her husband sat down to breakfast. It was more than half-past before Lesbia opened the door with the newspaper packet in her hand, looking more tired than a mere scurry would have made her, with her clothes all dusty and somewhat torn on one side, and the same side of her forehead bruised and badly scratched.

'Hallo, you've been down!' exclaimed Mr Whyte. 'Hope you're not much hurt?'

'Nothing to signify, thanks, Mr Whyte, only a little shaken, and a trifling headache. It was a bit of carelessness; I turned my head to listen to something I couldn't make out and don't understand now, and I rode right on to a big piece of brick and went a cropper over the handles. It was my own fault; bicyclists should have their eyes about them.'

'Whereabouts did it happen?' he inquired.

'On my way back, not a mile from here. I didn't feel up to mounting again, so I led my bike the rest of the way, and made it do crutch to support me as I crawled by its side. That is why I am so late: I should have been here twenty minutes ago.'

'Did anyone see you fall?' asked Mrs Whyte.

'Yes, a small boy carrying a bundle, who holloaed out, – ' 'Ulloa, guv'nor! 's that as 'ow yer stops yer express?"'

'Well, tell me now,' said Mr White, 'what was it you were listening to so intently as not to see the stone?'

For reply, Lesbia inquired with curiosity, – 'I say, have you a steam mill, or factory, or anything of that sort in this neighbourhood?'

'Steam mill or factory!' exclaimed Mr Whyte. 'No. Not unless one has sprung up during the night. Why?'

Because, as I rode along coming back, I heard distinctly a curious sort of vibrating hum which at first I thought might be the buzz of a hornet close to my ear, but that illusion didn't last long; I then supposed it must be that slow, monotonous musical grind, which is sometimes, you know, the effect to the ear of very large machinery clattering at a distance. But since you say there is none hereabouts, I can't divine what the noise was, nor where it came from; it seemed to come from all sides at once and to stick to me all the way here. Anyhow, it was by giving my attention to that I got thrown over. So much is certain.'

Mrs Whyte opened her eyes very wide at Lesbia, and an uneasy expression came over her face; but her husband burst out laughing.

'Bless your heart, my dear girl,' he said, 'that's the surf. If you lived at Bude all the year round, as we do, you'd hear that often enough. It's a particular set of the wind does it.'

'But, Mr Whyte, there's no surf this morning,' Lesbia objected. 'The sea's as smooth as glass, and, what's more, the tide's far out. It's only just beginning to flow now.'

'H'm, that's true, but I don't see what else can account for your humming sound, unless it was a sort of singing in the ears, a sound that had its source no farther off than your own head. Meanwhile, you can't breakfast on what the wild waves are saying. Here, I put down your cocoa, and your herrings, and eggs, and muffins, and all into the fender, for I thought you'd hardly do it by nine, in any case. It was very kind of you to go though, and I feel quite guilty. If it hadn't been for my insensate news-hunger, you wouldn't have had a spill. Now then, you can set to; I am sure you must be famished.'

Lesbia set to with a good appetite, after her ride and tumble. Presently she said, –

'Now, Mr Whyte, pray don't stand on ceremony with me; do open your paper – I know you're longing to.'

'Yes, do, John,' assented his wife; 'we should all like to hear what's going on, especially since this report about the French and Americ – There now, what on earth is making the windows rattle? Good gracious!'

'They're not rattling, Bessie dear,' said her husband; 'what's the matter, are *you* getting steam mill on the brain too?'

Then turning to Lesbia as he unfolded the paper, –

'Going to bathe this fine day, I suppose?'

'Yes, in the afternoon,' she replied, 'when the tide flows up. I shall wait till it fills my old pool behind the rocks, where I can get a good depth without having to struggle against currents, which is not very safe. I'm sorry it'll be my last dip, in all probability. I've enjoyed my swims in the ocean water, and feel the benefit of them; they've quite washed London out of me. Well, like all good things, they must – '

'Must what, you were going to say?' asked Mr Whyte, as Lesbia broke off her sentence and looked round.

'Surely,' she said, 'I heard that same noise again; didn't you hear something, Mrs Whyte?'

'I was just thinking so,' she answered; 'but I suppose John's right, it's only fancy. Anyhow, there can be no harm in taking a peep out of doors, just to satisfy my mind. I won't be a second.'

Before Mr Whyte could get his uncut sheet turned over to the telegram side, his wife came in again in a flutter.

'I'll just trouble you, John. Be so good as to come out on the terrace with me for a moment, and listen to your *surf*. All I have to say is, that if the surf at Bude is going to take to this sort of thing, I don't wish to live here any longer.'

Mr Whyte instantly dropped his *Daily Twaddler* in his arm-chair, and followed his wife and Lesbia to the terrace. There was no mistake. A dull, deep, throbbing boom, that was not at all like the plash and murmur of breakers, but had something peculiarly terrible about it, was filling the air and giving a sensation of making the ground tremble. They could not say whether it came from any particular quarter, or from overhead, or from underneath.

'The devil!' exclaimed Mr Whyte, now the most amazed of the party.

'I hope to goodness it's not an earthquake,' said his wife; 'one is so utterly helpless against an earthquake!'

'I hope not indeed,' answered Mr Whyte. 'I hardly think so – there's no upheaval or rocking. Still we had better stay where we are for the present, in case a shock *should* come and shake the house down; and we ought to call the servants out too until the crisis is past.'

The servants had already taken fright, and were coming toward the inmates on the terrace, Many other households along the Cornish coast grouped together out of doors, through fear of the earthquake. Some early excursionists who had mounted Hartland Point, hurried down and went inland, lest a sudden commotion might cause the point to fall bodily on the rocky shore. The lighthouse keeper on Lundy Island, some dozen miles north of Hartland Point, in the chops of the Bristol Channel, ran away clear of his tower and stood expecting it every minute to topple down in ruins. Southwards, at Tintagel and beyond, people on the cliff got away from them as fast as they could, not knowing how soon a great landslip might occur; for the fearful sound was growing sensibly louder. Our group on the terrace at the Bude Villa had ceased conversation, because no one felt inclined for levity, and there was nothing to the purpose to be said.

A sudden thought struck Lesbia; the Dream recurred to her mind in startling significance: and before anyone could remonstrate, she ran into the house, and came out again with the newspaper from her host's chair held open before her.

'Good heavens, Mr Whyte!' she exclaimed, pointing to the special despatch, 'this explains it all; it's not an earthquake – *it's a battle*! They are fighting already, fighting in the south of Ireland; and I know the place; I've been there. There! there! read about the landing of the allies near Cork Harbour, while I ride again into Stratton and get the very latest reports. Don't mind if I miss lunch, I couldn't eat any this awful day; you don't know how interested I feel about it.'

And, without waiting for reply, she had her bicycle out again, of which the handle-bar and one of the treadle-pins were slightly bent, and the steerage shaken very loose; but regardless of the state of her machine, or of her own bruises, in half a minute she was mounted and pedalling away again for Stratton as hard as she could.

CHAPTER XXIX.
THE 13TH OF OCTOBER 189 – .

LADY HUMNOHDIE was rather an early riser, and expected her family to be punctual to breakfast at half-past eight, especially in this busy and anxious time of the autumn session, when a family political discussion took place every morning, from which her husband sometimes gleaned some useful hints for his guidance.

'Very ugly news, Blanche,' he remarked, as they took their places at the table. 'I always feared these Irish rebellion-mongers would get us into hot water sooner or later. We made a mistake there; it would have been sounder policy to let them go with a good grace. Now we may have to let them go with a very bad one.'

'Bother the Irish, Hum!' was the reply. 'You've done all you could in recalling Lord Gurth from Asia. He knows the Irish well, and, depend upon it, he's a match for them and their French and Yankee allies.'

'Redhill's the man, beyond question,' replied her husband, 'and, as you say, we did the right thing in recalling him from Erzeroum. But such a force as he will have to cope with, by all accounts, is not driven into the sea at the first charge. I don't feel comfortable about it, I assure you.'

'I'm not comfortable either,' said Friga sulkily, as she took a cup of coffee from her mother, 'but it's not about Redhill and his army. I wish I could have been invited to Cornwall with Lesbia Newman; how lucky she is to escape from horrid London! What a nuisance an autumn session is!'

'I suppose you'd like to go to Ireland itself, Fri, if your precious Lesbia were there,' said her sister snappishly. 'The country may go to the dogs, so long as you and your inseparable can moon about together.'

'It may do that in any case, Hillie,' she answered; 'my staying in town will not prevent it.'

'Oh, come, Friga,' said her mother, 'don't *you* begin to croak, for Heaven's sake! or we shall all be in the dumps. There's reason for your father being annoyed, but your griefs are ridiculous.'

'The Lord knows what will happen if Redhill should be overpowered,' said the Marquis gloomily. 'We sha'n't hold Ireland, that's certain; and I don't want to frighten you, but we shall have our work cut out for us to hold England. The war must be stopped, or I shall throw up the sponge, and let a better man take my place. What the deuce possessed us to get into such a mess I can't think!'

'The Thoroughs wanted to keep us out of it,' remarked Friga, who was not in an amiable mood; 'but that, no doubt, would have been undignified for a Bungling Coalition.'

'But, Fri, dear,' remonstrated her mother, 'all women of caste are Bunglers.'

'I doubt it,' she replied; 'but even then, it is one thing to be a Bungler because one has thought out the subject and reached that conclusion, as papa has; quite another to be a Bungler simply because that sweet thing in Guardsmen, young Silverton, is a Bungler, and one admires his moustache.'

'What nonsense you talk, Friga!' said her mother, while Hilda, at whom the taunt was levelled, laughed. 'As if society were so frivolous as that! Women – that is, women who are in society – are Bunglers because bungling keeps up the decencies and amenities of life. I've no patience with your national reformers and agitators and mischief makers. Why must they go about the country, putting notions into people's heads that never had any, and upsetting the order which Providence has established from time immemorial?'

'I'll tweak Providence's nose if ever he has the impertinence to come ordering me about.'

'For shame, Friga!' said her mother; 'you have made me forget what I was going to say. Ah – as for your hoydens of girls like Lesbia Newman, they're the worst of the lot; they unsex each other, and they unsex men.'

'But then, you see, mamma,' said Hilda, with a peculiar look at her sister, 'unsexing is just what that wicked girl opposite me, and her wickeder absent friend, delight in. Don't you, Fri? But never mind, mamma, go on; it's so nice to hear all about the proprieties.'

'I am sorry you make game of me, Hilda,' said Lady Humnoddie bitterly, 'although I know, of course, that mothers have no claim upon their daughters' respect in these enlightened times. However, I think the days are coming when we shall keep a tight rein upon all this nonsense.'

'I think not,' said Lord Humnoddie.

'Yes we shall,' persisted his wife; 'we shall keep a tight rein upon all social and political tantrums. We English have always been a practical people, and we don't stand nonsense after a certain point.'

'What point, pray, mamma?' asked Friga.

'As for those Irish rebels,' pursued the Marchioness, 'I can hardly trust myself to speak of them and their doings. Never mind, when this war's over, and we've given a lesson to these foreign interlopers, their turn will come. We shall have to deal with Ireland once for all; and, in my opinion, the only way will be to deport the entire population, and colonise the island with sober English.'

'Unfortunately, sobriety is just the point in which your colonists might fail,' interposed Hilda.

'Well, it'll be a difficult and sad business, I know,' pursued her mother, 'but it'll be for the best in the long run, and I hope you will bring the matter before Parliament, Hum, at the first opportunity.'

'I should be afraid of Parliament framing a resolution to the effect that I should be advised to withdraw to that familiar satellite orb whence I appear to have strayed.'

'Quite right, papa,' remarked Friga, 'that would only be fitting.

'For now Ireland shall be free, says the Shan Van Voght;
For now Ireland shall be free, says the Shan Van Voght;
For Lord Gurth will be too rash,
And there'll be a pretty smash;
And then Ireland will be free, says the Shan Van Voght.'

Friga gave out this impromptu version of the old ditty, not humorously, but in a bold, loud, and strange voice which made her father and her sister start and look at her. But Lady Humnoddie was too full of her own prepossessions to heed it.

'Don't talk nonsense, Hum,' she replied, to her husband's last observation. 'You know very well that if you had the will of united England at your back, you could carry the measure through Parliament.'

'Ay, if. I could do many wonders with *if*. United England! Save the mark!'

'Well, if you don't, someone else must,' she said. 'The country, I'm very sure, will stand no more nonsense, and it'll have to be put a stop to. More tea, Hum?'

Brought up amid surroundings such as hers, a spoilt child of fortune and fashion, with no ambition higher than that of shining in the most outwardly brilliant but inwardlyshallow circles, and with no philanthropy wider than that which, it must be said, continually prompted her to help the needy with whom she came in contact, the Marchioness of Humnoddie was surely more to be pitied than blamed for these effusions of a light heart. Little did the frivolous, good-natured woman imagine, as she made her last foolish answer, that even while she was speaking the cannon of Queenstown began to send their deep thunder across the sea; that by the time she had taken her afternoon drive in the park, made her round of visits, and returned to dress for dinner, the Channel Fleet would be crippled, the flower of the army destroyed, the United Kingdom torn asunder, invasion threatening and revolution impending over England itself; and that but for an internal source of strength, unacknowledged, disowned, yet growing yearly, a merit which did not belong to any of the present rulers of this realm – in the crisis about to follow the great battle in Ireland, our British Empire had been fated to see the writing on the wall.

Nine A.M. had struck on the 13th of October 189 – .

CHAPTER XXX.
THE 13TH OF OCTOBER 189 – .

THE 13th of October 189 – . Mrs Newman stood in her garden at Dulham vicarage, tending a rich bed of late geraniums, upon which the autumn sun shed its softened glow from a clear, deep, blue sky. The leaves of the highroad elms outside the gate, under which, at the outset of our story, Lesbia had essayed her first bicycle mount, had begun to redden, and many already strewed the gravel walks; yet the breeze was a soft zephyr, and there was nothing in the air or in the scene suggestive of melancholy. Fidgfumblasquidiot was exercising Gossamer, who had come home with the rest of the party from London while his young mistress went to Cornwall. The bulldog took greatly to the half-wit, and she was not at all afraid of him, not even when, as she patted his head, he reared with his muddy paws against her white apron, which made her say 'Oh!' and look about her for ghosts.

But it was Lesbia's birthday, and she was not there; perhaps that was the reason why her mother, as she moved round the gay flowers, felt exceedingly depressed and anxious. There was no ostensible cause for this; she had heard from her daughter a day or two before, and by that account she was well and enjoying her seaside visit. What more could Mrs Newman desire; and yet she was apprehensive, she knew not why. Her brother the vicar had tried to talk her out of this uncomfortable frame of mind, and had ended by being himself infected with her fancies. But he carefully concealed it, and kept watch secretly for any letter or message which might arrive. Sure enough, just before luncheon time there was a ring at the house door, and a telegram was handed in. Mr Bristley took it with an air of indifference, but as soon as he was alone in his study, tore it open with trembling hands. He read it with amazement but at the same time with a feeling of intense relief. In another he was in the garden again with his sister.

'Lesbie's all right, Jane, please God, that is, all right herself. But I fear there's a great national disaster. Read that.'

Mrs Newman snatched it his from hand and read, –

'From L. Newman, Stratton, to Rev. S. T. Bristley, Dulham, Frogmore, 13th October 189 – . All is explained. Dreadful battle going on at Roche's Tower. We hear it from this coast; took it for earthquake. I start home to-morrow, all well. Use discretion about mother.'

CHAPTER XXXI.
THE 13TH OF OCTOBER 189 – .

As Lesbia, lame herself and driving her unsteady machine along at top speed, rushed again into Stratton, she heard the handbells and voices of criers, and saw groups of people gathered in the main street. Already in the near distance she had caught the words 'battle' and 'Ireland,' and now heard all clearly, as she dismounted with a backward spring amid the crowd. '*Great Battle by Land and Sea near Queenstown, Ireland! General Redhill and Admiral St George both engaged! The Invaders attacked in front and flank! Terrible fighting! Latest Dublin despatch! Great Battle in progress since nine o'clock this morning!*'

The noise of the criers, the excited talking at the doors of public-houses and elsewhere, prevented anything being heard here of the ominous sound which the westerly breeze was bringing from afar across the still water, but after hurrying to the post office and wiring to Dulham as we have seen, Lesbia, who was too excited to keep quiet anywhere, mounted her bicycle again, and in a minute or two was in the country on her way back to Bude, the deadly boom filling her ears all the while, as before. On arriving, she found every house had its occupants standing in front, listening with sombre faces. Mrs Whyte met her on the road some three hundred yards from the villa, and Lesbia dismounted that they might walk back together.

'It *is* that, Lesbia, eh?'

'Certainly it is, the battle of Roche's Tower. You will hardly believe me, Mrs Whyte, when I tell you that my mother had a weird day-dream about it more than two years ago, and that I went over the very ground myself this time last year.'

'How strange! Well, I would almost rather it had been an earthquake as we thought it was, than this; we might have escaped for the fright. A battle is worse. Think of the desolation left in so many homes, and the sufferings of the wounded!'

'Yes, it's very sad, Mrs Whyte,' answered the young girl, her luminous eyes moistening. 'Listen! the firing is getting heavier; it must be an awful battle.'

'What madness can have inspired our Ministry to embark in such a war, or our Legislature to sanction it?' said Mrs Whyte.

'For my part,' remarked her husband, who had just joined them, 'I believe they'll have a lesson, these people. I shouldn't be at all surprised if Redhill were to get a thrashing, and then Ireland will go. We ought to have let her go when we might with a good grace, then she would have stood by us. Now there'll be the devil to pay. But no doubt there are parties at home and abroad whom this game suits.'

'A pretty game indeed!' said Lesbia bitterly, as the roar of the artillery, some two hundred miles distant, swelled louder again.

'Yes, war's a dreadful thing,' said Mrs Whyte, with a sigh, 'and I do not see how any circumstances can ever justify it.'

'I don't know, Mrs Whyte,' said Lesbia; 'I think the cause of liberty justifies it, horrible as it is. But let us hope this battle may be the finish for ever, so far as England is concerned.'

'I shall not be at all surprised if it proves to be the finish so far as England is concerned,' said Mr Whyte dryly. 'However, I don't think we shall let our authorities carry their fun quite so far as the sack of London. A new Ministry and Parliament will simply have to make peace by reversing and disowning the acts of the present Government. It'll be a valuable but dear experience; the country will fare sumptuously on humble pie.'

'Please 'm', said Mrs Whyte's parlour-maid, in a tremulous voice, but encouraged by the word 'pie,' which had caught her ear as she came forward, 'I was to ask what you'd have for luncheon. Cook hasn't got anything hot ready; this dreadful thing has put us all out. There's the cold beef and – '

'All right, anything'll do, Susan; I don't think any of us will take much luncheon to-day.'

'No, indeed,' Lesbia assented; 'and it's getting worse! See, the windows rattle now, don't they, Mr Whyte?'

But if windows were rattling slightly on the Cornish coast, they were shivered into fragments at Queenstown itself. By this time very few panes of glass were left in the pretty hillside town overlooking the basin of Cork Cove, now shrouded in the battle smoke. The terrific cannonade on the water and on the hills beyond had worked almost as much havoc by its vibration as if it had been throwing shells into the town, which, as a matter of fact, was not hit once. The commotion of the falling glass scared the inhabitants out of their homes, and there was a general stampede to the hill top, whence the view of the great fight extended furthest. Cork, though out of sight of the battle, was but little less disturbed than Queenstown. Crowds, frantic with ardour, waving green flags, shouting national songs, cheering the various demagogues who harangued them from platforms, improvised on the tops of vehicles, bands playing, and processions forming, surging along the thoroughfares toward the Queenstown road and railway, and swaying against the pedestal of the placid statue of Father Mathew near the bridge – all this hubbub, which at another time would have been an uproar in itself, was now overwhelmed by a far mightier sound; for all day long the crackling thunder pealed, and tore, and shook the earth, from the awful scene of carnage only a few miles away.

To return to our friends at Bude.

'They're engaged by sea and land, you say,' observed Mr Whyte. 'I shouldn't have thought any landing could be effected until our fleet had first been beaten off.'

'Or surprised,' answered Lesbia. 'The enemy has forced entrance to Cork Harbour, and the two fleets are pounding away at each other inside the great basin, which no doubt makes a tremendous echo to heavy ordnance; while the armies are engaged in the valley between the long hills which extend northward from the ocean coast to the southern shore of the basin. I know all about it – I've been over the ground; and my mother had a dream or vision of this battle long ago.'

'Gracious! have I been harbouring a witch all this time?' said Mr Whyte, with a very forced laugh.

'Witch or not, you'll see the accounts will confirm what I say,' answered Lesbia positively. 'And now, dear friends,' she added, 'with your consent, I must run once more into Stratton to get the earliest news of the result – thanks, no, I couldn't eat or drink now, I couldn't fancy it, while death and wounds are sounding in my ears.'

'Won't you be over fatigued, dear?' said Mrs Whyte, in faint remonstrance.

'Fatigued! what are they *over there*?' replied Lesbia solemnly, pointing with one hand to the ocean horizon, whence the sullen roar boomed on, while she laid the other on the head of her bicycle and led it out again. She was very stiff and lame, and was made more so by a mismount, catching in her saddle and tipping down on the bruised side; but she picked up and went at it again with a will, and after a wobble or two across the road, was bowling along at the same risky pace as before.

'I believe that girl wishes she were in the battle herself,' said Mrs Whyte, looking after her. 'She might almost as well be.'

Arrived a third time in Stratton – it was now half-past two in the afternoon – she found that a further despatch was in the mouths of the criers. '*Gallant Attack along the whole line! The Enemy repulsed from left of his position with Heavy Loss! The Battle continues!*'

This raised the spirits of the very young people, and they gave vent to cheers. But to others the sobering reflection occurred that nothing could be counted upon so early in the day, and it was known that the British had to deal with a superior force.

Four o'clock. Another despatch cried. '*Terrible Fighting and Severe Loss! Lord Redhill still maintains his position! The Reserve called up! The Battle continues!*'

This looked very bad, Lesbia thought. Still maintains his position! Is *that* the fruit of the gallant attack along the whole line, and the partial victory on the right wing? Why call up the reserve? And never a word about Admiral St George and the fleet, although it was known that he had been engaged from the first! Bad! bad! Still these telegrams might be garbled by speculators. And giving two-pence to a boy to take charge of her bicycle, she moved restlessly about, talking with various groups, who, of course, knew no more than she did, perhaps less. The sun was beginning to get low and to throw long shadows; the breeze sank too.

Five o'clock. Another despatch cried, '*Great Slaughter! All the Reserve engaged! Admiral St George making splendid Defence! The Battle continues!*'

This was a damper for the most sanguine. Everyone felt the uselessness of trying to put a good face on the matter; there could be no doubt that the day was going against the brave but inadequate British force, which now for eight hours had been striving stubbornly against tremendous odds. Lesbia was seized with an impulse to ride back to Bude, but she had to get assistance to mount. Out once more in the quiet of the country again, she slackened speed to listen. The deep thunder from the west, after one awful peal, was sensibly decreasing, until, by the time she reached the villa just before dusk, she heard it no more. Somehow her spirits rose, and leaning her bicycle against the wall, she limped to the party still on the terrace, saying, –

'It's over – God knows with what result, I fear a disastrous one. But I'll have something to eat now, if I may; I've fasted long enough, and I can do *them* no good, poor fellows!'

'Dinner 'll be ready in two or three minutes,' said Mrs Whyte; 'you'll barely have time to house your bike, and wash your hands. I ordered it rather early, because none of us could eat any lunch.'

'Oh, very well; and, Mrs Whyte, I hope you won't scold me because I have wired home to say that I start tomorrow, as originally planned. I've enjoyed a long visit to you now, and I know my mother will be wanting me.'

'I'm so glad you've enjoyed your visit, and I hope it won't be your last, dear,' she replied. 'Well, I can quite understand your wish to get home and away from these terrible associations. We'll send you, bag and baggage, to the morning train.'

On retiring that night, Lesbia found that her morning's cropper had hurt her more than she had supposed during the excitement of the eventful day. Her right wrist was badly sprained, her right hip bruised and stiff, and she required the assistance of Mrs Whyte's maid to pack her portmanteau. Her first sleep was passed in a weird dream. She found herself on a line of high downs under a cloudy midnight, lit up by blood-red flames leaping from a brickkiln. In that lurid glare she could discern the forms of men and horses lying about on the ground, and of hooded female figures moving about and stooping down among them. She woke up with a scared sensation, but turning on her other side, fell into a heavy and dreamless sleep until Susan knocked at the door with hot water at a quarter to eight in the morning.

After breakfast, Mr Whyte drove her to the station at Stratton, carrying the bicycle on the luggage in the back of the pony-carriage, for its owner was in no condition to ride it. The rumours of a great reverse had already reached Bude before they started, and the morning papers, just come down to Stratton, confirmed the news.

'Gracious!' exclaimed Lesbia, holding out the *Daily Twaddler* at arm's-length, 'twenty-seven thousand *hors de combat* on our side; number of prisoners not mentioned; General Lord Gurth Redhill killed at the head of the cavalry, which was annihilated; the remnant of the disbanded army flying pell-mell toward Dublin; Admiral St George surrendered, with all of his ships that were not sunk – this is indeed worse than we had any idea of; there has not been such a disaster since Senlac!'

'The proof of the Bungler pudding is in the national eating, my dear,' said Mr Whyte quietly, thrusting his hands into his pockets. 'Perhaps this will satisfy the public appetite for some little time – say, until we can have the pleasure of a Battle of Queenstown fought in England itself. Meanwhile, we must see about your ticket. London, of course; where shall you stop?'

'At the Great Western Hotel. I have been there before. I shall call on the Hawknorbuzzards to-morrow, and hear all about it, and what is to be done; then I can go home by an afternoon train – but where are Solicitude and Perdition?'

'Solicitude and Perdition!'

'My portmanteau and umbrella. Oh, all right, in that corner. I call the portmanteau Solicitude, because I am always in a fidget to see it is not left behind, and the umbrella Perdition, because it is always getting lost. Here comes the train.'

Mr Whyte laughed.

'What trifles amuse us mortals at great crises!'

'Yes, indeed, Mr Whyte, you may well say so; it is not with me that solicitude and perdition have most concern at this terrible time. I suppose there will be a vast subscription to do what money can do for the sufferers. I will send you a line by first post on getting home. Good-bye, and many thanks.'

Three days afterwards a post-card announced her safe arrival at Dulham.

CHAPTER XXXII.

RETROSPECT – MARSHALLING THE FORCES.

A RETROSPECT here becomes necessary. The Irish Nationalists – that is, the vast majority of the inhabitants of the island – having abandoned all hope of getting their aspirations realised or even listened to while England was governed by the Bungling Coalition, had decided to take advantage of the quarrel to cast in their lot with the United States. Before this war, any one who might have suggested such a thing as the annexation to America of a small corner of Europe, would have been set down as a madman; but now that war had actually begun, the contingency came within the range of practical politics. If it could be achieved, it would repay the cost and risk of an expedition; and with the aid of France, its achievement seemed not impossible. Russia, too, would help the enterprise indirectly, by giving employment to all British forces which might otherwise have been drawn from the East. Lastly, the new dynamite rams, of which the American navy had as yet almost a monopoly, would render it practicable to transport a small army across the ocean to act as auxiliaries to a great French force held in readiness for a descent upon Ireland. Thus it came about that the first week in October an American expedition, with a great deal of manœuvring and but very little fighting on the high seas, accomplished the passage from New York to Brest, where the main French fleet from Cherbourg was awaited. Some little delay was experienced before the English Channel Fleet could be decoyed away so as to allow the junction of the Allies at Brest; but by dint of skilful feints appearing to threaten various towns on the English coast, the object was eventually attained. Immediately afterwards news was brought by a small steam yacht which had managed to slip out of Cork Harbour, that circumstances were favourable for a landing at that point.

After a calm dark night, the dawn of Saturday the 11th of October found the Allied armada – the united fleets being under the command of Admiral Brin, and the land forces under General La Roche – lying under the Irish cliffs a little east of Roche's Point. By the aid of the local guides, a body of five thousand infantry taken from both armies effected a landing at the little hamlet of Goyleen, the spring tide being very high and the water perfectly smooth. Thence, according to preconcerted plan, they marched along the highroad westward, pioneered by a squad of bicycling carbineers, mounted on low safety machines and dressed in plain clothes. Under their noiseless escort, the column passed the cross road in front of Trabolgan lodge gate [ref. Chap. XIII.]. Thence defiling up the narrow lane, formerly described, which ascends the hill westwards, and passing the hollow which, as the reader will remember, intervenes between that hill and Fort Carlisle, they contrived to capture that important fort by a *coup-de-main*, effecting the escalade at a weak point, where the dyke had been left unrepaired. Thus the entrance to the harbour was at least half secured, and presently, in the grey of the early morning, the garrison of Fort Camden, on the opposite or western end of the narrow strait, had the astonishment of seeing foreign war-ships defiling into the harbour right under their guns, and still more of being suddenly shelled by their old familiar friend, Fort Carlisle. A few British inferior war-vessels were lying inside the basin, and were quickly overpowered by the unlooked-for onset of the enemy. Thus, by sunrise on the 12th, the way in was completely laid open across the enfeebled fire of Fort Camden; and, with the following high tide, the whole army of about one hundred and ten thousand men effected a landing in good order at the village of Whitegate [ref. Chap. XIII.].

The reasons for selecting as a battle-field the promontory formed by the land diverging generally eastward and north-eastward from Roche's Point, were various; the principal being, in the first place, that Queenstown and Cork being friendly towns, it was not desired to inflict on them the damage of a fight; in the second place, the position of Roche's Tower precluded the danger of being outflanked, water enclosing it on three sides. Certainly, this also precluded the possibility of retreat; but there would be no question of retreat in the deadly struggle contemplated; it would be a question simply of victory or surrender. Again, the Allied commanders were well aware that if those on the English side were to resist the temptation of attack, and to fortify themselves somewhere in the interior to await the invaders, the latter might stay and amuse themselves at Roche's Tower until they were tired, and then advance against an enemy strongly posted and elaborately prepared for their reception. But from reliable information obtained through their Irish friends and aiders, they could count pretty surely upon provoking a pitched battle at once by the mere fact of their landing, and being attacked upon ground of their own choosing.

The only problem, therefore, was how to lay out the position to the best advantage before the enemy could come up. By the latest intelligence, they would have probably twenty-four hours at least, and could therefore set to work deliberately. After consulting his American ally, General Sackville, La Roche decided upon a plan made from a local map, which had previously been supplied to him from Cork.

The American contingent, only thirty thousand strong, and consisting wholly of infantry, was stationed at Whitegate; twenty thousand men in line holding that village, together with the wooded shoulder of the hill above it westward which commands a view of Queenstown [ref. Chap. XIII.], and ten thousand being held in reserve, along with five thousand French cavalry, in the hollow behind, on the road by which it will be remembered our heroine and her uncle, in their excursion, walked up from Whitegate to Fort Carlisle. This force of thirty-five thousand occupying the left of the invader's position, was placed under the American commander, whose special duty it was, aided by the fleet in the basin, to keep a firm grip upon the landing place.

The French then deployed along the whole ridge of the downs as far as Roche's Tower, throwing up redoubts and strengthening by embankments the stone walls of the pastures, some of which they loopholed. Their central or main body, thus arrayed in line, was forty-five thousand strong, and before laying out his right wing, General La Roche posted his reserve, cavalry and infantry, fifteen thousand, in the hollow in rear, the centre of the line being directly in front of that hollow, or at the point where the western arm of the

$$\text{A} \underset{\text{D}}{\overset{\text{B}}{\top}} \text{C}$$

(B C)runs up from the main road between Whitegate and Trabolgan [ref. Chap. XIII.]; finally, the mansion, grounds, and woods of Trobolgan itself were held by a French force of twenty-five thousand men, which, forming the right wing and touching the cliff all along, effectually guarded that flank from surprise. As already said, the disadvantage of the whole position was that it admitted of no retreat. The ships were not 'burnt,' but they would be useless for the purpose of escape; in fact, Admiral Brin could only cut his way out of the basin through the enemy's fleet. But the fact of being helped with heart and hand by a friendly population on shore makes a great material and moral difference to an invader.

This will appear the more vividly as we turn to see what the British Government was about. As soon as war with France was seen to be inevitable – or rather, as soon as the Bungling Coalition had decided upon it – General Lord Gurth Redhill was recalled in haste from Asia Minor, leaving Burnfingal and his ally Rhumbegar in the lurch. Nominally, they were ordered to entrench themselves well and hold their ground until aid could be spared, but they took these instructions *cum grano*, and commenced a prudent retreat. The Russians followed them up leisurely, and without harassing their rear. By this sorry expedient, the effective force for the defence of Ireland was raised to seventy-three thousand men, not more. With this insufficient army Lord Redhill marched by the most direct route from the Curragh toward Cork, while Admiral St George, with the main body of the Channel Fleet, steamed round to meet him at the harbour. The Admiral arrived first, and finding the allies already in possession of Roche's Point and Fort Carlisle and the whole of that side of the entrance to the harbour, he stood out and lay in the offing to wait for joint action with the land forces in dislodging the invader.

He had to waste a day, for General Redhill had yet to learn how effective guerilla warfare can be. His rear was harassed by swarms of plundering camp followers of both sexes; bridges were broken down and rails taken up; and since none but false warning could be had, so many trains were wrecked and so many lives and stores lost, that he was obliged to desist and convey everything by road and lane as it would have been in old times. But this did not mend matters much: wherever trees grew across his route, they fell with a crash and blocked the way;

very few of the scouts he sent forward on horse or bicycle came back; ammunition waggons blew up unaccountably, for no man was detected tampering with them; after dark, sudden volleys were fired into the troops passing narrow places, by bands of marauders who knew the country well and easily escaped; in short, the march was more or less of a fight and loss all the way. Eventually Midleton was reached, and the general position of the invader was ascertained. The wires of the southwestern main line had not been destroyed, and the British commander sent a small body, escorting telegraph clerks, to hold Mallow Junction, that this means of rapid communication with England might remain intact. Meanwhile, on the night of the IIth, a boat had been got out with despatches to the Admiral, instructing him to force entrance to the harbour on the morning of the 13th, by which time the army should be ready to co-operate with the fleet.

As remarked before, these tactics were very rash. With an inferior force in an unfriendly country, defensive operations only should have been undertaken until the invader had been placed in straits. But that sort of thing was not to the taste of Redhill nor of his men. Audacious foreigners were profaning the sacred soil of the kingdom, and they must be driven into the sea without ceremony; so caution was thrown to the winds, and glory was the order of the day.

Deploying from Midleton toward Roche's Point, so as to rest his left upon the cliff south of and contiguous to Trabolgan wood, and his right upon the slanting, copse-sprinkled ground which descends irregularly from the S.E. to White-while his centre occupied the crest where the main road (A B), the eastern arm of the

$$\begin{matrix} & B & \\ A & \mathsf{T} & C \\ & D & \end{matrix} \quad ,$$

runs between Trebolgan lodge and Goyleen – the same road by which the enemy had advanced to capture Fort Carlisle – Lord Redhill drew up in order of battle along the slopes opposite to the invader's high ridge, the hostile armies having between their respective centres that part of the same road which runs from Trabolgan to Whitegate along the bottom of the valley [ref. Chap. XIII.]. It was dark on the 12th October by the time the various corps were in their appointed places on the field, and under the clear starlight the blazing camp fires and flashing signals of the opposing hosts marked their respective positions along the two hills.

CHAPTER XXXIII.
THE DOUBLE BATTLE OF QUEENSTOWN.

SOON after eight o'clock on the morning of Monday the 13th of October 189–, Admiral St George, in command of as large a fleet as could be spared from the several maritime places about the world which it had become necessary to defend, passed Roche's Point and was piloted into the harbour under some vigorous objections in the form of shells from Fort Carlisle, which the enemy held almost overhead starboard. However, he not only ran the gauntlet of this fire without crippling damage, but even survived the far more serious ordeal of torpedoes; and shortly the two fleets were hot at it inside the basin between Queenstown and Whitegate, the Allies having this great advantage over the British, that they delivered their fire from a position sheltered on its flanks and taken up at leisure, while the English admiral had no time to make any arrangements, and hardly to come to the attack in any order whatever.

At the sound of the cannonade inside the harbour, which commenced a few minutes before nine, the defending forces on land were ordered to advance against an enemy who desired nothing better than to give them the warm reception upon which he had founded all his plans. The first shots were exchanged on the British left, where an onset was made against the wood immediately above Trabolgan House, eastward, which the invaders occupied. A sharp rifle fire rang through this thick plantation for some time without any visible result; at last, the English dashed in with fixed bayonets, and in a hand-to-hand conflict drove their enemies from tree to tree down the hill to the open pleasure-grounds of the mansion, and here a desperate combat raged; the English striving to carry by storm the garrisoned house. Every window was spitting fire upon them; the lower apartments were strongly barricaded, and a succession of fierce rushes against the house, first on one side then on another, was for a time repulsed with telling loss. But the French had not reckoned on their right wing being dislodged from the wooded hill opposite and driven in; hence reinforcements were not to hand for the moment. Meanwhile, the determined gallantry of two English battalions at last overpowered the house garrison, and after a stubborn cut-and-thrust struggle up the stairs, the British colours waved from the roof of the mansion.

Elated by this success, Lord Redhill prepared to advance the whole line. All his batteries which had been brought to bear upon the centre of the valley opened at once, while – the real movement – a strong body of cavalry, backed up by infantry, in fact, the whole of his right wing, swooped upon Whitegate and achieved a success even more brilliant than that which had just been gained on the left. Dashing along the road which acts as a sea wall in front of the village [ref. Chap. XIII.], they fell upon the Americans with a sudden shock and drove them pell-mell out of the village, forcing them to shelter in the wood which clothes the shoulder of the ridge and in the hollow behind it, where their reserve was stationed. Thus, both wings of the invader being already repulsed, the assault upon his centre began; but it failed, because the French centre was as good as impregnable. The crest of their hill was an *enceinte* of redoubts and wall-faced embankments which offered no weak point; while on the British side of the valley the hedgerows were not yet trampled down sufficiently to allow cavalry to advance unimpeded. At the onset, a hot encounter took place on the main road itself, at the very spot where our heroine had turned back in her walk a year before [ref. Chap. XIII.]; and here again the French got worsted and were forced up the hill, disputing the ground yard by yard; but as they retreated behind their strong places above, their artillery swept the hill side with a deadly fire; this was followed up by a simultaneous cavalry charge from the right and left centre which decimated the impetuous assailants, driving what remained of them back across the valley; and the British general feared for the moment that his own centre was broken. But La Roche's tactics were more patient and cautious, and he did not permit the counter-charge to be followed up.

It proved very soon that the carrying by assault of Whitegate, though it was certainly magnificent, was not war. It should not have been done until the success of the British fleet had been made sure of; and Admiral St George did not succeed. His position was altogether a weak one. He could not break the enemy's serried line of battle off Whitegate, strengthened as it was by the possession and fortification of the islet in front of the village; the new American dynamite rams darted about his ships like gadflies and inflicted great damage; lastly, he was rather annoyed than assisted by the blundering fire of Port Camden, which commanded his rearmost squadron, and whose shells, falling short of the enemy's vessels, did execution, when they did any at all, upon British ships. The consequence was that no support whatever could be given by the fleet to the attack on Whitegate. On the contrary, as soon as the American naval commander, whose division of the Allied fleet was posted inside, next the shore, understood what had happened, he opened a withering cannonade upon the village. Its effect became immediately visible in a stampede of the English; then the American corps which had been forced to take refuge among the reserve behind the wooded shoulder of the ridge, came on again in good order, re-occupied the shattered village, and even pushed its outposts further eastward, gaining ground.

Trabolgan was still held in the grip of the English who had stormed it; and their commander, seeing that matters stood badly on the right and on the centre, concentrated all the force he could spare upon that advanced post of his left. A battery was brought to bear upon the hillside below Roche's Tower from the opposite slope; cavalry was massed behind the wood on the same slope; and the wood itself was again filled with infantry, taking the place of the force which had gone forward and captured the house.

General La Roche, on his side, perceived too that the brunt of the fight would next be about Trabolgan, and subsequently either at Roche's Tower or on the opposite rising ground, according to which side should repulse the other. He therefore quietly drew off a considerable force, his now secure left wing, so as to leave his reserve intact for unforeseen emergencies, and hurried this force southwards along the rear of the ridge, between the line and the reserve, where it passed hidden from the enemy's view. It debouched at Roche's Tower, the infantry in front, just in time to engage in the fiercest contest of the day, with an English foot regiment which had poured across the low ground near the cliff and stormed the hill. This was a desperate move, because it must have been evident that a mass of men, if repulsed from Roche's Tower, must literally be driven into the sea over the cliff. And such was actually the result. A tremendous charge of the French cavalry cleared the ground, bearing down the tall signal-staff as an avalanche would a reed, and with a horrid smash, sacrificing many horses, as well as the limbs of their riders against the squat, round, white lighthouse, Roche's Tower [ref. Chap. XIII.].*But the charge did its work; the British regiment was driven over the cliff along with the foremost of its assailants; then the guns arrived at the spot, and it became an artillery duel between the opposing hills, each side seeking to clear the way for a decisive advance across the valley. But the Allies had the best of it; they were twenty thousand stronger than the British at this point in the field, and Providence was declaring for the big battalions. The French at Roche's Tower having both a superior force and a superior position, might assume the offensive at any moment, supported by cavalry, which the now trampled hedges would allow to act in the valley; and Lord Redhill could spare no additional force, without drawing away his reserve, which had to watch the Americans at Whitegate, who were preparing to attempt a flank movement.

This concentration of force by the invader at Roche's Tower sealed the fate of Trabolgan, verifying the prophetic words which our heroine had uttered on the spot a year before, '*The place is doomed.*' The intervening fringes of fir plantation having been now gapped by the artillery, aim could be taken at the mansion itself, which was still crammed from basement to roof with English soldiers. The roar of the guns was soon answered by the crash of masonry and the rising of smoke and flames from the ill-fated house, where the main staircase was one of the first parts to fall, involving in hopeless destruction most of those who were inside. And now, bit by bit, the solid wedge of the enemy's advance from Roche's Tower began to elbow out of the mansion grounds, and to push into the shelter of the wood above it, the English force which, since the morning, had held obstinately that point of vantage. And this, although the British battery, which was still in position near the cliff, mowed lanes in the assaulting column; because those gunners were exposed to a heavier cannonade, and from a greater elevation. Three o'clock found the wood above the burning house carried by the French; and the sharp ping of rifles filled it from end to end, as the fight grew on eastward like a rising tide, superior force prevailing steadily over stubborn endurance.

His right now gaining ground, and his centre secure, La Roche prepared to execute the flank movement on the left for which the Americans were eager, to avenge their early repulse. The rising water in the basin would now enable at least

---

*　　See *Frontispiece*.

the smaller vessels to co-operate with the advance by land along the harbour-side road eastwards. Accordingly, the twenty thousand Americans in line, together with five thousand French cavalry of the reserve, received orders to push forward and turn the English right flank, while the ten thousand American reserve came forward to occupy White-gate and maintain communications. It was now between four and five o'clock, and the attention of the British right wing was turning irresistibly to the crisis at Trabolgan, where the firing was becoming more furious every minute, the peppering of the rifles in the wood being overpowered by the booming of the big guns and the crackling explosions of the mitrailleuses. Suddenly they were surprised by a galling fire from a long fringe of trees on the right rear, and then by the sight of the Stars and Bars waving amid the smoke along their turned flank. The mischief was difficult to avoid; Lord Redhill was undermanned for his battlefield, and could hardly avoid one danger without running into another. Either he must have continued to give way on the left and centre, or by reinforcing them he must have exposed his right flank, as had now happened. The order flashed to the reserve, 'Change front half right back!' but the movement was executed under a murderous fire, and when at last the men fronted to the north-east, they had more than enough to hold their ground against the elevated position and greater numbers of the Americans. To support them with the centre was out of the question, while the centre itself was being forced upon the other side, and the left repulsed and driven in. There remained but one desperate chance – to carry the enemy's centre by a sudden onslaught, giving time to the assailants – when successful – to join with the reserve in maintaining the line of retreat. That did not mean victory, but it might give a chance of orderly retreat. Such a plan needs only to he stated to show its wild impracticability. The wise and humane course now would have been to send forward flags of truce, acknowledge a by no means disgraceful defeat, and surrender with the whole army. But the same temper which had prompted the would-be defenders of the unfriendly country to hurry on and stake their fortune on a pitched battle again prevailed over their better judgment, and the General called up the Life Guards, and formed them in column attack, thus weakening his reserve, and depriving it of its very faint chance of cutting a way out of the field.

'It's all over but the shouting, Barford,' he said, with a forced and livid smile, as the Colonel rode to his side; 'we're between the devil and the deep sea. Unless we can carry that ridge by assault, we must throw up the sponge.'

'Hopeless, General,' was the reply. 'But I see with you there's nothing else left. I believe my men would mutiny rather than surrender – but it rests with you; we wait orders.'

'Well, a soldier's death to us, old fellow, that's all.' Then, taking his place, – '*Attack in close column! Carry swords!*' The bristling steel flashed together.

'*Trot, march!*' The bugles sounded, and the French commander, on the opposing ridge, saw a great billow of cavalry coming end on down the slope to the valley in front of his centre.

'*Gallop!*' The bugles sounded, and the grass fields, by this time trampled into mud between their flattened hedgerows, quivered under the weight of the bounding mass, which flowed across the road, and began to ascend among the *débris* of breached and battered defences on the French hillside.

'*Charge!*' The bugles sounded, and up went the disciplined column, over all obstacles, compact, swift, and heavy as a rushing train, into the gaping jaws of destruction. The mitrailleuses were ready for them; there was a hell of flame and thunder; then a dense pall of white smoke, out of which, right and left, emerged a few score of mangled and shrieking horses, many dragging their dead riders in the stirrups, and all careering madly back across the valley, braining the scared wounded lying about, who tried painfully to get out of the way. This was the finish; the Life Guards had perished with the General, the reserve was broken up, the Americans were pressing on the rear; and now, under a panic no army could be expected to endure, the over-matched British troops gave up the vain struggle, and fled.

Admiral St George had been pounding away all day at the Allied fleet securely drawn up between the friendly shore of Queenstown and the guarded village of Whitegate. As explained already, he fought at immense disadvantage; it was no question of merely giving and taking hard knocks in the Nelson fashion. Still the English hammered away with their old pluck, clinging to the hope that success of the army on land might make up for the failure of the fleet; which indeed, from the patriotic point of view, would be the more important success after all. But when they saw the smoke of the American flank movement gaining onwards and onwards up the south-eastern slope; still more, when they perceived that the thunders of the battle were growing inland across the valley from the ridge of Roche's Tower, they knew that Redhill must have been outflanked, and that all was lost. Then the human instincts of life and safety took the place of emulation and self-sacrifice; they had clone all that men could do; and the Admiral signalled to cease firing, and struck his flag.

In a few minutes all was quiet on the water, and the heavy canopy of smoke lifted slowly from the basin of Cork Harbour, which lay calm and blue in the mellow October sunset. But, for two hours afterwards, the men in the ships could hear the roar of the pursuit on land rolling away past Midleton toward Youghal, until darkness put an end to slaughter and savagery, but not to untold miseries, which lay overborne by the headlong torrent of rout.

CHAPTER XXXIV.
NIGHT AND REFLECTIONS.

THE din of arms was past, and night settled down on the bloody field whereon lay shattered for ever – it would be absurd to say a hated tyranny, for, in spite of the Bungler reaction, there remained nowadays not a vestige of that – but a whole political and social system which had played its part and had its day, and which had how become a nuisance and a pest, blocking the way of a more enlightened civilisation which was waiting to spread far beyond the shores of Great Britain and Ireland.

The fight was over; the brave defenders of the lost cause were slain or dispersed, or worse, were lying huddled together in agonised and moaning heaps. The heavy pall of the battle smoke had even yet not lifted from the hills, but had become mingled with a sea fog, which melted down in a mild drizzle. There was no moon, but a lurid, flickering glare was thrown far and wide over the ghastly scene from the flames of burning Trabolgan, which, in the morning, had been a mansion, and was now a bonfire. The squat, round lighthouse, Roche's Tower, was no more; its stump showed a few feet above its surrounding ruins, laid low by the artillery; and the tall flagstaff by which our two friends had stood in their excursion a year ago [ref. Chap. XIII.] lay this night across a shoal of corpses. The flickering red light was in this spot unobstructed, for the fringe of pines on the hillside below had been shorn close by the shot and shell; and that light fell upon the wan features of the fallen, and upon their gory stains; while their groans, and the faint plash of the high tide against the rocks below, were the only sounds to break the stillness which had succeeded to the tumult of that fateful day.

Hard by the ruins of Roche's Tower, in the thick of the slaughtered, with his head resting on a part of the prostrate signal-staff, an English private of powerful build spoke in accents of pain to an equally stalwart comrade, who was doing his best to staunch the gash that was making a pool around him.

'Ah, Bill, my boy – beggared if this ain't sarve us roight for goin' a soldierin'. Why couldn't we stop at 'ome and do jobs loike about the river, and live a quiet life, instead o' listenin' like fools to your recruitin' sergeants a standin' drink and gettin' round a feller with a lot o' lies!'

'Oi'd never no more, Joe, dimd if a would,' groaned the other, in reply. 'This is what they calls milipery glory, this is. To lie ere with my 'ip smashed, and bleedin' to death as fast as fast, and moy poor Betsy a-thinkin' of me all the while, and 'opin her Bill's a-comin back to her after the war! Dim the war, and them that makes war, oi say. It makes lots of honest folks miserable, and does no good to no one. If ever oi gets well – but per'aps oi never shall, Joe – call me a turnip if ever yer sees me a-fightin' battles agin.'

'Curse them doctors, why don't 'ee come round?' gasped his comrade. 'Oi can't be a settin' my broken arm and rib for myself, can oi? Bother them chaps! they're no good.'

'Doctors wun't be o' no use to me, Joe,' whined the other, more faintly than before. 'Oi'm a goin', oi feel oi be. Oi'm a losin' all my blood, and oi can't stop it, and oi can't do without it, not even for my Betsy's sake – Who's this a-comin? Here! help!'

The hooded form of a Catholic Sister of Mercy was beside him, and in a moment she was kneeling on the gory turf and supporting his head in one hand, while with the other she moved him gently into a position adapted for an attempt to check the hemorrhage. But he was too far gone. Her companion had turned off to tend other piteous implorers among the hideous mass of human wreck. We cannot depict the heavenly compassion of these women, which soothed, where it could not stay, the departure of many a sufferer; suffice it to give poor Bill's last words.

'Oh, lady, yer be a angel, yer be indeed. I sees a many ladies like yer a-gatherin' round me, they're angels too. Yer'll find my Betsy, and comfort her – keep yer sweet 'and on my 'ead, lady – yes, just so – then I be 'appy and not afeard – '

And, under the wing of the Sister, the spirit of poor Bill, ex-bargee, passed into its next state, under the wing of the priestess of nature, the only true priestess, the only true Saviour. The other man next claimed her attention.

'Couldn't yer get me away into a 'orspital, ma'am?' groaned Joe, while the Sister, her garment lying across his brow, occupied herself in setting and binding his fractures.

'Yes, we will, my man,' she said soothingly, 'as soon as the ambulance comes round; but you must lie still and keep yourself quiet. There now, stay just as I have put you; take a drop out of this flask – that's enough for you just now; now lie still till I come again.'

Subsequently, Joe was removed, with a host of other wounded, to Cork, where he recovered, but, although in the prime of life, never was again the same strong working man that he had been.

We have thus described briefly two cases – and those by no means the worst – out of the thirty-three thousand – the loss of the Allies had been about six thousand – which were spread that night, either dead or in various stages of suffering, about the dreadful field; and even that list excludes the fallen on board the ships. It is a very, very old story, the horrors of a battle-field after the fight. It has been witnessed thousands of times, and who shall say that it may not have to recur many times yet? And still we boast of our civilisation; we are thankful that we are not as our fathers were, that the public mind is more sympathetic, and that philanthropic associations are doing much to alleviate the sufferings which in past times were simply neglected. There is something in this contention, no doubt;

but nevertheless we have as yet failed to eradicate the passions which provoke, and those which find their vent in, war. Nations do not trust one another; and so long as the existing social basis lasts, it is not likely that they ever will. Make believe as much as you please that the masculine half of society is the working and the ruling portion, this respectable fiction will not succeed in the future, any more than it has in the past, in neutralising the influence exerted by the other half. For better or worse, the moral character of men will continue to be moulded by the ideals which are set before them by women. The question then arises – what is the quality of those ideal? Is it of a kind tending to promote the common welfare, to merge international jealousies in community of properly human aims and interests, and to foster the love of peace? Is it not rather that of an artificial system of superstition and meanness; the falsification of spiritual truth, and the consequent perversion of the religious instinct, ramifying, like a poison in the blood, through every department of life, even the most secular, and discolouring the thoughts and emotions of all sorts of persons, even the most worldly? No man can be so absorbed in the cares of business that the influences of his home will have no effect on his character; even if he have no settled home, the female society he consorts with elsewhere will have much the same effect. And so long as his relations with that society are falsified, how can their effect be a good one? how can it be expected that the atmosphere of a subjected and distorted womanhood should be wholesome? The so-called virtues which it is the fashion to patronise when exhibited by women, are the virtues of the slave, not of the citizen; they borrow a little grace from being labelled womanly, but their real name is servile. And, after all, those who thoughtlessly foster this sort of thing, do not really admire it. They let it pass as a drawback of nature, – one of those things that cannot be helped, and give their attention only to picking out the few sweet plums which are to be found in the very unsavoury dish. But man cannot live on plums alone.

Nor is it any escape from responsibility to say that we must sit and wait until feminine nature changes and becomes something else than what it is. After all said and done, men must be here for something. If they had no business in the world, surely they would not have been put into it. Surely it is obvious enough that if on the one hand woman's influence is to determine, and does determine, the moral character of society, men, on the other hand, have their part to play in educating the source of that influence. There is no evidence to show that so long as two sexes are needed to propagate the race, the part of the father, the brother, or other male companion, is likely to count for nothing or little in the training of girls. On the contrary, we know that – for the present, at all events – it counts for much. Then our contention is that in order to be improved and elevated by feminine influence, men must feel women to be in all things *without exception* their equals – let alone the question of superiority – and that in order to feel them their equals, they must learn to make them so. They have not learnt it yet, though some feeble steps are being made in the right direction, and even these few steps already show splendid results. Whole-heartedness is requisite in this all-important matter; every prejudice must be uprooted, every morbid predilection scoured off; it must be recognised that 'womanliness' is not a harem superstition, to be set up as a standard of conduct and blindly adhered to, it is rather an attribute concerning which, owing to the world's past folly, we know very little indeed, but which is now to be revealed and developed as the goal of all knowledge whatsoever. By misuse of their opportunities given to educate their womankind to physical and intellectual equality with themselves, men have been hitherto held down in a condition where they are helplessly bound to expend in mutual enmity and destruction those energies which would have gone far to establish universal contentment; because there is a greater scourge even than war, that is, disease; and had women's capacities been made the most of, medical science must have been vastly in advance of the stage it has reached, and a sound mind in a sound body having become a general instead of an exceptional blessing, the soil from which war springs would have been cleared of that weed. It may still not be too late to make up lost time – the good signs already alluded to seem to indicate that it is not; but prolonged indifference would be fatal, because the day of salvation is limited, and when a people – especially a great and powerful people – has let it slip by unused, the beyond is not an automatic millennium, but a catastrophe.

The hackneyed word salvation reminds one that there remains another consideration which may be worth weighing by those who have not established to their satisfaction that there is no future life, and no judgment to come for waste of the present one, – no (metaphorical) 'lake of fire which is the second death.' If – whether by a series of more or less distressful lines in other forms, or by some other equally rational and natural mode – the Hereafter is to readjust by its rewards and punishments the seemingly unjust distribution of good and evil here – then those among us, men or women, who instead of helping purposely do what in them lies to hinder this work of the regeneration of human society by its female portion, may reasonably fear lest the authorities they will have to settle with *there* hold them personally responsible, in their degree, for the plagues of disease and war in the earth.

CHAPTER XXXV.
THE SEVERANCE OF IRELAND.

THE great pitched battle having now been decided on the ground chosen by the invaders, for reasons already stated, their advance could begin. A strong detachment at once crossed the water to occupy Queenstown, which place gave its victorious Allies a jubilant welcome, and illuminated at night, from the summit of the hill to the quays, notwithstanding that the glass of every window had been shivered to fragments by the vibration of the cannonade. Meanwhile, the main body worked round by land and bridges, and after leaving outposts at Mallow Junction to secure the important trunk line of railway to Dublin, entered Cork, whose inhabitants welcomed them with open arms. But time was valuable – it was necessary to keep striking while the iron was hot; so making the Cork and Queenstown district his base of operations, La Roche pushed on by forced marches, and reached Dublin with his advance guard on the fourth day after the battle. Here the fugitive remnant of the British troops had thought of a rally, in the hope of reinforcements; but the news of the great defeat had so paralysed the Home Administration, that none were forthcoming; and the next piece of news which enlivened the London papers, was the capitulation of Dublin on the 18th of October, or rather, its declaration for the enemy. There was nothing now to stop the march of the Allies northward; and in a very short time the last chance of retaining the Union in any form or degree, was taken away by the defection of Ulster; the majority in that province having come to see that their best course would be to make terms with the future Central Government of Ireland, the more especially as resistance, unsupported by England, would be worse than useless. The work of the invasion was now complete; on the last day of the month the American-Irish Declaration of Severance was despatched for the digestion of the British Cabinet, together with the other terms of peace, which included a heavy war indemnity, to be divided equally among the Allies.

Lord Humnoddie resigned, with all his colleagues, but no one could be found to form a Cabinet at this juncture; so the affairs of the country were managed for the moment by revolutionary mass meetings, which hurriedly delegated their authority to a Committee of Public Safety. First and foremost, peace was concluded, the costs were paid, and Ireland abandoned. It was a great blow to the pride of the dominant party in England; their only consolation was that matters might have been very much worse. After all, the battle had taken place in Ireland, not England; Great Britain was still intact, and perhaps her position among nations might not permanently suffer. France herself had borne a heavier disaster only a generation ago, and, instead of being crushed, had risen from it into a more solid national life.

Still it was not pleasant to reflect that what should have been conceded with a good grace, binding the two islands together in a more genuine union than had ever existed between them before, was now taken away by force; that through clinging stolidly to an insensate prejudice, half a kingdom had gone to the foreigner; for the incorporation of Ireland as one of the United States was hardly less than that, although, it is true, the foreigner in this case was one of kindred race, language, and political genius.

CHAPTER XXXVI.
AT RUDDYMERE AGAIN.

'PEACE is signed,' said Lord Humnoddie, as the two long acquainted families, his own and the Dulham party, were at afternoon tea in the great hall at Ruddymere, where they sat by preference. 'It's rather peace at any price than peace with honour, but there's no help for it. The thing took us all by surprise; I had just prepared a Home Rule scheme of my own to pacify Ireland, when the war broke out. I have the rough draft of it in that Japan cabinet.'

'Indeed! what a pity!' said Lesbia. 'Would you mind my seeing it, Lord Humnoddie?'

'I'll read you the sketch, if you like,' he answered, going to the drawer, and bringing out a sheet of manuscript. 'Here it is, then.

'*Article* 1. The Sovereign of England to retain the title *of* Queen or King of Great Britain and Ireland, but the Irish Government to have no connection with the English Government except through the Sovereign.

'*Article* 2. Ireland to be an independent State, but to claim the right of being defended by the Imperial army and navy in the event of war. In return for this claim, Ireland to furnish a certain number of men yearly to recruit the Imperial forces.

'*Article* 3. Ireland to be represented in the Imperial Parliament at Westminster by five delegates, one from each of the provinces and one from Dublin. These delegates to have the right of speaking and voting upon all questions, equally with English members. England, Wales, and Scotland to be represented in the Irish Parliament by seven delegates – one from London, three from the provinces, two from Scotland, and one from Wales. These delegates to have the right of speaking and voting upon all questions, equally with Irish members.

'*Article* 4. Ireland to be free to make her own fiscal arrangements, but to grant the province of Ulster a charter to make a special commercial treaty with England. In the event of the terms of such treaty not meeting the views of the Central Irish Government, custom-houses would be established along the inland frontier of Ulster, or the part of it affected by the treaty.

'*Article* 5. All persons visiting or residing in Ireland, to enjoy religious liberty not less than that enjoyed by all persons visiting or residing in England.

'I thought that would do,' he added, laying down the manuscript.

'Do!' exclaimed Lesbia. 'I should think so, indeed. Why, if only that measure had been brought forward, I believe Queenstown would never have been fought, and the kingdom would be still intact! Excuse me, Lord Humnoddie, but what on earth induced you to keep it back?'

The Marquis looked at his wife.

'That was rather my doing, Lesbie,' she said. 'I persuaded Hum to keep his Home Rule to himself, at all events until the Irish had had a whipping. I thought such concessions were more than they deserved, and it would have looked like giving in to a threat.'

'But it is we who have got the whipping, and we have had to give in, not to a threat, but to force,' replied Lesbia very quietly, but with sternness in her voice and face. 'I must say, Lady Humnoddie, that I should not like to have borne your part in this matter. I should almost feel myself – blood-guilty.'

It was a fault of our heroine's that when her feelings were stirred about sociology or politics, she was apt to give vent to them, without pausing to consider the weight of the projectile. Lady Humnoddie turned pale and was silent, and though too good-natured to resent what was said to her, she did not quite recover her spirits until the evening, after dinner. Mr Bristley himself was startled by his niece's observation, but felt its justice too much to remonstrate; he came to the rescue, however, as best he could.

'The old story, my lord,' he said, forcing a laugh. 'It happened to your predecessor, the very first Prime Minister. The woman whom thou gavest me, she gave me of the apple of Discord, and I did eat. It can't be undone now, any more than then, and it's no use crying over – to be practical, what do you think of the outlook at present?'

'Well,' he replied, 'the worst of the crisis will soon be over, let us hope. The indemnity is paid, the French army is quitting Ireland, which is handed over to the Americans, and perhaps the clouds of foreign war are passing away for good; but the Revolution is upon us in all its force, and our national idols, one after another, are toppling down and going under. My order is threatened with political and, it may be, social extinction; yours, too, Mr Bristley – '

'Let it go, Lord Humnoddie, let it go; don't spare it for my sake. By an Established Church the State is saddled with business wherewith it has no concern, while it is made to neglect things of importance within its rightful province. The days of State patronage and control of religion are numbered: no country will tolerate it much longer. If we sky-pilots cannot keep our heads above water without establishment, we had better sink. But what about the external relations of the country?'

'Well, you know, first we've got to pay the piper all round; next we are to hand over Egypt to France, our rights in the Suez Canal being guaranteed, if we choose to insist on them in preference to making a new canal further east. The Yankees will foot it in ould Oireland; and as for the Russian bear, he hugs for good Afghanistan in the east and Asia Minor in the west. Russia, in return, cedes to us a magnificent assortment of promises for the future. But, I fancy, she will soon have her own hands full; since every ruler who ascends the throne under the old regimen, knows that he signs his own death-warrant.'

'Some beside Russians think that Russia is to be the dominant country of the future, and to absorb Europe,' remarked his elder daughter.

'Possibly, Hillie; but she will have to traverse a big revolution first. If we here needed the physic, what does Russia? Anyhow, that question's not a pressing one. We have made a terrible mess of our affairs at home and abroad, and we must lie on our bed as we have made it, and be thankful it's no worse.'

'Who are the people on this revolutionary committee?' asked the younger girl.

'There's the list, Fri. I haven't the pleasure of knowing any of them, and don't wish to have.'

'I'll tell you what, Fri,' said her sister, winking at her, 'if the Revolution turns us all adrift, you and I shall have to start as professional beauties.'

'And in that capacity I hope you will visit Dulham,' joined in Lesbia, 'where Uncle Spines and I are going to set up the cult of Baal Peor.'

'Lesbia, for shame!' said her mother.

'Baal Berith will be more to the purpose, Lesbie,' observed her uncle. 'The Numen of the Covenant, the covenant of Divine Order, will serve us better than the Numen of Debauchery.'

'Never mind, we'll try them all round,' said Hilda.

'Girls, hold your tongues,' put in the Marchioness. 'We have it on the apostle's authority that the tongue is a fire, a world of iniquity. Is not that so, Mr Bristley?'

'And you have it on my authority that the apostle was a double-distilled donkey, down to the ground,' retorted the person appealed to. 'Nevertheless, he spoke truth sometimes for the sake of change, as in the instance you mention.'

'These be the clergy and the women of the future,' observed Lord Humnoddie, who had listened with some amusement.

'It was the man, not the parson, that spoke in me,' said Mr Bristley. 'The man considers the world around him; the parson is a guide to the sky.'

'And it was the woman, not the dollymops, that spoke in me,' said Hilda.

'Pray, what is a dollymops?' asked her father.

'A dollymops, papa, is a woman who trots out the proprieties,' explained Hilda.

'But sits heavily upon them while they trot,' added Friga.

'Lesbia,' said the Marchioness reproachfully, 'you've spoilt my Fri.'

'Spoil my own god-daughter, Lady Humnoddie! Never.'

'Your god-daughter! I should say you were a mother of quite the other sort,' she retorted. 'The old notion is that god-children are brought up by their sponsors in the fear of the Lord; how say you, Mr Bristley?'

'I say with you that that's a very old notion, Lady Humnoddie,' replied the vicar genially.

'And I say that Lesbie *does* bring me up in that fear,' added Friga. 'My fear about your god, dearest mamma, is that before long he will get – '

A shriek of laughter from the other two girls was loud enough to drown completely the remainder of Lady Friga's sentence. Probably, what she said was, 'will get his blessing disregarded.'

Seeing that this was a fresh discomfiture for her hostess, Lesbia said seriously, –

'Joking apart, Lady Humnoddie, I think that women of the world like you must perceive better than others, that the old notions look like being played out now. When from the Cornish coast I heard the cannon roar at Roche's Tower all that dreadful day, I seemed to listen to the knell of an epoch which indeed it is high time were dead.'

'I believe that too, Lesbie,' said her mother, 'else why should an event, which at the time was remote, have affected me in that supernatural manner? The first part of my dream has come true.'

'When the fruit hangs fully ripe,' said Mr Bristley, in slow and measured accents, 'any touch will bring it to the ground. Or, as was said of old, where the carcase is, thither will the vultures be gathered. It may be a battle lost in one place or another, at Dorking, at Guildford, at Queenstown – where you will; it may be a visitation of quite another, perhaps a direr, sort; but the teaching of history – notably of that Judaic history with which we are so familiar – goes to show that where national advantages have been abused, and national opportunities thrown away, the catastrophe – whatever form it is to take – is not very far off.'

'But if the decencies of life are to be upset, and good society ruined,' said the Marchioness bitterly, 'I shall give it up and go and live abroad.'

'I hope you may find there the personal relief you expect,' he returned, 'but the respite in any case can be only temporary. The revolution, I feel convinced, will spread from these shores, and effect, more or less, every part of Europe. You will everywhere see your chosen society changing around you, and increasing its distance from your sympathies. Far better, would it not be, to take the bull by the horns, and see what you can do to accommodate yourself to the times, and prepare for the future. The period will most likely be short, during which the wealthy and high-born can start with advantage over their competitors in the struggle for those things which make existence worth having. Hitherto, your order – mine too – has been as a caste set apart, nursed and favoured as if it belonged to a better world; and of that class the female portion has been the most petted, and, I must say, spoiled. They have been kept in a glass case, so to speak, treated partly as ornaments, partly as toys, partly as slaves; flattered, sonneted, grimaced at, lied to, regarded with mock homage, but not with sincere reverence; they have been thrown the sugared husks of life's enjoyments with an elegant bow, but debarred as much as possible from the nutritious inside; they have been overwhelmed with valueless offerings, but denied their rights. As my niece well says, it is time the doom of such an epoch were come; and it is come, I really believe.'

As all kept silence, the vicar turned to his wife.

'Well, now, Kitty dear, I mustn't tire the company with any more prosing. May we have our trap round?'

'Certainly,' replied Lord Humnoddie, ringing, 'and come over again soon; old friends should hang together at such a time, whatever their private theories.'

CHAPTER XXXVII.
LEADING TO THE SECOND PART.

'Hallo! visitors, bother! I must stop in for them,' said Lesbia to herself, for just as she was leading her bicycle down the vicarage garden, a day or two after the visit to Ruddymere, she saw a wagonette pull up at the garden gate, and a foot-man dismount from it. In a minute she recognised the visitors.

'Why, it's the Lockstables from their honeymoon, bringing Fri with them! How are you all? this is quite unexpected, come in – yes, yes, I can ride after-wards; you're just in time for a cup of tea with mamma and auntie, but Uncle Spines is out in the village; he was sent for. But how soon you've come back from Italy, Rose! you can't have done it properly in so short a time?'

'We didn't care to be gallivanting abroad any longer, with this great smash at home,' said Lockstable. 'What insanity made that unfortunate fellow Redhill throw away his life, and the lives of all those fine fellows, after the battle was lost?'

'They did nobly for their country, Athelstan,' said his wife.

'Country be shot!' was the reply. 'Catch me dying for my country! Not if I know it. My creed is, that a fellow's put here, not to die for his country, but to live for pudding and kisses, – eh, Rose?'

'Yes, that *is* your 'creed,' Athelstan, and I'm afraid you have no other,' answered his wife.

'There's some truth in what you say, though, Mr Lockstable,' remarked Lesbia. 'It was a manifestly useless, and, therefore, unjustifiable sacrifice.'

'Ah, you're a sensible young lady, Miss Newman. By the way, I've brought you a present from the Swiss, the actual weapon used by William Tell at Hastings, or anyhow, one fit to be used by your muscular arms, whenever you visit mountains with glaciers. Where the deuce an' all – ah, I left it in the carriage.'

'How d'you do, won't you come in?' said Mrs Bristley, advancing from the house and shaking hands with each. 'My husband will be sorry to miss you, but he may be in by five.'

'Here you are, Miss Newman,' said Lockstable, presenting her with a very workman-like ice-axe.

'Thanks endless; what a first-rate tool!' said Lesbia, taking it from his hands. 'But you needn't call me Miss Newman any longer, now that you are an append-age of my friend Rose.'

'Lesbia, then – you must get your uncle to take you to the Alps; it's just what you'd enjoy. I believe you'd go for Mont Blanc all alone, like that fellaw Jock o' Ballsack – '

'Jacques Balmat of Chamounix, I suppose you mean,' said Lesbia laughing. 'Balzac was a French novelist; and as for Jock o' Hazeldean, I'm sure I don't know who he was. But I shouldn't take Balmat's route; I should ascend from St Geovais by the Dôme, and return by the Côte, the Corridor, and the Bossous.'

'Not without a guide, Lesbie,' said Mrs Lockstable. 'It would be tempting Providence. The change of weather alone is a great danger on the high range. The local guides are well accustomed to observe it, and no one who values his life should venture on those heights without one.'

'No, by the cross of Christopher Columbus!' put in her husband. 'Why, I needed a guide inside a London 'bus yesterday, although Rose was with me. We were sitting near the door in one of the red pennies which run between 'Woyl Oak' and the Strand, you know. I took a fellow opposite me for one of the fellaws of my club, and shook hands with him violently. He was a perfect stranger, and stone-deaf into the bargain. Didn't he stare like an owl, and didn't our co-'bussers giggle!'

While the rest of the company were still chatting in the drawing-room, Friga led her intimate friend out again into the garden, and, taking her hand, said, –

'Lesbie, something has been haunting me ever since the news of the disaster of Queenstown, about which, I will confess to you, I care very little *politically*. That something is the interview which you and your uncle had some time ago with Cardinal Power, and which you gave me an account of. I understand your view, Lesbie, to be, that if women's rights are to be vindicated, the religious department must not be neglected; because it is mainly by appeals to the superstitious credulity and ignorance of the masses that our subjection has been maintained. You hold, do you not, that it is essential to the regeneration of society and a higher civilisation, that the spiritual dominion should pass out of the hands of those who have usurped it, and that the priestess of nature should also become the priestess by society's ordinances; and further, that the divine supremacy itself should be ascribed to our sex. Is that your doctrine?'

'Certainly, Fri; what of it?'

'Why, that on these grounds you have approached the Church of Rome through her chief representative here, as being the body most fitted to accept and act upon that view of the future of human religion, the one most competent and able to carry it into effect if she will.'

'Yes; what then?'

'Why, then I think it is time you followed up your first interview with the cardinal by another. If this revolution is going to shake society to pieces, the endurance of even his Church will be tried, the more especially if the rumours mentioned by the correspondent of the *Daily Twaddler* this morning should prove true, that an Italian woman of influence and position is getting up an agitation against the Church in Rome itself, which may end in a regular persecution.'

'Look here, then, Fri; if I go and call on the cardinal again, will you go with me?'

'I! Do you think that would be of any use, Lesbia? I sympathise with your aims as heartily as your uncle can, but my talents are not equal to his; in fact I am no orator, though I study a good deal.'

'I think it might be of service, Fri. The world's the world, and its motives are not always those of pure reason. Your father has lately been in a prominent position before it, while my uncle is only an obscure clever man.'

'My father!' said Friga, laughing. 'Yes; he *has* been in a prominent position before the world of late; very. More prominent than successful. However, if you think I might be useful to bait your hook, as a possible convert to Romanism, I'll go through the ceremony of calling with you, at all events.'

'That's settled then; we must arrange an opportunity. Now, how are you going home?'

'Direct. The wagonette will drop me at the park gate, and then take the Lockstables to Frogmore Station; they return to town this evening.'

'Well, I can ride my bike to the park gate, and then walk a bit with you. That'll give us a few minutes to consult about seeing the cardinal.'

CHAPTER XXXVIII.

THE PAPACY IN TROUBLE – THE PISA-VITRI PERSECUTION.

BEATRICE PISA-VITRI, a handsome, young Roman widow of birth and fortune, had, up to the year 189 – , been noted for her religious zeal, and her munificence toward the ancient Church with which she was connected, both by ties of kindred – her brother being a priest – and by her aristocratic family traditions. But at this date a change – or rather a development – took place gradually in her mind; she was seized by a desire to assert herself in matters hitherto held strictly ecclesiastical. This conduct on her part was met, first with mild remonstrance, then with open displeasure, reproof, and opposition from the clergy. The worse for them; their bigotry was as oil on the flame of Madame Pisa-Vitri's ambition, and turned her former devotion into a deadly hostility. It did more than that, however: it opened her eyes to the degrading position assigned to her sex in religious matters, and made her, like the heroine of this story, a champion of the cause. One morning the reading world of Rome was surprised by the appearance of a bulky pamphlet bearing her name as authoress, and entitled 'La Donna e la Chiesa,' in which doctrines were propounded which might have been taken for a translation into Italian of those summarised by Lesbia's friend in the preceding chapter. It had a rapid sale, first among her own friends, then among the élite of the society of Rome, then among the Italian public at large; eventually it was translated in French, and became the rage in Paris and other cities; finally it was done into English, and cheapened, and there was a heavy run upon it in London, and at all booksellers; and all this in less than a month. The book was a success, and a tremendous slap in the face to clerical authority, and to orthodoxy, clerical and lay.

The breach was now complete between Madame Pisa-Vitri and her once beloved Catholic Church; the work was put on the Index Expurgatorius, and the lesser excommunication was launched at the authoress herself. This was no more than she had calculated upon; but it roused the female society of which she was the brilliant centre; and enthusiastic meetings were held, where it was resolved that unless the papacy drew in its horns, and virtually apologised, the Roman ladies and women in general would henceforth refuse to attend mass or the confessional, and to visit or receive at their houses any of the clergy. Her brother expostulated with her, but all he got for his pains was being sternly forbidden the premises. Denunciation now raved from every pulpit against the rebellious daughters of the Church, but it was left for the present to rave away; for no one, as a rule, went to hear it, except scoffing males, who enjoyed it with grinning faces, and made scandalous scenes in the churches by lighting cigars in full view of the energetic preacher, which brought on a by no means *sotto voce* altercation with the suisses who attempted to turn them out.

Things had already reached this pass, when, as Madame Pisa-Vitri was passing in an open carriage through a crowd, a man shot at her with a revolver. The ball carried away a part of her mantilla, and then lodged harmless in the wall. Madame Pisa-Vitri did not start or utter a sound, but calmly turned her head with a nod and smile, indicating with out-stretched arm the nearest lamp-post. On this, accordingly, the ruffian was instantly strung up by the crowd – the police keeping discreetly out of the way – in a manner which exposed him to derision and pelting during his long death-agony.

There was no proof that the wretch was other than a half insane fanatic, acting for his own hand; but suspicion that he had been suborned, fastened – very unjustly, no doubt – on a certain portion of the regular clergy. And, as the signora had a large number of friends in the national parliament, ministers were only too glad to avail themselves of this pretext to introduce measures which should give effect to the popular indignation. A bill, ostensibly for suppression of the Budget of Public Worship, was brought in, and carried by a large majority; but, in reality, its clauses went much further than mere disestablishment and disendowment. They were secretly laid before Madame Pisa-Vitri herself, and amended by her, certainly not in the direction of leniency. The principal were as follows: The whole revenues of the Church in Italy to be confiscated, and the Catholic places of worship to be closed until the priests belonging to them should marry; all preaching and lecturing by unmarried priests to be prevented, forcibly if necessary; the Vatican and St Peter's to be taken possession of by the Government, and fitted up as a grand secular college for girls; lastly, military service was to be made compulsory upon seminarists as upon other youths; for this purpose, however, a special corps d'armée was to be created, enrolling clerical members only; so that the burden might be made tolerable to the conscripts, so far at least to exempt them from herding with their social inferiors and laymen. As a set-off against this privilege, however, Madame Pisa-Vitri devised a uniform for the clerical corps, which at first was hardly to their taste.

Here the persecution was stayed for the present; but another measure, the expulsion of the papacy from the kingdom, and the outlawry of any of those expelled if they attempted to return without leave, was in reserve for future emergencies. It depended on the pleasure of Madame Pisa-Vitri; for the circumstances of the time had made her the *de facto* ruler.

CHAPTER XXXIX.
SOME MINOR EFFECTS OF THE BRITISH REVOLUTION
OF 189 – . – OUSEBRIDGE.

THE distinctive character of Revolution, properly so called, as compared with constitutional reform, on the one hand, and with mere riot, on the other, is that society in revolution changes its principles of right and wrong. It is like a person turning on his heel; the objects which surround him may remain as they were, but his point of view is changed. Or, to take another simile, it resembles the situation of one revisiting at middle life the scenes of his early childhood. In one sense, they are the same scenes, but, in another sense, how completely altered! '*Cari luoghi, io vi trovai; ma quei dî non trovo più.*' A sudden gust of popular passion, rising against a time-honoured institution on account of a particular incidental provocation, may jeopardise it for the moment; but when the fit has passed, the institution will be found standing in its place. It is otherwise where a conviction has grown that the institution is intrinsically worthless, and that the reverence paid to it was a mistake. This is revolutionary change.

But the crash and ruin of venerable buildings, whether in the material or the moral world, is a more or less painful subject into which it is not necessary for the purposes of this story to go far. It will answer better to select seemingly small indications of a reversal of heart and mind on the part of English society, than to describe the cataclysms by which they were accompanied.

Among the *minor* effects, there was no one which more strikingly affected the tone of society through all its grades, than the thoroughgoing dislocation of the old-fashioned modes of female attire, and the rapid substitution of costumes at once healthful, comfortable, and becoming. Our heroine was no longer a solitary pioneer, hewing her way bravely through a mass of obloquy; girls both

younger and older than she were discarding their skirts and adopting, for everyday use, a knicker or tights costume, according to fancy, first for out-door
exercises only, then for all exercises, in-door or out-door, then for evening as well
as morning dress; and no remonstrances of old fogies of either sex could induce
them to return, except for occasions of solemnity where the dignity of a robe
was in place, to the condemned petticoats. This movement in the matter of dress
quickly entailed another one, but of more limited application. Riding astride
was encouraged by the institution of a 'Ladies' Bicycle Club' and a 'Ladies'
Reformed Horseback Association,' which sprang into existence and flourished
in the course of a single summer. Our heroine, and her friend Friga Hawknorbuzzard, here saw the fruits of an active propagandism at which they had worked
with renewed zeal since the catastrophe of Queenstown; but their success might
not have been so signal as it was, had their endeavours not been assisted by the
recognised leaders of fashion, who had the wisdom to keep touch of the foremost innovations, and to lose no time in espousing the winning cause. Never
did a fashion in dress spread more rapidly than this 'anti-skirt movement,' and a
new impetus was given by it to every kind of healthy exercise. Lawns and fields
presented scenes of feminine energy hitherto never witnessed unless in the artificial environment of the stage or circus, and which were transforming the life of
women, root and branch, and through them affecting for the better the manners
and ideas of men. The immemorial reign of the Weakervessel and the Dollymops was o'er; crinoline was unheard of, as was its bastard offspring, the hump
or dress-spoiler; the chignon displayed not its massive coil; the wasp-waist and
the stilt-heel were no longer admired, but were looked upon as horrid survivals of the mediæval torture-chamber; corset-makers had little custom but from
the very aged or diseased, the classical Spanish sash supplying the place of stays,
where required; the hollow modes of Paris were altogether beginning to find
the solid modes of London too strong for them, and had begun to shape their
course accordingly: in a word, the old-world fripperies and barbarisms were all
drifting away like November leaves before the north-wester. And with the new,
free, comfortable, and rational garments, and the vigorous enjoyments to which
they gave scope, the tone of girls' minds became braced, their tastes widened
and raised, their interest in public concerns, apart from personalities, aroused; in
short, their emancipation from the past completed, and their grasps of the future
assured. Superficial thinkers said that the sexes were changing places; but those
of deeper understanding saw that the elevation of woman to her proper place
would never degrade man below his, which indeed he had never yet filled; they
saw that within the area of the Revolution mankind was rising to a higher level,
and getting a wider and truer view of the world.

One part only of the revolutionary programme will probably jar upon the
feelings of the reader, as it did upon those whose unwelcome duty it was to carry

it out. The recognition of women's dignity made it imperative that personal out-rages against it should be put down with no irresolute hand. A fearful invention, called the Red Girl – a bronze girl in red garments, with the joints moving as in a living human being – administered the lash to offenders in that direction, with a tremendous but impartial severity such as no arm of flesh could use. But, fortunately, the terror of the machine proved, as a rule, a sufficient warning; and society was spared having to inflict a penalty which, in days when the develop-ment of feminine influence was promoting general kindness and forbearance, went very much against the grain.

We may now turn from that disagreeable topic to the most important among the minor effects at home of the British Revolution of 189 – . Already, under universal manhood and womanhood suffrage, a goodly sprinkling of the fore-most women had gained seats in the legislature, where they threw their weight solidly into every measure tending directly to the emancipation of their sex. A pressing, practical question had arisen, – what should be done with the funds created by the lapse of several bishoprics and other benefices of the late Establish-ment. The new law, hereafter to be referred to again, which gave the widows the refusal of their deceased husbands' ministration and emoluments, delayed the wholesale lapse; but even now there was a sufficient accumulation to start some national undertaking in consonance with modern views. After much debate, it was resolved to create a new and special national debt, to be paid off by the lapse of the church endowments. From ten to twelve millions sterling were to be devoted to founding a great university for women, where every profession and every trade could be thoroughly learnt at a moderate cost – in the case of girls on the foundation, free of cost. A commission was appointed to select and purchase a site, and eventually the midland town of Ousebridge, already much resorted to for educational purposes, was fixed upon as being a convenient distance from the metropolis, fairly central for the rest of England, and possessing a gravelly and sandy soil, a good river, and other advantages. Here, accordingly, was built a vast college, the nucleus of a future group destined to eclipse both Oxford and Cambridge in its influence on English society, destined to be the nursery of a new order, the order of women free at last, and lacking only the training to enter upon their inheritance and rule the world, rule it no longer indirectly by the fawning and cajolery and chicanery which are the instruments of an enslaved race, but directly and openly in their own right and – if need should ever arise – by those resources which Science was yearly more and more transferring from the, as yet, bigger frames of half-civilised men to those most intelligent in her ways.

A staff of thoroughly qualified teachers was drawn from the most cultivated grades of society, particular stress being laid on their personal character and cir-cumstances; all the male professors being required to be married men living with their wives, in order that no favouritism, or suspicion of it, might interfere with their relations to the students. The girls who were to form the Foundation College of the university were selected exclusively from the well-born in straitened circumstances, and this not from any sentiments which might be described as snobbish, but in order that a tone of refined simplicity might be taken by the institution at its start; that the first impression made on the townspeople of Ousebridge by the novel experiment might be a favourable one; and that the new ideas and fashions might penetrate outer society with the greater force.

The Foundation College was to be free; the other colleges which in course of time would cluster round it, would bear their own expenses, like other educational establishments; it was important that the undertaking should set out with a class of students chosen only for their fitness to the ends in view, and unhampered by other considerations. It was a fair compact; the college to provide first-rate education, living, and healthy sports; the girls, on their part, to wear the college uniform during their resident membership, and to do their best to reform outside society on their own model. Thus for five years each student at Ousebridge had guaranteed to her a life of work and recreation such as girls have a right to expect – a right which was yielded to them now, probably for the first time in human history.

The colour chosen for the university was a rich crimson, as Oxford and Cambridge have their respective blues; the badge was an oval with a golden arrow in it, pointing upwards, and the word *Deira* below it. The uniform for Foundation College, which was filled mostly with younger girls, was a dark-blue serge knicker suit with crimson beretta cap and stockings, but other colleges could have their own colours; the gown, of course, was common to all, for the hours of study and lectures in school, and for walking about the town. University officers were, of course, appointed to see that the liberty of students to go almost where they pleased did not lead to abuses and scandal, which would have weakened the influence it was the main object of the institution to extend. We say the main object, because mere learning, of one sort and another, could be acquired elsewhere. Learned women who were learned and nothing more, would be no new thing; the object now was not only to make them learned and intelligent in their respective chosen callings, but also to eradicate from them what the world, but a few years back, had miscalled 'womanliness,' – to harden them in character as in muscle, – to bruise out of them their frivolity and soft-headedness, and silly mannerisms and coquetry and mischievous thoughtlessness and all other pseudo-feminine habits, the heritage of prehistoric degradation, which had been the means of keeping eastern nations in barbarism, Europe in semi-barbarism, and, finally of bringing England – though the foremost country in recognising women's rights – to Queenstown and the Revolution. So at last in Ousebridge our heroine saw that she would find a congenial society, the female society of a new era, whose members, whatever career they might choose, would at all events be prepared for it by the cultivation of a vigorous physical and moral constitution, unhampered by stolid prejudices and impossible compromises.

These minor effects of the Revolution, which have been selected for mention as pertinent to the story, if they were but little straws, showed at any rate that the wind had set in favour of making a *tabula rasa* of the old civilisation. The example soon proved contagious; the Spirit of the Revolution spread like a prairie fire among other nations. But space will not permit our following it abroad, nor even going far beyond this cursory glimpse of its work at home, which work, it need hardly be said, made a clean sweep, once for all, of women's disabilities of every sort, social, political, professional, religious. They could now compete with men on a fair field and no favour, in every existing or possible walk of life.

CHAPTER XL.
DISESTABLISHED, BUT VIVIFIED.

HAD the long-talked-of disestablishment of the Church of England been carried out in the years preceding the Revolution of 189 – , that great, highly-cultivated, and in some sense national religious body would simply have been reduced to the level of other denominations; and no place or pretext would have been found now for violent innovations affecting it, and it alone. Family ties, formed in parsonages, but ramifying thence all through the upper strata of English society, would have counted heavily against depriving the established clergy of their social status after they were disestablished; courtesy and regard would have made good the loss of caste decreed by the law, and probably the zeal of adherents would have more than made good the pecuniary loss by disendowment.

But, as Napoleon is reported to have said, *Les Anglais sont toujours trop tard*. As in the case of Irish Home Rule, so in this case the needful change, instead of being made in good time with a good grace, was deferred until it became compulsory and came with a crash. And now in the *mêlée* of the Revolution, the disestablished and disendowed clergy felt that they had no longer any professional dignity to lose, and had nothing but a flimsy, dubious fence of religious, or rather doctrinal, principle between themselves and the inducement to run riot among those allurements of this life which formerly it had been their business to denounce. That in many cases the fence broke down, and some singular results followed its breaking, is no matter for surprise, but the contrary; in a subsequent chapter we shall instance the most important of these cases.

Yet, after all, it would have been a pity had the change come quietly, instead of being precipitated by the Revolution; two considerations will show this. In the first place, as things were now, a meteoric display of talent which had been buried under the mounds of uniformity and routine – talent as various as the variety of faces – shot forth from thousands of rustic retreats, where its existence bad been unsuspected. Incumbents whom their neighbours had never imagined to be anything beyond hum-drum country parsons proved to be artists, mechanicians, agriculturists, economists, financiers, lawyers, first-rate men of business, the real character could now come out from under the parson's cloth, because, the etiquette and prejudices having been swept away, every clergyman felt that he could put off his clerical profession at pleasure, or make it merely auxiliary to the occupation which his heart really was in. No doubt there were those to be found whose heart was really in a religious life, but they were not plentiful; the iron mask undone revealed a class of men the far greater part of whom had adopted the profession from motives more or less worldly.

But in the second place, the Revolution had promulgated a law which gave the married clergy a direct interest in disestablishment. Every clergyman's widow could now enjoy for her life-time the income and residence of her deceased husband, on condition of succeeding him in his clerical office and undertaking, either in her own person or in that of a sister or daughter, the whole offices of the ministry without exception. This could be in no case difficult, because the ritual could now be altered in any manner or direction according to the opinions and taste of each individual minister, male or female, and no authority could impugn this right. More than this, a clergyman could at any time appoint any competent woman to undertake for him the whole or any part of his services, including the ministration of sacraments. It may well be supposed that the optional institution of clergywomen in place of clergymen produced a powerful effect upon large portions of society. For instance, the churches filled with men who before had turned their backs upon everything religious; for the sake of kneeling to girls as their ministers, they would put up with forms of words which they could not endorse. Whatever the National Church may have been during its reign, at its lapse it was become an undeniable blessing, a lever of genuine progress.

CHAPTER XLI.

CLENCHING THE NAIL, AND THE CORONA OP THE DREAM UPON THE CARDINAL.

CARDINAL POWER sat alone in his front drawing-room at Archbishop's House, fatigued with preaching a long sermon at Sunday vespers at one of the Kensington churches, and depressed by lugubrious thoughts inevitably suggested by the bad news from headquarters which we have already sketched. Even independently of that, it seemed to him that the Catholic interest was on the wane. True, it had been so before many times in history, but this time the conditions were different. In former ages persecution was looked upon as a fiery trial out of which the faithful emerged more strong in their faith than ever; now it had no such effect; on the contrary, its effect was to show men the disagreeable side of a profession of religion about which they were not very keen, even on its pleasant side. It did not evoke their indignation against the persecutor, nor their chivalrous zeal for the persecuted; it merely set them thinking that perhaps they had better leave the other world alone, and look more sharply after their interests in this. The practical result of such a change of mind was a diminution of the material support hitherto given to the Church; services were less well attended, and those who did come gave less at the offertory. It looked as if Catholicism were going into a decline, dying of neglect and inanition, through the growing coldness of its members, who had caught the spirit of the age and of the Revolution, and become sceptical, and apathetic, and self-willed. Radicalism in politics, and atheism regarding religion, those were the winning forces of to-day; how were they to be encountered? for the old armoury of sacerdotal intimidation was either laughed to scorn, or used as an argument to justify persecution of the Church. Clearly this state of things must be put an end to somehow, or it would soon put an end to the ancient priesthood, not by the rack, and dungeon, and faggot, and all that ugly sort of romance, but by the modern prosaic and far more efficacious method of simply taking away the means of subsistence. In these days, the secular arm of the church is money; and if the laity are going to refuse to pay for the salvation of their souls, what is to be done? There is only one thing to be done – their devotion must be bought back at any price, any sacrifice, any conceivable compact with heaven, earth, or hell. But is there any price which will buy it? How if there be none? Then the days of Catholicism, of Christianity, of religion, are numbered.

Such were the prelate's sage but not cheerful reflections, as he leant back in his favourite easy chair, and bent his gaze at that part of the room where our heroine and her uncle had sat in their memorable interview with him in days that were recent, yet separated from the present time by Queenstown, the Revolution, and the Italian persecution. At this moment the servant entered with two cards, and the prelate, taking them off the salver to drop them carelessly into the card basket, read with surprise the names of Lady Friga Hawknorbuzzard, and Miss Newman.

'Ask the ladies to come up, if you please, and bring tea at once. If anyone else calls, say I am engaged.'

'I must apologise for this sudden intrusion on your Eminence on Sunday,' said Friga, 'but tin's is not a visit of ceremony; we wanted to find you at home. You know my friend Lesbia Newman – rather too well, perhaps – it is she who persuaded me to invade you like this.'

'As an influential pioneer of the new dispensation, I suppose,' said the cardinal, coming forward with extended hand, and a smile upon his careworn face, which was paler than when our heroine last saw him.

'Not influential, Cardinal Power; I wish I were; I should know how to exert my influence.'

'Because the most important way she could exert it just now, would be over your Eminence,' said Lesbia.

'I know you think so, Miss Newman,' replied the cardinal. 'But first and foremost, let me give you some tea. And where is Mr Bristley? Not unwell, I hope?'

'No, my uncle is quite well, thanks, Cardinal Power; but he is not in town. We two came up together on purpose to see you, and with his knowledge.'

'From which it is not difficult to surmise the object of your visit,' said the cardinal. 'Do you know, I was just thinking of you when the man brought in your card. But seeing Lady Friga with you is quite an unexpected pleasure.'

'Thinking of me! And, pray, what were you thinking about me, Cardinal Power?' asked Lesbia, looking at him straight and searchingly.

The cardinal saw the imprudence of his confession; but there was no receding.

'I was – balancing the – pros and cons.'

'Of what?'

'Why, of the – the whole question, in fact.'

'Then I think,' said Lesbia, laughing, 'that it is a pity there is not a fourth person present to assist the rise and fall of your Eminence's scales. I don't mean my uncle; I refer to a lady. Need I name her?'

'You mean that sorceress Madame Pisa-Vitri. She is bent on the destruction of the Church, Miss Newman.'

'I hope not, Cardinal Power, because if she is bent upon it, she will probably compass it.'

'A pretty state of things indeed, for the Catholic Roman Church to have to grovel in the dust before a – combination of this kind!' said the prelate bitterly. He had it on the tip of his tongue to say 'before a woman,' but checked himself in time.

'But I do not understand, Cardinal Power,' said Lesbia, 'how the balancing in your mind of the question of your Church's future made you think of me, as you say it did. What have I to do with the pros and cons?'

She said this in order to help him out; but her look told him plainly that she *did* understand. He therefore felt no awkwardness in plunging forthwith *in medias res.*

'You have this to do with them, Miss Newman, that the suggestions you made to me on a former occasion about Madonna-worship – I say *you*, because I look upon you and your uncle as one in this connection – may now, by the force of circumstances, be worth considering. We are as an ox fallen into a pit, and we must be pulled out, though it be the Sabbath.'

'I see. Infallibility must accommodate itself to the exigencies of a fallible world,' said Lesbia, at which both the others chuckled. 'Well, better late than never, Cardinal Power. If his Holiness could be induced to say as much to

Signora Pisa-Vitri as you have now insinuated to me, all might yet be well. You say she is bent on destroying the Church; I don't believe it. I believe she is bent on nothing more than compelling the Church to do its duty. She is within her right in using her power relentlessly, for she is a Catholic. I – speaking to you as a non-Catholic – can but suggest and advise.'

'Suggest and advise!' exclaimed the cardinal, laughing in his turn. 'But, my dear Miss Newman, you suggest earthquakes and advise floods. Do you look upon it as a small matter between ourselves that the Catholic Church of Rome should tell her faithful people all round the globe that the worship of Christ has been found to be a mistake, and that henceforward they are to go in for Venus?'

'Small or great, Cardinal Power,' took up Friga, who thought it time to let him see that she was of one mind with her friend, 'that's about the state of the case. Better go in for Venus than for another sort of dissipation, especially that passive sort which consists in being scattered to the winds. *Cogitavit Domina dissipare murum filiæ Sion.* That is the earthquake and the flood you have to fear and to avoid.'

The prelate looked at her in some surprise, then he asked, –

'I presume, then, that you reject Christianity altogether, Lady Friga?'

'I reject it in its present form,' she replied, 'because it embodies the old curse of man-worship. But let that be put an end to, and the place of Christ may still be found beneath that of his mother; it may be recognised by those who are willing to include Hadrian's cult of Antinous in the economy of the spiritual world.'

'So much for masculine divinity,' observed the cardinal, with quiet sarcasm. 'I may perhaps, however, be permitted to hope, Lady Friga, that when the new Christianity is promulgated, it will not be found to insist upon Anti-nomianism as necessary to salvation?'

'I think we need hardly settle that point now, cardinal,' said Lesbia. 'Begin at the beginning; establish divine order first, and see to its corollaries afterwards.'

'Let doctrine take what shape it will, Cardinal Power,' added Friga, 'the practical consideration is this, that a new and disobedient generation is growing up around you – I almost belong to it myself. This rising generation will insist upon your schools being ordered to its liking. It will not be enough for you to take Catholicism in its present unsatisfactory shape and wrap it up in a cover of good music and evening parties and entertainments, and pleasant outing's with pleasant companions on holidays; you must recast the faith itself and make it palatable, not merely disguise it, otherwise your pupils will swallow the jam, but take care to spit out the pill.'

The cardinal looked up for a moment, and smiled at this realistic metaphor; then he asked, addressing both his visitors, –

'But with what face could I go to the Church or to the world, and say that Christianity must yield its place to Venus?'

Lesbia at once replied, –

'I cannot admit, Cardinal Power, that the worship of the Madonna, such as your Church is called upon to practise, and to some little extent does already practise, is accurately described as the cult of Venus. Love and beauty may be the sceptre of womanhood; but they are not womanhood itself. I cannot even recognise them as the sceptre, unless you are prepared to assign to those two words a vastly nobler meaning than they have hitherto borne in vulgar parlance. If by love you are prepared to signify that lifting up of the heart toward a superior being which finds its delight in the feeling of self-abasement to her, and cares for sensual gratifications only so far as they can be made by careful study and dicipline the most direct and apt vehicles of that adoration; and if by beauty you intend, not a mere harmony of form and quality, which may be found in various other things after their kind, but the very essence and substance of godhead itself, looking out at you in those kinds of beauty which are peculiar to women – well and good. In that case, I may personally not object to employing the old name Venus. But all this is very different from those gross, brutish ideas with which the name is commonly associated. For example, what do your Don Juans, your rich men about town, who can buy as many women as are to be bought for money, know of the higher pleasures which I have specified? Nothing. To them a woman is 'pretty,' or 'nice,' or 'jolly,' just as a cigar or a bottle of wine is in good condition; they set about the conquest of a 'fine' woman as they would kill a fine salmon; they attach about as much idea of the sacramental to women as a dog does, probably not so much. *Sacrament!* It's sport, sir, rattling sport, nothing more. Pledge it merrily, fill your glasses! No, no, Cardinal Power, you must not call Our Lady Venus; it will not do. The name is misleading; in your mouth or mine it might mean something holy; in the mouth of the world in general it would mean only what is coarse and degrading. As much passionate adoration of Her as you will – the more the better; but it must be *sanctified* passion; the animal instincts must be subdued to the service of Divine Order, or they are sacrilegious.'

'I am glad to hear you say that, Miss Newman,' said the cardinal; 'we understand each other better now. And I will own that you have both given me much, very much, to think of.'

'That is something gained, Cardinal Power,' said Lesbia; 'only I trust, for the sake of the whole religious world, and in particular for your grand old Church, which surely would not have been preserved to our times unless to fulfil some great mission, that the words we have unskilfully spoken to you to-day may bear fruit in action. There is no time to lose; the Revolution is washing round your base, and if you lift no finger to strengthen yourselves, you will soon be undermined past remedy.'

This brought back the troubles which had beset the prelate's mind before his visitors came. To disperse them he raised his eyes to Lesbia's with an expression of reverence he had never worn toward any mortal.

'And this, then, is to be the end of the great Christian Religion, now near eighteen centuries old!' he said slowly and dreamily.

'*Ruat Christiana Religio, vivat Ecclesia!*' cried Lesbia, in that weird foreign voice which changed her personality, as she started to her feet, her eyes flashing fire.

The cardinal's hands dropped by his sides as he rose; the girl's seized them; and as they lay locked in her strong clasp, his consciousness seemed to reel; and all that took place afterwards, even to the visitors' leave-taking, was to him as if done in a day-dream. A rainbow-hued mist obscured his sight, shutting out the walls of his drawing-room, though he could see the windows through it; and Lesbia's concluding words, though spoken gently in her natural voice, were accompanied by, and almost drowned in, the growing music of a sacred march, which sounded in his ears unaccountably; it certainly did not proceed from any band playing in the neighbouring streets.

'Let that be your banner-scroll, Cardinal Archbishop,' she said, 'in the struggle which is before you. One man against the powers of evil still ascendant in your hierarchy. No matter; you will conquer and break them, for She will sustain your arm. *Domina illuminatio mea et salus mea; quem timebo? Domina protectrix vitæ meæ; a quo trepidabo? Si consistant adversum me castra, non timebit cor meum: si exurgat adversum me prælium, in Hâc ego sperabo.*'

The Legate again passed a sleepless night, and morning found him still distracted between conflicting views of interest. Totally as he had succumbed to our heroine's witchery at the time, he did not in his heart believe in the new worship of the Madonna, any more than he did in the old worship of Christ and the Trinity. The question for him was simply, which would pay? Would he become the more marked man by helping to bolster up the moribund creed, or by boldly hacking it down with his own hand? His servant, knocking at the door with hot water, brought in a telegram which decided him.

'Please to put up all I require for a month, the same as last time,' said Cardinal Power. 'I leave by this evening's mail from Charing Cross.'

CHAPTER XLII.
THE AXE TO THE ROOT OF THE TREE.

As Cardinal Power sat in a saloon carriage of the *grande rapide*, rushing through the night across France, he could not close his eyes until the small hours were past, oppressed by the weighty thoughts which filled his mind ever since our heroine and her friend took leave of him at his house in Westminster. Yet the present journey was not made solely as a result of that interview. The telegram we saw delivered to him by his servant on the morning after the two girls' visit, had apprised him of the consummation of the crisis at Rome. The persecuted Papacy had just received the last vial of lovely Beatrice's wrath, in the form of a notice to quit Italy, 'bag and baggage,' within forty-eight hours, on pain of imprisonment with hard labour. Cardinal Power, on reading the message, shed no filial tears over the discomfiture of his Master's Vicar; but, on the contrary, muttered to himself, 'Now's my time, then, if that girl is right. Catch them on the edge of the gulf, and throw them. The Lord shall reign for ever and ever, but I will govern meanwhile.'

His mind was made up; he had grasped the possibilities of the situation, and resolved to become master of it; and as the flying train carried him Romewards, he pondered the manner of making known to the Roman curia his change of mind, which no doubt would startle them almost as much as that of Madame Pisa-Vitri. One thing seemed clear; his demeanour must be bold. The venture might retrieve the fortunes of his Church, and mark him as her most distinguished son; while if it failed, if he were to be rebuffed and disowned as a heretic – why, schism had rent the old structure in twain before; and a new and more formidable one, which he would conduct, should rend it in pieces. A Catholic and a prelate, if you please; but a man of ambition first. A Christian, of course, no doubt; but neither Christ, nor all his apostolic successors, should stand in Cardinal Power's light, if he could help it. That was settled, and now he could go to sleep, just as grey morning began to spread over the meadows and blossoming orchards of the southern provinces.

It was the morning of the second day after the Cardinal had left England; consternation was rife at the Vatican, for the blow had fallen suddenly. The Pope held consultation with his most trusted advisers in his audience-chamber, which was besieged by a number of old inmates of the vast palace, whom the stern summons of the police had routed out of their seclusion, as smoke drives crawling insects out of the crannies of a wall. The day had come when, by the decree of the Government, which practically was ruled by Madame Pisa-Vitri, the papacy, with all its belongings, must quit its ancient home by sunset. A long special train would convey the company at that hour to Civita Vecchia, where a large and well-appointed steamer would lie ready to start for any destination out of the Italian dominions, and within a few days' voyage, which the exiled pontiff might fix on for his abode. The meeting in the audience-chamber was an excited one for such an assembly; in the hour of common adversity, much etiquette was thrown aside. The difference of opinion turned on the pressing question of removal, some preferring one destination, some another. The discussion was at its height, and the pontiff was undecided whose advice to follow, when suddenly the British Legate walked in unannounced.

After the formal salutations were over, he said, speaking in French, on account of the presence of various foreign prelates whom he recognised, –

'Holy Father, and brethren priests and dignitaries, – I have come hither, as in duty bound, upon receipt of the disastrous intelligence which reached me two days ago. It is not the first time that the hand of the persecutor has been heavy upon us, nor the first time that a Pope has been driven from Rome; but though not the first, I believe it is the most serious. The foundations are cast down; our priesthood is forcibly suspended from its functions, except on condition of violating that law of celibacy which has been its principle of cohesion through centuries of trial; the training of the young is taken away from us; and the 'devout female sex,' as we have been accustomed to call it, is learning rebellion and the spirit of domination, so that its influence is no longer on the Lord's side' – here the prelate paused, produced a snuff-box and deliberately took a pinch, to the surprise and impatience of his august audience, to whom the action appeared singularly out of place; then, shutting the box with a loud snap, and returning it to his pocket – 'Hem! no longer on the Lord's side. They are actually going to take this ancient building away from the Vicar of Christ, and turn it into a school for the training of young women into further rebellion, the training of them into such courses as that of our persecutress Madame Pisa-Vitri. How will it fare with holy Church when her daughters all trample upon her neck? Then they are taking her sons, too; the priests, the Levites, are being secularised; barrack life is their lot for two precious years, and they who were being trained for the altar parade the streets in a grotesque uniform, and fill the taverns with profane songs and jests. All this might be borne; but they are taking away our livelihood, by making it depend on the voluntary offerings of those who are daily becoming more estranged from us, and who insist upon our reversing all the customs and morals which our great history has handed down. Turn whither you will, ruin stares us in the face, insult is heaped upon us, and our total destruction within a very short time can only be averted by a miracle. *Egressus est a filia Sion omnis decor ejus: facti sunt principes ejus velut arietes non invementes pascua; et abierunt alsque fortitudine ante faciem subsequentis.*'

The cardinal resumed his seat, but had quite marred the effect of this magnificent passage from the Lamentation, by taking out his snuff-box again in the middle of it.

'But, Cardinal Power, have you no advice to offer in the emergency?' asked the pontiff mildly. 'Our evils are only too apparent; we would gladly hear how they are to be met.'

'That is what I am ready to do, Holy Father,' he replied, rising again, 'but I feared to encroach upon the rights of other speakers. However, since you graciously give me leave, I will state my views as to the Church's future. To assist you out of the present trouble is not in my power: I cannot work miracles of *that* kind. You will all have to leave this place in a few hours for a foreign land, and you do not need me to tell you that any show of resistance could only expose you to popular derision, and fill the comic newspapers of the week with amusing pictures. There is nothing for it but to submit with dignity and go. With your consent, I will go with you, for I have a mission which must not be neglected. Do you wish to hear, brethren, what that mission is, the accomplishment of which can, it is my belief, save the Church; or would you rather wait until I can speak to you about it at more leisure and in quiet?'

As the feeling of the assembly was evidently in favour of hearing something of Cardinal Power's ideas at once, he skilfully broached the all-embracing subject upon which our heroine, aided first by her uncle and later by her friend, had succeeded in forming his mind. Amazement at the novel doctrine, coming from one in his position, was depicted on every countenance; and when the speaker, warming as he proceeded, concluded with a torrent of newly found but not the less fervent – or fervently acted – devotion to the Queen of Heaven, the Pope himself, under the fiery influence, rose to his feet and heard the remainder standing. There was a deep silence of some seconds, then the pontiff asked calmly, as he resumed his seat, –

'But, Cardinal Power, the innovation you advocate, would it not subvert the Christian religion altogether?'

'*Ruat Christiana religio, vivat Ecclesia!*' thundered the cardinal, stamping his foot with vehemence, a thing he had never been known to do before, even in private. But he spoke as one controlled by a guiding spirit; could Lesbia Newman have been present, she would have thought hers had passed into him.

Everyone sat as petrified, until the Pope spoke again in his quiet tones.

'But, Cardinal Power, would the Church accept life on such terms?'

The cardinal answered in slow, measured accents, –

'Holy Father, if the Church will not accept life on those terms, who will be the gainer by her decease? The gainer will be some modern sect, ready to make its fortune by pandering to carnal lusts unfettered by lofty spiritual aims or by any feeling of *noblesse oblige*. And even while I speak to you here to-day such a sect, under the name of Mylittists, which I fear uses religion only as a cloak for licentiousness, has sprung up in London out of the *débris* of the shattered Establishment, and is pushing its way with such rapid success that – '

'Pardon, your Eminence,' interrupted one of the Italian prelates, 'but surely you do not ask Rome to vie in the race for popularity with this or that sect of infidels?'

'With this or that one, no, Cardinal Borsa,' he answered, 'but to compete with the whole world of sects is just what Rome must do, or how shall she survive, how lift up her head out of the present disasters and still worse ones that may be yet to come? You do wrong to sneer at popularity; it is our breath of life, our last and only resource. Now look here, brethren,' he continued, in a louder and sterner voice, 'should my views prove unacceptable to the reverend assembly I have the honour of addressing at this moment, there is another influential quarter where they may possibly be more favourably received – I will lay them before Madame Pisa-Vitri.'

His hearers all turned their faces, and most of them shifted uneasily in their seats, but nothing was said.

'It would not be the first time,' pursued the cardinal, in the same stern voice, 'that a staunch friend has been turned into a dangerous enemy. The case of Madame Pisa-Vitri herself is an instance. She was your devoted adherent; now you have the pleasure of feeling her claws. You may have to feel mine too, if her ladyship and I should become allied, united in the determination to reform holy Church more drastically than ever Luther or anyone else did. It would be the last schism you will ever suffer, for the sufficient reason that it would be fatal. I can count upon a large following in England, and especially in Ireland; for thousands who are not now Catholics will be ready to adopt *my* Catholicism. In Italy, your own home, you are overthrown already; how long will it be before intelligent France shapes her course to the wind? What will become of the Papacy, disestablished, disendowed, exiled, torn by schism and beaten by a rival who sits in its seat and flourishes in its place? Therefore beware! You leave the kingdom this night because you have provoked Beatrice Pisa-Vitri. Submit to her, and she may pardon you. But if you provoke me too, I will see that she does not pardon you, and that you never come back.'

The cardinal resumed his seat amid a chilling silence, followed by a low murmur of disapprobation, as the gravity of the situation forced itself upon the minds of his hearers. The pontiff alone remained unruffled and absorbed in deep thought. Presently he rose, and, holding up his hand for silence among the murmurers, said gently, –

'Be not disturbed, brethren, by the over-zeal of his Eminence our nuncio to England, but rather lay to heart those discreet words of Gamaliel, 'If this counsel or this work be of men, it will be overthrown; but if it be of God, ye cannot overthrow it, lest haply ye be found godfighters.' We may accept it as certain, that if in the future the Catholic Church is to bear rule at all, it must be a rule by love.'

'Are we to understand, then,' inquired the French prelate, 'that this startling heresy – so it seems to us – commends itself to the approval of your Holiness?'

'It is too great a question to decide off-hand, Monseigneur de Rheims,' replied the Pope; 'it will be necessary to convoke an Æcumenical Council. We have now to meet the exigencies of the day, and there are but three hours for our preparations. I salute you, brethren; the audience is at an end.'

No more questions were asked, but the assembly, quite taken aback by the turn of affairs, regarded the pontiff in mute wonder as he passed out of the chamber. The French prelate alone found voice, –

'Æcumenical Council upon *that!* The head of the Church wills it! Then brethren, we may say *Actum est de fide Christi.*'

'*Et salua facta est Ecclesia,*' replied Cardinal Power, also passing out, with a gleam of triumph on his face.

A few hours afterwards the gibbous moon laid clear-cut black shadows from the guarded Vatican, but a broad belt of rippling shimmer upon the ground swell of the Mediterranean, over which the steamship rolled on her outward way to England.

CHAPTER XLIII.

MR MOUNTJOY GIVES OUR FRIENDS A BIT OF HIS MIND.

'ANYTHING in the paper, Lesbia?' asked Mr Bristley, as he came to their break-fast-table in the coffee-room of the Great Western Hotel, Paddington, where his niece had seated herself a few minutes before. It was the tenth day after the visit of the two girls to the cardinal. Friga had left for Ruddymere on the morrow of the visit, and Lesbia met her uncle, who had come up for a short stay, at their accustomed hotel.

'News? yes indeed there is, Uncle Spines; what do you say to this?' handing him the despatch sheet of the *Times.* Mr Bristley read, '*The Catholic Crisis. Arrival of the Pope. The members of the papal court, with numerous foreign prelates, landed at Plymouth this morning after a smooth passage. They will probably proceed by an afternoon train to London, where preparations have been made for their entertainment.*'

'I suppose they'll reach this station after dark; and, of course, whatever train they come by, there'll be a crowd to stare at them,' he added. 'Now you'll have a chance to close with them at head-quarters, Lesbie.'

'No, Cardinal Power will do that for me, if it be not already done,' she replied. 'I can do nothing in this matter without his aid; should he need mine, which is not likely, he will write to me. My part is done, for the present; now about this other business; we had better call on Mr Mountjoy, if we want to get a place in the gallery next Sunday. I expect they'll be pretty full.'

'Yes, we might go this morning; in the afternoon, he's almost sure to be out.'

A little before noon they rang at Mr Mountjoy's door in Northbourne Terrace, and were shown into his study, where he was sitting at a writing-table piled with MS. He rose with alacrity to receive his visitors.

'Bless my soul Abdullam! – my dear Bristley, and Miss Newman – how you are developed! What an age it is since we met!'

'Abdullam – is that what you call me?' asked Mr Bristley, as they shook hands. 'Ah, I twig; good, very good. A new set of the letters, eh! Not the *Servant of the World,* but the *Father of Dulham.* Very neat.'

'Or if you read Adullam,' said Mr Mountjoy, 'then like the stream in the song, you go on *for ever*; at any rate, your work will. But I have another appellation for you two – Light and Leading.'

'My light is undoubtedly due to my uncle's leading, Mr Mountjoy,' said Lesbia. 'I have lately been trying to shed it in an important direction; a short time will show whether successfully or not. But it is *your* leading we are come about; we want tickets for the gallery next Sunday, if you have any to spare.'

'You are just in time, I have these two left. But, Miss Newman, may I not hope to see you enshrined in the costume of the Sea-born, with some worthy suppliant at your feet? We work for the same ends, you know.'

'You work for my ends, – the elevation of my sex, Mr Mountjoy?' said Lesbia seriously. 'Well, I thought you did; I was sure of it. But I should like to understand exactly *how* the Mylittic ritual is to elevate woman.'

'If, Miss Newman,' he replied, slowly and earnestly, 'I were to reply, by putting an end to what is commonly called the social evil, you would tell me that I am a dreamer, and that my project is Utopia. You would say the hundred thousand women who nightly crowd the pavement of this vast metropolis are not to be diverted from their courses, be they good or bad, by a musical performance in a church, under a name taken from a Greek historian, and connected with the preaching of doctrines which, right or wrong, are 'Greek' to them. So be it. I am aware of that. But all movements for the amelioration of society have small beginnings; and it seems to me that the soundest of beginnings is example, example set by the classes who are supposed to have paid for and obtained a superior education. It is my belief that if the ladies, or some of them, whose influence over what is called 'good society' determines the moral code of the sphere wherein they habitually move – if these ladies can be induced to think, and to let the world know that they think, that the old code of morals as between the sexes is a mischievous error throughout, and that the right or wrong of these inclinations consists in their use or their abuse, their use for the elevation of woman in Divine Order – '

'I am glad to hear you employ the right word, Mr Mountjoy,' interrupted Mr Bristley.

'Their use for her elevation,' resumed the other, 'their abuse for her degradation, then I contend that the world of fashion will soon shift its couches, and fall in with the newer and nobler mortality, and 'a new heart and a new spirit' will come to it, and it will recognise in enlightened women its true teachers, and will commit to the flames its old false and foolish notions, and the false religion upon which they rested.

'Time they did!' exclaimed Mr Bristley. 'When I think of all the sickly twaddle hawked about by those blubberly old lubbers, I feel a thickening sensation in the toe of my boot.'

'Not in thy soul, but in thy sole, harsh Jew,' said Mr Mountjoy, laughing.

'Yes, I confess it does raise the family porcupine in me,' replied Mr Bristley. 'Although, mind you, it is only fair to remember that the Christian morality, by its blundering monogamic theories, has done more, theoretically at least, for woman's dignity than other creeds have.'

'But about the social evil, Mr Mountjoy?' said Lesbia.

'Well, Miss Newman,' he replied, 'in the first place, why and in what sense is it an evil? It is an evil because, and in so far as, in its present conditions, it operates for the degradation of women. But under other conditions it need not do so. I am not now referring to the material uncleanness with which so much of it is mixed up, nor to the horrid plagues arising therefrom. Sanitary regulations, carefully organised and strictly enforced, can do away with all that. But when I speak of the degradation of women, I mean their moral degradation by means of being placed in false relations toward men. What is society's present standard of female virtue? We have it in the words of Shakspeare; you remember that when Desdemona is accused of playing false to Othello and is called by a scurrilous name, she protests against it, saying that she keeps herself 'for my lord, from any other foul unlawful touch.' Now that sort of thing is what I complain of, and what I call the degradation of woman. Woman's dignity is *in herself*, not 'for my lord.' The false doctrine that woman's place is to shine with borrowed lustre, – to be glorified by her good relations with man and not by her own inherent worth; the doctrine that her virtue consists in making her person the property of a man; this doctrine, I say, is the head and front of her degradation. No doubt the celibate life is the higher one for those women who are fitted for it by their temperament; but for those who are not, there is honour in the other walk, that of the matron. And I say that it is contrary to nature and to common sense that a matron should be bound to one man against her will. Nature indicates that if either sex ought to be bound, it is ours. Polygamy is unnatural as well as unjust; polyandry, whether unjust or not, is natural. Without going further into this, it is obvious to anyone whose understanding has not been abused, that to bind women by a false code of virtue, which outrages nature and tramples on common sense, is about the most deliberate crime of which society can be guilty.'

'Slay and spare not,' said Lesbia, smiling. 'But still, Mr Mountjoy, what have your church services to do with all this?'

'I am coming to that,' he replied, 'and in doing so I shall answer the question as to how the social evil degrades women. The degradation consists in the *theological* character which has been artificially impressed upon the whole question. That theological character is a perversion and a misrepresentation throughout. It is the devilry of the priestcraft of past ages. For, let it once be assumed – as those theocracies did assume – that woman is spiritually man's inferior, and there is then no limit to the proprietary rights he may not claim over her on that false assumption. She becomes a marketable commodity in his hands.'

'That's very severe, Mr Mountjoy,' said Lesbia. 'I cannot but think you paint the world blacker than it is. And I still wait to hear how your services are to supply the remedy.'

'They cannot do so directly and immediately, Miss Newman,' he replied, 'but they bear upon the matter in this way. They set up as an object of reverence those very things which have been the object of irreverent handling by those who indulge in them, and of insensate abuse by those who do not. The force of example, I have already said, is that to which I look as the remedy for the evil character of the social evil. When a certain number of women in high social circles shall have made it clear that they have discarded the old false teaching, and that they intend to make the religious element in human nature not the enemy, but the servant, of their affections and desires, you may depend upon it that other classes will see their opening, and will combine to insist upon religion being pressed into *their* service also. In short, we intend to show that Hedonism must be the religion of the future. That is my remedy, Miss Newman, and when it has worked, society will look back upon the state of things in which we now live complacently as belonging to an era of barbarism and abomination, even as we of to-day look back upon cannibalism or the torture. But the initiative lies with us, the more cultivated and influential classes; and that is why I consider that every lady who is brave enough to enter my church as a Mylittist, is a champion of her sex's right in the most thorough and effective way, because her presence amounts to a formal claim that henceforward woman, and not man, shall lay down the law in the matter of woman's morality.'

'Provided, you mean, that her line of life is the matron's and not the maiden's,' suggested Lesbia.

'In either or any case,' he answered.

'Well, we shall judge for ourselves on Sunday, Mountjoy,' said Mr Bristley. 'Now we must be going, and thanks for the tickets.'

CHAPTER XLIV.
IN CHURCH WITH THE MYLITTISTS.

ELEVEN A.M. on the following Sunday found our two friends among a number of other visitors admitted by card, looking down from the gallery in the spacious church. The service commenced as usual with the choir chanting in the original Greek the opening verses of the Johannic gospel, which contain in wonderfully few words the whole doctrine of transcendent philosophy, that is, the unreality of matter. This was followed by the regular special psalms, also in the original Hebrew of David; next came the extempore sermon. Not to weary the reader, we shall give only the finishing sentences.

'The rule of Divine Order,' said the preacher, in conclusion, 'is that *all* relations of the kind specified must be those of reverence toward woman, and that the degree of delight in communion with her must rise or fall with the intensity of that reverence or worship. Thus, and thus only, do we really 'crucify the old man and abolish the whole body of sin,' namely, by creating in ourselves the New Man of Divine Order, whose code of theology is at once as simple as that of the nursling, and as complex as that of the archangel. The man regenerate by Divine Order needs no creeds and catechisms to be thrust down his throat; his wisdom comes spontaneously, according to the mould of his mind and temperament. Yet let none imagine that the work of self-discipline in Divine Order is light and easy; how can it be? For it is no less than the struggle of an animal in human shape to convert himself – into a human being proper, the struggle of one who is carnally minded to become spiritually minded, because he has come to perceive that to be carnally minded is death, while to be spiritually minded is life and light and liberty, the only pleasure which fully satisfies and which never palls.

'I do not see, then, my friends, that I can usefully detain you any longer this morning. You know that the purpose of these services is not to let society down into vulgar licentiousness, but, on the contrary, to raise it into the purity and beauty of Divine Order. But please to bear this in mind, that amatory inter-course between women and men can never be of a neutral character. If it do not raise you upwards, it will drag you downwards; it is either a sacrament or a profanation. Let us pray then to Her whose image stands before you on the high altar that Her spirit may guide us aright. It is only the feminine Wisdom who can decide which desires are harmful and which are beneficial, and under what conditions they may become the one or the other. If the teachers of old were right in their opinion that all are harmful together, then we may be sure that the higher education of women will lead them to stamp out those inclinations, both in themselves and in men. While if, on the other hand, few or none are harm-ful when properly regulated, then we shall have walked in a vain shadow and disquieted ourselves for nought, by listening to those self-appointed and utterly misguided apostles of a false theology and, in this respect, false morality.'

'He's right anyhow in acting in the latter assumption,' observed Mr Bristley to his niece, in a rather loud whisper.

'Perhaps so,' she returned.

'To the care and guidance of Mylitta,' ended the preacher, 'I now commit you, my hearers, in thought, word, and deed. Grant, O Mother and Daughter of the Universe, to thy faithful people pardon and peace, that they may be cleansed from all their sins and serve thee with a quiet mind; that they may be nourished with thy grace, and ever grow in thy holy wisdom more and more, until they reach to thine eternal glory!'

The choir chanted an elaborate Amen; and as Mr Mountjoy descended from the pulpit to his stall in the chancel, the orchestra and organ struck up Mozart's wellknown minuet in *Don Juan*, and presently the choir sang to that rich and voluptuous music a special hymn of the Mylittic ritual, with solos in it for the different voices. It was curious to observe the solemnifying effect of this upon the faces of the congregation; so many of whom had been accustomed to associate the same air only with the adventures of vulgar and brutal intrigue. The sound of the minuet was the regular signal for the corps de ballet to mount the raised dais which stood in the centre of the chancel before the statute of Mylitta. Eight girls, of magnificent figure and clothed outwardly in sea-blue gauze, walked the minuet, in full view from every part of the church; and the ladies who at the same signal had entered their vestry came forth in the thick white and blue Mylittic robe, to take their places each in the door of her confessional, and to receive there the homage of their appointed suppliants for the day, who came to kneel at their feet.

'Splendid!' exclaimed Mr Bristley rapturously.

'This ritual,' said Lesbia, 'must be very costly, but it is the sort of thing most likely to draw the purse-strings of wealthy people. I heard by a side wind that Dr Fairfax, the ex-Bishop of London, sent a cheque for one hundred pounds towards the expenses of the choir.' And there he is, sure enough! on the north side of the chancel boxes. And who's the lady he's worshipping?' she added, raising her opera-glass, which she had had the forethought to bring with her. 'Yes, upon my life! Rose Lockstable! Oh, Rose, the proper and pious Rose Lockstable, a Mylittist! Won't I roast her!'

'The Lord gave the Establishment, and our Lady Mylitta hath taken it away, and its priests bear rule by their means,' said Mr Bristley, loud enough to be heard by all his neighbours in the gallery, which in a few minutes was cleared, and some of the visitors waited in a shelter outside the church to see the Mylittists come out, which they did in about three-quarters of an hour, the ladies coming in a body and the gentlemen dispersing to their homes.

'Good-morning, Rose the Mylittist!' said Lesbia, shaking hands with her cordially. 'I hope you have thoroughly enjoyed yourself?'

'And I trust,' added Mr Bristley, 'that his disestablished and disendowed lordship has been established in the skies and endowed with your grace, Mrs Lockstable?'

Rose did not at first know what to answer; after a few seconds, she said, –

'There's no denying that Mr Mountjoy has succeeded in converting both me and Dr Fairfax to his views, so far as to acknowledge that religious men ought to be made the confidants of religious women. They call it here shriving, but it is rather – a – '

'Yes, yes, we quite understand,' said Mr Bristley, bowing to her, while he rubbed his hands over one another.

'You're incorrigible, Mr Bristley,' said Rose, biting her lips.

'By no means,' he returned, 'and there's nothing I should enjoy more than being corrected by you; I envy Dr Fairfax his shrift.'

'I say, Mylitta, what does your husband think of it all, eh?' asked Lesbia, nudging her friend maliciously.

'Oh, Athelstan – bless you! he doesn't interfere; we don't agree about religion – he votes it all a bore, except the dinners on feast days; and so, as we can't agree, we agree to differ. So long as I let him spend Sunday morning smoking in bed, and the rest of the day at his club, he says nothing about my spending it where I like, especially at a fashionable place of worship. Not that it would make much difference, if he did.'

'While I think of it, Rose,' said Lesbia, 'we intend getting up a sort of rout and dance – if the weather will permit a tent ballroom on the lawn – at Dulham on Friday week. I hope you'll both be able to come? We have already over thirty acceptances.'

'Yes, you must manage to come, Mrs Lockstable,' Mr Bristley joined in; 'we should miss you greatly; I look upon you now as one of the elect.'

CHAPTER XLV.
A PARTY AT HOME.

It has not been mentioned that our heroine had matriculated at Ousebridge, and become an undergraduate of New College, the first college erected after the original one, which was called Foundation College. She enjoyed the life thoroughly, and was the leading spirit of the place in all things that savoured of its principal purpose, the eradication of the old ideas and standards of feminine vocation. Undoubtedly, before the days of Ousebridge, Girton and Newnham and other institutions had been praiseworthy moves in the right direction, but the authorities in those places had been content with the improvement in studies, and had been willing to compromise with the old regimen in other matters; whereas at Ousebridge the object was to obliterate every artificial distinction between the sexes which had been in the past, or might be in the future, used to the detriment of the female sex. And it was in aiding such a purpose that our heroine's strength lay. She was no abnormal genius; she was simply a healthily developed girl, strong physically, mentally, and spiritually; a pattern for girls in general, so soon as society shall have been led – or driven – to do women justice.

It was the Easter vacation, and the only pleasant sunny afternoon that had yet occurred in it. Two of Lesbia's college friends were staying at Dulham for the occasion; and many guests for the day, a few from London and the rest from the neighbourhood, had assembled, some in the vicarage garden, where a pavilion for the evening dance had been erected, with the porcupine flag floating above it, and others in the rooms of the house. Lady Hilda Hawknorbuzzard had had to drag her mother and sister to the party, but once there, they enjoyed it. Presently Hilda asked, –

'And how's Fidgfumblasquidiot the brilliant? I didn't see her as we came in.'

'Oh, she's very well,' replied Lesbia, 'and in an ecstasy ever since post time this morning, because some thoughtful person has sent her an old Christmas card, addressed to 'Miss Grewel;' the poetry runs thusly: –

> 'A happy new Christmas to you,
> With your nose pink and thine eyes blue!
> And may each merry New Year
> With roses those white cheeks smear!'

Fidge thinks it very grand. But you haven't heard her last exploit. Finest thing. We drove her with us to Frogmore the other day for an outing; and while she was walking down the High Street with me, as we passed Bummingby's, it occurred to her to ask if my bicycle wasn't getting worn out. 'Yes, Fidge,' I said; 'thank you for reminding me. I must grow a new one. Here's threepence; just go to the market gardener's over there, and ask him for an ounce of bicycle seed.' Off starts Fidge, dutifully and without misgiving. In two or three minutes she comes back and returns me the coppers. 'Well, Fidge?' 'Please 'm, the man's stupid; he stared at me and laughed, said he hadn't got any bicycle seed, but he could supply me with some bicycle eggs from a mare's nest, if that would do as well. So I said I must come and ask you first.'

'Delightful Fidge!' exclaimed Hilda; 'give me the refusal of her, Lesbie, if ever she's for sale.'

'Now, Lesbie, I haven't had two words with you yet,' said Lady Humnoddie, as she joined them. 'What did you do in town this time? See anybody or anything?'

'Yes, Lady Humnoddie, everybody and everything. That is, you know, everybody who is anybody, and everything that is anything. We saw a lot of fashionable marriages.'

'Bless me, Lesbie! you're turning dollymops like me! I shouldn't have thought you'd care about fashionable marriages or fashionable anything. But where did you see them? – at St George's, Hanover Square?'

'Why no, Lady Humnoddie, not at St George's, Hanover Square, but at St Mylitta's, Northbourne Terrace. I omitted to mention that the marriages, though extremely fashionable, were only temporary, and that they appeared to be contracted mostly between married men and other men's wives. But this may have been an optical illusion.'

This was said pointedly at Rose Lockstable, who was just then within earshot.

'Don't you believe that wicked girl's stories, Lady Humnoddie,' said she, coming forward. 'Lesbie has no more sense of propriety than her monster Gossamer there.'

'Oh yes, I have, Rose, much more,' remonstrated Lesbia. 'You should have seen Goss romping with Fidge's great tom-cat Bollflax, yesterday morning. Boll was determined to get his teeth into Goss's back, and at last he did. Goss didn't seem to be the least hurt, quite the contrary; never saw a dog so good-natured in his play.'

'Was there any mark afterwards?' asked Rose.

'Really, I didn't look,' replied Lesbia.

'We are told in Holy Writ that the lion shall lie down with the lamb,' observed Mr Bristley; 'but when cats and dogs take to mutual backbiting, it is quite a new school for scandal.'

'Here comes my worse half,' said Rose. 'Well, Athelstan, I won't ask, 'Who's your fat friend?' as Brummel did, but, who's your slim one? Didn't I see a spare young man get out of the trap with you?'

'Yes, to be sure, Rose, don't you know Dandidimmons by this time?' replied her husband testily. 'As I knew you were coming with cousin Blanche, I thought I might as well give him a lift. We've had a jolly discussion about a joint trip to Italy in the autumn. Of course, you won't say no.'

'Not if it's a great pleasure to you,' answered his wife doubtfully, 'but you're not a first-rate linguist, Athelstan, and you've quite enough to do to make your own way abroad, without having to act as interpreter to a green young tourist.'

'There's no need for interpreters nowadays, my dear Rose,' replied her husband. 'They'll give you your change right, I fancy, at the chief railway refreshment stations; and any one can see the Hums and Damns at the little houses all along the line. What more do you want?'

'Some people travel with ulterior objects, Mr Lockstable,' observed Lesbia snickering, 'but, after all, there's no blessing like a contented mind. Hallo! how are you, Julius Cæs – I mean, Mr Dandidimmons?' putting out her hand to the young man's, and giving him a grip, which – but that it was salve to the passion he secretly felt for her – would have been enough to make him howl.

'Call me Julius Csesar or anything else you like, Miss Newman,' he answered; 'any name is pleasant from your mouth. How splendid you look in that dress!'

'Splendid! of course I do. Fine parsnips butter fine birds, don't they? But there are two of my chums in the same, and you'd see the whole flight of us if you came to Ousebridge. This is the college uniform.'

'Well, I will say that the process of changing the sex of gurls is a beautiful one.'

'Developing the sex of girls, not changing it, Julius. Perfect womanhood includes, not differs from, masculine attributes.'

'Jove! that is thundering queer, bai Jove!' said Julius, endeavouring to make his moustache bear the weight of the new idea, by vigorously twirling the former. 'But I say, Miss Newman, do you go in for such masculine attributes as smoking and billiard rooms, for instance, at Ousebridge?'

'Yes, everything; come on visitors' day in term-time, and I'll show you over. But now let me see if you recognise a former acquaintance of mine, – that girl leaning against the rope, the taller of the two in uniform.'

'Miss Blemmyketts an Ousian! She! Never should have thought it!' exclaimed Julius.

'Yes,' said Lesbia; 'her friends thought it worth while to lose her company for the sake of the education. They haven't fixed up anything in Yankeeland yet to equal Ousebridge, although I've no doubt they will, and perhaps beat us. But come and talk to her.'

'Yes – a – presently, with pleasure – but I just want to say a word to a fellow over there.'

Julius made his escape, and Lesbia crossed over alone.

'Guess that young masher's afraid of me, eh, Lesbie?' said the American, who had observed the move. 'Most of the sort are.'

'Yet he's not a bad sort either, Letty,' replied her friend. 'He has no brain to spare, but what little he has is malleable.'

'Ah! I'm glad you've not forgotten us, Mr O'Logan,' said Lesbia, advancing to shake hands with her acquaintance. of Killarney. 'So good of you to run down; I hope you'll find Dulham and Frogmore endurable till to-morrow.'

'Purgatory and h – hem! would be endurable, with you to lighten them, Miss Newman,' answered the Irishman.

'But I hope you don't regard Dulham and Frogmore in that light?' said Lesbia, laughing.

'No, no, not at all. Binns's is a very comfortable little inn, – always bicycling men there to smoke and talk with you in the evening. And I should be glad to stay longer, but my engagements forbid.'

'Well, Mr O'Logan,' resumed Lesbia, 'how your forebodings have come true!'

'And sorry we are for it, at the bottom of our hearts, I can assure you,' he returned. 'True, English and Americans are the same race, still the new country cannot be as the old, any more than a second wife or husband can be as the first. But what were we to do? The bigoted stupidity of your majority here prevailed over your intelligent minority, and the result – Queenstown! Well, the lesson won't have to be repeated, that's a little comfort. The world in general is beginning to shake down on new couches, and after all, things might have been a great deal worse. Introduce me, will you kindly, Miss Newman, to your American friend; I should like to hear what she thinks about Yankeefied Ireland.'

The introduction was made, and Letitia soon engaged in earnest conversation with her new acquaintance. In reply to his direct question, she said, –

'I guess, sir, we shall keep you as long as you want, and no longer. Keeping the Irish against their will is like treading down an octopus, or poking smoke out of a door with a fork.'

'You are discreet, Miss Blemmyketts,' answered O'Logan. 'We are the closest friends, and the most dangerous enemies. The reason is not far to seek. You can't deny that the Irishman is, after all, the – a – well, it's a difficult thing for me to say, but – you know what I mean.'

'I'm sure I don't, Mr O'Logan,' said Lesbia. 'Come, out with it! don't be modest!'

'Well, in fact – why disguise it? – the paragon of God's creation – there it is.'

'Guess he's the loudest animal at blowing his own trumpet,' laughed Letitia.

The dancing presently commenced, and Mr Lockstable happened to lead off the first waltz with his cousin Hilda. He was rather moody at the moment, and danced silently for a long turn. When at last they stopped to rest in a corner, he said to his partner, with sudden geniality, –

'Do you know – I'm going to sneeze – do you know h – h – h – ha SHUB! do you know, h – ha SHUB! that seven years ago, ha SHUB! I danced at a ball on the Continent – in fact, at the Casino, the Etablissmong des Bang, you know, at Blown-sir-mayor, in this very evening suit in which I'm now waltzing with you. Hope to start a new one next month; seven years complete.'

Hilda laughed in his face.

'What a funny man you are! I hope the lower portion is not too worn to hold out till our dance is over? But, I say, what were you doing at Boulogne? I shouldn't have thought it was the sort of place you'd care about.'

'Ah well,' he replied, 'there was gossip and caffyshantongs and squibs and balloons and boat-races and horse-races and balls and operas; but I wasn't much in the town itself. I stayed about a month in a crockery-cupboard of an inn, at the hamlet of Whacking-gong* on the Calais road, about five miles from Blown, which I was told would be central for my trout-fishing excursions. It was cheap and nasty.'

'Here, Rose, I say!' Hilda called Mrs Lockstable's attention, as she and her partner came to a halt near them; 'here's this husband of yours changes his evening clothes once in seven years, like his skin. I tell him he'll come to grief with them in public before long.'

Rose laughed, and waltzed off again.

'Who's she dancing with, do you know?' Hilda asked.

'Oh, yes, that's Captain Clapper,' replied Lockstable, 'a member of my club, and the most imperturbable cool hand you ever saw. What do you think? While the Battle of Queenstown was at its height, happening to be on sick-leave at the time, he offered 5 to 2 on the enemy! Someone at the club took him; and when the telegrams told us how the awful day had ended, he seemed quite consoled for his country's disaster by having won his bet. And even now he's always rather pleased to hear the subject brought up. I fancy he made a good thing by speculating for the fall – I say, Clapper! 'as Rose stopped him in the same place near

---

*   Wacquinghent.

them, 'allow me to introduce you to my cousin Lady Hilda Hawknorbuzzard. I'm telling her some things about Queenstown, you know.'

'Getting rather an old subject now, isn't it, Lady Hilda?' said Captain Clapper. *'But 'twas a famous defeat* – eh?'

'For shame, Captain Clapper!' laughed Hilda. 'You've neither patriotism yourself, nor respect for its greatest examples.'

'Ah, my patriotism's the modern sort, the patriotism of the market. I made a few shillings over the affair.'

'Well,' observed Hilda, 'I'm not sure it isn't the most harmless sort, after all. Swinburne says slumber is sweeter than tears. We're getting cosmopolitan now; patriotism is going the way family pride has gone.'

'And many other old things are gone,' added Rose. 'The platforms of religion and morals are being new-planked; perhaps it was high time.'

'Only it is our turn to lay the new planks,' put in Lesbia, who stopped beside them at the moment, in her waltz with Julius Dandidimmons, whom she had whirled quite out of breath and made giddy. 'Men have tried and failed. But about Queenstown, this is the second time we English have gained more real good from a crushing defeat than from our most brilliant victories. Hastings made us a world-leading nation; Queenstown, there is every reason to hope, has made us a world-bettering nation. But who comes here? Why, Rose! it's your spiritual suppliant, the Bishop of Disestablishment! Happy to make your personal acquaintance, Dr Fairfax,' she said, advancing to shake hands with him; 'I saw you lately, but not to speak to, at the church of Saint Mylitta, you know. I heard from Mrs Lockstable that we might possibly have this honour. Meanwhile, I should have said, my lord.'

'Nay, nay, lord me no lords, Miss Newman,' replied the personage addressed. 'I wish no man to say of me now, Ah, lord, or Ah, his glory. It's a relief to doff titles, I assure you. What's the use of titles without power? they're only in one's way. It is true that I am indebted to Mrs Lock-stable for the pleasure of this visit; but the immediate reason for my coming down into the neighbourhood is some law affairs in which I rashly offered to assist my dark friend over there, who is talking to your uncle. But I don't regret it now.'

'You are quartered for the night at Frogmore, I presume,' said Lesbia.

'Yes, our business is there, with a lawyer of the name of Lyttelhurst.'

'Oh, I know him well,' said Lesbia; 'he's the chief of my bicycle club, and we expected him here. But our friend is quite a negro, is he not?

'Yes,' answered Dr Fairfax; 'he's a Nubian by birth, and now a missionary of disestablishment! a converted heathen, and, like all converts, a zealot. His name is Babtweak – Evangelicus Trigonometrosius Babtweak; he's very well off, and consequently well received in soceity; but how he made his money, Heaven knows.'

'Perhaps they know better still at the opposition shop,' suggested Lesbia. 'I suppose he made it by preaching the gospel to the poor, and practising Baal to the rich.'

'If that had been the case, I should hardly have known him,' said the ex-bishop; but with a twinkle in his eye that did not escape Lesbia.

'Not know him! Why not, Dr Fairfax? If he could, why shouldn't he do so? Money's money all the world over, don't you think? And don't you think that the world's good word is at all times and in all places to be bought with it? What saith the wise man? Get wisdom, get understanding; but with all thy getting get riches. And again he saith, – Blessed is the sinner that converteth to much wealth the error of his ways; for he hath saved his soul from death, and he shall hide a multitude of sins.'

'It *is* just as well to hide them, is it not?' answered the ex-bishop, gazing at her with unfeigned admiration. 'Upon my word, Miss Newman, it's a great pity they hadn't your assistance in compiling the New Version. You'd have smoothed over every difficulty. Meanwhile, are you ready for me to present my Nubian to you? You'll like him better than you think.'

'Yes, but just let him finish his confab with my uncle; he's getting some newer ideas into his fine curly pate than I can give him. I'm sorry that press of business has prevented Mr Aluminium Mountjoy from coming here to meet you. I understand that something like ten thousand applicants are refused admittance to his church every Sunday. He'll have to build two or three new churches at least. The bell again – the cry is still they come.'

Meanwhile the vicar and the Nubian were conversing with animation.

'No, sir, no good to be a missionary any more,' said the negro; 'gospel's knocked on the head. Universal free secular education has scuttled Christianity.'

'Therefore you must go and preach a new gospel, Mr Babtweak,' replied the vicar. 'You see for yourself that the old one's played out; where's the good of sticking to the sinking ship? The gospel of woman's priesthood is the gospel of the future; go and preach that. There's your ex-diocesan, Dr Fairfax, with my niece on the other side of the room, come and hear what his opinion is. He's a man without prejudices; and if what he says does not convince you, I will give you a note of introduction to Mr Aluminium Mountjoy, when you return to town.'

But before they could cross to Lesbia's group, she had gone to meet the late arrival.

'Oh, Mr Guineabush,' she said, 'here you are at last! we'd almost given you up. But where's your wife?'

'Somewhere astern,' he replied; 'she's fussing people still about that old parrot.'

'What – have you lost him?'

'Yes, I'm afraid so; we can't find him anywhere. It was the hunt after him that made us so late in starting.'

'Well, I'm sorry too, for my own sake as well as yours. Not only was he associated in my recollection with dear Goss, who you see is flourishing, and might take a prize, I should think, but also the old parrot reminded me of a memorable conversation, heard long ago, between two bargees at Poplar's Weir. The men and their language were very rough, but so simple and naïf, that I quite took a fancy to them, and was very sorry to hear that one of them had perished, and the other had been crippled on the field of Queenstown. What a dreadful thing war is! That men should spend on mutual destruction the energies given them to be employed for their own and the general welfare! but let us hope the end is in sight, though it has been long in coming. But who's that with Mrs Guineabush? How are you, Mrs Guineabush? and this is quite an unexpected pleasure, Sir Richard; we understood you were away.'

'I was, Miss Newman,' replied Sir Richard Robins; 'I only came back this afternoon, and found your mother's note, about five o'clock. What an age since we've met! But I see Miss Blemmyketts over there, and I hope I shall see her with you once more in your old place in the hunting-field next season. It'll be a revival of good old days that I thought were gone for ever, and fox-hunting along with them. What times we have been through, Miss Newman! what times! Did any country ever go through such a convulsion as ours, and survive at all? But it does survive after a fashion: the character of old England dies hard.'

'Bother old England! it's welcome to die, if only my parrot were alive!' exclaimed Mrs Guineabush.

'Depend upon it, he's only strayed away to some neighbouring wood, Mrs Guineabush,' said Lesbia, to comfort her. 'He'll come back when he gets lonely and hungry. I wish I could think the same of Ireland!'

'I say, Miss Newman,' observed Sir Richard, 'your college fare agrees with you; they don't starve you at Ousebridge evidently; you're a more muscular Christian than ever.'

'Yes; well, they give us everything good of its kind there,' she replied, – 'old beef and old mutton, instead of stuff that's half veal or half lamb, and all the malt liquor direct from the breweries, not filtered through the retail trade. The bread, too, is made of pure flour, without any of your lightening messes. That's why the living there is so wholesome.'

'But you'll miss it all very much when you leave.'

'No doubt, but meanwhile we get a good foundation. And perhaps the good example will spread, and people will not be so ready as they are to swallow trash without inquiry.'

'To turn to a widely different topic,' said Sir Richard, 'what's the meaning of the Pope and his satellites coming to London?'

But Lesbia was not to be drawn out upon that subject by the old squire. She merely replied, –

'Really, I can tell you no more about that than you can tell me. Their quarrel with the Countess Pisa-Vitri having led to their expulsion, I suppose they find London the likeliest warm corner.'

'Except one, perhaps,' added the M.F.H., grinning, as he moved off to another group.

CHAPTER XLVI.

THE SAME – MR BRISTLEY ON OLD AND NEW STYLE.

'Would you tell me the right time, Lesbie? my watch has stopped!' said Lady Friga, stopping her partner near our heroine, in the walk round after a quadrille.

'Twenty-two fifty,' replied Lesbia.

'Eh?' said Friga, looking puzzled.

'Fifty minutes past twenty-two. Or, as we said before the Deluge, ten minutes to eleven p.m.,' Lesbia explained.

'Oh, I see, you've got one of the new twenty-four-hour watches; they're the correct thing, of course. I must get one too.'

'You've no need to get a new watch, Fri; all you need do is to have the figures added which come after 12, putting them on the dial under the others, 13 under 1, 14 under 2, 15 under 3, and so on until you come to the last, 24 under 12. That's the cheap way, and it's what I've done, you see.'

'We have had the twenty-four-hour clock for some time on our side of the splash,' remarked Letitia; 'I'm glad it's likely to become Európian. But it's not a great matter, after all; they're talking now of our international convention to do away with the Christian era and devise a new method of dividing and reckoning time which shall suit all the world, independently of religious creeds, every one of which has proved a will-o'-the-wisp. I guess they'll suppress the week altogether and the month too, unless the lunar month can be turned to account, which is doubtful.'

'Yes, weeks are a baseless invention, having nothing in nature that represents them,' observed Mr Bristley, who was standing near. 'The era of N.O. (Novax Ordinis) which is to supplant the A.D., will have to be strictly scientific. No respect will be paid to tradition, least of all theological tradition. Months, weeks, days, and hours will all have to pass into the crucible of science, and no slip-slop makeshifts will be allowed. The world will have to get over its childish habit of reckoning the year by the degrees of light and darkness, heat and cold; those methods may be good for poetry, but they will not do for business. If sidereal time be exact and invariable, while solar time is inexact and variable, every prejudice of habit will have to be discarded, and we must accustom ourselves to having New Year's Day fall sometimes in the height of summer sometimes in the depth of winter, just as we have accustomed ourselves to have, say four o'clock fall at one season in light and heat, at another season in darkness and cold. Provided that the division of time – as by the sidereal year and the sidereal day – be the same and invariable for all parts of the globe and for all time – mankind will have to clear their local predilections out of the way, to make room for that mode of reckoning.

'Guess that'll be something like common sense,' remarked Letitia.

'Yes,' rejoined Mr Bristley; 'for it is a patent fact that the existing modes of reckoning the year and its divisions, whether in Christian or other countries, however much those modes may have been worked into a plausible system by the ingenuity of obsequious men of letters – they do, in the last resort, rest upon the self-willed stupidity and ignorance of some despot or augur. The sky-pilot has over-ridden the astronomer in his own department. And the fact must be faced, that if exact science and religion are to clash, it will be religion that goes to the wall.'

'Boldly said, for a sky-pilot!' observed his niece.

'However,' resumed Mr Bristley, unheeding the interruption, 'I must at the same time say for myself personally, that I do like to have one thing or another; I hate what's neither fish, flesh, fowl, nor good red herring. Don't be off with the old love, say I, before you're on with the new. So long as we do keep up the Christian era at all – and your convention, Letitia, may not find the world prepared to throw it over for some years yet – why did we go and spoil the poetical associations and upset the quietness of life by a change of style in the year 1752, just because some other countries had been fools enough to humour the fads of a superstitious old pope who wanted to make Easter fit in with some lunatic craze or other?'

'That is not respectful to Infallibility, Mr Bristley,' observed Friga.

'I'll tell you what,' returned the vicar, who was not in a reverential mood, 'if Infallibility doesn't clear out of my way, when my time comes to join the glorious company whence it claims its titles, I'll make it see more stars than ever the astronomers did whose intelligence it seems to have obfuscated. But seriously, Lady Friga, don't you see that the change from the old style of a hundred odd years back to the current style of to-day has been a piece of botch tinkering and patching which has spoilt everything and mended nothing? Granted that the solstice may be brought into a nearer harmony with the fiction of Christmas and the purely arbitrary date of New Year's Day – '

'Yes, I suppose the new style is rather truer to the sun,' put in Friga.

'Beggar the sun!' rapped out Lesbia, in her loudest tones, forgetting where she was, in the excitement of the moment, for she joined heartily in her uncle's contempt for the current calendar. All faces in that end of the ballroom turned, and there was a general roar of laughter. Lesbia's aunt put on her propriety stare; and an old paterfamilias, invited because he was a neighbour of thirty years' standing and had known Mrs Bristley before her marriage – not only stared, but blushed.

'Now then, Mr Leckinsopp!' said Lesbia, making as though she were going to pat him on the back, 'what's up with you? You look as uncomfortable as if you were leading out a sixty to mount in a gale!'

'Leading what, my dear Lesbia?'

'Oh, Mr Leckinsopp, I really must tell you a story about Miss Newman,' interrupted Julius Dandidimmons, who had come near Lesbia again when he saw that Letitia was out of the way. 'At the last Frogmore annual flower-show there was a young fellow about my age, but a head and shoulders taller – six feet three at the very least – anyhow, a visitor and a stranger. Up walks Miss Newman straight to him, eyes him from head to foot as if she were inspecting a horse, pronounces aloud the word 'Sixty,' then turns on her heel and rejoins her party. The fellow stared, as you may suppose, and I heard him say to himself, 'Devilish free and easy gurl, that! Me sixty! I'll pay her in her own coin presently.' And presently he did; as Miss Newman happened to pass near him, he planted himself astride of her course, stared her in the face, and said in a loud, deep voice, 'Forty-five.' 'Forty-five!' returns Miss Newman promptly. 'Bless you, man, fifty-two!' 'Nonsense!' exclaims the fellow, quite taken aback. 'You can't possibly be fifty-two; you don't look more than fifteen!' But it turned out, on mutual explanation, that it was the height of bicycles, and not the respective ages of herself and the tall chap, that Miss Newman was talking about.'

'Why, of course, Julius; who cares about age, except as it affects muscle?' said Lesbia. 'But now, Mr Leckinsopp, I want to know what it was that made the rose i the bud feed on your damask cheek just now.'

'I – a – I'm rather amused to hear such expressions from a young lady as you made use of just now about the sun,' he answered sheepishly.

'Well, it's the sun's fault,' retorted Lesbia; 'what made the lumbering old thing get in my way? But, Fri, my girl, what makes *you* take the part of the stupid new style? There's nothing to be said for it.'

'Nothing,' assented Mr Bristley. 'Or, at any rate, so very little, that it was, in my opinion, a huge blunder to make the change. Let us have scientific truth in wholeness and consistency on a grand scale; that no rational man will gainsay. But do not let us spoil the beauty and homeliness of the old merely to make way for a shallow thing of shreds and patches. The poetry of the seasons has been quite destroyed by the silly innovation. May – the month of Mary – has been doubly dislocated. It now begins and ends twelve days too soon; it begins before the trees have had time to put on their first young green, or the cowslips to flower, and it ends just as everything is getting into full bloom, but yet is not far enough advanced to proclaim leafy June. Again, Christmas now comes before the lengthening of the day is sufficiently apparent to give one the feeling of having left the dark time behind, and generally before the frost and snow have had a chance. Easter, being a moveable festivity, is not affected; but Michaelmas and the goose-fair come before autumn shows on the boughs, and before the birds have had time to get into condition. For sportsman now the 12th of August and the 1st of September and of October arrive before the game has got properly strong on the wing; in short, every old custom, and every time-honoured association, has been thrown out of gear, for no good or practical purpose whatever. Russia and Greece only have had the good sense to stand firm and resist an innovation which represented nothing in the way of genuine improvement, but only a fidgety pedantry.'

'Still, Mr Bristley,' observed Friga, 'there are dates connected with the Gregorian style which are associated with much we set store by in our national history, such as Waterloo on the 18th of June, Trafalgar on the 5th of October – '

'Or Queenstown on the 13th, to finish,' returned the vicar. 'Yes, but would not these several dates be equally 'glorious' if they were called the 6th of June, the 23rd of September, and the 1st of October, as they are called in Russia? You see the date of an event, such as a battle, a birth, or what not, is as good for one nominal date as for another: old style or new style is no matter. But we are accustomed to associate the progress of the calendar months with that of the seasons, the growth of light and heat, or of darkness and cold, and with the effects of those changes on vegetation. That is why I complain that the change of style has uselessly taken much of the poetry out of life. By all means, I grant you, let us have a rigorous, strict, thoroughly exact, and scientific mode of reckoning and marking time, such as the sidereal system, one which by its irrefragable mathematical certainty shall command the assent of all educated mankind and be wholly independent of creeds and traditions. Be it so, by all means; the sooner the better. As rational beings, we are bound to give up our cherished fancies, when the question is between them and the proclamation to all the world of a clear, common truth which sheds light and creates stability. That of course. It needs not to be argued. But to go marring the beauty of dear old associations, taking the comfort and geniality out of social life, spoiling whatever there is of poetry in the changing seasons, and in their effects upon vegetable and animal nature, by such a peddling, puddling, pettifogging, basimecu alteration as that perpetrated by those geese the mediæval papists, and afterwards copied here, from ape-like mimicry and weakness – really, I cannot characterise it in any words fit to be heard in this assembly. The Russians half-barbarous, say we? They may be, but at any rate they have managed to keep sane upon a point on which the world in general has gone crazy.'

'Well, Mr Bristley, well! I hope you feel better,' laughed Friga, taking his hands in her own as she faced him closely. 'Come here, do, somebody with a broom – you, Mr Lock-stable – and sweep up the shreds of the new style.'

'Not I; let 'em be,' answered Athelstan. 'For my part, I quite agree with Bristley. The mischief that's been done to all that's jolly in life by the change of style, is enough to make a goblin dernd's particular hair to stand on end, like bristles on the faithful porcupine, as Hamlet says.'

'You're a great Shaksperian, Lockstable,' laughed the vicar, 'only I hope you don't mean to be personal?'

Lesbia, who had been dancing most of the evening, now wished for a little quiet chat with Friga about the latter's impending matriculation at Ousebridge, but she met her retiring with Letitia to a quiet part of the garden, where the two remained until Lady Humnoddie's carriage was sent for.

As the party broke up, old Mr Leckinsopp came forward to say to Lesbia, –

'I am sorry to have seemed put out just now, but if the truth must be told, your expletive was only a pretext. The real cause of my ill-humour was that I have had a violent quarrel with my wife to-day, which makes me disagreeable to everyone.'

'Really, Mr Leckinsopp! I am surprised at that, I must say. People look upon you two as model man and wife who never knew what it was to have a tiff.'

'Yes, and I hope that, generally speaking, we are so,' he answered. 'But I will tell you frankly, as an old acquaintance, what it was that came between us. We were disputing whether to have roast goose or boiled turkey for dinner the Christmas after next. And to this hour we are not agreed about it.'

'Then,' said Lesbia 'you don't agree with Talleyrand's advice, '*Ne jamais faire aujourd'hui ce qui peut-être remis à demain.*''

CHAPTER XLVII.
THE COUNCIL OF LONDON, A.D. 1900.

IT was a foregone conclusion. *Perish Christianity, but live the Church* / our hero-ine's dictum to the cardinal, had prevailed, the papacy had comprehended the situation, which, indeed, had become even more formidable for Catholicism than on the day of departure from Rome. For the French Chamber, partly because the exile from Italy looked like the *coup de grâce*, but partly also because it was influ-enced by the clever intrigues of Madame Pisa-Vitri, who had brought her talents and her rancour to Paris, suppressed the Budget of Public Worship by a heavy majority; thus the whole clergy of France were thrown at a stroke upon voluntary support for their livelihood, which support, however, flowed in so ungrudgingly that it was doubtful whether the clergy were not in some respects better off than before. Still, their position was now dependent upon their popularity, and the moral effect of the change could not be otherwise than far-reaching.

The Æcumenical Council held in London had lasted nearly a week, and various dignitaries of the Church summoned from the principal Catholic com-munities of the world, had spoken on the proposed Definition; but it will suffice to translate two of the shorter speeches, one from each side.

The Archbishop of Paris thus addressed the assembly: –

'Holy Father and venerable brethren in Council, – I regret to raise a dissentient voice, but ought we to take so momentous a step, without knowing what we are about? I shall not take up your time by discussing abstract theology; that has already been done enough during this long and solemn debate; I shall address myself to a single practical aspect of the question. Have you well considered what the promulgation of this dogma of the Godhead of Our Lady will involve? It will necessitate the early ordination of a number of priestesses. Not mere vestals nor acolytes, mind you, but *priestesses*, women invested with full power to celebrate mass, to hear confession and give absolution, extreme unction, in short, to administer all the sacraments. Our laymen will clamour for it, and our women will see that they are mistresses of the situation, and will command it. Shall we not, think you, find this a little sudden? So far as Catholicism is concerned, our sex will be supplanted and subjugated. So be it, perhaps you will reply; we are willing to bow our necks under that yoke. Very well, but are you sure that when women shall reign supreme in spiritual concerns, they will use their power well? My experience as a Frenchman does not incline me to believe that it will be so in France. We have there too long seen feminine influence enlisted on the side of bigotry; indeed it is well for us priests that it has been so, for without the sustaining hand of Frenchwomen France had ere this ceased altogether to be Catholic. But when I am told that emancipated women will light all the lamps of science, especially sanitary science, will raise art to the place of divinity, abolish war and armaments, and work together without jealousy or egoism for the universal happiness, I can but smile sadly at the sanguine temperament of those who talk thus. I have reason to fear, on the contrary, that the women of the future will prove to be like those of the past, the irreclaimable slaves of inherited prejudices, working for political and social reaction, making class feeling and even personal selfishness the basis of all their actions, and dragging modern civilisation down again into the slough of barbarous antiquity. But, fathers assembled, it will then be too late to retrace the false step we shall have taken; no power on earth, perhaps no power anywhere, will be able to bottle up again the evil genius we shall have let loose; and it is for this reason that I feel constrained to reserve my vote in favour of the Definition, at any rate until the general sense of the Council shall have pronounced decidedly against me.'

It was a relief to Cardinal Power's feelings that his turn to speak came next. He drew out of the breast of his robe a small statuette of a female figure, presumably a Madonna, and held it on high in his right hand as he faced the assembly.

'*Domina illuminatio mea et salus mea; quem timebo? Domina protectrix vitæ; a quo trepidabo? Si consistant adversum me castra, non timebit cor meum; si exsurgat adversum me prælium, in Hâc ego sperabo.* Why does my brother of Paris fear the power of liberated and elevated womanhood? That we do not yet know what it is, I grant; but all the evidence we have on the subject points one way, which is this, that just in proportion as man has raised woman, so she has raised him; and only as he has degraded her has she debased him. The barbarism which the Archbishop of Paris deprecates is the effect and token, not of predominant feminine influence, but of its absence; except, indeed, where that influence has been perverted; then the effects are undoubtedly worse than if it were absent. The slave develops low cunning because it is his only resource, and the status of women in the world hitherto has been a gilded and painted slavery. If there be danger to be apprehended from giving power to women, it is on that account alone; but remove the slave's habits, and you remove the danger. The Archbishop of Paris, and those who think with him, do not seem to perceive that they are in this dilemma. Either our attempt to set up woman-worship in place of man-worship will fail, or, if it succeed, experience warrants us in expecting from its results the opposite of those which the Archbishop of Paris apprehends. We shall not have unhottled an evil genius, but, on the contrary, brought a good genius to combat the evil one whose course has been a failure and a disaster throughout. But even if this were not so, even if I were to allow that the spiritual emancipation of Catholic women would let loose an evil genius, there would still, after all, remain the great world of non-Catholics and non-Christians, who surely would be strong enough to neutralise the evil. Such fears are therefore chimerical, and I give my vote for the Definition because I believe it to be the only way to save the Church, which is now beset with real and pressing dangers, not merely threatened by a remote and imaginary one like that. As regards the institution of priestesses, I shall welcome that too, because I see in it a prospect of winning to the fold many-thousands of souls stronger and more worth having than those who have deserted us.'

Cardinal Power resumed his seat, and was followed by other prelates, whose orations the reader may be spared. The upshot of the Council was a majority so overwhelming in favour of the Dogma, that the Archbishop of Paris and the few who had sided with him thought it best to avoid being marked men in an invidious cause, by waiving their personal objections. The practical unanimity of the Council being thus established, it only remained for the Pope as its president to promulgate formally a bull embodying the decision arrived at, whereof the following is an idiomatic translation: –

THE BULL PROPTEREA QUOD ANTIQUIS.

We Melchisedec II. by the grace and consecration of Our Divine Lady and the Holy Trinity Vicar of Christ and High Priest of the Holy Catholic Apostolic Church Pontifex Maximus and Bishop of Rome Do hereby ex cathedra and with sanction and mandate of the Sanhedrin and of the bishops and pastors of the Church in solemn Æcumenical Council assembled and speaking with the infallible voice of the Church declare

THAT WHEREAS throughout past ages the Divine Wisdom hath allotted to the nations of mankind such religious dispensations as were commensurate with their undeveloped slate in things spiritual leading them gradually through the darkness of barbarous cults and afterwards through the dispensation of the Hebrew patriarchs and prophets unto the present phrase of the Catholic Church in the dispensation of Christ our Lord and His successors the Bishops of Rome each preceding dispensation thus giving place to a higher one accordingly as the Church became capable of receiving it AND WHEREAS *the culminating dispensation of all could not be given forth from the Divine counsels until the time had come when the eyes of mankind should open naturally to see the truth concerning the Divine Nature and Image as shown in the perfections of womanhood* AND WHEREAS *this truth hath ever more and more of late years been tacitly recognised in the devotions of the faithful in all lands even to the extent of causing multitudes who are neglectful of mass and confession to come and kneel at the shrines of Our Blessed Lady and to draw with them into the fold many who had kept aloof in enmity* AND WHEREAS *the weighty pressure of the said devotion to the Queen of Heaven hath come to bear with such force upon the pastors of the Church that they can no longer doubt that it is a mandate and a new revelation from on high fulfilling the words of Christ our Lord that that which hath been told into the ear shall be proclaimed upon the housetops*

THEREFORE *be it known unto all men now henceforth and for ever that the Holy Catholic Apostolic and Roman Church shall now and for evermore adore Our Divine Lady as being in Herself the Unity of the Trinity, Supreme God, world without end* AND FURTHER *that the faithful shall be bound to receive and acknowledge such Priestesses of Our Divine Mother as the Church shall see fit to ordain and shall render to them honour and obedience not less than hitherto hath been rendered unto men the priests of the Church.*[7]

We command that a solemn office be held and a Miserere mei Dea in observance of this Definition be sung in all the churches of the faithful throughout the world and we bestow upon all persons whatsoever who shall attend this office our apostolic benediction.

Given at our Æcumenical Council of London A.D. 1900.

CHAPTER XLVIII.
THE RE-SETTLING OF THE WATERS.

THE convulsion, looking to all its effects, had been a violent one, and the old order was shattered beyond recovery; yet the British Revolution of 189 – was working for the good of the nation and of the world better than any national triumph could have done; thus verifying what Victor Hugo had written half a century before, '*Les nations sont grandes, Dieu merci! en dehors de la bonne ou mauvaise fortune d'un capitaine.*' The dissolution of the old pattern of empire purchased cheaply the new domain of social improvement; and, after all, when we ask what sort of greatness the country had lost, the answer comes that it was only a discredited sort, – one which the awakening public conscience was beginning to look askance at. There was a prospect now that nations might at last learn to trust one another, not because human nature was radically altered, but because it was against the interest of each to be out of touch with the general sentiment of the others. Public opinion, which formerly belonged to cliques, subsequently to the mass of the people, was now becoming international. And all this because the British Revolution had broken the cast-iron shell and let a ray of the truth illumine the darkness and purify the bad air within.

It might indeed be said in biblical metaphor that this time, at any rate, the ten righteous had been found in Sodom. However misdealing might prevail in high places commonly supposed to be temples of integrity; however covertly venal justice had become; however hypocritical morality had remained; though the State might be rotten almost to the core – yet the actual core was sound: its soundness was evinced by one thing which sufficed. Behind clouds of iniquity, England had a great light to show, – that she had done more, take it altogether, than any other country hitherto, to raise her womankind, or allow it to rise, out of the mire of prehistoric servitude; and it was from this cause alone that the Battle of Queenstown had opened to her the noblest of missions, instead of placing her, as it otherwise must have done, on the list of great empires blotted out.

For it may well be doubted whether the decline and fall of any one of the great empires of history came about, or could have come about, apart from the paralysing action of internal foes; it is rather the division of the house against itself than assault from outside, which is the secret of its fate. A State may be strong even though split up into parties, provided that those parties acknowledge some rallying-cry to which they will sink their differences from the common defence. But if there be one party among them imbued with such implacable resentment against the State itself as not only to be deaf to the call, but actually to welcome the common danger – then assuredly the mischief which that one can work will overbalance the good done by the patriotism of the rest.

And had the great naval and military disaster befallen a people influenced – for the influence of women is ubiquitous, we had almost said omnipotent – by such a generation as that to which our heroine's nearest relatives and some other females in this story belonged, the impulses of revenge and hatred, bred by mortification, would have prevailed in the national councils, and would have made an enemy deadly and permanent – permanent until such time as the question were set at rest for ever by some catastrophe nearer home and more fatal than Queenstown. But the rising generation among whose pioneers Lesbia Newman was one, cared for no imperialism which did not benefit the races ruled; the influence of her and her like was for peace and progress, without regard to defeats or triumphs of arms belonging to the woeful past. And the nation, fitted by the trials of Revolution to imbibe the better spirit thus engendered, soon found that the source of apprehended ruin had, on the contrary, become a source of strength, the resort and the home of sound, if retrospective, patriotism and more genuine conservative instincts than during that turbulent period when it was formerly a portion of dominions on which the sun, notwithstanding the catastrophe, had not even now begun to set.

Besides, over the head of territorial questions and dynastic disputes, a feeling was gaining ascendancy, that the old-fashioned patriotism, as meaning the love of one's country at the expense of other countries, is not so very exalted a virtue after all; that the sympathies of modern man should be cosmopolitan. For if the worship of womanhood in its apotheosis was to supersede that of the old gods, be they one, three, or more, how could any portion of the apotheosis be antagonistic to another portion? And if not, where would be room for that rivalry between nations which the old idea of patriotism implied? Before the establishment of this common bond, there had been no more fertile source of strife than religous belief; but if all creeds were to be practically fused into one, international hostility could never more take any but the most sordid ground. So the less said about patriotism in future the better. Nobler aims and higher ideals were now coming to the front; and as the day-spring from on high grew apace, the evil phantasms of the past fled before it, and with them vanished those standards of honour which superstitious stupidity had set up. One human family bound together by fact not fancy, one demonstrable religion, one moral code, following nature instead of the craft of augurs and the tyranny of despots – such was the platform to which the new society should climb, throwing aside its childish things.

Dona nobis pacem. Already a great calm was broadening down over the world, because the abomination of desolation, the usurper of divine attributes and honours, the false god and true devil, the grim, huge, hideous, overshadowing, bearded idol of a thousand centuries or more, tottered to its fall; and the ineradicable religious instinct of mankind was turning from that nightmare to shelter under the wings of Eternal Wisdom, whose worship, now about to be inaugurated by the recognition of Her image and representative, caused the sunshine of peace beyond understanding to be felt from the spiritual to the temporal sphere, from innermost to outermost of the rind of human nature we call civilisation.

CHAPTER XLIX.
RECONCILIATION.

'YES. That is all which the spiritual interests of mankind require at the hands of the Roman Church,' said Lesbia gravely, as she laid a printed copy of the papal document upon the breakfast-table at Dulham vicarage. 'I only hope that Madame Pisa-Vitri will see it in the same light. We must get an introduction to her,

Uncle Spines – she is still in Paris – and talk the matter over, and persuade her to receive Cardinal Power. He would like nothing better, I know, than to figure again conspicuously as the leading man.'

'Well, if I don't go myself, I will send you Lesbie,' replied her uncle. 'Perhaps your friend Lady Friga would accompany you, and be of more service in some ways than I could. But what's that other letter there, which you have not yet opened?'

'From Cardinal Power, I declare – just as we were talking about him!'

'Well, what does he say?' asked Mr Bristley, as soon as his niece had had time to read the letter.

'All's well; there is no need for any of us to go to Paris. Madame Pisa-Vitri herself has written to him, saying that she considers the Council of London and its result as a full and sufficient atonement for all the past errors of the Church; that she assumes all differences between herself and the papacy to be at an end; and that in that case she will use her influence with the Italian Government to allow the Pope to return to Rome, on well-defined conditions. I suspect, Uncle Spines, that the conditions will include her own ordination as a priestess, or appointment to some post of still greater responsibility and power; be that as it may, Cardinal Power is willing, and the rest will be obliged, to eat whatever shew-bread it may please Madame Pisa-Vitri to bake for their consumption.'

'Does the cardinal mention anything about the ordaining of priestesses?' asked the vicar.

'Yes, they have already chosen the first English one, the Lady Superior of Hildenboro.' * She will have completed her probation by the beginning of winter, and as soon as she is ordained, I must go to her and be baptised into the Church. I cannot consistently refuse, nor can you, uncle.'

'I have no wish to refuse,' he replied. 'I was always ready to meet Rome half way. It will entail upon me the necessity of converting this neighbourhood, but I do not apprehend much difficulty in that *now*. Does the cardinal say anything else?'

'Yes, he congratulates me upon being one of the few who had lived to witness the realisation of their progressive ideas. But I shall tell him in reply, that in the first place an individual can only be the mouthpiece of the age; secondly, that the idea owes at least as much to you as to me, if indeed either of us were the real chief actor.'

'You say well there, Lesbie; the real chief actors are not denizens of this world, although probably they may have been so.'

'The last piece of intelligence in the cardinal's letter, said Lesbia, 'is that they are to get back Westminster Abbey. They have been hankering after it ever since the days of Cardinal Wiseman, and now at last they have done something to deserve the reward.'

---

*   A village on the South-Eastern Railway, which might possess a convent.

'I suppose,' said Mr Bristley, 'it will be a race between non-established Rome and dis-established Anglicanism, as they call it, for all the fine cathedrals of the kingdom. It would be a sin to let them go to ruin; somebody must have them. Madonna and Mylitta – which of the two forms of woman-worship will get the best of it in this country?'

'If one may forecast the future,' replied his niece, 'I should say that Mylittism will be very soon merged in Catholicism as a special congregation. Depend upon it, Rome will not have rivals, if by latitudinarianism she can avoid it.'

'Latitudinarianism is a fine word, and may be made to mean a good deal,' said Mr Bristley, laughing.

'Let it mean all it can,' said Lesbia; 'the leap has been taken. Moreover, are we not told that no man having put his hand to the plough and looking back – '

'Is fit for the kingdom of Mylitta,' put in the vicar. 'But seriously, Lesbie, it does seem at last as if the horizon were clearing all round. The great convulsion has not wrought the misery we all feared it would. Enormous changes have come about, but the classes concerned are adapting themselves to the new conditions, and are not harassed by those who agitated for those conditions. An element of what might almost be called conservatism is tempering the zeal of revolutionaries; we may soon look to see all the wounds which are still open bound up, all the sores healed. The great battle upon which it all hinged is already ancient history, it has left no international rancour; the constitutional landmarks which had been overthrown are being silently replaced by new ones not wholly unlike them, only better. Much that excited mere blind animosity now receives fair consideration; the clash of interests is less loud; jarring and discord of all sorts go more against the grain. Yes, the horizon is decidedly clearing; it was high time it should. We may fairly hope that the world has passed the dark hour which precedes the dawn, and that those lines of Swinburne are in course of being realised: –

> 'Liberty! what of the night? –
> I see not the red rains fall,
> Hear not the tempest at all,
>   Nor thunder in heaven any more:
>   All the distance is white
> With the soundless feet of the sun
> Night, with the woes that it wore,
>   Night is over and done.'

CHAPTER L.

BEFORE WESTMINSTER ABBEY.

'So you are going to be a vestal, mademoiselle,' said Madame Pisa-Vitri, speaking in French, to our heroine as they sat together in the former's private apartments at the Grand Hotel, Charing Cross, months after the conversation of the preceding chapter, on a raw and foggy afternoon in the beginning of December. 'What, may I ask, will be the duties of the office?'

'They are not onerous, madame la comtesse,' she replied; 'we shall have to sit as 'orient' above or near the altar in churches where we attend service, wearing the robe of our office and receiving by implication the reverences of all those who bow to the altar in entering or leaving church; also we shall hold the post of honour in every Catholic procession. But the office is not assumed under a vow of celibacy, like nunhood or sisterhood; it can be surrendered should a girl wish to marry, or otherwise feel that she is unfit for it. Nor does it necessarily entail abstinence from lay pursuits and distractions.'

'How many of you are to be appointed for the Definition ceremony next week?' asked the countess.

'Twelve, including myself and my friend Lady Friga Hawknorbuzzard, all resident Ousians,' answered Lesbia. 'It was thought necessary thus to mark the adherence of the Church to the new *régime* in the education of girls.'

'Very necessary,' assented Madame Pisa-Vitri, with emphasis.

'But you, madame, what a change in your attitude too!' observed Lesbia. 'Your impending ordination as a priestess, must have been a bitter leek for the papacy to eat.'

'Well for them they had no bitterer,' returned the Italian, with some sternness. 'But let us not revive animosities: all that is past and gone. Moreover, they write to me that I am become very popular among the clergy at home and the seminarists, who are doing their two years' military service in the uniform which I had the honour to design for them. It seems that they parade the streets shouting '*Evviva Beatrice! Beatrice ed il dietro di San Pietro!*' And they have no idea of allowing the institution to drop. They like it; the military duties are light, and it is two years' refreshing holiday from the dull clerical career. And they make all the better clergy for having been men of the world for a space.'

'What a droll creature you are, my dear countess! Excuse me, I can't help laughing,' said Lesbia, drawing her chair to the side of the other, and taking one of her hands, which was yielded readily enough.

'Well, you in your way, my Lesbia – permit me to call you so – and I in mine, I think we have done our serious part,' said Beatrice.

'When will the return to Rome take place?' Lesbia asked, after a pause.

'As soon as this great ceremony is over, or rather after the Octave of the Immaculate Conception and the Definition,' answered her friend. 'You must bring the uncle of whom you say so much to visit me at this hotel; and afterwards I hope you will both be my guests in Rome. I will go with you and inspect your Ousebridge, and you must come and give your opinion and advice upon our Roman college.'

'A thousand thanks, dear countess, I will do the first at once. I will bring him to-morrow, if that will suit.'

A mild and sunny 8th of December saw a concourse of some fifty thousand persons gathered on the open space near Westminster Abbey. The inauguration of a new religious era had been opened in the forenoon with the celebration of high mass by the first ordained priestess, assisted by the Pope himself and the British Legate, a ceremony which virtually surrendered the chief priest's office into woman's hands. It was followed by the reception into the Church, by the same priestess, of the twelve girls, and their investiture with the order and insignia of vestals. But the crowning ceremony was to be the afternoon pontifical vespers, to be concluded with a solemn procession round the interior of the church, in honour of the Definition of the Dogma. Each vestal had her special colour assigned, the robe and train-mantilla being of white cashmere, the apron and fillet of the special colour. To our heroine was awarded the marine blue of the Sea-born, as a special honour for the active part she had taken in the cause. Friga, as the next in honour, had the colour of her University, blood-red crimson; a third had the green of spring, a fourth gold-yellow, and so on, a single colour being worn with the white by each vestal.

The procession was originally intended to go round the interior of the church merely, a choir of young girls in white leading it and singing the revised Litany of Our Lady, the vestals being seated on thrones borne aloft on the shoulders of the bishops, some eighty of whom had come to the Æcumenical Council; the train-mantilla of each vestal being supported behind by a cardinal, the British Legate holding up that of our heroine. The Chief Priestess and the supreme Pontiff would remain in their respective places at the high altar until the procession reached it again.

However, as the day approached, public interest became so keenly excited throughout the Catholic world – special trains and steamers being announced to run from all parts of the Continent – that eventually it was decided to have the procession, not only in the church but *to* it, from some convenient place of assembly, so that all spectators might witness it. An immense brass band, amalgamated from all the best of the country, was engaged to accompany the procession. The weather, of course, must count for much under the changed programme, and on the night of the 7th there was a heavy gale with torrents of rain, which continued until sunrise; then short smart showers succeeded at intervals, and it looked very doubtful for the outdoor part of the ceremony. But before eleven a.m. the clouds lifted, a lovely day succeeded, and in a very short time a great sea of heads spread over the open space and lined the approach to the Abbey. The families of the twelve vestals, with other privileged persons, had seats within the church, as well as a certain space reserved for them outside, in front of the main porch, so that they could see the procession as it came, and then follow it in to take their seats for the grand vespers.

'Wonderful days, sir!' observed the father of one of the vestals to Mr Bristley, who stood near him outside the porch.' Who would have believed that you and I should live to see the Roman Church re-enter Westminster Abbey, after so long an exclusion, and in this manner too!'

'This manner, my dear sir?' was the reply; 'but don't you see that this was the only manner possible? How could the papacy ever have got back the Abbey, how could it ever have kept its archaic head above water at all, except by boldly appealing to the deepest-seated of popular sentiments?'

'And by boldly throwing Christianity overboard,' added the other, with a grin.

'If necessary,' answered Mr Bristley, in a serious tone. 'But it may not be necessary – time will show. Rendering Her due to the Mother of God, we shall not rob the Son of Man of that which is rightfully his. His interests are now Hers; his hour is come. But looking only to the Nazarene personally, I believe he would repudiate what we glibly call Christianity, and would say to its respectable and fashionable and orthodox professors, 'Ye are of your father the devil, and the works of your father ye will do.' While to those who seek the truth in sincerity, even though they be called heathen, his other words apply, 'Not every one that saith unto me, Lord, Lord' – not every one who is sprinkled with a rite and ticketed with a creed, is my true disciple, but he who, with or without any theological system, leads a humanitarian life. If circumcision and uncircumcision avail not, no more shall Christianity nor unchristianity. The thing needful is to become a New Man, the NEW MAN of DIVINE ORDER.'

At this juncture, faithful little Fidge, who had implored her young mistress to get her taken with the family to London and to the ceremony, and who looked remarkably graceful in her simple cap and snow-white apron upon a dark blue frock, having left her over-wraps in the seat, touched Mrs Newman's arm, saying excitedly, –

'Please 'm, the procession's coming; I'm sure I hear the music!'

'I heard it before you spoke, Fidge,' answered Mrs Newman, 'and, God bless me! they're playing the Priest's March in *Athalie!*'

From that moment the whole scene appeared to Mrs Newman to float before her as if it were unreal. The gorgeous procession, the full pomp and panoply of the ancient Roman Church, aided by the wealth of English adherents, now came in sight; the tramp of the stirring music swelled louder, and the vast crowd knelt to the glorified vestals with a common impulse. As the twelve thrones, carried on high, passed through the portal, Lesbia's rustic little maid, simpleton as she was in the things of this world, gazed up into her young mistress's face with a rapt expression that was truly angelic, a gleam *of* the Divine Nature breaking forth even from such a very lowly type of it as she. The kneeling crowd rose as the last chords died away down the aisles of the interior, but there was more to see yet; for overhead the rainbow spanned the towers of the Abbey with a brilliancy probably never before known in smoky London, and indeed seldom seen anywhere, Certainly, the weather for the last few hours had been very exceptional; still the coincidence was impressive, even for the least imaginative and superstitious among that motley multitude.

Two hours afterwards, Mrs Newman clasped her daughter in her arms, while a burst of tears gave her oppressed brain relief.

'Praised be God, my own darling Lesbie, for these most wonderful events! A weight, if an unreal one, is taken off my mind. The Dream is all fulfilled now, and still I have you safe.'

EDITORIAL NOTES

1. Lesbia seems to have been riding the then popular 'ordinary' bicycles. These had a front wheel that could be up to five feet from the ground.
2. Queenstown, now known as Cobh, was a naval station and an embarkation point for passenger liners on the New York to Liverpool route.
3. 'The National Party' was the Irish National Land League, founded in 1879 with Charles Stewart Parnell as the first president. It became the main proponent of the Irish interest at Westminster.
4. The Married Woman's Property Act of 1882 gave women the right to acquire, to hold, and to dispose of any real or personal property.
5. Raffaele Cadorna was an Italian general who distinguished himself in the War with Austria in 1866.
6. An insurrection in what was known as the Egyptian Sudan and the destruction of the Egyptian forces on 5 November 1883 caused the British government to intervene. General Gordon, a popular hero and a distinguished soldier, was sent as governor-general to Khartoum, which was soon surrendered by the followers of the Mahdi. The attempt to relieve Khartoum was a calamitous failure that almost brought down the Gladstone administration.
7. Dalton manages to ignore the theology of the Trinity and the dogmas of the Nicene Creed in this final episode. The proposition is so extravagant, so alien to the tradition of the Christian churches, that it is not possible to take the new doctrine seriously.

AUTHORS AND EDITIONS

Frontispiece

Frontispiece from Albert Robida, Le *Vingtième Siècle* (Paris: Georges Décaux, 1883), p. 16.

Walter Besant: The Revolt of Man

The text used here is the later and revised ninth edition: William Blackwood, Edinburgh and London, 1890.

Walter Besant (1836 – 1901) was a Cambridge graduate, 18th wrangler in 1859. His career began in education, first as a professor of the Loyal College in Mauritius 1861 – 7, then as Secretary to the Palestine Exploration Fund, and Chairman of the Society of Authors from 1884 – 92. His sympathy for the poor was reflected in writings such as *All Sorts and Conditions of Men* (1882) and in *The Children of Gibeon* (1886). He wrote several popular novels, biographies such as *Rabelais* (1879), and several important histories of the development of London.

Henry Robert Samuel Dalton: *Lesbia Newman*

The text is from the first and only edition of 1889. Its author, Henry Robert Samuel Dalton (1835 – 1902?), was born in Bridgnorth, Shropshire. His father, Henry Dalton, was a clergyman of the Church of England and had been appointed to the perpetual curacy of St Leonard's church, Bridgnorth in 1832. The young Dalton came up to Christ Church, Oxford, at the age of 17. After an undistinguished career he graduated with a pass degree in 1855. He does not appear to have followed his father and sought ordination, possibly because the Reverend Henry Dalton had been summoned on 27 November 1834 to answer charges of disobeying the commands of his ordinance, preaching in public, and spreading opinions and beliefs contrary to the doctrine of the Church of England. For these offences the Consistory Court deprived him of his perpetual curacy. Thereupon he seceded from the Church of England and with his followers in Bridgnorth formed a congregation of the Catholic Apostolic Church which had been established by Edward Irving after he had been excommunicated by the Presbytery of London.

The life of Henry Robert Samuel Dalton is almost a complete blank. His college never heard from him after graduation and the college archivist reports that he did not respond to the appeal for the restoration of Christ Church cathedral in 1870. He published five books which included *Education for Girls* and *Religion and Priestcraft*. He seems to have inherited his combative, assertive style of writing from his father.